the
Winston Brothers

ALSO BY PENNY REID

WINSTON BROTHERS SERIES
Beauty and the Mustache (#0.5)
Truth or Beard (#1)
Grin and Beard It (#2)
Beard Science (#3)
Beard in Mind (#4)
Beard in Hiding (#4.5)
Dr. Strange Beard (#5)
Beard with Me (#6)
Beard Necessities (#7)

Truth or Beard

Penny Reid

Truth or Beard

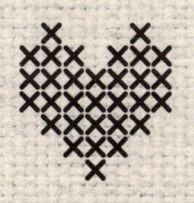

PENNY REID

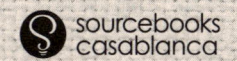

sourcebooks
casablanca

Copyright © 2015, 2025 by Penny Reid
Cover and internal design © 2025 by Sourcebooks
Cover design by Stephanie Gafron/Sourcebooks
Cover images © V_Sot_Visual_Content/Shutterstock, Lemonsoup14/Shutterstock, TWINS DESIGN STUDIO/Shutterstock
Internal design by Tara Jaggers/Sourcebooks
Winston brothers paper doll and map illustrations © Blythe Russo
Emoji art © streptococcus/Adobe Stock

Sourcebooks and the colophon are registered trademarks of Sourcebooks.

All rights reserved. No part of this book may be reproduced in any form or by any electronic or mechanical means including information storage and retrieval systems—except in the case of brief quotations embodied in critical articles or reviews—without permission in writing from its publisher, Sourcebooks.

The characters and events portrayed in this book are fictitious or are used fictitiously. Any similarity to real persons, living or dead, is purely coincidental and not intended by the author.

All brand names and product names used in this book are trademarks, registered trademarks, or trade names of their respective holders. Sourcebooks is not associated with any product or vendor in this book.

Published by Sourcebooks Casablanca, an imprint of Sourcebooks
P.O. Box 4410, Naperville, Illinois 60567-410
(630) 961-3900
sourcebooks.com

Originally self-published in 2015 by Penny Reid.

Cataloging-in-Publication Data is on file with the Library of Congress.

The authorized representative in the EEA is Dorling Kindersley Verlag GmbH. Arnulfstr. 124, 80636 Munich, Germany

Printed and bound in the UK and distributed by
Dorling Kindersley Limited, London
001-348810-Jan/25
CPI 10 9 8 7 6 5 4 3 2 1

*For those who travel without a destination,
here's hoping you take the time to feed
your heart as well as your spirit.*

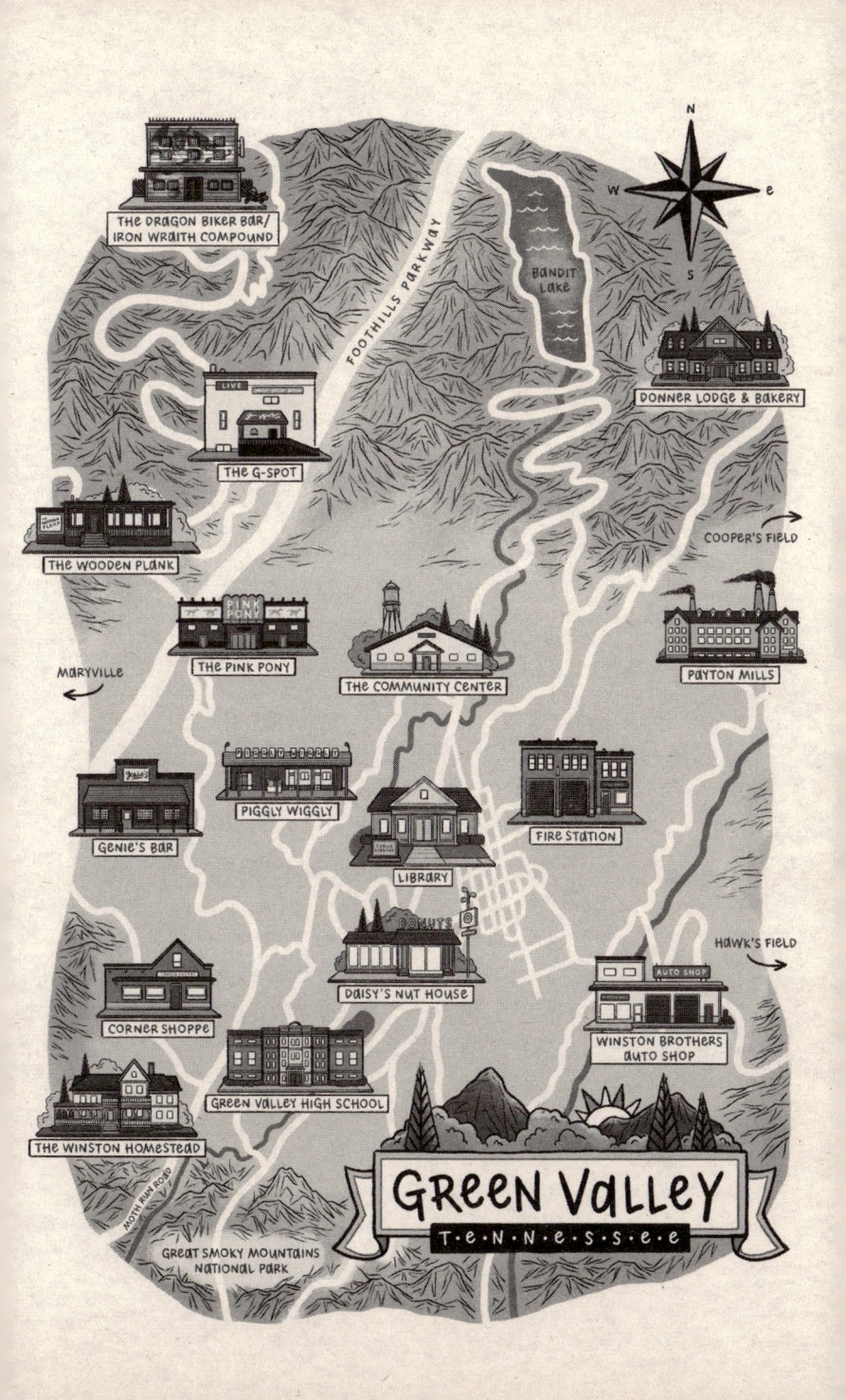

Green Valley, Tennessee

- The Dragon Biker Bar / Iron Wraith Compound
- The G-Spot
- Donner Lodge & Bakery
- The Wooden Plank
- Cooper's Field
- The Pink Pony
- The Community Center
- Payton Mills
- Maryville
- Genie's Bar
- Piggly Wiggly
- Library
- Fire Station
- Hawk's Field
- Daisy's Nut House
- Corner Shoppe
- Winston Brothers Auto Shop
- Green Valley High School
- The Winston Homestead
- Moth Run Road
- Bandit Lake
- Foothills Parkway
- Great Smoky Mountains National Park

Jessica

1

> "Not all those who wander are lost."
>
> —J.R.R. TOLKIEN, *THE FELLOWSHIP OF THE RING*

I PULLED INTO THE GREEN Valley Community Center parking lot and scared the crap out of five senior citizens.

Even though it was Halloween, inducing heart attacks in the geriatric population was not on my agenda. Unfortunately for everyone within earshot, my truck made a ghastly, high-pitched whining sound. This happened whenever it idled.

The group of five jumped—obviously startled—and glared at me. Soon their glares morphed into wrinkled squints of befuddlement, their eyes moving over my appearance from my perch. It took them a few minutes, but they recognized me.

Everyone in Green Valley, Tennessee, knew who I was.

Nevertheless, I imagined they were not expecting to see Jessica James, the twenty-two-year-old daughter of Sheriff Jeffrey James and sister of Sheriff's Deputy Jackson James, dressed in a long white beard and sitting behind the wheel of an ancient Ford Super Duty F-350 XL.

In my defense, it wasn't my monster truck. It was my mother's. I was currently between automobiles, and she'd just upgraded to a newer, bigger, more intimidating model. Something she could plaster with bumper stickers that said:

Have You Kissed Your Sheriff Today? and

Don't Drink and DERIVE, Alcohol and Calculus Don't Mix, and

Eat Steak!! The West Wasn't Won with Salad.

As the local sheriff's wife, mother to a police officer (my brother) and a math teacher (me), and the daughter of a cattle rancher, I think she felt it her duty to use the wide canvas of her truck as a mobile pro-police, pro-mathematics, and pro-beef billboard.

I waited patiently for the seniors to look their fill, giving them a small smile they wouldn't see behind my beard. Being stared at didn't bother me much. After a few more minutes of confused gawking, the gang of seniors shuffled off like a herd of turtles toward the entrance to the community center, casting cautiously confused glances over their shoulders.

As quickly as I could, I maneuvered the beast into a space at the edge of the lot. Since inheriting the truck, I usually parked on the edge of parking lots so as not to be that person who drives an oversized vehicle and takes up two spaces.

I adjusted my beard, tossing the three-foot white length over my shoulder, and grabbed my gray cape and wizard hat. Then I tried not to fall out of the truck or flash anyone on my hike down from the driver's seat. Luckily, my costume also called for a long staff; I leveraged the polished wood to aid my descent. The rest of my costume was negligible—a one-piece miniskirt sheath dress with a low-cut front—which made stretching and moving simple.

I was halfway across the lot, lost in delighted mental preparation for my father and brother's scowls of disapproval, when I heard my name.

"Jessica, wait up." I turned and waved when I found my coworker and friend Claire jogging toward me.

"I thought that was you. I saw the staff and cape." She slowed as she neared, her eyes moving over the rest of my costume. "You've made some…modifications."

"Yes." I nodded proudly, grinning at her warily amused expression. Claire hadn't changed since work; she was still wearing an adorable Raggedy Ann costume. Lucky for her, she already had bright-red hair and freckles. All she had to do was put her long locks in pigtails, then add the overalls and the white cap.

"Do you like what I've done?" I twisted to one side, then the other to show off my new garment and my high-heeled strappy sandals.

"Are you still Gandalf? Or what are you supposed to be?"

"Yeah, I'm still Gandalf. But now I'm *sexy* Gandalf." I wagged my eyebrows.

Claire covered her mouth with a white-gloved hand, then snorted. "Oh my God. You are a nut."

A sinister giggle escaped my lips. I'm not much of a giggler unless I've done something sinister. "Well, I couldn't wear it to work. But I love the irony of it, you know? All those stupid Halloween costumes that women are expected to wear, like *sexy nurse* and *sexy witch* and *sexy bee*. I've actually seen a sexy bee costume. Am I missing something? Is there a subset of men who get off thinking about pollinators?"

"I agree. You can't wear the sexy Gandalf costume to work. In addition to being against the dress code, you're already starring in the sex fantasies of all your male students as their hot calculus teacher. If you'd worn sexy Gandalf at school instead of regular Gandalf, I think they'd go home feeling confused about their sexuality."

I laughed and shook my head, thinking how odd the last three months had been.

Like me, Claire was a Green Valley native; also like me, she'd moved back to town after college. However, where I was here only temporarily—just for the few years until I paid off my student debt—Claire was here to stay. She'd become the drama and band teacher during my senior year of high school. Now we were coworkers. With her gorgeous red hair, light-blue eyes, and strikingly beautiful face, during my senior year as well as now, she was labeled *the hot drama teacher*.

I shivered as a gust of late autumn wind met my excess of bare skin.

"Come on." Claire looped her arm through mine. "Let's get inside before you freeze your beard off."

I followed her into the old school building. As we neared, I heard the telltale sounds of folk music drifting out of the open double doors.

It was Friday night, and that meant nearly every able-bodied person in a thirty-mile radius was gathering for the jam session at the Green Valley Community Center. As it was Halloween, the place had been decorated with paper skeletons, carved pumpkins, and orange and black streamers. The old school had been converted only seven years earlier, and the jam sessions started shortly thereafter.

Everyone in Green Valley would start their evening here. Even if it hadn't been Halloween, married folks with kids would leave first, followed by the elderly. Then the older teenagers would go off, likely to Cooper's Field for a drunken bonfire. The adult, unmarried, and childless would leave next.

I was clumsily and hesitantly trying to find my way in this new single-adult subgroup.

Before I left for college, I was part of the Cooper's Field, teenager, drunken bonfire subset, even though I usually didn't stay long and never got drunk. But I always managed to find a boy to kiss before I left.

In my present predicament, where each individual from the unattached adult cluster (to which I now belonged) ended the evening would depend heavily on that person's personal goals. If the goal was to have good, clean fun, then you typically went to Genie's Country Western Bar for dancing and darts. If the goal was to get laid, then you typically went to the Wooden Plank, a biker bar just on the edge of town. If the goal was to get laid and cause trouble, then maybe get laid again, you went to the Dragon Biker Bar, several miles outside of town and home to the Iron Wraiths biker club.

Or, if you were like me—no longer an angst-filled, rebellious adolescent looking for boys to kiss—and the goal was to relax and grade a week's worth of calculus assignments, you went home, put on flannel pj's, and turned on the Travel Channel for background noise and inspiration.

I spotted my father before he spotted me as a crowd had gathered; he was speaking animatedly to someone I couldn't see. My daddy was standing at the table just inside the entrance where a big glass bowl had been placed to collect donations. He was, as always, wearing his uniform.

Claire stood on her tiptoes, then tried leaning to the side to gauge the cause of the crowd. "Looks like they're doing trick-or-treating. I see a bunch of kids in costume, and there's a bucket of candy at the table."

I nodded, glancing down one of the short hallways, then the other. Music came from only one of the rooms, but there was a mass of kids going in and out of the five classrooms, each with either a decorated pillowcase or an orange plastic jack-o'-lantern bucket to hold their treats.

I leaned close to Claire to suggest we skip the line and make our donations later when my eyes snagged on a red-haired, bearded man coming out of one of the classrooms, holding the hand of a blond little girl—not more than seven—dressed like Tinker Bell.

I felt a shock—a jolt from my throat—travel down my collarbone to my fingertips, then weave through my chest and belly. I lost my breath on a startled gasp. The shock was followed by a suffusion of spreading warmth and levels of intense self-consciousness, the magnitude of which I hadn't experienced in years.

My eyes greedily traveled over every inch of him, dressed

in blue Dickies coveralls that had been pulled off his sculpted torso, the long sleeves now tied around his waist to keep the pants portion from falling down; they were dotted with grease stains and dirt at the knee and thigh. He also wore a bright-white T-shirt and black work boots. His thick red hair was longish and askew, like he'd just run his fingers through it…or someone else had just run their fingers through it.

Beau Winston.

I knew it was Beau and not his twin, Duane, for three reasons. He was smiling at the little girl. Beau always smiled. Duane never smiled.

Also, he appeared to be helping the little girl in some way. Beau was friendly and outgoing. Duane was moody, quiet, and sullen.

And lastly, my body knew the difference. I'd always been reduced to a blubbering mess of teenage hormones at the sight of Beau. In contrast, Duane, though identical in looks, raised my blood pressure and made me a blubbering mess of self-conscious irritation.

My adolescent crush—nay, my adolescent *obsession*—was walking toward us, his attention focused solely on the child next to him. He looked like a ginger-bearded James Dean, only taller and broader. I think I forgot how to breathe. He was so dreamy. He was so dreamy, and I'd forgotten how much I disliked the word *dreamy*.

"Jess." I felt Claire nudge me with a sharp elbow. "Jessica, what's wrong?"

The way some preteens lose their minds for boy bands, rock stars, and hot celebrities was how I always lost my marbles for Beau. It all started when he climbed a tree to save my cat. I was eight. He was ten. He'd kissed me on the cheek. He'd wiped my tears. He'd held my hand. He'd hugged me close.

He was my hero. He'd saved my cat.

I wondered for a flash whether there was something truly wrong with me, whether there were other twentysomething women out there who still experienced paralysis at the sight of their first crush.

Shouldn't I have outgrown this by now?

My voice was a weak whisper, and my mouth was dry when I finally answered Claire's question, tipping my head just slightly toward the pair. "That's Beau Winston."

There was a little pause, and I knew Claire was looking past me to where I'd indicated.

"No." She squeezed my arm with hers. "No, that's Duane Winston."

I shook my head, forced myself to look away, and met Claire's eyes. "No, that's Beau."

Claire's mouth hooked to the side as she studied my features; I'm sure my face had gone mostly pink, a by-product of being blessed with freckles and an insane, persistent crush on the nicest, sweetest, funniest guy in the world. I wasn't embarrassed, but I was impressively flushed. Growing up, whenever I'd been in the same room with Beau, he'd had that effect on me. Full-on butterflies in the stomach and music only I could hear.

"I'm telling you, that's Duane. Beau's hair is shorter."

"Nope." I shook my head again, more resolutely this time as I tried to regulate my breathing and body temperature. "I go a different kind of haywire around Duane. That must be Beau."

In fact, Duane and I didn't much get along. During the same episode that initiated and solidified my lifelong adoration of Beau, my aversion for Duane had also been established. While Beau was climbing the tree to save my cat, Duane was throwing rocks at the branch. While Beau had been kissing my cheek, Duane had been rolling his eyes.

I could tell Claire was trying not to laugh as she added, "Cripes, you weren't kidding when you told me you had a crush on that boy. Is this the first time you've seen either of them since high school?"

"No. I saw Beau once at the Piggly Wiggly during my sophomore year of college when I was home for winter break. He was buying bacon and green beans, and I stood behind him in line."

She stopped trying to hide her smile and grinned. "This is fascinating to watch."

"What is?"

"You, struck stupid. I mean, you're Jessica James. You have this plan that ensures lifelong freedom from commitment. All you ever talk about is traveling the world. You're home just long enough to pay off loans and gain experience for your résumé. Yet here you are, harboring a treasured memory of an encounter in the Green Valley Piggly Wiggly with Beau Winston. I bet you can recall that conversation word for word."

I stared at her, wanting to deny it, but also not wanting to lie. She was right. I could recall the conversation word for word, action for action. He'd turned to me and asked if I'd mind passing him a gum package that was just out of his reach. I tried to shrug, but I'm sure it looked more like a minor seizure. Then I fumbled for the gum, accidentally knocking an array of breath mints to the floor.

He'd knelt and helped me pick up the felled mints, our hands had touched, I'd almost fainted, and I was certainly bright red. Then he smiled at me. I almost fainted again. Then he helped me stand, and I almost had a heart attack.

He'd asked, "Hey, Jess…are you okay?" dipping his head close to mine, his amazing blue eyes all sparkly and lovely and concerned.

I'd nodded, not able to speak because his hands were still on my forearms, and I'd gazed up at him. Butterflies and music only I could hear—that time it was "Eternal Flame" by the Bangles—drowned out the sound of his voice and the next words from his mouth. I did see that his lips curved in a barely there smile as he'd studied me.

Then my brother, Jackson, appeared and ruined everything by telling Beau to mind his own business. Beau shrugged—an actual shrug, not a semi-seizure—and turned back to the cashier. He'd paid for his bacon, green beans, and gum, and then left.

The thing was, I was not a shy person. Not at all. I considered myself confident and levelheaded. I had a brother, so boys were not a mystery to me. But Beau Winston had always rendered me beyond completely tongue-tied. He rendered me stupid.

I was, in a word, completely ridiculous.

Okay, that was two words. I was so ridiculous, I'd lost the ability to count.

"Jess, seriously…are you all right? Your face is turning bright red." Claire squeezed my arm, drawing my attention away from the sound of my blood pressure.

"Yeah." I knew I sounded weak. "Just let me know when he's gone."

"You're not going to talk to him?"

I shook my head quickly.

Her nose wrinkled; her eyes flicked over my shoulder briefly, presumably to his approaching form. She squeezed my arm again. "I've never seen you like this. This is not the Jessica James I know."

"I can't help it. If I talk to him, I might faint."

Claire *tsk*ed. "Two weeks ago, when we were in Nashville, you walked up to that sexy stranger outside the club and kissed him."

"You bet me ten dollars to do it. Plus it's not like that with Beau. Plus that guy was flirting with me. Plus I like kissing."

"What do you mean? You don't want to kiss Beau?"

I whispered frantically, "Of course I *want* to kiss him, but only in theory. Who is your famous crush? If a super-hot Hollywood actor who also happened to be a great person wanted to take you home—and the lights stayed on during the deed—what would you do? I mean, not in theory. Honestly, what would you do?"

Claire looked at me for a long moment, then asked, "Would I get a heads-up a few months ahead of time? So I could eat low carb and start working out?"

"No."

"Then, honestly, I'd run the other way."

"Exactly! I don't know how to describe it. It's like if he actually wanted to kiss me, I think I'd die of mortification."

"So you think of Beau like a celebrity or something?"

"It's complicated. I have similar—but not exactly the same—feelings for Intrepid Inger, Gottfried Wilhelm Leibniz, and Tina Fey."

"Intrepid Inger? Isn't she that solo travel blogger you're always talking about?"

"Yes. She is she."

"Who is Gottfried Wilhelm Leibniz?"

"The father of calculus. He's dead."

Claire twisted her lips to the side, and she looked like she was trying not to laugh.

I shrugged helplessly. "I know. I'm a math nerd."

"Yes. You are a math nerd. But you're a math nerd who can totally pull off a sexy Gandalf costume."

"Oh my God. I forgot!" My hand flew to my beard. "Maybe he won't recognize me."

Claire made a short sound of impatience. "Let me get this straight. You'll kiss a random guy on the street with nothing but sass. But if you had to talk to one of your hero crushes—a famous woman travel blogger, the father of calculus, arguably the funniest woman alive, or Beau Winston—you develop aphasia and faint?"

I nodded.

"Honey, Beau Winston puts his pants on one leg at a time. He's completely normal. Why the hero worship? Go talk to him."

"Every time I saw him while we were growing up, he was always doing something brave, heroic, or remarkably kind. Did I tell you he saved my cat? And one time I saw him rescue two little boys from a rattlesnake. And one time he—"

"I get it. You've spent years building him up in your head."

"I can't talk to him. Not yet. Maybe one day, after some extreme mental preparation." My whisper was harsh, urgent.

"Yes, you can."

"No. Really. I can't." I felt my eyes widen to their maximum diameter. "I've never successfully carried on a conversation with Beau Winston. It's not just the fact that I've built him up in my head. I have a terrible record of failure where he is concerned. Every time I try to speak, my brain forgets English, and I start slurring Swahili or Swedish or Swiss. He thinks I'm a total idiot."

"People of Switzerland don't speak *Swiss*. They speak German, French, Italian, and Romansh."

"See? I'm becoming dumber with each second."

I sucked in a breath because I could hear his voice now; he was speaking to the little girl, and the sound was so fantastically charming it caused my stomach to pitch, then lurch like I was in a small boat in the middle of the ocean. I placed my hand over my belly and braced my feet apart.

When he entered my peripheral vision, my attention was drawn to him like a magnet. He was still smiling, but it was smaller, polite. He was handing the little girl off to a lady I recognized as Mrs. MacIntyre, the lead librarian at the local branch in town. Tinker Bell must be her granddaughter.

She said something about a chicken or a rooster. He said something in response. They laughed. I stared, letting the velvety sound wash over me. Once again I was caught on a big wave in the middle of the ocean—pitch, lurch.

Then it happened. His eyes flickered to the side, likely feeling my stalker stare, and he did a double take. His gaze ensnared mine. My throat worked without success, and I was a heat wave of cognizance. His stare narrowed as I continued to meet his gaze.

God, I was such a creeper.

I wanted to look away, but I physically could not. He so rarely looked at me. I felt like I was falling, my surroundings fading away—everything except *him*, and his goodness and magnanimity and blue, blue, blue eyes.

Annoyingly, the music only I could hear whenever he

was near started playing between my ears—this time it was "Dreamweaver" by Gary Wright—therefore I missed the sound of his voice when he said, "Hey, Jessica."

Instead, I guesstimated what he'd said based on the movement of his lips, and subsequently tried my best to turn down the volume in my head. I nodded at him, still unable to look away.

Then, horrified, I watched as he excused himself from Mrs. MacIntyre and Tinker Bell, and walked to where I was standing with Claire. I swayed a little, took a step backward as he advanced; Claire slipped her arm through mine and fit herself against my side. She probably thought I was going to either faint or make a run for it.

Unfortunately, I managed neither by the time he made it to where we were standing.

"Hey…Beau," Claire said, the hesitation in her voice obvious. "You are Beau, right? Or are you Duane?"

He gave us a crooked smile that looked completely delectable and mischievous, his eyes darting between us. "You can't tell the difference?"

Claire returned his smile with a small one of her own. Beau's charm was contagious and addictive. I'd once overheard my daddy tell my momma that the six Winston boys had inherited their father's ability to charm snakes, the IRS, and women.

I was also smiling, although mine probably looked dazed and weird. I was thankful for the long gray beard around my mouth. I hoped it camouflaged my expression of dazed, worshipful adoration.

"I'm pretty sure you're Duane," Claire said, then indicated me with a tilt of her head. "But Jess thinks you're Beau."

His eyes moved back to mine—somehow more intense, interested, and piercing than they'd been before—and he swept them up and down me again. On the return pass I saw what I thought might be appreciation, and that's when I remembered I was wearing my ironic sexy Gandalf costume, which basically hid nothing except my face and hair.

The point of the costume was to irritate my daddy and Jackson and amuse myself with delightful irony while doing so. I may no longer be the bratty teenager who left home four years ago, but I still enjoyed little tokens of rebellion against the overprotective males in my family. It hadn't occurred to me until that very moment someone who mattered might look at me, my curves in this scrap of fabric, and see more sexy than irony.

"What's this costume, Jessica? Are you a wizard?" His lips tugged to the side, but his tone deepened when he added, "I like it."

The tenor of his voice paired with the words sent a new jolt racing through my body. But it was different than anything I'd felt in his proximity before. This wasn't me going gaga for a childhood hero crush.

This feeling was...mature.

I gripped Claire tighter in surprise.

"She's sexy Gandalf. She was going to be a sexy bee, but the shop sold out of pollinator costumes."

Beau laughed—a sound that, for reasons unknown, I felt in my uterus—and reached for the beard at my navel. The back of his fingers brushed against my stomach as he plucked the length of synthetic facial hair from my inconsequential sheath of a costume.

"The beard adds a certain something..." He tugged just gently and winked at me.

Of course, my response was to stare at him mutely because the grin plus wink plus the light touch of his fingers meant I was terribly confused. Instead of outgrowing my crush, apparently I was now unwillingly compounding my adoration by adding new, very *adult* feelings. Some odd little corner of my brain briefly thought about the logistics of wearing this long white beard always, every day.

"Hey, if you tug her beard, she gets to tug yours," Claire teased.

His smile growing, the redhead stepped forward and into my space, his eyes at half-mast as they glittered down at me. "Go ahead, Jessica… Touch it."

He said my name like it was a secret. Beau's words and nearness stole my breath.

I could *smell* him, and it just made me want to…want to… I don't even know what. I'd had boyfriends before, guys I liked, but the sudden depth and breadth of my dirty, sordid thoughts took me by surprise and I felt a hot flood of confused alarm in my chest.

Beau's eyes seemed to flicker, then flare as though he could read my thoughts; they dropped to my lips.

Once again, a new rush of something not at all hero-worshippy made my stomach twist. My female reaction to his maleness made no sense!

Well, it made some sense.

Both Winston twins were seriously good-looking. It hadn't escaped my notice how he'd walked just moments before, how his hips moved, the way his T-shirt pulled over his pectoral muscles and was tight where the short sleeves ended at his biceps.

"I am so sorry about your momma, son." A voice to my

right and his left pulled our attention away from each other. We both turned our heads to find Mr. McClure, our local fire chief and Claire's father-in-law, standing there with his hand outstretched. Beau looked down at it and then, taking a step away from me, accepted the offered hand as the man continued. "She was a good woman, and she'll be missed."

I shook myself a little, a spark of sobriety cutting its way through "Dreamweaver." The Winstons had lost their mother not more than four weeks ago. Bethany Winston hadn't been more than forty-seven. It was very sad and had been quite sudden. I hadn't gone to the funeral as I was sick with flu, but apparently everyone else in town had shown up to pay their respects to Mrs. Winston, her six sons, and her daughter.

"Thank you, sir." Beau nodded once. The heat of his earlier expression was now extinguished, replaced with a tight-lipped smile and a shuttered gaze.

Mr. McClure nodded at Beau, then turned to Claire and me. He greeted us warmly, stepping forward to give Claire a kiss on the cheek. During this intermission, I felt Beau's eyes follow my movements. I gave myself a mental high-five for keeping my attention on Claire's father-in-law.

After hellos were exchanged, Mr. McClure narrowed his eyes at Claire, "Claire, did you lock your car?"

I thought it was cute how Mr. McClure looked after Claire like she was his daughter; it warmed my heart. Claire had married her childhood sweetheart. Her husband, Ben McClure, had been in the army; he'd died overseas a few years ago.

Claire nodded and her lips curved in a warm and patient smile. "Yes, sir. I locked my car."

To my surprise, Mr. McClure swung his blue eyes to me, "Jessica, did you lock your car?"

I blinked at him, caught off guard, and glanced at Claire.

"There's been some thefts," Claire explained, "and not just tourists, like usual. Jennifer Sylvester's new BMW went missing last week."

"Her momma told me she had a banana cake in the front seat, too." Mr. McClure *exhaled a short huff*, like the real crime was the disappearing banana cake, then turned his attention back to Beau. "Are your brothers here?"

"Yes, sir. Everyone but, uh"—his eyes flickered to mine then back to Mr. McClure—"everyone but my twin."

"I see." He nodded, glancing down the hallway toward the sound of music. "I need to talk to your brother Cletus about the transmission work he did."

Beau stood a little taller. "Is there something wrong?"

Beau, Duane, and their older brother Cletus owned the Winston Brothers Auto Shop in town, hence the blue, grease-stained coveralls he currently wore.

When I was growing up, most new-to-town people had trouble keeping all the Winston boys' names straight. I used to describe the family as follows:

Jethro has brown hair and true hazel eyes—though sometimes they look almost gray. He's the oldest and the most likely to give you a sweet smile while he steals your car and/or wallet.

Billy is the second oldest. His hair is a darker brown and his eyes are a bright, startling blue. He's the most serious and responsible (and incidentally the worst tempered) of the bunch.

Next comes Cletus, number three: shortest, brown beard, olive-green eyes. You can tell him apart from Jethro because he doesn't smile often and his beard is longer. Instead of stealing your car, he's more likely to take apart your toaster and tell you how it works. And he's always been a little…odd. Sweet, but odd. As an example, he'd started attending my first period advanced placement calculus class two months ago. Apparently, he'd talked to my principal and had been cleared to sit in for the rest of the year.

Ashley is number four. She's the girl and looks just like a beauty contestant version of Billy.

Then the identical twins—Beau and Duane—with their red beards and blue eyes. Good luck telling them apart if they don't talk, but if they do, Beau's the friendly one.

Last but not least is Roscoe. He's a mixture of Jethro and Billy—big smiles that hide a more serious nature. He's also a huge and indiscriminate flirt (or at least he was when I last knew him).

The fire chief shook his head. "No, no. It's not for my truck, son. It's Red, the fire engine. He's helping me get the old girl running again for the Christmas parade."

"Ah. I see. Yeah, Cletus is playing his banjo." Beau tossed his thumb over his shoulder. "Only one room is jamming so far tonight; I think everyone else is waiting until the trick-or-treating is over."

Mr. McClure glanced in the direction Beau had indicated. "I'll go sit in then and wait for a break." He turned a friendly smile to Claire and me. "Girls, I'd be honored to be your escort."

Claire nodded for both of us, but before she could verbally accept the offer, Beau reached out and grabbed my arm lightning fast.

"Claire, you go on." Beau pulled me away from my friend in a smooth motion. "I'd like to catch up with Jess. See y'all later."

He didn't wait for Claire or me to react.

Before I knew what was happening, he'd slipped his rough palm into mine, grasped my fingers, and turned toward the converted cafeteria, tugging me after him. I was so shocked by the sensation of his skin and the electric current running up my arm that I followed mutely because I could only focus on where our palms touched.

I loved the feel of him. In truth I was in danger of climbing him. I just wanted to be near him, touch him, snuggle against him. He was so epically enticing.

We wove through the crowd as I tried to memorize the feeling of his hand grasping mine. I had difficulty drawing breath; my stomach was an eruption of suspiciously amorous butterflies. People said hi—to both him and me—but we didn't pause. I was his shadow as Beau led me to the buffet table. I dreaded reaching it because he would likely release me. To my surprise we kept on walking.

He didn't glance back at me as we skirted around a table laden with lemonade and sweet tea, heading behind a curtain that ran the length of one wall—from ceiling to floor—and obscured a set of stairs leading to a small stage. The stage, likewise, was hidden by the curtain. Beau didn't pause once we were up the steps or on the stage. Instead he continued tugging until he had me to one side backstage, completely hidden by the curtain, around a corner, and behind a wall.

It was dark and my eyes required several seconds to adjust; likewise, my brain hadn't yet caught up with where we were and how we'd arrived here, not to mention who I was with. A single overhead light source cast our surroundings in a grayish murkiness. I nearly tripped over my own feet when Beau turned, placed his hands suddenly on my hips, and backed me into the wall.

I felt solid concrete behind me. Beau and all his heroic gorgeousness loomed before me, scant inches away. His glittering eyes ensnared mine. Then and only then did he stop.

I was so confused—really, *discombobulated* was the word for it. This was like something out of a music video fantasy. (Did I forget to mention that my daydreams actually present themselves as music videos à la Paula Abdul's "Rush, Rush," complete with glowing, imperfection-blurring lens filters?) I could only gaze up at him in wonder.

He leaned forward, and his forehead hit the rim of my hat. Scowling, he pulled it, the wig, and the beard from my head, dropping them to the floor.

"I like this costume," he said in a low voice as his hands reclaimed their spot, his thumbs rubbing the area just above my hips like he was entitled to touch me and my body however he liked. The heat from his palms sent spiking shivers to my lower belly. "But I do not enjoy that hat."

I'd known Beau for almost fifteen years, but had never imagined a moment like this, not in my wildest dreams. I hadn't been lying when I'd told Claire my crush on Beau was complicated. My daydreams involved him and me saving people together, a team of rescuers—like the one time I watched as he saved two little boys from a rattlesnake. He'd always been patient, verging on saintly.

Basically, they were the neutered fantasies of a young girl with extreme hero worship.

But Beau didn't look patient or saintly now, and he felt very, very real. Even in the murky dimness, his eyes sparkled like sapphires, like they possessed their own internal radiance.

His hands slid up my body, then pushed my cape over my shoulders with a whisper-light touch. He removed the staff from my hand. I watched as Beau leaned it against the wall with care, his boots scuffing against the wooden floor.

"Jessica James, you've been giving me hot looks that are difficult to ignore." He said this in a near growl, leaning a fraction of an inch closer.

I didn't respond. I didn't know what a *hot look* was, what it meant, or how to make it on purpose. Regardless, I surmised my inadvertent hot looks were responsible for our alone time. My heart twisted, then leapt as he wet his bottom lip just before drawing the succulent flesh into his mouth, between his teeth, and biting.

That's right, bite that lip.

I almost groaned.

I was maniacally and fiercely aroused, and I was completely ill-equipped to deal with these feelings.

A broken hymen while horseback riding at thirteen; lots of random kisses with random guys for fun and practice; a few inconsequential and forgettable gropings in high school and college; a drunken, laconic coupling in my dorm room with my physics lab TA last year. These were the pithy total of my adult sexual exploits.

In all honesty, I'd enjoyed the horse ride more than the man ride. At least the horse had been a stallion. Looking back, my lab TA was more like a Shetland pony—hairy and small.

Truly, I didn't know what I was doing, what *we* were doing. This was beyond bizarre. If the father of calculus or Intrepid Inger had brought me backstage at the Green Valley Community Center, I doubt I would be having such divergent thoughts.

Instinct told me to tackle Beau, maul him before he discovered his error and tousled my hair like I was still a twelve-year-old. At the very least, the crazy part of my brain had made up its mind to tempt his mouth down to my chest. Nothing fantastic had ever happened to my nipples before. I was pretty sure I'd die a happy woman after Beau Winston did something fantastic to my nipples.

Speaking of nipples, I didn't realize I'd brought Beau's hand from my hip to my breast until hot sparks of desire radiated from where I pressed his palm against me, the only barriers between our skin my lace bra and the thin fabric of my dress.

Beau stared at me, his mouth parted in stunned surprise. His eyebrows jumped, and his eyes widened at my forward gesture. I arched forward, again without consciously meaning to, straining to close the distance between our bodies, wanting to feel his hard against my soft.

And then I learned what a *hot look* was.

Because Beau Winston was giving me a hot look.

I wanted to label it as incendiary, but as it was the first hot look I'd ever been aware of receiving, I decided instead to make his hot look the baseline by which all other hot looks would be measured.

I didn't get much time to mull over what units of measurement I would apply to hot looks—would it be Celsius? Calories? Watts? Voltage? Or lumens?—because Beau did three things, driving all thought and ability to reason from my brain.

First, his fingers at my breast worked, massaged, and caressed while his thumb brushed over the nipple. His hand felt greedy, rough, and fantastic.

Second, his other hand reached around, gripped my bottom, and squeezed as he brought me against him.

Third, he kissed me. Beau Winston was a helluva good kisser.

And, oh God, parts of me tensed, clenched, and braced in a completely new way, a way that made no sense at all, but sent all the amorous flutters diving straight to my pelvis and heat to my lungs. I was abruptly starring in the music video for Beyoncé's "Naughty Girl" and desperately trying to figure out how to get Beau's clothes off.

He dominated, pushing me against the wall, his hands under my dress, on the bare skin of my hips then into my lace underwear, grabbing my bare ass. Nothing about him was soft. He was hard edges, solid granite everywhere I touched. And I touched him. I touched him in a fevered frenzy because I didn't know what the hell was going on or when it would stop. I hoped never. Peripherally, I heard my wizard's staff clatter to the ground.

I'd always thought of Beau as a really, really nice guy. But he didn't kiss like a nice guy. Not saintly in the least.

He kissed with dangerous and punishing hunger, his mouth greedy and demanding. He bit me—my bottom lip—then soothed and tasted the abused flesh with his tongue while grinding his hips against mine, his hard length growing against my belly.

"Fuck, Jess…" he growled, then pulled his mouth from mine, his breathing labored. He bent to bite my jaw, lick my ear, suck the soft skin into his hot mouth while one hand pushed my little gray dress up to expose my lace-clad breasts. The fingers of his other hand danced around the hem of my panties but moved no farther. I felt his hesitation and I clawed him. I dug my nails into his shoulders and bucked instinctively, wanting him to touch me.

The non-crazy part of my brain told me I was going to be seriously mortified by my behavior at some point in the future, but crazy was now the overwhelming majority. Sanity had lost the popular vote.

In response to my crazy, he tugged the cup of my bra down. Then his wet mouth was on the center of my breast. Then his tongue swirled over my nipple as a tortured-sounding moan rumbled in the back of his throat. Then I panted because it *was* fantastic.

I reached for his white shirt, drawing him closer, and tried to roughly pull it off. He acquiesced, helping me remove the material, as my fingertips fumbled for the hem of his boxers, then delved inside. This was easily accomplished since the coveralls were only loosely held up by the long sleeves tied around his waist. My hand closed around his hard length, and he sucked in a startled-sounding breath, releasing it raggedly as I stroked him.

"Oh God…" he breathed, his eyes moving back to mine. I'd expected to find them dazed with desire; instead he looked a little shocked, panicked even. "Wait, wait a minute."

He reached for my wrist, and I saw his intentions clear as day. We were moving too fast. He was going to put on the brakes.

But the thing was, crazy didn't want brakes. Crazy wanted acceleration. Crazy wanted velocity. Crazy wanted reckless, heedless, crazy, passionate sex with Beau Winston. And crazy wanted it right now, against this wall, at the Green Valley Community Center, while children trick-or-treated and Mrs. Sylvester traded recipes for blueberry muffins, ignorant to the fervent and erotic moment on the other side.

I stroked him again, pressing my chest to his and lifting on my tiptoes to bite his neck. He shuddered, moaned, his hips instinctively jutting forward and into my palm even as his fingers tightened around my wrist and gently tried to force my withdrawal.

Instead, with my dress bunched up under my armpits, I rubbed my body against his; my thumb circled the head of his erection. With my other hand, I brought his fingers back to my panties, pressing them over the fabric and against my center, and I nipped at his parted lips.

His breathing was labored, and he moaned again, cursing. Beau's eyes were squeezed shut like he was trying to separate himself from what was happening, like he was trying to strengthen his resolve…like he was losing control.

Abruptly, and with an audible growl, he yanked my hand out of his boxers and turned, walking ten steps farther backstage and away from me.

I felt the loss of his heat first, then the loss of his touch. I didn't try to pursue him because I felt dizzy, disoriented, and out of breath. Instead I leaned against the wall at my back, closing my eyes. My body hummed and protested the loss of promised fulfillment. I don't know how long I stood there, gulping air and trying to figure out what had just happened and why it ended.

Eventually I heard him say, "Goddammit…" Again, like a restrained roar, his voice closer than I'd expected.

I opened my eyes and found him standing a few feet away, shirtless, hands on his hips. His chest visibly rose and fell as he breathed. His gaze flickered over my body, then to the floor of the stage. Numbly, I adjusted my bra to conceal my breasts and tugged my tiny dress down to my thighs, allowing myself to devour his muscled torso, the ridges of his stomach, the plane of his hard chest.

I wanted to touch him again.

"Jessica, you *have got* to stop looking at me like that." He sounded irritated, desperate, catching me by surprise and pulling my eyes back to his.

I was startled to find that his teeth were clenched, his eyes were flashing; however, despite that he'd just reprimanded me for how I was looking at him, Beau was giving me an extremely hot look. Regardless of his words and the fact he'd been the one to end our frantic grope-fest, he appeared torn. He appeared to be struggling.

He appeared to want me very, very badly.

I stared at him, mystified. The realization of his want paired with the reality of the last several minutes caught up with the here and now. He was watching me as I was watching him. My stare was undoubtedly one of inviting and anxious expectation; whereas his glare oscillated between blatant desire peppered heavily with longing and then fierce frustration.

I waited silently, witnessed his resolve waver, watching his eyes lose focus as they stared beseechingly at mine. He was still breathing hard.

He took a step forward as though pulled, stumbling in a daze, had no choice; words tumbled from his lips in a rush, "Jessica, I'm not who you think I am and—fuck it all—but I want you, I've always wanted you, and I can't do this without you knowing—"

"Duane, you dummy. Are you back here?" a man called from my left, and I heard the telltale sound of boots on steps.

My eyes bulged.

My jaw dropped.

My breath caught in my throat.

And my head whipped to the side and toward the newcomer.

It wasn't that I feared getting caught in a heated moment, not at all. The cause of my intense shock was the sound of the approaching voice. It was Beau's voice.

"Are you back there?" The steps slowed, then stopped. Beau once more called out to Duane, "Should I…? Uh, do you need some privacy?"

My body jolted as understanding punched me in the stomach. The ice bucket of reality quelled any hot looks or hot feelings and I was left cold. So very, very cold. I turned my attention back to the man of my dreams.

Except *he* wasn't.

My companion was most definitely *not* Beau Winston—hero, world's nicest guy. No, no, no. This man was not Beau. This man was Duane.

And this man had just done *fantastic* things to my nipples.

Jessica

2

> "The road that is built in hope is more pleasant to the traveler than the road built in despair, even though they both lead to the same destination."
>
> —MARION ZIMMER BRADLEY,
> *THE FALL OF ATLANTIS*

AS SOON AS OUR EYES tangled, Duane winced—almost like I'd sucker punched him—and he turned away. I watched his muscled torso and chest rise and fall with an expansive breath just before he plucked his shirt from the floor and pulled it on.

He cleared his throat, then called out, "Yeah, a little privacy would be nice."

"Who's back there with you? Is it Tina?" Beau's deep, velvety chuckle met my ears, and my stomach twisted painfully.

I felt like I was going to be sick. My eyes drifted shut; the back of my head hit the wall behind me. My chest seized. I was so stupid. I wished for a black hole to open up under my feet and swallow me, send me to the other side of the universe.

Tina was, of course, Tina Patterson. Duane's girlfriend. Or ex-girlfriend. Really, keeping up with their on-again, off-again relationship was inviting whiplash. She was also my first cousin on my daddy's side as well as my best friend in elementary and middle school, but we'd gone in different directions since.

"None of your business, dummy. Go away," Duane answered his twin; his voice sounded thick, gravelly, and I felt his eyes on me though mine remained firmly closed.

"All right, all right. Fine. Tell Tina I say hi, but we're leaving for Bandit Lake in twenty minutes." Beau's response was paired with the sound of boots descending the stairs.

The first notes of a new song played between my ears: Radiohead's "Creep." Ice entered my veins even as a mortified flush spread up my neck, over my cheeks to the top of my head. Gritting my teeth, I opened my eyes and glared at Duane Winston.

If he thought I'd been giving him hot looks before, then my look now was the polar opposite. I was aiming for the equivalent of midnight at the Arctic pole during the winter solstice.

His hands were on his hips, and I watched him slowly nibble on his bottom lip like he was tasting it, like he was tasting me. His eyes were on the floor of the stage, his breath beginning to even, though not yet completely normalized.

A weird thought occurred to me, making me feel hot with guilt and shame: I'd cheated on Beau, betrayed him in some way. Really, this was just more of my crazy thinking because my infatuation with Beau had always been extremely one-sided. I may have been ridiculous, but I was not deluded.

Regardless, the guilt, shame, and anger I was feeling meant I'd never wanted to stab and/or maim someone as much as I wanted to stab and/or maim Duane Winston in that moment. Therefore I was not surprised when I said the words I was thinking.

"You are such a bastard."

His eyes lifted then, glittering sapphires that held just a whisper of bitter amusement buried under another hot look.

"Now she speaks," he said flatly.

"What? What are you talking about?"

"Now you speak," he accused, sounding so different to my ears.

Instead of the friendly and adorable Beau, I heard Duane. Sarcastic, sullen, snappish Duane.

"This whole time, since I walked over to you and Claire, you haven't said a single word. Not when I took you away from your friend, not when I pulled you through the cafeteria, not when I brought you here, not when I had my hand in your panties and your tits in my mouth. But now, miraculously you find your voice."

God, how I loathed him.

"You are *such* a *bastard*!" I repeated, louder and a little more violently this time as I pointedly tried to ignore the confusing, swirling, humming desire that still twisted in my belly. I used the lingering passion to fuel my anger.

"Nice to see you again, Jess. I admit, you've filled out very nicely"—his eyes blazed a path from my strappy sandals to my breasts—"but you're just as bratty as ever."

I charged forward and pushed against his chest. "You lying asshat! I thought you were Beau."

Before I could claw his eyes out, Duane caught my wrists and walked me backward against the wall, holding my arms hostage over my head, his body trapping me, keeping me in place. I tried to knee him in the groin, but he deftly sidestepped and pressed his legs against mine to keep them immobile.

"Ah, there now, Princess, we'll have none of that."

This unfortunate position meant that his impressive erection was digging into my abdomen and my breasts were flattened against his chest. Again, confusing, swirling, humming desire ignited, and I clenched my jaw to keep from rubbing my torso along his. Our eyes locked. His look was still hot but now tempered with something else, something that felt like contempt flavored with bitterness.

"I hope you wander into a hornet's nest and die of an acetylcholine overdose," I spat.

"You say the prettiest things."

"Let me go!"

"Not until you calm down." These words sounded exceedingly reasonable.

"Calm down? *Calm down?*" I bellowed because I'd never been so angry in my entire life. I didn't know how I was going to calm down. I might never calm down. I might spend the rest of my life as the five-foot-six, blond, female version of the Incredible Hulk (so, She-Hulk, but not a lawyer). I wanted to smash everything, starting with Duane Winston.

"Yes. Calm down."

"I AM NEVER GOING TO CALM DOWN!" I shouted in his face.

"THEN WE'LL STAND HERE FOREVER!" he shouted in my face.

I glared at him. He glared back. A storm of feelings whirled around and between us. I despised him, yet some nonsensical—obviously mentally ill—part of myself felt relief at the discovery of his duplicitousness.

Duane had never made me dreamy-eyed because he was definitely *not* heroic. Duane had made me tongue-tied, but only because he'd always made me mad. He wasn't perfect;

he was real. And he was an arrogant ass. Yeah, he was sinfully good-looking, but he was also argumentative and aggravating.

Nevertheless, and because crazy brain was obviously still in charge, I desperately wanted him to kiss me again. Kiss me and touch me and pull my hair and bite the softest parts of my body. I wanted his hungry mouth and greedy fingers.

I wanted him.

His eyes—made even more brilliant by his anger—narrowed as he watched me, moved between mine, then darted to my lips. I wondered if he could read my thoughts. I wondered if I was still throwing him inadvertent hot looks. I wondered at the unfairness of his eyes. He had such pretty eyes, blue and glittering, mesmerizing… It was a shame they belonged to Satan.

"I hate you," I whispered, feeling confused, defensive, and therefore spiteful.

Duane's fingers loosened just a smidge where he held me, and his thumb stroked the inside of my wrist. I shivered, and I hated myself for the involuntary response.

He cocked an eyebrow and whispered gently, softly, "I hate you too, Jess. I hate you so very, very much…"

Inexplicably, my breathing quickened. Further muddling matters, Duane's pretty eyes were fastened on my mouth, and his mouth was lowering—inch by excruciating inch—closer to mine. As though pulled, as though our lips were still magnetized. I lifted my chin.

Then, like before, he pulled away. Again I felt the loss of his heat first, but this time I felt like he'd also thrown me off a bridge. I was free-falling into nothing. As well, his eyes—instead of unfocused with desire—were mocking and hard.

He shrugged, stuffing his hands into his pockets, his lips

twisted to the side in a derisive sneer. "Did you forget? I'm not Beau."

I drew myself up, straightened my spine, braced my feet apart, and shot him daggers as I said, "Obviously you're not Beau. He doesn't have to lie about who he is in order for me to like him."

Duane's flinch was subtle; if I'd blinked, I would have missed it. The muscle at his temple jumped, and his eyes hardened further. He looked like he was going to toss me another insult, so I bent and retrieved my beard, staff, and hat. My cape swirled around my shoulders. I was intent on getting as far away from him as possible, as soon as possible.

"You know what? Never mind. Just…just go away, and leave me alone." I turned, tucking my hat under my arm, and managed three paces toward the curtain before Duane's hand caught me by the wrist.

"What are you doing?" he asked.

I tried to shake him off, but his grip tightened. "I'm leaving."

"Not that way, you're not."

I huffed, still not looking at him. "Why not?"

Without answering me, Duane turned me around, then slipped his hand in mine. I promptly planted my feet in place and pulled my palm out of his grip.

He turned suddenly and charged me, cursing under his breath before spearing me with a menacing glower and barely restrained fury. "Listen, Princess, my brothers are probably waiting for me out there. If we leave the way we came in, they're all going to see us. Together. And that includes Beau. Now do you understand?"

I frowned at him, absorbing his harshly spoken statement.

At length I nodded once, reluctantly realizing I would have to accept his help in order to avoid an epic walk of shame. "So... how do I get out of here?"

"Follow me." He moved like he was going to touch my hand again, but I pulled it out of his reach and took a step back. His eyes shot scorching flames at my retreat.

"You don't need to hold my hand in order for me to follow you." I crossed my arms over my chest, closed my cape around me, and lifted my chin. "Lead the way, *Duane*."

He studied me and his eyes dimmed, grew remote and guarded. Inexplicably, my stomach flipped, and I felt oddly remorseful.

After a protracted moment, Duane swallowed. His voice was thick and gravelly when he finally said, "Sure thing, Princess." Then he turned away from me toward some unseen exit, his stride unhurried, languid, and confident, and sexy as hell.

I hesitated for a single second, then followed reluctantly. I couldn't help but admire his backside—the nice curve of his bottom—the width of his strong shoulders, how his waist tapered at his hips, and how he walked.

I kept thinking about his heavenly kisses, his divine, rough hands on my body, and his hot mouth on my skin. I pushed those thoughts away, but they were replaced with the memory of how great he'd felt in my hands—long and smooth and hard and thick—and how close I'd come to having him inside me. I bit my lip to stifle a pitiful groan, feeling out of breath and dizzy from the mere possibility.

Despite how I loathed him, I knew now that riding Duane would not be like anything I'd ever experienced. He was no Shetland pony. He was a stallion. And I despised myself a little for still wanting him. I was all mixed up.

And, worst of all, I would have to live my life trying to suppress the memory of Duane Winston doing fantastic things to my nipples.

♥

Cletus Winston took a step back from my truck and scratched his beard. He looked to me, where I hovered anxiously by my open driver's side door, and said, "Catastrophic engine failure."

I blinked at him. "What?"

"Catastrophic engine failure. You have it."

Feeling abruptly winded, I croaked, "That doesn't sound good."

"It's not good. It's bad," he said simply.

I shifted from foot to foot, trying to keep my teeth from chattering. Now at ten o'clock and bitterly cold outside, I was still dressed as sexy Gandalf. I was sure my nipples were as hard as frozen peas and gave my chest a lovely headlight effect. To Cletus's credit, he didn't appear to be interested in my boobtacular headlights.

"What can I do?" I asked, grimacing at the small desperate quality of my voice. The evening's events were catching up with me.

After Duane had led me outside from a hidden exit behind the stage, I'd taken off without looking back and reentered the community center from the front door. Immediately, my brother and father saw me and proceeded to throw disapproving glares at my skimpy costume.

I welcomed the distraction because every part of me missed the feeling of Duane's hands and mouth. All evening I shivered, but it wasn't from cold. I tried my best to ignore it. I was unsettled.

I'd effectively put off Claire's pointed questions. I'd excelled at chitchat with my students' parents—despite my ironic costume choice—and I'd successfully avoided seeing both Duane and Beau. Granted, based on what Beau had said about leaving for Bandit Lake, they were probably long gone from the community center well before I tried to leave. Duane was probably off with my cousin Tina, giving her his hot looks and kisses…

Ugh!

I shook myself out of my weird musings about Duane—who I most certainly *did not* care about—and tried to focus on something else, anything else.

I'd even sat still long enough to listen to Cletus Winston play his banjo solo in one of the music rooms during an oddly charming folk rendition of Michael Jackson's "Thriller."

But I was tired, and my head was muddled, and I was tired of my head being muddled, and my monster truck wouldn't start. Thankfully, just as I was about to give up hope, Cletus was walking by my truck with his banjo case tucked under his arm.

He recognized me from my perch, and stopped. Without asking any questions, he motioned for me to pop the release and took a flashlight out of his pants pocket. Then he delved under my hood.

At present he was shaking his head, his lips twisting to the side. "Your timing belt broke. You need a new engine."

"I need a new engine?" I asked dumbly.

"You need a new engine and a new timing belt."

All the wind left my lungs in a whoosh, and I staggered

a bit to the side. I was dizzy, mostly because there were little dollar signs flying around my head. I couldn't afford a new engine. I couldn't afford a car. I had student loans out the wazoo and a new car would mean delaying all my plans.

In an instant, Cletus was at my elbow, his hand wrapping around my waist.

He must've realized I was about to fall down, because he scooped me up in his arms and said, "You'll have to grab my banjo and carry it on your lap."

"What?" I stared up at him, at his brown beard and his perma-serious eyes.

"My banjo case…you'll need to carry it on your lap. I can't carry both you and the case unless I put you over my shoulder. But I think that would be counterproductive, seeing as your skirt is extremely short and has already hiked up around your thighs."

I glanced down at myself and found his words to be an understatement. I'd taken my cape off earlier. Along with my beard, hat, and staff, it was in the cab of the truck. Therefore I was basically mooning the darkened parking lot.

"I'm sorry, I'm sorry." I shook my head to clear it. "Just… just put me down. I'll figure something out."

Cletus deposited my feet on the ground but didn't move away. "Did your daddy already leave?"

I nodded. My dad and brother would be on duty tonight. I had no desire to call them for a ride.

"That's too bad. I meant to talk to him about the mail sorter down at the station. It's due for maintenance. Do you happen to know if they're having any troubles?"

Non sequiturs and rapid subject changes weren't unusual for Cletus, so I shook my head, having no idea what he was talking about. "I'm sorry, I have no idea."

"Hmm… Well, what about your momma?"

"She's visiting my aunt Louisa in Texas, who has cancer, so I don't know how long Momma will be out there." My teeth chattered and I glared at the monster truck.

Aunt Louisa had no children and had never been married. She'd lived alone in a huge house on a horse farm in Texas for the last fifteen or so years. My momma and I had visited for a few weeks every summer, and I'd spent my entire summers during college keeping my aunt company and running errands. Sometimes she'd come to our house for Christmas.

She was the kind of person who kept others at an arm's length. Even after spending months with her, I never felt like I really knew her. But my momma and aunt were very close.

I heard Cletus sigh. With his arm still around my waist, he walked us both to his banjo case and picked it up. "Well, looks like you're coming with me. Do you have a sweater or something?"

"Naw, Cletus. I don't want to be a bother."

His hand gripped me tighter. "Nonsense. You're no bother. But I have to make a stop before I take you home. What about that sweater? A coat maybe?"

"I have a wizard cape in the truck," I offered weakly. "I wouldn't have driven it tonight if I thought the problem was this serious. I didn't expect it to break down."

"They never do." Cletus grunted and kicked my driver's side door shut; he then pushed me gently against it. "Hold still," he said, placing his banjo back on the ground. He took off his red and black flannel jacket and handed it to me.

I thought about pushing it away, but something about his deadpan expression told me not to argue.

"Thanks, Cletus."

"You're welcome, Miss James."

I frowned at the formal salutation. Cletus Winston was the third oldest of the Winston kids and was a full six or seven years older than me. "You can call me Jessica, you know."

"Nope. You're my teacher. It wouldn't be fit." He grabbed his banjo case in one arm, me with the other, and marched us to his car.

"Wait." I glanced over my shoulder. "I didn't lock the truck."

Cletus shrugged. "I wouldn't fret too much about it. In order for someone to steal the beast, they'd have to install a new engine."

♥

After the seventeenth switchback, I lost count. Cletus was taking me up the mountain to check on a friend's house before he could take me home.

We fell into a surprisingly companionable silence as he focused on navigating his Geo Prizm. That was also surprising—Cletus's car choice. Here was a guy who worked on cars for a living. He, Duane, and Beau found old classics and fixed them up to sell at a hefty premium. According to my daddy, the Winston Brothers Auto Shop was doing gangbusters business.

And Cletus was driving a 1990 Geo Prizm painted primer gray.

I tried to use the quiet time to ponder my own car situation, figure out a solution. Instead I spent ninety-nine percent of my brainpower slapping away thoughts of Duane Winston and his tongue. He really did have a lovely tongue. Unlike most of my previous kiss encounters, Duane seemed to be a man that actually knew what he was doing with his tongue. He *used* it in the most delightful ways.

I was a little stunned and disoriented when we pulled into a gravel driveway at the very top of the mountain and Cletus put the car in neutral to park.

"We're here," he said, engaging the emergency brake, the sound punctuating his words. "You should come with me. I don't know how long I'll be, and I don't like the idea of leaving you in the car by yourself."

I shrugged and looked around at the inky darkness. I had no idea where we were and couldn't find my way back if my life and the future of chocolate hung in the balance.

"I'm sure I'll be fine. Looks like there's not another person out here for miles."

"That may be," he said, his eyes flickering over to mine before he twisted in his seat to pull out a large canvas bag from behind him, "but there are bears out here. This is a reliable car, but it won't keep out bears."

My eyes widened at the thought, and I quickly opened my door when he opened his. I followed him to a big house with a wraparound porch. All the lights were off.

"Whose house is this?" I asked, taking in the pretty white trim.

"Dr. Runous, the game warden from DC. He's on a trek with my brother Jethro at present in North Carolina. Should be back close to Christmas, I suspect."

"And you're looking after the place?"

Cletus gave a noncommittal shrug and veered away from the porch into the darkness. "More like I'm keeping an eye on the two people who are supposed to be looking after the place."

I stumbled on something I couldn't see, causing Cletus to halt and turn. He fit his hand in mine, then used the contact to pass me a flashlight. "Here, I got my hands full with this stuff." He let go of my hand and picked up the canvas bag he'd momentarily placed at his feet. "Maybe you could make yourself useful by shining the light ahead of us."

I got the impression Cletus could see just fine without the flashlight, but was perhaps looking to give me an excuse to use it. I gave him a grateful smile and clicked it on, shining the light ahead, and was surprised when I saw a wooden boardwalk with a rail directly in front of us.

"Where does this go?"

"Down to the lake." Cletus began walking again, his boots connecting with the wood of the boardwalk, making a distinct thudding sound. His movements were swift while mine were hesitant as I tried to see by the glow of the flashlight; therefore, he was soon twenty or more feet ahead of me. I realized we were approaching stairs that descended into a black nothing.

"Which lake?" I asked, hesitating again.

"Bandit Lake," he threw over his shoulder just before falling out of sight.

I stopped, suddenly unable to move, and whispered to myself, "Bandit Lake…"

Beau and Duane were at Bandit Lake.

My heart rate skyrocketed, and despite the fact my legs were bare and I was in strappy high heels, I felt abruptly hot and anxious. I didn't know what to do, so I stood stone-still, my flashlight shining in the direction where Cletus had disappeared. I couldn't go forward, so I lingered, feeling paralyzed and fretful for an indeterminate period of time.

I kept thinking, *What if he's there?* But I didn't know which *he* I meant.

Did I mean Beau? Or did I mean Duane?

Forward likely led to the twins—one made me tongue-tied and the other...*the other...*

A rustling from behind caused me to jump, pulling me out of my musings and back to the present, a small squeak escaping my throat. I was still flushed, but I shivered, my heart now thundering in my chest. It might have been a bear. It might have been a possum. I tried to calm down. But then an owl hooted, and my squeak turned into a yelp.

Winston twins or not, anything was preferable to being stranded alone in the darkness on a moonless Halloween night in the middle of nowhere. Swallowing the lump in my throat, I ventured forward and down the steps, pausing briefly to take off my shoes when I realized they were keeping me from moving at maximum speed.

I sprinted forward, a feeling of dread in my chest. Every few feet I thought I heard the sound of steps behind me. This only made me move recklessly faster. A lump formed in my throat when I realized I should have reached Cletus already, but the stairs were never ending. The light in front of me seemed to waver. My hands were shaking. I clenched my jaw, telling myself to relax.

But then I heard the steps again, and this time they were unmistakable. Someone—or something—*was* behind me, and it was moving faster than I was. Panic and dread and every tortuous emotion clawed at my lungs, which were now on fire, and I had only one thought. I needed to get *away*.

I descended another two full flights, the sound at my back growing louder, and a scream started building in my throat.

But just before I released it, a hand closed around my mouth, and an arm wrapped around my middle, easily lifting me off my feet.

I thrashed against the strong hold, dropping both my shoes and the flashlight in my struggle. Blind fear took the place of sense, and I bit one of the fingers over my mouth with gusty violence.

"Ow! Dammit, that hurt!" I felt the hard chest behind me vibrate as the hand was removed from my mouth. I recognized that the voice of my captor belonged to either Duane or Beau Winston.

Therefore I froze.

"Who the hell are you, and what the hell are you doing here, and why the hell did you bite me?"

I swallowed, tearing my lip through my teeth. My back was still to his front, my feet still not touching the ground.

Tentatively, I asked, "Duane?"

He stilled, and I felt some of the tension leave his arms. Slowly, carefully, gently he set me down and turned me to face him. I could just make out a shadow of his features in the starlight.

"Jessica?" he asked, his hands on my shoulders. "Jessica James?"

"Yes. Yes, it's me." I swallowed my last word, my knees feeling weak as adrenaline left my body. I was so relieved. Despite our lengthy history of mutual dislike and his trickery earlier in the evening, my chest flooded with warmth at the sight of him. I couldn't ever remember being so happy to see the outline of another person in my whole life.

"Are you okay?" he asked, his voice soft and concerned.

Overcome, I lunged forward and threw my arms around

him, burying my face in his neck. I knew I was behaving like a lunatic, but I'd spent the whole night thinking about him. I needed him to hold me; even if he didn't like me, I needed him.

He shushed me, his arms coming around my body, his hand petting my hair. "It's all right, Jessica. I got you now."

I had no idea how much time passed as we stood holding each other. I know I snuggled shamelessly closer, eliciting a short velvety chuckle from him.

And then, just as I was beginning to relax and decide what to do next, he surprised me by saying, "Jessica, I'm not Duane, honey. I'm Beau."

As soon as the words left his mouth, but before I could react, before I distinguished whether what I felt was joy or disappointment, the screams started.

Duane

3

> "Let love find you. Don't go looking for it. The best way to attract a mate is to post an ad on Craigslist titled, 'Have lube, will travel.'"
>
> —JAROD KINTZ, *LOVE QUOTES FOR THE AGES. SPECIFICALLY AGES 18–81.*

I KNEW THE EXACT MOMENT I fell for Jessica James. I remember it clear as day.

Even though I hadn't set eyes on her for years, time and distance hadn't dulled the memory. The constancy of my regard for Jessica just made her presence now in Green Valley feel transitory, like she was slipping through my fingers.

I was sixteen. She was fourteen. I'd shoved her off a dock into the river. Instead of screaming or freaking out, she'd grabbed my leg on her way down and pulled me under too, dragging me out to the middle.

I was in swim shorts, and she was in her Sunday school dress. While we were struggling under the water, she'd pulled my shorts down and off, then escaped. Seeing as how she'd been on the swim team since elementary school, she was the better swimmer, even in a Sunday school dress.

Jessica had climbed onto the bank. Her blond hair had been wet, tangled around her face, down her back. Her white dress had clung to her body making every young curve visible, and she'd taken off. She'd always been real pretty, but so had lots of other girls. Spitting mad, I ran after her, not caring one lick that I was naked.

I'd caught her easily enough—I was the better runner, faster—and tackled her to the ground. I'd pinned her hands above her head and searched them. They were empty.

"Where are my shorts?" I'd demanded, furious.

Her body had shook beneath mine; she was laughing. She was laughing so hard she could hardly breathe, and I remember thinking she was beautiful.

Then she'd said, "I threw them in a tree."

I'd watched her again losing her breath to laughter, and I couldn't stop my smile. "You threw them in a tree?" I asked, feeling a touch of wonder at her cleverness.

"Yeah," she'd said, her smile wide and crooked, "you think being mean is enough. Being mean *and* being smart is better."

That was the moment. That was when it happened.

Though I grew up seeing her nearly every day, I hadn't noticed she was a girl—or the existence of any other girl— until I was nearly thirteen. By then it was too late. She disliked me. But she worshipped my brother. He didn't see her, not really. Not like I did.

Sure, we'd argued since childhood. But that's what kids do when they're in a pack of wild children. I'd always liked her, maybe had a crush on her, but I fell hard the day she threw my swim trunks into a tree.

Presently, I was sitting two hundred feet from Bandit Lake, staring at the bonfire Beau and I had built hours before and feeling downright sorry for myself. I stood, shaking my head, and pushed the memory aside. I glanced at my cup. It was empty.

Usually I'd take the Road Runner out to clear my head; if I wasn't going fast, then I wasn't really driving, and that car was built for speed. But I wasn't going to chance mountain roads when I was two bourbon shots shy of drunk.

I was refilling my cup when Cletus suddenly appeared at the edge of the bonfire and gave me a fright. He was a floating head, his body invisible. I was the first to see him, and he scared the breath outta me. I inhaled sharply and jumped about three feet. He also made me spill the bourbon.

"Dammit, Cletus!" I closed my eyes, concentrated on slowing my pulse.

Then one of the girls screamed. Then another. Soon they were all screaming. I sighed because they were irritating.

Cattle, I thought. It was an uncharitable thought. My mother would have been disappointed. I felt a little pull under my lowermost left rib. Her death was still fresh, I couldn't think about it without hurting someplace, and it seemed like I was always thinking about it.

I opened my eyes, grinding my teeth, and set about the task of pacifying the screamers. "It's Cletus, my brother. Tina, listen to me, Tina—it's just Cletus."

Tina's screams continued until I covered her mouth with my hand. Her brown eyes were wide and worried as she glanced from me to my older brother. When I was sure she wasn't going to scream again, I took my palm away.

"Cletus?" she parroted, frowning. Her face was framed by a black and yellow wig; her cleavage was spilling out of the sexy bee costume she wore as she gathered gulping breaths.

"Yeah. It's Cletus. Just Cletus." I glanced at him. He wasn't helping the situation by hovering just beyond the glow of the fire, his eyes eerily wide. I pressed my lips together to keep from laughing. He must've been wearing a black turtleneck because he really did look like a floating head.

The other guys had also stood, but were now shaking off the brief fright and moving forward to welcome my brother.

In all, there were about twenty-five people gathered, almost an equal number of guys and girls. The bonfire had been Beau's idea, and he'd promised to keep the party small. Twenty-five felt like a crowd. The mood I was in, I would have preferred five or six…or one.

Tina wrapped her arms around me, giggling into my chest. She was two vodka shots past drunk, and she was pissing me off. "Duane, baby. Hold me, I'm scared."

I placed my arm around her shoulders, mostly to keep her from falling into the flames and ruining everyone's good time, and walked her over to a blanket. My plan to remove her from my side proved difficult, because she seemed to have grown two more arms. Each time I removed one, another three took its place. Too late, I realized this was because she was climbing me with her legs.

Tina and I had been seeing each other on and off for going on five years. I'd called it quits once and for all four months ago. This was the first time I'd seen her since.

"Come on, Tina." I pushed her away, cursing my brother for inviting her in the first place.

Looking back, five years with Tina was four years and eleven months too long. She'd never been my girl, but she liked to tell people she was. Sure, she was pretty enough, beautiful even. She had a free-spirited wildness that had been fun for about ten minutes. She also had the body of an exotic dancer—because she was one—and never lacked enthusiasm when we fucked.

But that's all it had ever been—fucking.

And five years of fucking around was more than enough.

Tina was shrewd but willfully ignorant. I couldn't talk to her about anything, because she didn't want to know anything. I once bought her a copy of my favorite book and found out later she'd used it as kindling for a fire.

Hell, I'd been ready to shoot that horse four years ago. But she'd become a bad habit. She was easy and soft and persistent. And that had been enough to keep me from turning her away.

Until last July.

Until I found out from Jackson James that his sister was moving back to town.

With a firm grip, I finally succeeded in removing Tina's nails, setting her on the blanket and away from me.

"Stay there," I ordered, then walked around the circle of flames to greet my brother, throwing my paper cup in the fire. Tina climbing on me was incentive enough to sober up. I heard her call my name, but ignored it. Two shots shy of drunk was where I wanted to stop, especially since I was still frustrated from earlier events.

"It's me, your brother Cletus," he said unnecessarily—as he was prone to do—dropping a canvas bag to the ground at his feet.

I felt my lips tug to the side. He was wearing a black turtleneck and black pants.

"Hey, are you sticking around?"

"Nah, just dropping off the supplies Beau wanted."

I studied him. He looked cold. "You want to warm up next to the fire before you go?"

"Sure. Maybe for a bit."

"Where's your jacket?"

"I gave my jacket to a lady in need. She'll be along shortly."

I didn't get a chance to question him further because he lifted his chin to the crowd. "Who are these people?"

"Mostly Beau's friends." I scanned several unfamiliar faces. "You know how he is; he has more friends than a tree has leaves. Some are from Merryville, a few came over from the Cades Cove side."

I knew the moment his eyes found Tina because they turned mean. "What's she doing here? You back with her?"

"No," I said, feeling revulsion at the thought. "No way."

He nodded, frowning in an atypical display of dislike. "Good, 'cause she's crazier than a road lizard."

I didn't even have three seconds to register or feel surprise at Cletus's words before Beau reappeared at the edge of the bonfire, drawing everyone's attention to him and the girl he had tucked under his arm.

If Cletus's statement had surprised me, then the sight of Jessica James pressed against my twin nearly knocked me flat on my ass.

Time slowed. I couldn't breathe. My vision turned red. My throat and chest burned. I wanted to punch something… or someone.

"What the fuck…?" My thoughts escaped on a breath, and a deep, piercing pain twisted in my gut. Thankfully, only Cletus had heard my curse.

"Oh, yeah. Catastrophic Engine Failure." Cletus lifted his chin toward Jessica as though *Catastrophic Engine Failure* was her name. "I'm taking Miss James home."

I turned my glare to Cletus and snapped, "What do you mean, you're taking her home?"

His stare narrowed, and he openly studied me. I hated it when he did this. When Cletus put his mind to something, he could see everything. I averted my eyes but then instantly regretted it, because Jessica was looking straight at me. Images of her bare tits, her hot looks, bringing my hand to her flimsy panties played through my mind's eye.

I swallowed so I wouldn't groan, thankful I'd changed into jeans because, fucking hell, I was abruptly hard. Again my gut twisted; again I couldn't breathe. I fought to distance myself from her gaze, but she reeled me in. Her mouth, her eyes, her body—my bait. Jessica was so much more than beautiful, and with Jessica I'd always wanted so much more than fucking around.

I hadn't wanted things to escalate backstage at the community center; that wasn't my intent or my goal. It was a kiss I was after, just a single kiss. I'd wanted her mouth on mine; I'd wanted that memory to replace the mourning and melancholy. Watching my momma's slow decline over the last weeks and months, I'd been so sad for so long and the ferocity of wanting Jessica had made me a little crazy tonight.

When she'd thought I was Beau, her big brown eyes had been trusting, adoring. She'd never looked at me like that before. *It was addictive.* I wanted her to do it again. But my terrible prospects were dwindling. I'd been practicing my speech for months, waiting for the right time, but now I'd blown my careful planning on one kiss. And yet, part of me thought it had been worth it.

Her skin had been soft, like a petal or silk. The memory of touching, tasting, and holding Jessica—and having her return the force of my attentions—was still fresh. As was the suffocating misery of her rejection and my destructive foolishness.

I didn't blame her for hating me, not at all. And now I reckoned it would be the only time she'd allow anything akin to affection between us. Taking her backstage had been a spur-of-the-moment decision, temporary insanity, and—in retrospect—a shitty, selfish one too.

You tricked her... I swallowed around a sourness, the acrid flavor of guilt and remorse. *Damn it.*

I needed to get my head on straight. I needed to apologize. I *would* apologize. My mother had raised us better than to disrespect women. I hadn't been myself since her death just a few weeks ago. But losing the heart and soul of our family was no excuse for mistreating anyone.

And Jessica didn't need to worry; I'd never do anything like that again. Spur of the moment was well beyond my typical comfort zone. I liked to know what to expect. I liked the certainty that came with a well-laid plan.

Presently, I balled my hands into fists and forced my mind to blank. Even so, my eyes were drawn to her lips. They'd always been a little slanted, higher on one side than the other. This imperfection only added to her appeal. It made her look like she was thinking about a private joke, like she was ready to laugh.

My eyes lowered to her neck before I forced myself to stop. If I moved them any lower, I would be thinking about her naked again. So I brought my eyes back to hers.

She wasn't looking at me with trust now. I couldn't read her expression, but it appeared to be founded in unkind thoughts.

I wiped my own expression clean. I was caught in her

web. Worse, she didn't even know she'd caught me. And even if she had known, she couldn't care less.

"Everyone, most of you already know her, but in case you don't, this is Jessica James," Beau announced with his usual charm. He glanced down at her, and she removed her eyes from mine to look at my brother. He smiled. She returned it, but hers looked shy. I had the distinct sensation I'd swallowed rocks.

"Jessica, this is everyone."

People waved. A few stood up to greet her, including Tina. Vaguely I remembered they were somehow related, cousins maybe.

But I could only stare. I felt like I'd been planted, roots had grown out of my feet. I couldn't look away. She was wearing a man's jacket—I suspected Cletus's by the look of it—but her long toned legs were still bare to her thighs, and she had no shoes.

"I think we'll stay for a while," Cletus announced.

"Fine," I said, realizing too late it sounded like a growl.

"Good."

"Okay then."

"Excellent," he said, rubbing his hands together. He had the outward appearance of calm. Boredom even. But I knew my brother well enough to know his tells. Rubbing his hands together meant he was near giddy. My suspicions were confirmed when he added, "In fact, we should all play a game."

I scowled at him, still wanting to punch something, and he was closest.

"Hey, Beau." Cletus ignored me, stepping forward. "Duane wants to play truth or dare."

I set my jaw, grimacing. Several chimed in with their

support for this terrible idea. Before long, someone had placed a cup in Jessica's hand, the crowd was huddled together, and truths were being shared like STDs and unsolicited advice.

I withdrew to the edge of the group, sitting with my knees up and my elbows resting on them. I couldn't help but watch Beau with Jessica. Each time she smiled at him was like rubbing salt on a wound or shoving a hot poker up my nose.

She was sitting close to Beau; his arm was around her. They were laughing together. I wanted to gouge my eyes out.

And yet, I deserved the torture, didn't I? I'd been the one to trick her. Jessica had done nothing amiss and I'd done everything wrong. *Still doesn't make it easy to watch.*

Just when I'd had enough and was thinking about leaving—taking that fast drive—Tina turned to me and said, "Duane baby, truth or dare?"

She cast me a seductive gaze, her eyes flirtatious as she sucked on her index finger. It did nothing for me.

I shrugged and said, "I'm not playing."

"Come on. It was your idea." Tina pouted, appealing to the crowd.

I felt myself grimace as I ground out, "Fine. Dare."

Most people chose truth, but I'd always preferred dare.

I'd never had the good sense to be afraid of perilous situations like most people. I'd been bungee jumping, drag racing, skydiving—none of which had ever set my blood pumping beyond a mild degree. The more dangerous my circumstances, the more focused I became. I couldn't think of doing a single thing that scared me, and I'd *never* embarrassed easily.

However, right this minute, talking about myself in front of Jessica felt downright terrifying.

Tina squealed and clapped. "Yay! Okay, good. I was

hoping you'd pick dare. I dare you to come over here and kiss me."

Someone, probably an idiot, called out, "I'll take that dare."

I tried not to gag.

My attention moved to Jessica. I don't know why I did it. Some part of me, likely the asshole part that enjoys feeling like shit, wanted to see her reaction—or nonreaction.

But to my surprise, she wasn't gazing at Beau. She was looking at Tina, and she looked like she wanted to bury Tina alive. The intensity of her glare, the ice behind it, caught me off guard. Suddenly, kissing Tina didn't seem quite so revolting.

"All right," I drawled.

Jessica's eyes flickered to mine. Before she was able to hide it, I saw misery and shock. And, if I wasn't mistaken, I also saw jealousy. Encouraged by the possibility that Jess might care a little about who I was kissing, I stood and picked my way through the crowd, then knelt in front of Tina.

I had a decision to make.

I could give her a quick peck and move the game forward.

Or, I could kiss Tina like I wanted to kiss Jess. I could exploit the situation and potentially push Jess out of her comfort zone, hopefully provoking some response. Something to give me a reason to hope.

Decision made, I grabbed Tina by the neck, and I kissed the hell out of her.

Pretending Tina Patterson was Jessica James was like pretending tofu was steak. Despite the disparity in quality, texture, and taste, I soldiered on. I tapped into a hell of a lot of pent-up sexual frustration and had to restrain her hands when I felt them reach for my dick.

The crowd had made noises at first, egging me on. But then they grew quiet, and I heard a few whispered comments, "Damn, that boy can kiss" and "I'm next" and "Remind me to use my next turn on Duane."

As soon as I finished, I lifted my eyes to Jess, and what I saw made my chest hurt. But this time, it was a good hurt.

Her glare was affixed to mine; her face was bright red. Her usual charming smirk was replaced with a deep frown. Beyond all that, she was giving me a hot look.

I wiped my mouth with the back of my hand and stood, holding her gaze, and leaving Tina dazed on the blanket.

"It's your turn, Duane," Cletus's voice broke the silence. He sounded cheerful…for Cletus. "Pick anyone you want, anyone at all."

I nodded, my eyes never leaving Jessica's, and gritted my teeth in preparation for what I was going to do next, my mind homing in on my target. It would require courage, the kind that risks public rejection.

"Jessica." Her name on my lips sounded too loud.

I had an odd thought just then, that I should only ever whisper her name, and that she should always be close enough to hear it.

"Truth or dare?" I whispered.

Her gaze narrowed. Even beneath the thick coat she wore, I could see her chest rise and fall with her breath. To drive my point home, I allowed my eyes to flicker meaningfully to Beau. I hoped she'd interpret the movement as an implied threat to expose her feelings for him.

For the record, I would never do that. I would have to be a complete idiot to do that. If Beau had any idea, he'd be a jackass to let her go. Also, it would be a betrayal. I didn't want to betray Jessica. I'd already disrespected her in a way I'd never forgive myself for.

No, I only wanted to cherish her.

"Dare," she said, like she was daring me and not the other way around.

I kept my relief from showing but did allow myself a smirk. "Okay. Dare it is."

Again I picked my way through the crowd, and again I knelt down on the blanket; this time I was kneeling next to Jess, and she was adorably ruffled, unable to hide her anger.

"I dare you to come with me and go skinny-dipping in Bandit Lake for the next hour."

Her brown eyes widened, rimmed with shock, and the crowd erupted in opinions. I heard someone say, "I should have thought of that one; that's a good one."

"Well?" I pushed, burying my eagerness under an expression of boredom. "What's it going to be?"

Finally she sputtered, "An hour? That lake is near freezing; we'll get hypothermia."

"Okay, thirty minutes then."

"Thirty minutes?"

"Fifteen. Final offer. Or else you have to choose truth."

A wrinkle formed above her nose, and she stared at me. Then, abruptly, she lifted her chin and said with venom, "Fine. I accept."

She stood, unzipped her jacket, tossed it to Cletus, then jogged out of the circle of the bonfire's light. I was too surprised to move at first, but then Beau punched me in the shoulder.

"What are you waiting for, dumbass? Go get her."

I stared at my brother and he stared back, giving me an excited, encouraging smile. And I saw what I'd been blind to earlier. Beau wasn't interested in Jessica, not because she wasn't beautiful or amazing. She was. She was gorgeous. She was smart and clever. She was breathtaking. She was also too good for either of us.

Beau wasn't interested in Jess because he knew how I felt. Of course he did. We were twins. He must've always known.

We exchanged a brotherly grin, and he punched me again. "Go on, get."

I nodded once, then stood, toeing my boots off and pulling both my sweater and shirt over my head. I left everything but my pants in a pile on the ground, grabbed a still-folded blanket, then sprinted into the woods after Jessica James.

I was always running after her, but this time—if she'd give me the time of day—I wasn't going to let her get away.

Jessica

4

> "The journey of a thousand miles begins with a single step."
>
> —LAO TZU, *TAO TE CHING*

I'VE NEVER BEEN A LIAR. I'm not that creative and I lack the energy required. I'm not even very good at lying to myself. That's probably why I currently felt like my brain was being torn in two.

I didn't like that I wanted Duane Winston, but there it was. He'd done something to me, awoke some slumbering feral female creature, and now I was pathetic with thinking about him. And it wasn't just wanting his kiss, his touch, his body, and maybe even a bit of his sassy back talk. I was thinking about *him* and our interactions growing up and all the countless hours we'd spent in each other's company not getting along.

To make matters even more muddled, whatever he'd done to me backstage at the community center had apparently miraculously broken the Beau spell—at least for the night. I wasn't sure if this was a good or a bad thing. On one hand, I'd always known my feelings for Beau were based on an unhealthy and unrealistic infatuation.

On the other hand, at least Beau had been nice to me. No sassy back talk from Beau Winston—only friendly smiles, honesty, and kindness—which was why I'd hero-worshipped him for so long.

But now…almost nothing. When Beau had found me in the dark and told me who he was, the first thing I felt was disappointment he wasn't Duane. No music only I could hear. No reducing me to a blubbering, slurring Swahili speaker. Just disappointment.

How that was even possible after twelve years of obsessive behavior made me question my mental health. Likely, I should have been questioning it long before now.

I slowed my jog to a walk, guessing that the edge of the lake was nearby and cursing myself for not bringing a flashlight. The short run was good, but not enough. It had expelled merely a modicum of the restless energy coursing through my system, making me feel fried, dried, and crispy.

The problem was my brain was tearing in two because my feelings for Duane were not consensual.

Did I want to feel like a jealous, raging, seething she-witch when Duane had kissed my sexy-bee cousin, who also just happened to be his ex-girlfriend *and* a smokin'-hot stripper?

No. No, I did not. I didn't want to feel this way. I wanted to feel nothing. But I didn't feel nothing. I felt like he'd reached inside my chest, closed his fist around my heart, and was slowly squeezing it. I also felt like plucking the wings off Tina's costume.

He'd kissed her. He'd kissed her *just* like he'd kissed me.

Obviously Duane made a habit of kissing the hell out of women, all women. That's probably why he was such a good kisser. Lots and lots of practice.

This was the thought circling around and around my brain. The image of them, of his mouth moving against hers, was branded in my vision, making my insides cold and eclipsing my ability to reason.

My first instinct had been to march over to them and pull them apart by the nose. I'd seen my mother do this once to my cousins when they were fighting. She'd put her index finger in one nostril of each of their noses and tugged them apart. They'd never fought at our house again. All she had to do was wiggle her index fingers in the air. Tina would have known what it meant.

I slowed my pace further, not sure if the sensation beneath my feet was cold damp, or just cold. Three steps later I realized it was cold damp. I'd reached the edge of the lake. I turned, my hands out, and walked a few steps back to the last tree I'd passed and leaned against it, waiting for Duane to show up.

I heard his footfalls, not too far off now. His approach made my insides tense in a delicious and disquieting way. I balled my hands into fists and squeezed my eyes shut, giving myself a mental talking-to. Despite the fact it was near forty degrees, I was not cold. In fact, my skin and my lungs and my belly felt like they were on fire. I guess anger, intense aggravation, and frenetic lust will do that to a person.

I needed time. I needed distance.

We'd *just* kissed less than five hours ago. I was being stupid. Feeling territorial about Duane Winston made no sense. I wasn't in Green Valley for the long haul; I was here to pay off my student loans, gain teaching experience, and then move on and out and see the world.

One does not make life-altering decisions based on a single, solitary make-out session, especially when I'd been kissing Duane thinking he was Beau.

Maybe, I reasoned, Duane wasn't a great kisser. Maybe I'd built the whole thing up because I'd been working under a mistaken-identity misconception.

I told myself that these bizarre cravings would disappear just as quickly as they'd encroached upon my sanity. I told myself that tomorrow everything would be back to normal. Duane was irritating, challenging. Beau was nice. Even if my obsessive crush for Beau never resurfaced, my strange surge of feelings for Duane was likely fleeting.

I had a plan and my momma hadn't raised me to be stupid. End of story.

"Jess…"

I stiffened at the whispered sound of my name and was surprised to find him so close. Standing straighter, I turned, offering him my profile. I must've been so lost in my head that I didn't hear his final approach.

"Hey," I whispered back, then frowned, glancing at him. "Wait, why are we whispering?"

He didn't respond. Instead, he walked slowly forward and reduced the space between us. I could tell by his outline that he was shirtless. This revelation elicited a barely contained moan because, dammit, I wanted to touch him again.

I turned completely just as he stopped two feet from my position.

He blurted, "Jess, can we…? Can I…?"

I listened as he abruptly paused, then released a loud

breath. He sounded frustrated. I couldn't see his face so I had no idea what his intentions were or what he was thinking. I waited a beat for him to complete his thought. Five seconds turned into twenty, the quiet broken only by owls hooting in the distance, the wind through the trees, and the gentle lapping of the lake against the water's edge.

I sensed that he moved, and a moment later, I felt his hand brush against mine. Already taut with nerves and my continuing internal boxing match, I flinched away from his touch, mostly because it was unexpected.

At my involuntary reaction, he shifted a step back and pulled his hands through his hair. I don't know why I felt embarrassed, but I did. Maybe because I wanted to grab his hand, not recoil from it. But then, how pathetic was I?

He'd just kissed another girl—one he had history with and might be dating—right in front of me, no more than ten minutes ago.

Less than five hours ago, he'd pretended to be his brother and I'd held his penis in my hand. I'd stroked it, for hootenanny's sake! I'd given him a penis stroke under false pretenses. I should be running in the opposite direction. Instead I was girl-stupid for a guy who thought I was a brat.

He was right, of course. I was a brat sometimes. But I didn't want him to think I was a brat.

I cleared my throat, sought the steadiness of the hemlock tree at my back, and said, "Let's get this over with."

I reached for the hem of my dress and pulled it over my head, folding it for no reason in particular and placing it at the roots of the tree. Next I unclasped my bra, hesitated for just a split second, then dropped it on top of the dress.

At this point I stopped because I heard the sound of Duane

undoing his zipper and my belly filled with lava. Hot, hot, hot molten lava. My body tensed and braced. I didn't realize it at first, but I was holding my breath. I strained my ears and listened as he pushed the fabric of his pants down to his ankles, then bent to remove them completely.

He was now naked.

Meanwhile my thumbs were hooked in my panties, and now I was a frozen, chaotic river of lava. I wasn't sure if I was actually capable of movement while Duane was naked. It felt…dangerous.

He cleared his throat, and I saw by his outline that his hands were on his hips. "You can leave your underwear on, if you want."

I'll admit, I was staring at the region of his pelvic area before he spoke, hoping against hope that my untapped superpower of night vision would suddenly reveal itself. Alas, it was too dark and all I saw was shadow. I tore my eyes away from his midsection and lifted them to his face. I could just make out the stars reflecting his glittery eyes.

I shook my head, expelling my breath, his offer spurring me into movement. "No, you said skinny-dipping. I don't want you crying foul later."

"I wouldn't."

I made no response.

"Jessica, I wouldn't," he pressed.

"I don't believe you," I countered quietly, giving him my back as I pulled my underwear down my legs and laid them on the rest of the pile.

The hairs on the back of my neck prickled. Though I couldn't see well in the dark, I suspected he could see just fine. This thought drove me suddenly forward, toward the lake, my arms covering my breasts. I made it to my stomach before I stopped, trying to catch the breath driven out of me by the abrupt, icy submersion. The lake was colder than a witch's tit, and I was now freezing. My body gave a convulsive shake and my brain screamed, *What are you doing? Don't you know this lake is near freezing? You've lost your mind!*

All that molten lava of confusion and upheaval had been replaced with survival instinct and repulsion for the frigid water. It's true what's said about cold showers.

The sound of a splash and a string of curses signified Duane's foray into the water. I urged my feet to move, but they wouldn't. I was so cold. My teeth chattered and my shoulders shook.

Then I felt him behind me, hovering. And when I say *I felt him behind me*, I mean his front was so close to my back that I felt the heat of his skin. The water was a smidge warmer, though we weren't touching.

"Is this f-f-far enough?" I asked, annoyed with myself for being too much of a chicken to venture farther.

"Jessica, I have to tell you something."

I bunched my shoulders, holding myself tighter. His hot breath spilling over my neck, paired with the autocratic tone of his voice, made me shiver.

"Go right ahead. We got fifteen m-m-minutes to kill."

I felt the water around my stomach swirl just as he closed the remaining inches between us, his chest hitting my upper back, his groin my bottom. I stiffened, then tried to move away, but one arm wrapped around my shoulders, the other around my rib cage above the water, holding me in place.

"Jess, this lake is so fucking cold. Please just let me hold you."

"W-w-well, this w-w-was your idea."

"I know. And I don't regret it, but shut up for a minute so I can tell you something."

I huffed. "Don't tell me to shut up."

"Sorry—I'm sorry, you're right. I shouldn't have said that. It's just I'm so cold I think I'm losing my mind."

If my teeth weren't chattering so hard I think I would have smiled. "F-f-fine. Go ahead."

"Jess." His fingers dug into my skin and his arms tightened on my body. "I am sorry I tricked you into kis—into coming with me backstage. I–I shouldn't have done that. It was wrong, I was wrong, and I'm very sorry. I hope you'll find it in your heart to forgive me, but I absolutely understand if you can't."

Well.

I don't know what I'd been expecting, but I hadn't been expecting that.

Before I could form thought or words, he quickly added, "Tina and I aren't together anymore. I ended things with her for good months ago."

I stiffened, again surprised, but not wanting to acknowledge, even to myself, that these words pleased me.

He continued. "Now, you and I, we've known each other since we were kids."

At this point, I leaned in to him and admitted inwardly that I was very glad he'd decided to hold me.

When he spoke next, his words were rushed and they sounded rehearsed. "You've never liked me much and I get why, I do. But we're not kids anymore. You've been gone for four years, off to college, and now you're back, doing good work at the school. You're different, you've changed, and I'm different now too, a business owner. I think it's time we call a truce and start over."

I blinked into the darkness, trying to process his words, and noticing suddenly—now that we were motionless—how the stars were reflected back at the sky by the surface of the lake. If we held perfectly still, it was like being in the center of space, stars above, stars below. I tilted my head backward unthinkingly and it fell against Duane's shoulder, resting there as I gazed at the heavens.

It took him about a half minute, but then he dipped his head and pressed his cheek against mine.

"I'm glad you agree," he whispered into the silence, apparently taking my small action as agreement. His lips moved against me as he spoke, his beard tickling the sensitive skin of my neck.

Despite myself I laughed lightly, because even though I was freezing, I could appreciate the bizarreness of the situation. Here I was, standing in a near-freezing lake with Duane Winston, oddly enjoying myself. The last time we'd been alone together in a body of water, it was the river during the summer of my fourteenth year. I'd de-panted him and thrown his swimsuit in a tree. Now we were both de-panted and freezing.

Nothing about it made any sense. I needed it to make sense, so I asked him to explain it to me.

"Duane, you remember when we *were* kids? And we used to argue about everything? I mean, it didn't matter what it was. If I said the sky was blue, you would say it was purple."

"Sometimes the sky is purple. Right now it's indigo, almost black. You can't just make a unilateral statement that the sky is blue."

"See? This is what I'm talking about. I don't know if we can call a truce. All we know how to do is argue."

"You say that like it's a bad thing."

"Isn't it?"

"Jessica," he whispered, "arguing with you is one of my *favorite* things to do."

My heart set off at a gallop and my breath caught in my throat. It wasn't his words so much as how he said them, all soft and sincere. I had to blink several times to keep from melting against him. How it was possible for me to melt when I was surrounded on three sides by near-freezing water made me again question my mental fitness.

I cleared my throat and endeavored to stay focused. "One of your favorite things to do? You mean like playing practical jokes on me? I think you're trying to rewrite the past."

Again, I felt his small smile on my skin. "You liked playing jokes on me, too. Don't deny it."

Without really meaning to, I found myself grinning and reminiscing. "I liked your reaction to the jokes, like that time I switched out the cake part of your strawberry shortcake with a sponge and you took a bite."

"Or how about the time you tricked me into thinking you were eating flies?"

I giggled. "That's right, I'd forgotten about that. Best use of raisins ever. And you were so grossed out, I thought you were going to throw up."

We were quiet for a stretch, perhaps both lost to our memories of each other. It occurred to me that maybe he wasn't trying to rewrite the past. Maybe he was encouraging me to see our shared history in a new light.

I was speaking my thoughts before I realized words had left

my mouth. "I loved how you'd lose your temper and threaten me with retribution."

"Exactly. And I always kept my promises."

"Yes, you did…"

We were quiet again, the sound of gently lapping water against the embankment our only companion. But then his hands slid lower, grazing my hips and providing just the right amount of sobriety.

I shook my head and leaned a fraction of an inch forward, clearing my throat before speaking my mind. "If we did start over, why do you even want to be friends with me? Didn't you call me a brat earlier?"

He nodded and his arms shifted, which made his hold feel more like a hug. "Yeah, I called you a brat because you were acting like one."

I grunted my irritation. "I wasn't the one who lied and I'm allowed to be angry. I don't know…" I stopped, swallowed, and debated my next words before continuing. "I don't know if I'm ready to forgive you."

"Even though I asked for forgiveness, I reckon I'm not sorry it happened."

"You're not sorry?" My voice sounded loud and screechy to my ears, and I gritted my teeth. Despite being surrounded by frigid temperatures, my blood pressure spiked.

"Nope. Not sorry we kissed."

I laughed again, but this time it was because I was peeved. "So you're telling me you're not sorry for making me think you were Beau?"

He shrugged, nuzzled my neck, warming me. My brain told me to stop him, but my body vetoed that with, *To hell with pride, I'm freezing!*

At length he said, "For the record, I never said I was Beau and you didn't ask."

I opened my mouth and a small sound of incredulity escaped. "You're unbelievable."

He ignored my statement. "And I don't want to be your friend."

"You don't want to be my friend? Then what are we talking about?"

"We're talking about starting over."

"To what purpose?"

He hesitated for just a second; then he said, "Because we should see each other more often. I think we're suited."

I wasn't surprised.

I was flabbergasted.

I was sure I must've heard him wrong.

Then I realized my mouth was wide-open.

Then I realized a full minute had passed and I'd said nothing.

I blinked at the stars in the sky. "I'm sorry, I think I must misunderstand your meaning. So…what do you mean?"

"Just what I said. We're suited for each other."

"You think we're suited?"

"Yes."

"For what? Debating the color of the sky? Practical-joke wars?"

"Sure, if that's what you want to do or talk about. I'm going to take you out."

"Out? Out where?"

"To nice restaurants, to movies, camping, for ice cream—on dates."

"On dates?"

"We could go to Genie's, go dancing."

"You dance?"

"Yes, I dance, when it's good music and I'm in the mood."

"You would dance with me?"

"Hell yes. I'd dance with you right now if you'd let me and I wasn't freezing my balls off."

I laughed again, shaking my head because this entire conversation had taken a detour to Unexpectedville. I couldn't comprehend the idea that Duane Winston thought we were *suited* for each other.

In what universe would he ever think such things?

And why did these things he said *not* sound crazy? And why did these things he said make my heart twirl with excitement?

"I don't… I can't…" I didn't know what to say and I didn't know what to think.

The evening had been too eventful and I hadn't a spare moment to digest what had occurred. Obviously, I needed time and I needed distance. I wasn't staying in Green Valley, not more than a few years *at most*. Being suited with Duane Winston had the potential of being a huge confounding complication. My eyes were on the prize, namely leaving town with no debt, no regrets, *or* reasons to stay.

I cleared my throat and whispered, "I think it's been fifteen minutes."

When I pulled away, he let me go. Cold water hit my lower back and thighs, replacing the warmth and protection of Duane's body. Hugging myself, I turned toward the forest and forced my stiff legs to move. This did not go well. I stumbled, slipped on a rock, and crashed sideways into the water.

The wind was knocked out of me as I hit the lake, forced from my lungs by the shock of cold. Immediately my legs straightened, pushing my head up and out. Just as I was gathering a greedy gulp of air, I felt Duane's hands reach around my side and lift me off my feet and out of the water, cradling my front to him in a princess carry.

When I found my voice, I said through chattering teeth, "Put me down."

He didn't respond, just continued trudging to the embankment.

"Duane Winston, put me down." I felt breathless, confused, dizzy. Pressed together like we were, and without the chilly water keeping me sober, my body was warming to his. Our skin was slippery, my breasts against his chiseled chest, his strong arms around me. I was too exhausted to be aroused, but it felt improper.

Improper? Really? Now you're feeling improper? I'd traded lunacy for sense.

"I'll put you down, but I don't want you running off and throwing my pants in a tree."

"You deserved that." I knew to which adolescent encounter he referred, and I couldn't help a very little smile at the memory.

"Yes, I did." He nodded, then hoisted me a few inches in the air like I was a sack of potatoes, readjusting his grip when I came down.

We were out of the water now, some feet into the forest, and I was just about to complain again when he set me down gently, but wrapped a big paw around my upper arm.

"My clothes are back there." I tugged half-heartedly away, my body too cold and tired to put up much of a fight. Goose bumps had broken out everywhere and I was shaking violently.

Duane bent to retrieve something. In one smooth motion

he released my arm, shook out what I realized was a large blanket, and tossed it over his shoulders. He then yanked me forward and wrapped me in the soft fabric and his embrace.

"You need to dry off, warm up first," he said, rubbing my bare back. It was then I realized how cold he was, that he too was shaking.

Without consideration or caution, I snuggled closer, instinctively wanting to give and share warmth. I hugged him, rubbed the broad muscles of his back, and buried my face in his neck. Yes, we were naked. But first and foremost we were near-frozen, heat-seeking bodies.

Practicality won out over the lunacy of prudishness.

The blanket must've been huge because it covered us from his neck and the tips of my ears and pooled around our feet, giving the impression of a cocoon. I was grateful he'd planned ahead. Whereas I'd just run off into the woods, relying on my anger and inexplicable jealousy to keep me warm.

The memory of and the reason for my earlier ire reared its ugly head: a flash of an image, Duane's expert kisses shared with his ex. He was still clutching the blanket around us, holding me close, rubbing feeling into my arms and back. His hands were big and divine, strong and skillful. His heart beat against my cheek. His smooth skin, his granite stomach and shoulders under my fingertips made me feel greedy and muddled.

He was muddling me and I began to hear my brain soundtrack, this time it was "Touch Me" by The Doors.

Suddenly I was warm, we both were, and it was much faster than I'd anticipated. As true physiological numbness receded, his hands on my body ignited something else. Soon the shared heat changed from necessary for survival to something evocative and abruptly ripe with decadent tension. His hands slowed and I realized belatedly that my breath had quickened. I wasn't aroused; it wasn't like before. I was…caught. This time my heart was involved, not the crazy part of my brain.

I glanced up at him, found him watching me. His eyes reflected the stars, and I was close enough to see they were on my lips.

"Jessica," he whispered, swallowed, his hands now motionless on my waist.

I shook my head slightly; really, the small movement was me telling myself to cease feeling. Duane was all around me, and he felt intoxicatingly good. I need to end this, whatever it was.

So I blurted, "I'm not kissing you."

His eyes lifted to mine, his expression unreadable, but I felt him tense.

I huffed. "You lied to me. You pretended to be your brother—"

He cut me off, yanked his head back. "And you want Beau." His tone was cold.

I gripped his biceps to keep him from moving away. "No, no—that's not it. It's the lie, and my sexy-bee cousin."

"Your sexy-bee cousin?"

"Yes. Tina Patterson, my dad's sister's daughter. Remember her? You kissed her. You kissed her *right after* you and I…" I couldn't finish because I was confusing myself. I used to kiss boys all the time and it never meant anything. Yet I couldn't finish my sentence because I was beginning to think Duane's earlier kiss—even shrouded in a veil of deceit—had meant something to me.

He licked his lips before he asked, as though reading my mind, "Did our kiss mean something to you? Not"—he shook his head and glanced around the darkness—"not when you thought I was my brother, but after, when you found out it was me?"

I answered honestly, my words pouring out of me. "I don't know. I honestly don't. And I don't get why you're pushing this so hard now. I feel like I don't know you at all. One minute you're the Duane Winston who throws rocks at my cat, kissing another girl, making me feel like I have heartburn, arguing about the color of the sky, and the next minute you're telling me we're suited for each other. I don't trust you."

"Jessica, we're standing in the forest naked. You trust me a little."

I pushed against his chest lightly, shaking my head, tired and exasperated and not ready to let him go. It was the strangest of combinations.

"Of course I trust you that way. I know you'd never murder me or take advantage—well, take *too much* advantage. I mean, you did get a penis stroke out of me earlier and did really fantastic things to my nipples." A little shiver raced through me at the memory. "But now that I think about it, you stopped me before I could—"

"Jessica, please stop talking."
"What? Why?"
"Because you're making everything…really hard."

We stood motionless for a long moment as understanding dawned. His words held a delicious double meaning, and even in the inky darkness, I could tell he was struggling. I wavered back and forth between wanting him to do something and hoping he wouldn't. Our breath mingled. His fingers dug into my hips.

Then his eyes closed and he set me away. He didn't let the blanket slip. Instead he pulled it from his shoulders, stepping out of our little oven, and wrapped it firmly around my shoulders, tucking it under my chin. I was mummified in our residual warmth.

Duane left and quickly located his pants. I watched his outline pull them on, then move to the tree where I'd discarded my clothes. He brought them back and held them out.

"Here," he said.

Once I had the folded pile, I sensed him turn away.

I stared at the back of his neck for a beat, just the dim outline visible to me, then slowly began the process of getting dressed.

I rewound through the evening and our time together, all of my actions. I was too honest. He made me feel naive and mindless. I wasn't used to the disorientation brought on by excellent-quality physical intimacy. Plus, he and I *knew* each other. We had years of history.

Maybe my immature, fantasy-based feelings for Beau had dispelled so abruptly because I'd been given a taste of reality, of an *actual* adult liaison. The way Duane touched me felt like a brand.

The beginnings of an uncomfortable blush crept their way up my neck to my cheeks. When I was finished dressing, I cleared my throat and glanced at him. I could just make out the shape of his bare back.

"I'm all done."

He twisted, his eyes moved over my body still wrapped in the blanket, and he nodded. "Okay, let's get back."

Duane took a few steps, carrying him maybe ten feet, but then stopped. I hadn't yet moved as I was more or less swimming in a sea of mental melancholy. He might be right, we might be suited, but so what? Nothing could ever come of it other than a few months—at best, years—of being together.

In my typical fashion of getting ahead of myself, my mind leapt to a time two years from now when I would be ready to leave Green Valley. What if Duane and I were extremely well suited? What if we became serious? What if I couldn't leave him?

I glanced up just in time to sense, then see him returning to where I stood. Instinctively, I took a step back, but he held me by my arms and halted my retreat.

"Tina, your cousin," he said, his voice thick with both hesitation and ferocity.

"Yes, Tina is my cousin."

"She dared me to kiss her."

I pressed my lips together and swallowed, feeling again like I had heartburn. "You *did* kiss her, and she's your ex-girlfriend."

"She was never my girl."

I didn't want to argue semantics. "Right, you've been with Tina since before I left for college, but she was never your girl. What about her?"

He hesitated for a beat, then said, "You remember who I was with before you left for college?"

I responded through gritted teeth, "Duane, what about Tina?"

He seemed to shake himself before starting again. "Tina..." He nodded, then took another step, bringing him firmly inside my personal space. "When I kissed her earlier, it didn't mean anything."

"Well, it looked like something to me."

"It wasn't. Not with her. But with you, at the community center, I meant what I said. I've always wanted you. And I am sorry you didn't know it was me, because you deserve better than that and..." His voice lost its fierce edge, but roughened; his next words emerged sounding like an aching confession. "I'd really like for there to be a next time."

Jessica

5

> "Maybe you had to leave in order to really miss a place; maybe you had to travel to figure out how beloved your starting point was."
>
> —JODI PICOULT, *HANDLE WITH CARE*

I WAS DISTRACTED.

Not even *Rick Steves' Europe* could hold my attention.

It was all Duane's fault. His words' and lips', and hands', and eyes', and his penis's fault.

He had a nice one; at least it had felt nice in comparison to the only other penis of my acquaintance, thick and long and smooth and rock-hard. I didn't get a peek at it backstage or when he'd dared me to go skinny-dipping. However, I could recall with surprising clarity what it looked like when we were younger, when he'd been naked chasing me through the woods, or the time before that when a bunch of us went skinny-dipping in the waterfalls near Burgess. He was circumcised. I'd noted it as a teenager because I'd just finished eighth-grade health class (also known as sex education).

I never expected to be fixating on Duane's circumcised

penis. Yet there I was, sitting at my desk at work, grading pop quizzes, trying to recall the glorious weight of him in my hand...

How irritating, because now I was having a lusty hot flash.

I groaned, letting my red pen drop as my face fell into my hands.

How had I even arrived here in this purgatory? Yes, I was drooling over the memory of his sexual magnetism from afar. But it was more than that. So much more. And this *more* was beyond distressing. Duane's admission—that our time backstage at the community center had been something he'd wanted for a long time and he wanted a repeat—felt overwhelming.

I'd known him forever. I knew all about him, or I thought I did.

His confession felt like finding out my cat—Sir Edmund Hillary, named after that dude who climbed Mount Everest with Tenzing Norgay—could talk and wanted to give me a tongue bath. At best, Sir Hillary was indifferent to my existence. At worst, he may have been plotting my demise. He was an audacious calico psychopath, always pushing his litter box from its place beside the toilet in the bathroom to directly in front of the shower, but only when I was in the shower...

Anyway, I decided I was cursed by the spirit of J.R.R. Tolkien for my ironic sexy Gandalf blasphemy. That's why I couldn't stop thinking about Duane Winston's body parts and his perplexing suggestion that we were suited.

Five days had passed since Halloween and my busy, bizarre night. Of course I'd avoided him since. What would I say? What could I say?

Hi, Duane. I don't know whether I like you or not, and you confuse the hell out of me, but I'd like to buy you a piece of pie so we can argue about the color of the sky. Let's schedule that.

Or how about: *Hello, Duane. I obviously lack self-respect and common sense because—even though you kissed my cousin, your sexy stripper ex-girlfriend, right in front of me—I don't find that weird or creepy or disrespectful. Let's go out for ice cream cones so I can watch you lick yours.*

Making matters more muddled, Tina had cornered me Sunday afternoon at Daisy's Nut House. My daddy and I had gone out for breakfast after Sunday service. She'd been super friendly. She wanted to get together, hang out, do cousin stuff.

We hadn't really spoken to each other since we were thirteen. I hadn't been cool enough to be her friend when we were in high school. When I went to college and she started working as an exotic dancer, we'd rarely interacted, and then only during family get-togethers.

But now she wanted to reestablish a relationship.

And I was having oddly whimsical and amorous thoughts about her ex-boyfriend.

"So, are you ready to tell me what happened when you disappeared with one of the Winston twins?"

I didn't look up at Claire's question, even though she startled me a little. I could tell by the direction of her voice that she was standing in the doorway of my classroom.

"How long have you been standing there?"

"Long enough to watch you stare into space for several minutes before plunking your head into your hands and making those lovely moaning sounds. I can't decide what the sounds mean, but they sure are interesting."

I shook my head and peered at her through my fingers. "A circumcised penis."

I was gratified when she choked on air. "Ah...what?"

"A circumcised penis. That's what happened. And some hot looks, hotter kisses, truth or dare, then maybe we're suited—I don't know—skinny-dipping and rubbing for warmth and—"

"Stop, stop right there." She held her hands up. "We can't have this kind of conversation at work."

"Why not? Is it against policy?"

"Not precisely, but drinking while at work is a big no-no."

"I'm not drinking."

"But *I'd* like to be a little tipsy if we're going to talk about the Winston brothers and whether or not they're circumcised."

I let my hands drop and gave her a little smile. "You went to school with Billy and Cletus, sandwiched between the two, right? Billy a grade above, Cletus a grade behind?"

She nodded and said quietly, "Yes, but I know Jethro best. He and Ben were best friends."

I could feel my smile turn sad before I could stop it, and regretted the unintentional pity that must've shown in my eyes. Claire looked away and cleared her throat, looking equal parts resigned and impatient.

"Ben used to joke he didn't have the patience to learn the Winston boys' names, so he called all of Jethro's brothers 'Jethro Jr.'" Claire addressed this to her feet and paired it with a small laugh.

I smirked at Ben's pragmatism as I studied my friend, how her face had fallen even though she tried to smile.

Claire had no family to speak of... Actually, by that I mean her daddy was the club president of the local motorcycle gang, the Iron Wraiths. As well, her momma was his old lady. But together or separate, those two were the definition of *dysfunctional*. As far as I knew, Claire had no contact with her parents.

I assumed she was still living in Green Valley because she wanted to stay near her husband's family. She accompanied them to church every Sunday, and her house was within a block of theirs.

She'd been a local beauty growing up—she even had those awesome high cheekbones that magazines talk about, with the little hollow above the jaw—but she had sad eyes. Add to her stunning good looks being the most laid-back, kind, generous, and all around talented person I'd ever met. For example, she had the most beautiful singing voice and should have been in Nashville singing, or in New York or Milan living the life of a muse or a model or a concert pianist.

Meanwhile, I couldn't carry a tune in a bucket.

I'd been in the thespians my sophomore through senior year of high school and was therefore labeled as one of those drama kids—for my school, that basically meant weird and funny. Plus, I was universally acknowledged as the county math whiz, having led our school's team to Math Bowl victory three times.

I didn't marry my childhood sweetheart because I didn't have one, though I kissed lots of boys because I liked kissing boys. Kissing boys also had the delightful by-product of aggravating my father and overprotective brother. Essentially, I'd left home for college an antsy, angsty, but well-mannered good girl. So, a typical teenager.

But upon my return to Green Valley High School (just a short four years later), same school with the same social order and subsets, I'd now become a new stereotype.

I was *the hot math teacher*.

I'd never thought of myself as the *hot* anything. Don't get me wrong, I had a perfectly fine self-image. But I guess in comparison to Mr. Tranten—the previous and now recently retired math teacher—the fact I had boobs and was under eighty-five meant I might as well have been Charlize Theron.

"Well, come on," Claire finally said. "Come home with me and you can tell me all about it. I just need wine first."

"I can't." I glanced at the wall clock at the front of the room. "I have to wait for my brother to pick me up. My beast of a truck is still parked at the community center with 'catastrophic engine failure.' He's driving me home."

Claire's eyes darted back to mine; she studied my face with a question in her expression. "Uh…no, it's not."

"What?"

"The beast, your truck. It's not at the community center. It was towed."

Panic seized my chest and my hands balled into fists. "No, it couldn't have. Could it?" I'd talked to Mr. McClure about keeping the truck at the center until I could afford the towing and repair costs; he'd assured me it was no trouble.

"Calm down." She lifted her hands and walked farther into the classroom.

"I can't afford impound costs. Why would they tow it? Your father-in-law said it was fine."

"It's not at the impound, Jess. I saw it this morning in the parking lot of the Winston Brothers Auto Shop. It's not at the impound. Calm yourself."

I flinched at this news, blinked furiously. "What…? Why would they do that?"

Claire chuckled, and I didn't miss the amusement or the

wicked glint in her eye when she responded. "Probably has something to do with that circumcised penis."

♥

I was going to get tipsy. I needed at least two glasses of wine. But first, I was going to find out what in the name of tarnation was going on.

I called my brother and left a message telling him I would be out with Claire. I did not tell him Claire was driving me over to the Winston Brothers Auto Shop. Jackson and the Winston boys did not get along, mostly because everyone knew Jethro Winston—the oldest—used to steal cars and neither my daddy nor my brother had ever been able to make the charges stick.

It also had something to do with their sister, Ashley Winston, and Jackson acting like a fool about her in high school.

I remembered Ashley growing up, mostly because she was so darn pretty and sweet. Just the nicest girl in the history of forever. I think most people expected her to be catty because she was so pretty, but she was the opposite.

I pulled at my bottom lip with my thumb and index finger, my narrowed eyes seeing nothing of the colorful foliage umbrellas framing the mountain road. Fall color was out in full force and would be for the next few weeks, assuming we didn't get any unseasonal snow.

I'd be lying if I said the Smoky Mountain landscape wasn't a big draw and factor in my decision to return home after college. The other two main contributing factors were my family and the student loan deferment plan for STEM (science, technology, engineering, and mathematics) teachers who taught in underserved areas. Living at home helped me save money and pay off my student loans. And I was the only high school calculus teacher outside Knoxville for fifty miles in every direction.

My predecessor, Mr. Tranten, had taught math as high as Algebra II. This was the first year high-achieving math students in our area and the surrounding valleys weren't bused off to Knoxville for trigonometry and calculus.

But ever since I was a little girl, I'd dreamt of seeing the world, experiencing it, and not as a tourist. I wanted to be a world traveler. I'd craved freedom and adventure. Being home now felt like preparing for launch. I'd been savoring the time with my family, storing memories, because—if all my painstaking planning came to fruition—I wouldn't be seeing them much in the coming years.

"We're here."

Claire's pronouncement pulled me from my thoughts. I stared out the windshield as she placed her car in park and turned off the ignition, glaring at the open garage of the auto shop. I saw a pair of boots sticking out from underneath the car, and my heart kept asking my head, *What if that's Duane?* My head kept putting my heart off, saying, *We'll cross that circumcised penis when we get to it...*

"Are you going to get out of the car?"

I shook my head. "I haven't decided yet."

Claire sighed. "The sooner you get this sorted, the sooner we can go back to my place and drink wine."

"Well, that settles it," I said distractedly, still not moving.

She paused, likely waiting for me to do something; I could feel her eyes on me. "Jess, what are you stalling for? What are you afraid of?"

Just as the words left her mouth, two redheaded and bearded

male specimens of mighty fineness sauntered out of the garage. The boots under the car were a decoy, likely Cletus. My breath caught and I held it, my eyes widening behind my sunglasses.

The twins were both dressed in sky-blue coveralls and black work boots, with a white undershirt peeking out at the collar. Claire had been wrong last Friday; their hair was approximately the same length and so were their beards. Even the grease stains on their hands and clothes seemed identical. I forgave myself a little for my mix-up on Halloween.

They *looked* exactly the same, and I hadn't seen either of them for going on three years.

Regardless, now I knew immediately which of the two was Duane. If I'd given myself a moment at the community center, I would have been able to figure it out. Duane carried himself differently than Beau. He always had; how he stood, where he looked, and the line of his mouth were in stark contrast to his sociable brother.

Beau swaggered even as he stood still, glanced around at his surroundings, his brow untroubled, and his smile was easy.

Duane held himself straight and aloof, his eyes never leaving his brother's, as though Duane only ever focused on one thing at a time. His slight squint made him appear deep in thought as Beau chatted cheerfully. Duane's smile was almost reluctant. I'd noticed the reluctant smile on Friday, too. His smiles were reserved, secretive, like he rationed them.

I glanced between the two brothers and didn't have to wait long to figure out whether the mystical Beau voodoo spell had truly been broken.

It had.

I looked at Beau now and felt a placid, warm fondness. He really was such a nice guy.

Another sign of Beau's diminished power: I looked at Duane and felt powerfully and irrationally irritated, flustered, and insecure. These weren't unusual reactions to his proximity; however, each swelled inside me with a sudden surprising fierceness and was paired with something new—abrupt and intense longing.

Duane hadn't made any attempt at contact over the last five days. Of course neither had I. After his admission at the lake, we walked back to the bonfire in strained silence, my hand in his. Releasing me as we approached, he disappeared after depositing me with Cletus, telling his brother to take me home. He'd walked out of the ring of light provided by the fire, and that was the last time I'd seen him…if you didn't count all the odd dreams I'd been having about him since.

"Which one, Jess?"

I started, Claire's question interrupting my aggrieved reflections, and responded without pulling my gaze from the twins. "I'm going to sound like a looney bird when I admit this, but... Duane."

"Well, I'll be..." I knew she was fighting a smile.

"I know, right? I'm a crazy person. Obviously I can't trust myself, what with my flighty impulses. Next week I'll probably be batshit crazy for Cletus."

"Well, Cletus is adorable. You could do a lot worse."

"Yes, I could. Maybe I'll just decide to be infatuated with Cletus."

I tried to make light of my feelings, but I knew it wasn't that easy. My emotions for Duane were wrapped in years of *knowing* him—animosity, begrudging respect, and five days of agitated pining. Our history was complicated enough, multifarious enough, for me to be wary that the feelings could be genuine and lasting.

Claire chuckled, placed her hand over one of mine, and squeezed. "Must be rough, liking the look of him so much when you obviously dislike him so."

"I don't dislike him." I shook my head, searching for the right words to explain what I felt for Duane. "I mean, I did...I did kind of dislike him when we were growing up. He was never nice to me like Beau was. But he talked to me more than Beau did, a lot more. He seemed to go out of his way to argue with me all the time."

"And now?"

"Now..." I shrugged. "Now I don't know him anymore, not really. I mean, assuming nothing's changed since I left for college, I know his favorite ice cream flavor is rocky road; I know he's got a scar on his right arm from climbing over Mr. Tanner's junkyard fence when he was thirteen and that it required a tetanus shot and stitches. I know he drives way too fast and, last I knew, had never lost a race at the Canyon. I know he whistles Darth Vader's theme song from Star Wars when he washes his car or fixes his car or does anything in rote. I know he takes his coffee black and doesn't like the taste of carbonated beverages—that kind of stuff."

"Seems like you know a lot."

I shrugged again. "Just stupid stuff you pick up when you grow up with someone."

"How does Beau take his coffee?"

My eyes slid to Claire's and I frowned at her. "I don't know; why?"

"Does Beau whistle when he fixes cars?"

I shook my head, lifting my eyebrows in the universal sign of ignorance. "How should I know?"

I could tell she was hiding a grin when she responded. "Are you sure you had a crush on Beau? Or did you maybe like Duane all along, but felt Beau was a safer choice?"

My mouth fell open—not a whole lot, just enough to be gaping—and my eyes narrowed as a small sound of disbelief tumbled from my lips. "What? No…no." I shook my head again, with more vehemence this time. "No, no, no."

"Jess, Duane still races cars down at the Canyon and he's still undefeated—mostly because he takes crazy chances and fear doesn't seem to register. Over the summer he killed a rattlesnake at the community center."

"So?"

"So, he walked right over to it, stepped on its head, then reached for it with his bare hands."

"Then he's stupid."

"No. Lord knows he's no fool. He knew what he was doing. He just doesn't seem to have a healthy fear of deadly snakes, or of getting killed at the drag races either. Beau *is* the safer choice. I can understand how you might've been drawn to Duane all along, but—"

"No. No. Just no."

"They're *identical*."

"Looking. They're identical looking. They're not identical people."

"Yeah, but by your own admission, you actually knew Duane growing up. You knew about him; you spent time with him. Yet your crush was on Beau?"

"He was the nice one," I grumbled.

Claire laughed, rolling her eyes. "Maybe. Or maybe he was the safe one."

I turned away from her and back to the brothers in question. They were leaning into the hood of a vintage car, their red heads obscured; however, I had an excellent view of their backsides.

I huffed with indignation, not liking Claire's rewriting of my history (mostly because it made sense). "Listen, Dr. Phil, I don't know why we're even talking about this yet. Neither of us have had enough wine for this conversation. Although I could sit in this car and ogle Duane Winston's fine ass all day from afar, I need to find out why my truck is here and what's to be done about it."

"I agree."

"Good." I nodded, reaching for the door handle, finally having enough incentive impetus to eject myself from my seat.

"I, too, could sit here all day and ogle Duane Winston's fine ass from afar." Claire said this just as my feet hit the ground. Before I could administer my reproachful glare, she was out of the car with her door shut, striding purposefully toward the twins.

"Hey, boys!" she called immediately, drawing their attention and giving me no time to prepare my game face.

My steps faltered as they looked over their shoulders, Duane's glare catching on Claire first, then flickering to me. His expression didn't change, not precisely. Rather, I had all of his focus. Once his eyes latched on to me, they didn't waver.

Apprehension warred with anticipation, and both caused a lump to form in my throat. Try as I might, I was unable to hold Duane's gaze and I looked away, preferring instead Beau's lazy, easy smile as he grinned at both Claire and me with straightforward, undemanding affability.

"Hello, beautiful ladies," Beau drawled, pulling a rag from his pocket and wiping his hands.

"Hey, Beau. Duane." Claire stopped about four feet from where they loitered in front of the car. I saw her dip her head toward Duane as I came to stand next to her.

"Hi, Claire," Duane said, and just the sound of his voice made me feel like someone had lit a match in my belly, the warmth spreading to my fingertips in a shock. My eyes flickered to his, then away. He was still looking at me, all intense and focused, but otherwise expressionless.

He was unsettling. I was unsettled.

"Hey…guys," I said lamely, like a lame person, to the patch on Duane's coveralls that told me his name was *Duane*. Determined, I pushed past my uneasiness and cleared my throat, opting to speak to Beau instead.

The irony was not lost on me.

"I couldn't help but notice that my truck is parked out front."

Beau's eyes were the color of the summer sky as he

regarded me, his mouth pulled to the side in a plainly amused smirk. "Yep."

I couldn't help but return the smile as his were still infectious. "Last I knew, the truck was still parked at the community center with catastrophic engine troubles."

"Not *troubles*, sweetheart." Beau's tone was gentle and replete with sympathy. "You've still got catastrophic engine failure. You need a new engine."

I stuffed my hands in the back pockets of my khaki skirt and shifted on my feet. "I know that. But I don't have the money right now to get a new engine."

"We figured as much," Duane cut in, stepping forward so he was shoulder to shoulder with his brother and directly in front of me. "We'd like to buy the truck from you, if you're willing."

I waited two seconds before lifting my gaze to Duane's, needing time to gather my faculties. When I met his stare, I was glad I'd taken the time to prepare. If Beau's eyes were the tranquil summer sky, then Duane's were a tempest at sea—a stormy aquamarine.

"Duane," I said unnecessarily, and a little dreamily, on an exhaled breath.

His attention drifted over my face and his non-expression softened. "Hi, Jessica."

My heart gave a little leap. Even though his features were completely absent a smile, I felt one—a blasted shy, wistful one—tug at my lips. "Hi, Duane."

Then silence.

I wasn't aware of it at first because I'd tumbled into an aquamarine tempest. My mind was fully occupied with memories of Halloween night, of his hands on me, his mouth on mine, the hot velvet touch of his tongue. Preoccupation with my memories became something else—fixation on a wish…I think—and my chest felt heavy and full.

I only became aware of the quiet when it was broken.

"Claire, can I take a look under your hood? I think, uh, one of your engine mounts might be loose. I heard a rattling sound when you pulled up," Beau said, as he took Claire's elbow in hand and walked her toward her truck, not waiting for a response.

If she made one, I swear I didn't hear it. The soundtrack in my brain had started again. This time Roberta Flack's "First Time Ever I Saw Your Face" was playing, the music swelling, carrying my sense out to sea.

Duane and I were now basically alone, giving each other hot looks.

Duane

6

"Don't let your luggage define your travels. Each life unravels differently."

—SHANE KOYCZAN, "WE ARE MORE"

I WAS GOING TO KISS her.

But first I was going to strangle her.

"Duane…" She said my name again in that breathless way, making my neck itch and my throat tighten.

Jessica was looking at me expectantly. Her big amber eyes on mine like I was the center of her world. I liked it too much. It was also irritating because I didn't know what it meant, what she was thinking. She hadn't said a damn word to me on our walk back from the lake. She hadn't called me. We hadn't spoken since Friday.

Five days. Five days without touching or tasting her.

I was going to kiss her while I strangled her.

"Yeah?" I said, the edge of my irritation clear. I wasn't trying to hide it; there was no need. One way or the other, we were coming to an agreement that involved something definite, not definitely maybes. Better she knew I wasn't planning on rolling over unless it involved her beneath me.

Jessica blinked at me, likely because of my tone, and I watched her shake herself a little like I'd startled her.

"Uh, so…the truck." She cleared her throat, her eyes sliding to the side and away from me.

"What about the truck?"

"You towed it."

"Yes, I did." I allowed myself a moment to look at her body. She was wearing a thin pink shirt with buttons down the front, with a lacy white tank top under. It was tucked into a tan skirt that ended at her knees. She was also wearing brown high-heeled boots, the kind that don't make sense.

Boots are for working, for walking through wet mud, for keeping feet from getting shredded by broken glass and falling machine parts. Boots with spiked heels were just as practical as sandals with steel toes.

Still not looking at me, she asked, "So, you want to buy it?" Her voice was different, higher pitched.

"That's what I just said." Again, my irritation was clear.

Her eyes cut to mine, throwing me splinters of frustration. "Well, there's no need to be rude, Duane."

"I'm sorry, was I being rude?" I couldn't help myself, I took a full step forward, forcing her to lift her chin to keep eye contact. "Should I have called?"

"Yes," she ground out. "You can't just tow other people's cars without asking."

"Excuse me, Princess. But Mike McClure called me and asked if I minded moving the truck here. I figured he was calling on your behalf."

"No, he wasn't calling on my behalf. If I wanted to call you, I would have just called you."

I felt those words in my stomach, just under my ribs, a quick slice. I'm sure I winced because her expression changed, but before she could explain away her meaning, I cut her off.

"Fine, I get you, loud and clear."

"Duane—"

I lifted my hands to keep her from talking. She was so lovely, even her voice was pretty. But suddenly I couldn't wait for her to leave and put me out of this misery of being with her when she wasn't interested in being mine.

"We want to buy the truck and I'm willing to offer you a fair amount."

"Would you just hold on a sec?" Jessica took my hand between hers, her grip surprisingly strong, her skin against mine sending a shock up my arm. I ignored it and ground my teeth.

"You can use the money for a new car, something smaller that gets better mileage."

Paying no heed, Jessica took a half step forward, catching me unaware. One second she was glaring at me; the next she was lifting to her tiptoes and brushing her lips against mine. That was it. I was done for.

I was surprised, so it took me a second to respond.

But I was also motivated, so it only took me a second to respond.

I gripped her arm, staying any possible escape, and moved to deepen the kiss. Surprising me again, she moaned and opened her mouth, her hot little tongue searching for mine. I growled and I didn't regret it.

I'd been thinking about her sweet curves, her silky skin,

perfect fucking breasts, and round luscious ass for five days. Five days of an unending, tortured hard-on. I was impressed the only thing I did was growl, because what I wanted to do was throw her over my shoulder, take her to the room above the office, handcuff her to the chair, strip her naked, and listen to her moan, cry, and scream my name.

It didn't have to be my name. Also acceptable: *Oh God*, and *Yes, please*, and *Don't stop*, and *Harderfastermore*.

You get the picture.

I doubted her sheriff father or deputy brother would be pleased with that course of action, but I can't say I cared much about their feelings on the subject.

Jessica's hand released mine, slipped around my back, kneading and searching, pressing her soft body to mine, pulling against the hold I had on her arm. I relinquished her and grabbed a handful of her ass, snaking my other arm around her waist.

I needed leverage. We needed privacy. I needed to put her against something so I could do more of what I wanted to do. To that end, I lifted her slightly off her feet and carried her into the shop, past Cletus's boots, past the Toyota he was working on, past the rusty Master Lock toolbox on wheels, and into the supply room off the garage.

For her part, she never stopped kissing me. Tilting her head to one side and pressing herself to my chest, Jessica licked and bit my ear, giving me little sighs and enthusiastic moans. She also wrapped her arm around my neck and further accommodated our relocation by bending her legs, making it easier to traverse the obstacle course of the shop.

Once inside the supply room, I slammed the door and immediately turned and pressed her against it. Her hands came to the zipper at the front of my coveralls at my throat and fumbled for the tab.

Now, in that moment shut in the little room, surrounded by shelves of greasy cylinders, busted pistons, and an array of crankshafts, I admit I thought about hiking up her skirt, sliding into her sweet body, and taking her hard and fast against the door.

I thought about it. I did.

But I didn't want to do that.

I wanted to marry this girl.

That was the truth of it. And maybe one day, after we'd been married for a while, I'd pull her in here and bend her over the table at the back and we'd have a real good time. Maybe we'd do it every Wednesday…when she was my wife.

But not now. Not yet. Not when I'm needing to be taken seriously and respected. That's why, when I spotted the grease stain on the upper arm of her pretty top, most certainly left by my hand, I felt my engine cool and a good dose of sobriety chilled my veins.

I grabbed her hands before they could work the zipper of my coveralls down to my hips and brought them over her head. It was hard to think with her hands on me. It was also hard to think with her mouth doing its voodoo, so I bent my head to her neck and bit a spot on her shoulder. I took the opportunity to breathe her in and found this was a mistake if I wanted a clear head.

After placing one more kiss against her jaw, I lifted my head for some cooler air while trying to ignore her rapid pants of excitement and the beat of her heart against my ribs. We were pressed together knees to chest. I still held her wrists but I lowered them to her sides. My eyes were closed. I needed more than a minute, so I took it, and reminded myself that being shortsighted can ruin the long game.

Jess was the first to speak. "You're really good at that."

"At what?" I lifted my eyelids, careful to keep my stare affixed to the sobering dark stain on her shirt. I frowned when I saw there was more than one stain; she had streaks of grease everywhere I'd touched her.

"Kissing, touching me, making me hot."

My mouth curved slightly at her honesty as I backed up a half step to see how dirty I'd made her. Jess had always been so honest, to a fault really. She was honest when it would have served her better to be guarded. She was so honest that I worried for her.

But for now I was grateful for this peculiarity in her character.

Knowing I had myself under control, and recognizing I was going to need to replace her entire outfit, I finally met her eyes and released her wrists. "Thanks, Jess."

But her attention was on my mouth and her hands slipped back to my torso, gripping my jumpsuit like she didn't want me to go too far. "We should do it again."

I didn't try to hide my smile. Rather I leaned one palm on the door behind her and placed the other possessively on her hip; her skirt was already ruined and I liked the feel of her body beneath my hand. "Sounds good to me."

I kissed her nose. The bridge of it had always been covered with brown freckles, but they'd faded since she was a teenager. Standing close like we were, I could see them.

"When?" Her nails dug into my sides through my coveralls, her tone urgent.

"What are you doing tonight?" I smiled at her pushiness. "Want to go see a movie?"

Jessica blinked, her eyebrows pulling together in a small frown. "Movie? No. Not unless it's an empty movie theater."

"Jess…" I shook my head, and searched her face to see if she was joking. She wasn't. My neck itched again and the beginnings of a cold uncertainty trickled down my back. "Jess, there are lots of good movies playing now. Let me take you out to dinner."

She stared at me. I stared back, waiting. I could see her mind working, but what she was thinking, I had no idea. Her fingers relaxed, letting me go, but the rest of her body soon stiffened. Then I saw a flash of pensiveness in her brown eyes. I didn't like how she'd grown distant while I still held her, but I held on anyway.

"I can't tonight." She swallowed, her eyes moved between mine, then away; she looked increasingly agitated. "Claire and I have plans. We're going to drink wine."

My eyes narrowed and my blood pressure steadily increased the longer we stood there, me touching her, but Jessica was already far away. "Jess…"

"Yes?" Her voice was weak.

I cupped her jaw and cheeks, forcing her to look at me and leaving smudges on her skin. "In case you haven't caught on yet, I'd like to take you out."

She lifted her hands, covered one of mine, and held on to the wrist of the other. I was happy to see some of the rising panic recede as I continued. "I want to go to a place that serves food, where neither of us have to do the cleanup or the dishes, and talk to you."

"What do you want to talk about?"

"I don't care, I honestly don't. As long as I'm talking to you."

This won me a quick smile and it went a long way toward easing my cold doubt. She bit her lip, chewed on it, her big brown eyes even bigger than normal. Then she nodded.

And I finally breathed, releasing her. "Good."

She nodded again, her eyes lighting up, her pretty mouth slanting with a roundabout smile. "Good," she repeated, then pressed her lips to mine for a fast kiss. "This is good."

I nodded too, her sudden happiness like aloe to a sunburn, and then proclaimed the understatement of the century. "I'm glad."

"Okay then, it's a date. Duane Winston and Jessica James are going on a date."

I laughed because she was too adorable, and her words solidified something I'd wanted for years; finally the angry hard-on in my boxers didn't feel so pointless.

"Yes. That's what's happening." I rubbed my nose along hers, gave her another soft kiss. "The only question is when and where?"

"Oh…" Her gaze turned hazy, unfocused, and drifted over my shoulder. "I could pack a picnic for Saturday afternoon."

I thought about that, about not seeing her the rest of this week. I decided it was probably too soon to say I'd miss her if I didn't see her between now and Saturday.

"Saturday is good. Let's do Saturday," I said. "And I'll pack the picnic." I'd been thinking about this for a long time and I'd decided years ago that if I ever got the chance, I'd take her out proper, pay for dinner—even if it was a picnic.

"You don't have to do that."

"I want to."

"Fine. Let me bring drinks at least." Her hand sought mine, entwined our fingers, and squeezed.

The simple movement and connection was dizzying, and it caught me off guard. I opened my mouth to respond but found I'd forgotten what she'd just said.

Her eyes searched mine, her small smile still in place. Obviously she mistook my speechlessness because she soothed, "Don't worry, I know you prefer Guinness to Budweiser." Then she dropped her voice to a sweet whisper and leaned a bit closer. "Your secret is safe with me."

♥

I grinned at Jessica James's backside as she walked away because she had a big old brown grease stain on the left side of her skirt where I'd palmed her ass.

"Damn, Duane, you got big hands." Cletus sauntered up next to me, wiping his own hands on a rag.

My grin became a frown and I shot my brother a look. "Don't be looking at Jess's ass."

"I'm not looking at her ass. I remind you, sir, she *is* my calculus teacher." Cletus lifted his chin toward Jessica's departing form. "I'm looking at the palm print on her ass."

I returned my eyes to my girl just as she twisted at the waist and sent me a shy grin over her shoulder, setting my heart off on a goose chase.

Jessica hadn't cared two nickels when I'd pointed out the hand marks to her just before she'd left. When I suggested I give her one of my clean shirts to cover the evidence of our groping, she looked at me like I was crazy.

Instead she surprised me by laughing at the incriminating smudges. She also laughed about the fact that the rest of her clothes were ruined by my dirty paw prints—everything but her impractical boots—and waved away my insistence to replace the outfit. She seemed to be delighted by her rumpled state, and her eyes burned brighter after she saw how disheveled she was.

"Hold your hand up." In my peripheral vision, I saw Cletus lift his palm toward me, suspending it between us.

I kept my eyes on Jessica, the sexy sway of her hips, how her long blond hair was blown over her shoulder as she walked to Claire's car. She held her head high, and the big smile she gave me from across the parking lot as she opened the passenger door to Claire McClure's Chevy almost knocked me off my feet.

This girl was flaunting the fact we'd just made out in the supply room.

"I will not hold my hand up," I said absentmindedly.

"Come on, I want to see who has bigger hands."

"Shut up, Cletus. I'm not going to hold your hand."

I thought about calling to her before she shut the door. I also thought about doing a victory lap around the garage. Instead I settled for watching Jess and Claire pull out of the lot, make a left, and disappear down the road.

"I don't want to hold your hand. I want to compare our anthropic units."

"Quit it."

Beau stopped in front of us, his expression blank. "Cletus, you finished with that Toyota yet? We need to leave soon if we're going to make it to Nashville today."

Cletus's attention moved between me and Beau; he let his hand drop. "Listen, I think it'd be best if we just cleared the air now before things progress any further with Duane and Catastrophic Engine Failure."

"Who?"

"Miss James."

I felt my eyes narrow on my older brother. I hoped he wasn't about to say what I figured he was going to say. I was in no mood—not now, not ever—to discuss Jessica's infatuation with Beau. An infatuation, I noted, that appeared to be over as of last Friday's bonfire.

"No need." Beau shook his head rather emphatically. "No air to clear."

"Come on now. No use ignoring things." Cletus was using his grandfather voice as he placed his greasy fingers on Beau's shoulder. "I think we'd all feel better if everything were out in the open. I know I would."

My stare shifted to my twin and I felt a spike of alarm. "What's he talking about, Beau?"

"I don't rightly know, Duane."

Cletus put his other hand on my shoulder and nodded solemnly. "The truth is, Duane—and I know this might be hard to hear—but the fact of the matter is, and you know I think Catastrophic Engine Failure is a sufficient teacher of calculus, but that doesn't negate the fact that—"

"Just spit it out, Cletus!"

"Fine. We all hate Jessica's brother, Jackson James."

I blinked at Cletus, then Beau and I blinked at each other. As much as two people could read each other's minds, Beau and I could. He and I shared a brief, silent conversation where the following was shared:

Both of us: *Of course we hate Jackass James.*

Me: *Didn't he give you a speeding ticket over the summer?*

Beau: *Yes.*

Me: *Jackass*

Beau: *By the way, I've always known you had a thing for Jess, since we were kids. I would never do anything to get in the way of you two being together* (or something along these lines).

Me: *Thanks. I appreciate that.*

Beau: *But you owe me one, because she's hot, funny, and sweet* (or something like this).

Me: *Fine. I owe you one.*

Beau: *Good. Glad we have that settled.*

"Stop it." Cletus snapped his fingers in front of our faces. "I hate it when you two mind-meld through your eyeballs."

Beau sighed. "Cletus, I think we're all clear on the fact that no one in our family has any patience for Jackson James. After that shit he pulled with our sister when they were teenagers—"

"And all the times he arrested Jethro for stealing cars," I chimed in.

"In all fairness, though, Jethro likely did steal those cars," Cletus added offhandedly.

"Jethro was never convicted," I added unnecessarily, wanting to defend my oldest brother.

"Exactly." Beau sounded exasperated. "Plus Jackson still brings it up all the time. I saw Jackson at the Wooden Plank two weeks ago and he made some dumbass remark about Jennifer Sylvester's new BMW being stolen and whether Jethro had been investigated as a suspect."

"And that's just him being a douchebag because Jethro has been straitlaced for over four years, and Jackson won't let it go. Plus, Jethro hates bananas," I added unnecessarily. Everyone knew Jennifer Sylvester had a banana cake in her front seat when the car was stolen. I could feel myself getting worked up and knew Beau was feeling similarly irritated.

Neither Beau nor I could drive on the Parkway without

getting pulled over by Jackson James. It didn't matter if we were speeding or not. I always figured this was because Jackson still felt teenage torment about my sister's lack of interest in his dumb ass during high school. But recently I was beginning to think Jessica's older brother was just a bored little shit of a man, drunk on small-town power.

"Right. Well, we all agree." Cletus rested his hands on his hips, nodding thoughtfully. "But no amount of wishing is going to change the fact that Jackson James is unsavory and that Catastro…I mean, Miss James is his sister."

"So what's your point?" I crossed my arms over my chest and frowned at my brother. He always had a point—usually it was a good one—but it just took forever for him to get there.

"My point is that you need be cautious of Jackson. Because once he finds out your intentions toward his sister, things will not be pretty."

"I have no ill intentions."

"I know you don't, but—"

"But nothing. The truth is that girl is it for me."

"I know, Duane." Cletus's expression flattened, like he was losing patience. "She's your 1968 Plymouth Barracuda. Everyone knows that. Well, everyone that matters. All I'm saying is, don't expect him to give you his blessing."

"I don't need his blessing."

"Cletus is right." Beau's tone turned uncharacteristically serious, his wide eyes drilled into mine. "Jackson ain't gonna like this one bit. And he's a right sneaky bastard. Just watch your back."

"He'll make problems for you, if he can," Cletus continued. "So just let me know if you need help making problems for him in return."

This statement surprised me. And by the looks of it, this statement surprised Beau as well.

Beau mimicked my stance, crossing his arms over his chest and leveling Cletus with a narrowed stare. "Just what is that supposed to mean?"

"Just what I said." Cletus shrugged, looking and sounding innocent. That's one of the things about Cletus. He's real good at looking innocent. Sometimes I forgot Cletus could spot a sneak so well because he was the king of sneaks. I was just glad he was on my side this time.

"Now, Beau, enough of this dillydallying." Cletus stole Beau's rag from his front pocket and wiped his hands, glancing around the shop as though he was making sure everything was in order. "Are we going to Nashville today, or what?"

Duane

7

"I am happy to report that in the war between reality and romance, reality is not the stronger."

—JOHN STEINBECK, *TRAVELS WITH CHARLEY: IN SEARCH OF AMERICA*

I WASN'T PAYING ATTENTION TO my surroundings because I was distracted by pleasant thoughts.

And I suppose that's why I didn't hear the motorcycles park around the back of the shop or know I had company until they were already inside the garage. I heard an obnoxious laugh, loud and long, alerting me to the unexpected arrival. I lifted my eyes just in time to see Repo—one of my deadbeat father's biker brothers—pick up Cletus's favorite socket wrench and toss it back to the toolbox with a loud clang.

Just behind Repo was Dirty Dave, the owner of the obnoxious laugh, another member of the Iron Wraiths, and a real jackass. He was called Dirty Dave because he was dirty. And he stank.

I sighed my aggravation and set down the carburetor I was fixing. As enjoyable as Jessica's visit had been that afternoon,

I knew without a doubt these callers were going to inspire my ire.

Dirty Dave was just a douchebag lackey.

But Repo was a man of importance within the Iron Wraiths. I'd known him since I was little. He even had dinner at my momma's table on occasion, and gave each of us boys a bowie knife for our tenth birthday. Once upon a time I looked up to this man.

But as an adult, I considered him a con man and pariah.

"Hello, son," Repo said, lifting his chin in my general direction as his eyes scanned the shop.

I reached to the side to switch off the Bluetooth speaker for my iPhone. Repo had a real raspy voice. I could barely make out what he was saying half the time in a quiet room. The shop was suddenly filled with the quiet sounds of a Tennessee night and the unwelcome sounds of motorcycle boots scuffing on cement.

"Repo. Dirty Dave. What do y'all want?" I didn't bother to wipe my hands because I had no plans to shake theirs.

"Now, is that any way to speak to your Uncle Repo?" He smiled, his salt-and-pepper beard framing bright-white teeth. This one reminded me of my daddy, with all the charm of a snake in the grass.

I glanced at the wall clock behind him; it was almost 11:30 p.m. I'd lost track of time.

"You aren't my uncle, old man," I answered flatly.

No. This man was most assuredly *not* any family relation of mine. Though my daddy considered the members of the Iron Wraiths to be his brothers, these men were less than nothing to me and I wanted them to know it.

"Ah, you're not Beau," Dirty Dave chirped from his spot

next to Repo. He seemed to be looking at me with new eyes. "We were hoping for Beau. He's so much nicer than you, plus he knows when to show respect."

"Be that as it may, I'm trying to finish up here. So if you two will get to the point?" I set my hands on my hips, lifting my eyebrows, hoping they'd get my message to hurry it up.

"Now hold on a minute," Repo rasped, lifting his hands up as though I needed to calm down. "We're here with a business proposition. One I'm real sure you're going to want to hear."

"Not interested." In an effort to show the alluded-to respect, I decided not to say, *Not interested, asshole. Now go fuck yourself.*

See? Very respectful.

"Just listen up."

"No. You can leave the way you came in." I flicked my hand toward the back of the shop, then turned back to the carburetor and the well-lit table where it rested.

"You can't say no to money, boy." Dirty Dave lifted his voice.

"I'll say no to anything involving the Iron Wraiths." I shrugged, showing the boredom I felt. I knew they were used to seeing fear and inspiring awe. The Iron Wraiths weren't a joke; the club president was a criminal mastermind and a crazy fucker to boot. These weren't good guys. But I'd never been able to muster up even the slightest trepidation where dumbasses were concerned—even dangerous ones.

"Why's that?" This came from Repo. In my peripheral vision, I saw the pair halt their slow progress into the shop, standing close and to my right.

"Because everything you do is illegal."

"So? You race cars at the Canyon, right? Rumor is you're

one crazy motherfucker in the pit and make buckets of cash doing it. That sure as hell ain't legal."

"Racing for easy money is one thing; getting involved with your kind is another. I'm not my worthless father, and I'm not interested in making money off other people's misery."

"How about making money to keep your family safe?"

A chill spread down my spine, making me stand straighter. I turned a questioning glare on Repo first, then Dave. I found Dirty Dave giving me a dirty smile. I faced them.

"Is that a threat?"

"No," said Repo.

"Hell yeah," said Dave.

Repo cut in before I could order them out again. "Now hold on. We're not planning to hurt anybody. But you want to keep your family out of jail, then you need to hear us out."

"Keep my family out of jail? What are you talking about?"

Dirty Dave nodded once as he said, "Jethro."

"Jethro?" I scowled at this. "No, no. I ain't buying it. He washed his hands of y'all years ago."

"Yeah, but before he did, he stole us a lot of cars." Dirty Dave said this with measured glee.

"So what?" I spat. "You're going to turn him in now? If you do that, then you're admitting to your own guilt."

"Boy, didn't I say *listen*?" Repo's words were clipped in an unusual display of exasperation.

I threw my hands up and leaned my hip against the table, figuring that letting the man say his piece was the only way I was going to get them to leave. "Sure. Fine. Speak."

"So your momma…" Repo paused. My eyes must've betrayed my spike in anger at the mention of my mother because he held his hands up again like I needed to calm down.

"I'm not down talking your momma, boy. I'm just saying, your momma died a month ago, rest her soul."

I swallowed a lump of emotion, unable to stop thinking about my momma's last days, how the cancer had taken her from us. I missed her: her kindness, her sweetness. I rallied against a sudden flash of nostalgia, knowing now—with these morons—was not the time to dwell on these thoughts.

"This is not news to me, Repo."

"Yeah, but we been keeping our distance out of respect, giving you and yours time to grieve. We gave you a month. She was a good woman."

"I'm not interested in your thoughts on my momma." These words arrived through clenched teeth. He needed to wrap this shit up.

"Okay now, but here's the thing. Brick and Mortar, the two Iron Wraiths brothers your sister got arrested after your momma's funeral—"

I cut him off. "They got themselves arrested *because* they were trying to kidnap Ashley and Billy from the funeral."

"And Brick and Mortar were only there trying to help your daddy because your momma tricked him out of his money." Dirty Dave pointed his thick index finger at me. I wanted to snip it off with twenty-four-gauge wire cutters.

"That's not how it happened. That money doesn't belong to Darrell Winston. It never did."

"Darrell is your daddy, boy. He and your momma had seven babies together, were married for years. That's a long time, a lot of history, and a lot of kids for a man to wait for his fair share. Then your sister's boyfriend, that park ranger—"

"Drew Runous isn't Ashley's boyfriend and he isn't a park ranger. He's a game warden."

"Whatever. Drew Runous swoops in and sweet-talks your momma into signing over all her money. Now, how can you blame your daddy for trying to get what's his?"

I had to grit my teeth to keep from hollering. Dirty Dave's version of events was far from reality.

The truth was my *daddy*, Darrell Winston, was a no-good, rotten sonofabitch. In addition to riding with the Iron Wraiths, he was a con man and an abuser. He'd married Momma for her money when she was sixteen—because she came from lots of money. He'd also beaten her and cheated on her. Habitually. And every time she tried to divorce him, he'd used us kids to keep her from following through.

Finally, she outsmarted Darrell by filing for a separation from him, then selling all her belongings—her family's house and all possessions therein—to a family friend named Drew Runous for a thousand dollars, thereby removing it all from my father's reach. She also signed over all her bank accounts and our trust funds.

That left Darrell spitting angry. But there was nothing he could do because Momma was already dead by the time he found out. So he showed up at my mother's funeral with two of his Iron Wraiths brothers—Brick and Mortar—and tried to kidnap Ashley and Billy. He'd likely been desperate and couldn't think of another way to get his hands on Momma's money.

Luckily he and his biker friends were stopped, but not before Ashley shot one of them in the leg. All three—Darrell, Brick, and Mortar—were presently awaiting trial and would hopefully serve serious prison time.

"What does Brick and Mortar trying to kidnap my family have to do with anything? Why are you here?"

"'Cause, *Duane*, Brick and Mortar were our mechanics. Now they're gone, we've got nobody to take over their work. That's where you boys and this shop come in." Dirty Dave gestured to the inside of the garage.

"So, what? You want me to fix your bikes?"

"No, son. You might not like it, but your daddy is one of us. That means you're family too, and you owe us. Brick and Mortar were our *mechanics*…"

I blinked at Repo, knowing I was missing the point, and waited for him to fill in the blanks.

When he saw I didn't understand his meaning, he huffed, then spelled it out. "They ran the chop shop. They dismantled the cars. They took our stolen goods and made them transportable."

"You and your brother Beau, the two of you are going to take over running our chop shop." Dirty Dave connected the dots for me even as the picture Repo painted clarified in my head.

A sound of repulsion and disbelief escaped my mouth before I could stop it, followed by, "Oh, *hell* no."

"Hell yes, boy."

"Hell. No. And stop calling me *boy*." I was three seconds away from punching Dirty Dave in the jaw.

Repo must've seen my patience snap because he stepped forward between Dave and me, again holding his hands up. "Now, you need to listen to reason. We got evidence against your brother Jethro that'll put him away for life. Not for years, *for life*."

"Bullshit."

"No. No bullshit," Dirty Dave denied from behind Repo. "This shit is real."

My attention was split between them; I was looking for any sign of subterfuge. "Like I said before, you incriminate him for those stolen cars, then you're incriminating yourself."

"No. Not with this." Repo reached into his leather jacket and pulled out a thumb drive. He offered it to me.

I glared at him instead of taking it. "What is it?"

"Jethro got out of the Wraiths three years ago, and the video on this drive will show you how he bought his freedom. In the scheme of things, it was a small price. But this small price carries a hefty federal sentence *if* the police were to find out what he did."

I narrowed my eyes, feeling equal parts suspicion and panic. "What did he do?"

Repo pushed the thumb drive against my chest, forcing me to take it. "Watch this. Then you'll know. Then, when you see things our way, you call us."

The flash drive landed in the palm of my hand and I glared at Repo, wanting to crush it under my boot and despising the fact I couldn't.

The older man scratched his facial hair as he studied me, the solemnity of his expression increasing until, with grave severity, he added in a low voice, "Don't be stupid. There's no reason to include your brother Billy in this. He don't need to know."

I didn't say so, but I agreed with Repo on this one. Billy's answer would be to go directly to the police, all the while waving his middle finger at the Iron Wraiths. Billy loved Jethro, but he hated the Wraiths more. In fact, I was pretty sure Billy hated the Wraiths more than he loved anything— except maybe our momma. But with her death, Billy's regard for Momma was a moot point.

"But," Dirty Dave stepped around his biker brother and waved his fat finger at my chest, "you got two weeks, *Duane*. Two weeks to decide, or else we send an anonymous tip to Sheriff James and you can visit Jethro on the weekends…at the Federal Correctional Institution in Memphis."

♥

I did nothing with the thumb drive at first except hide it. When I got home that night, I researched thumb drives and whether they could be used to install spyware or cause mischief on my personal computer. Everything I read made me nervous.

I thought about calling Jethro or Drew, but decided against it. Jethro was now a law-abiding park ranger for Great Smoky Mountains National Park and Drew was his boss. They were currently together on a trek in the mountains some two hundred miles away, and only reachable via satellite phone.

I was also feeling paranoid and didn't think it prudent to have a telephone conversation about my brother's previous illegal activities. Discussing matters with Jethro would have to wait until he got back from the mountains.

In the end, I decided to talk to Beau—and only Beau— about everything when he and Cletus arrived home on Saturday. There was no reason to include my other brothers in the discussion. Worst-case scenario, if it turned out that the only way to keep Jethro out of prison was conscription of the Winston Brothers Auto Shop, then Beau and I would have to do it alone. I didn't want anyone else getting caught up in this tangle.

The fewer people who knew about this business with the

Iron Wraiths, the better. Billy, Cletus, and Roscoe could plead true ignorance if Beau and I were caught.

Before I went to sleep, I further decided to drive into Knoxville in search of a pawn shop as soon as dawn broke the next morning.

On my way into town I grabbed a doughnut and caffeine fix from Daisy's Nut House, an early-riser café for locals of Green Valley. The warm jelly-filled pastry paired with her drip coffee did a bit to settle my uncommon nerves. Though I still felt cautious, so I decided not to search for a pawn shop using my iPhone or computer, deciding it was better to leave no computer trail of my activities…just in case.

Thankfully, I found a shop that looked promising called Discount Larry's Gun and Pawn. Because these places always have surveillance cameras, I parked across the street and pulled on my brother Roscoe's Yankees baseball hat (something I wouldn't be caught dead wearing) and nondescript blue hoodie.

I kept my head down as I entered and did a fast sweep of the merchandise, finding what I was searching for almost immediately. I paid in cash and left the shop quickly, having shared no words with the proprietor.

I jogged back to my car. I then took the long road back to Green Valley, but stopped by Mr. Tanner's junkyard on my way. It was there, down the tree-lined dirt road to one side of the junkyard, that I opened the old laptop I'd just purchased from the pawn shop, and watched the video.

What I saw made me want to murder my oldest brother.

And when Beau got home on Saturday, he could help me figure out how to hide Jethro's body.

Jessica

8

> "If you really want to escape the things that harass you, what you're needing is not to be in a different place but to be a different person."
>
> —LUCIUS ANNAEUS SENECA,
> *LETTERS FROM A STOIC*

NOBODY EVER EXPECTS A MUSTANG convertible.

Especially not Duane Winston leaning against a dark-blue Mustang convertible with a white top and racing stripe. The convertible had a white top and racing stripe, not Duane. He was wearing faded, bootcut blue jeans that fit nice and snug over his hips and a charcoal-colored thermal. As I approached—after I recovered from my surprise—I noticed the shirt's color made his eyes appear almost gray.

He wasn't smiling, but I did have all his focus, and Duane's focus made me self-conscious and unsteady. Therefore, my smile was dreamy and reflexive.

"What are you doing here?" I gestured to the high school parking lot. It was Thursday afternoon, and I'd just received a text message from my brother, Jackson. He was on his way to pick me up so I was coming outside to wait.

Instead of answering my question, Duane leaned forward, placed his hand on my hip, and gave me a soft kiss that stole my breath and made every inch of my skin hot.

Then he leaned away, his hand falling back to his side, and answered simply, "I'm bringing you your car."

My mouth fell open for obvious reasons and I blinked at him. "My...my car?"

"Yes." He gave me just the faintest shadow of a grin. "Your car. You can keep it if you want, or you can give it back when you find something better."

"What are you talking about?" My attention moved past him to the gorgeous vintage automobile. He'd backed it into a parking space at the front of the school. I didn't know much about cars, but this car was beautiful.

"While we negotiate a price for your truck, you need a car for getting around, back and forth to work. Take this one for as long as you like."

I struggled to form both words and thought. Finally I managed. "Duane, first of all...whose car is this? I mean, who does it belong to? Won't they miss it?"

"No. It's one of mine. I hardly use it." He reached for my hand and placed the keys in my palm.

"One of yours?"

"Yeah."

I couldn't stop blinking at him. "I can't take your car."

He shrugged. "Sure you can."

"It's a classic! I mean, I'm no expert on cars, but this isn't a recent model. This must be over thirty years old."

"About fifty years, actually. It's a 1966 Mustang 289."

Now I was blinking and shaking my head, and my thoughts were a breathy whisper when they slipped out. "You're crazy."

He finally smiled, though it was swift and gone almost as quickly as it had appeared. I made a mental note that Duane Winston liked it when I called him crazy.

"Take it for a test drive." His hands were on me again, steering me to the driver's side door. He opened it and gently pushed me inside, taking the bag from my shoulder and setting it on the floor behind my seat.

Meanwhile, I was greedily devouring the inside of the classic car with my eyes, unthinkingly slipping the keys into the ignition, pressing the clutch, and turning it on. It was… majestic. Something about the car almost felt alive, even sitting idle, humming beneath my fingers, anxious for the road.

Duane claimed the passenger seat and I glanced at him, finding his attention affixed to my face and a warmth there that made my heart race.

"What?" I narrowed my eyes at him.

"Are you going to touch it or drive it?"

"Honestly? I haven't made up my mind." I stroked the steering wheel. It was covered in soft white leather. In fact, all the upholstery was white leather; the inside smelled like leather and Duane's cologne. "I don't think… I mean, I don't know if I can."

"Don't you know how to drive a stick?"

"Yes. But that's not what I meant." I let go of the wheel and faced him, clasping my hands together on my lap so I wouldn't reach for it again. "I mean, I don't understand what's going on. I should get a rental car in Knoxville until I find a replacement for the truck, something newer."

"No. You shouldn't." He wasn't smiling now. In fact, he looked frustrated. "That'd be a waste of money. This Mustang is a classic, yes. And, sure, it has over six hundred thousand miles on it. But I've rebuilt the engine, and most of the other parts are new. It has new tires, brakes, suspension. It runs as good as a new car; I wouldn't let you drive anything unsafe. You're not going to have any problems with it, and it handles the mountain roads real well."

I shook my head and reached for his hand, seeing he'd mistaken my meaning. "That's not what I meant. I trust that this car handles like it looks—beautifully."

"Then what's the problem?"

"The problem is this car is a *classic*. It is far too valuable for me to use as a loaner."

"Then it's not a loaner. I'm giving it to you. It's yours."

My mouth fell open again and a small sound of confused protest escaped. "Duane."

"Jess."

"You can't be serious."

"I am serious." He looked serious.

"Why are you doing this?"

"Because you need a car and I have four." He shrugged.

"You could sell it. I'm sure it's worth a bundle."

"I can't sell it because I just gave it to you."

I gritted my teeth before hollering, "*You can't give me a car!*"

He lifted his voice to match the volume of mine. "*I just did!*"

I stared at him, the stubborn set of his square jaw, the way his left eyebrow was slightly raised in challenge. He was so stubborn and irritating…and cute. And sweet. And thoughtful. And presumptuous.

"I'm not taking it," I said finally, shaking my head. "It wouldn't be right."

"Quit being so stubborn."

"Being rational isn't being stubborn. You can't just go around giving people cars. You're not Oprah."

Duane's lips flattened in a way that made me think he was trying not to laugh because his eyes were shining. "What gave me away? Was it the red hair?"

Without thinking, and in a way reminiscent of our bickering childhood, I responded flatly, "No. It was the feel of your circumcised penis last week."

Duane lost his battle with laughter and threw his head back, eliciting an unbidden smile from me. I exhaled a chuckle and rolled my eyes, feeling remarkably pleased I'd made him laugh. I think I was even blushing, which was strange. Making Duane Winston laugh flushed me with pleasure, or maybe it was the intoxicating sight of how much he seemed to enjoy it, enjoy being with me.

Still with a wide grin—which in and of itself looked foreign and therefore dazzling on his face—he said, "But before last week, you still had doubts as to my identity?"

"Well, I've never seen you and Oprah in the same room together. Plus you both have your *favorite things* lists." I was making reference to his statement last Friday, that arguing with me was one of his favorite things.

"Do you have a *favorite things* list?"

"Wouldn't you like to know?" My neck was abruptly hot.

He lifted an eyebrow. "You've been thinking on my trouser department, haven't you?"

Flustered, I shook my head. "Getting back to the topic at hand—"

"Is it? At *hand*? I wasn't aware."

"Duane Winston!" I tried to sound shocked and foreboding,

but my involuntary answering smile was ruining the effect. "I'm attempting to be serious. Stop trying to muddle me."

"If I were trying to muddle you, then you'd know it."

I *tsk*ed, then huffed. "When'd you get so sassy?"

"When'd you get so serious?"

"I'm not! I just can't accept this car."

"Can't or won't?"

"Same thing."

"Nope. Not the same." He plucked my hand from where it rested on my lap and held it in both of his, sending a warm, delightful sensation of loveliness up my arm and around my brain. "Jessica James, you're going to have to get used to me wanting to take care of you and fix your troubles."

"I'm not a damsel. I don't need rescuing."

"I know. You're capable and stubborn, and I like that about you a whole lot. But maybe you could pretend to be a little less capable from time to time?"

"To what end?"

"So I get to feel good about rescuing you."

I smirked at this logic. His request actually reminded me of my mom and dad. Sometimes my mother would pretend she couldn't open a jar in the kitchen or that she needed help lifting something heavy. When I'd called her on it, she'd said, "Nothing wrong with making your man feel needed. If your aunt Louisa had done the same, then she wouldn't be so lonely in that big house of hers."

"Let me help," he implored. "Use this car."

"I don't want to take advantage."

All trace of his earlier smile had vanished and he appeared to be completely sincere. "You won't be. It'll settle my mind, knowing you're driving something I built."

I sighed, considering him and his request. "So, it would be a loaner?"

"Sure." He shrugged noncommittally. "If that's what you want to call it."

"And what do you expect in return?"

"Pardon me?" he asked, looking confused tinged with horrified. "I don't want anything."

I narrowed my eyes further and teased, "Tell me, Oprah, what are you after? Penis strokes? More frigid skinny-dipping? What?"

Catching on, Duane's eyes lowered to my mouth; his held just a hint of a smile as he responded, "I'll take a rain check on the stroking and skinny-dipping, but how about a kiss?"

I'd already wanted to kiss him.

So I did.

I grabbed a fistful of his gray thermal and tugged, bringing his lips to mine suddenly, and I kissed him.

BAM!

Infuriatingly, he didn't seem at all surprised. He quickly took control, one hand fisting in my hair, angling my head as he liked, the other digging into my hip as he pulled me closer. He licked my lips and surged forward, giving the impression of requesting entrance without actually waiting for my consent.

It didn't matter. My pleasure moan gave me away, a sound of surrender. His hot mouth moved over mine, the sweep of his tongue sending a thrill straight down my spine, making me feel frenzied and cherished at the same time.

But then the *whoop whoop* of a police car scared the bejeebus out of me, and I jumped away. Duane released me as I spun toward the sound, my heart in my throat.

"What the hell is going on here?" I found my brother,

Jackson, barking and glaring at us. He'd pulled his cruiser parallel to the Mustang and rolled down his window.

I sighed, closing my eyes, and letting my head fall back on the headrest. I swallowed before I reprimanded my brother. "Jackson! You scared me half to death."

"I repeat, what the hell is going on here?" Jackson didn't sound repentant; he sounded irate.

I shook my head without opening my eyes, couldn't help the laugh that bubbled up from my chest. "What does it look like?"

"Jessica…" he warned, his voice rough.

I opened my eyes and grinned at my older brother, pressing the clutch and shifting the beautiful car into first gear. I'd be lying if I said I wasn't thoroughly enjoying his shocked expression.

My brother's eyes narrowed in warning. "Don't you dare. Have you lost your mind?"

"No, I haven't lost my mind. I've found a car, and look! It has a Duane in it. Now if you'll excuse me, my Duane and I really must be going."

And with that, I pulled out of the space Duane had backed into and turned the car in the opposite direction of home.

♥

He was right: the car handled beautifully.

This car was powerful and light. My beast truck was powerful but heavy. The Mustang was actually fun to drive. I'd never driven a car like it before, one with personality and eager responsiveness, like the automobile was a willing and eager participant in its motion. Driving felt like more than just traveling from one place to the next. It felt like an experience. An odd thought entered my head thirty minutes after first pressing on the gas pedal: I was falling in love with this car.

Duane was quiet while I drove. I didn't know where I was taking us and his silence felt introspective. Every once in a while, I felt his eyes on me, but he kept his hands to himself.

I made no attempt at conversation, partially because the windows were down and the rush of wind meant I would have to shout to be heard. The other reason was because the silence felt comfortable.

We crossed the mountain, taking the Parkway to Cades Cove, and I pulled into the picnic area, searching for a parking spot farthest from the rest of the cars, trucks, and campers. At the tip of the loop I spotted an isolated spot where no tourists appeared to be nearby. I pulled in and cut the ignition, but left the keys where they were.

Without the hum of the engine and the roar of the wind, the near soundlessness that surrounded us felt deafening and heavy, like the end of a ballad. But soon the whisper of flowing water, rustling of leaves, and song of birds met my ears and alleviated the hefty stillness that had settled between us.

I glanced at Duane from the corner of my eye and found him watching me. Not staring, just watching, like he was waiting to see what I would do next. His expression was inscrutable and therefore unsettling.

I cleared my throat, clasping my hands on my lap, and gave him a small smile. It likely looked guilty, because I felt a little guilty for the way I'd used Duane to irritate my brother.

"Are you still doing that?" he asked, shifting in his seat until his back half rested against the passenger side door, like he needed distance to see me clearly.

"Still doing what?" I tucked my hair—now likely a crazy mess—behind my ears and met his eyes directly.

"Still trying to upset the men in your family?"

I huffed a laugh and answered honestly, "Yes. I guess I am. It's just too much fun, getting Jackson all riled up."

"I understand the desire to annoy your brother, because he is annoying. But your daddy…he's a good man, steady, hard worker. You should cut him a break."

"I know. I am and I do…mostly. But in all fairness, if my father had found us kissing in the parking lot, he probably wouldn't have turned on his siren and pitched a fit. He'd have invited you over for dinner."

"And I would have accepted." Duane nodded at his own assertion and added, "I want to do this right."

Something about the way he said the words filled me with both pleasure and dread.

On Wednesday after leaving the Winston Brothers Auto Shop—with the benefit of wine, Claire's analysis, and hindsight—I started to be of the mind that Duane Winston wanted to court me. Courting meant a long-term relationship with marriage and a white picket fence being the end goal. Marriage and white picket fences terrified me because they sounded like the end of freedom, the end of my dreams.

Suddenly, the inside of the car felt stifling. I tore my eyes from his, opened my door, and exited the car, walking to the hood and pausing, not sure where I was going. I listened as he also exited, his door closing, the sound of his boots crossing to me, crunching over gravel and crispy leaves.

Duane fit his hand in mine and I looked up at him. He frowned at me—not an upset frown, just a thoughtful one—and tugged on our connected fingers. "Let's go for a walk."

I acquiesced and allowed him to lead me over the log barriers and boulders, down the path to a stream. Something about his presence and touch, the way he moved with confidence, the broadness of his shoulders, and his inherent strength calmed me. I found myself settling into the moment, deciding not to think too far into the future.

Tall trees rose high overhead on either side of the embankment and crystal-clear water displayed colorful rounded stones paving the shallow riverbed. I smiled at the sight of several children farther down picking their way across the rocks. Their chatter and laughter carried to us, even though they were at least fifty yards away.

Duane let go of my fingers and crouched down. I watched as he untied the laces of his boots and I understood his plan at once. I turned, found a boulder, and perched at the edge of it, slipping off my comfortable work shoes and math-themed socks and setting them on the rock.

The water would be cold, but that was no matter. I wasn't planning on falling in this time.

When we both had our shoes off, we held hands again and waded into the stream. It was only calf deep at the lowest spot, but it was relatively wide. In the spring it would be deeper, the water would move faster, and I wouldn't be able to wear my sensible black pencil skirt without getting it wet.

"You okay?" Duane asked, his thoughtful frown still in place.

I nodded and bent down to retrieve a blue rock from beneath the water and straightened. I held the stone up to the sun and studied the veins of white running through it.

Then, apropos of nothing, I said, "When I was ten, my daddy bought me a three-year subscription to *National Geographic* magazine for my birthday."

I glanced at Duane, found his thoughtful frown had been replaced by a thoughtful almost-smile. "Is that so?"

I nodded, releasing his hand so I could walk a bit farther into the stream. "Yes. According to him, I'd wanted the magazine since I was four and a half. I first saw it at the library and asked Santa Claus for it every year. And it wasn't the kid version either. I didn't want the kid version. I wanted the real thing."

"Why did you want it so much?"

"I loved seeing pictures and reading stories about the world, especially the places I didn't know existed. I spent hours getting lost in the pages, imagining myself scuba diving in Fiji, hand-harvesting saffron in Greece, or working with Jane Goodall's chimpanzees in Africa." I glanced at him over my shoulder, wanting to see his reaction.

"Chimpanzees?" His smile grew.

"Yes. In Africa."

The brightness in Duane's eyes grew radiant and felt almost overwhelming. He appeared to be pleased—more than pleased—yet I was surprised he didn't look at all amused. Just interested and happy. Had I ever seen that look directed at me before?

"Do you still have a subscription?"

I shook my head. "No. My momma was cleaning my room about a year later and she saw the magazine had what she considered dirty pictures. Specifically, naked photographs of men and women, members of isolated tribes in South America."

"Oh no!" Now he looked amused in addition to interested and happy. "What happened?"

"At first she was livid and made me go talk to Reverend Seymour about what I'd seen."

Duane grimaced, like he was bracing for the worst. I waved his concern away as I turned to face him.

"It was fine. He'd listened patiently while I'd burned scarlet red, describing all the various body parts I'd been exposed to and my feelings on the subject of modesty."

Duane laughed, really a chuckle, and stuffed his hands in his pockets. I liked the way his laugh sounded against the symphony of whispering water, rustling leaves, and birdsong. I also liked the way he looked, ankle deep in a pure mountain stream, the blue sky and tall trees behind him.

Again, I found myself settling into the moment, taking a mental snapshot of his happy and handsome face. An inadvertent sigh escaped my lips because I was happy, too. Duane Winston was a good listener.

I think I was staring, lost in the vision of him and a daydream, because when he spoke next, the sound startled me a bit.

"Did Reverend Seymour take the magazines?"

I shook my head, mostly to clear it, and glanced at my toes. My feet were cold, but the cold felt good. "No. Eventually, he handed the magazine back to my mother and told her there wasn't anything wrong with me learning about the world, but there might be if I formed my own conclusions without guidance. He suggested she use the magazines as an opportunity to discuss the world with me, that we should go through the articles together, and she should answer any questions I might have."

"Well...that's good, right?"

I met his gaze again, gave him a rueful half smile. "When the magazines came after that, my momma kept them locked in her closet until she could find time to go through them with me. For the first few months we'd sit down together after dinner and she'd explain things from her perspective even when I didn't ask. I liked the one-on-one time with Momma, but it wasn't the same, you know? The magazines lost their magic. I couldn't become lost in pages and pictures and possible adventures when each article was dissected for faults and ungodliness."

Duane's thoughtful frown was back. I had all his focus and holding his weighty gaze was difficult. He was searching mine, and something about his persistent interest made me feel vulnerable. Regardless, I held his stare with a half smile and eventually shrugged, blowing out a deep breath.

"I think my momma sensed my growing dissatisfaction, because after a time the magazines just piled up in her closet. They didn't renew the subscription."

"I'm sorry." He sounded sorry.

My half smile grew and I shook my head. "Don't be. It didn't matter much because by then I was making monthly trips to the library and reading *National Geographic* along with *Condé Nast Traveler* and *Wanderlust* magazines." The library was also where I discovered internet travel blogs and first became a fan of Intrepid Inger.

"I remember seeing you there, always the first Saturday of the month."

"That's right. That's when the magazines came in." I studied him for a beat, more than a little surprised by the excellence of his memory. At length I decided to add, "I remember seeing you there, too. One time you switched out my travel magazines with urology journals. Do you remember that?"

He nodded, one of his eyebrows lifted while he bit his lip as though to keep from laughing. "I remember."

I squinted at him, unable to help my smile. "You were always there, helping your momma shelve books. You and Roscoe, sometimes Cletus."

His eyes lost some of their focus, like he was recalling the memory. A foggy kind of smile passed behind his features, but it was abruptly replaced with dark melancholy, like the memory caused him pain. As well, he looked tired, bone-deep tired, almost like he hadn't slept in days. I don't know how I'd missed it before.

Impulsively, I crossed back to him and wrapped my arms around his waist, laying my cheek on his shoulder and squeezing. "I'm so sorry about your momma, Duane. She was a sweet lady and everyone misses her. Please let me know if there's anything I can do."

He returned my embrace without hesitation, bringing me flush against him. I snuggled closer to his warmth, wanting to share some of my own, hoping I was giving him comfort.

"Thank you, Jessica," he whispered into my hair, squeezing me, and repeating, "Thank you."

We stood like that for a while; I don't precisely know how long. But it was long enough for my mind to wander and for my thoughts to turn forward, to the future, to how nice it would be to have access to Duane hugs daily. How dichotomously comfortable and thrilling it was to touch him, be touched by him.

And how perfectly we fit together.

Jessica

9

"All my days I have longed equally to travel the right road and to take my own errant path."

—SIGRID UNDSET, *KRISTIN LAVRANSDATTER*

"I GUESS YOU'RE GETTING READY for your date."

I turned and found my brother standing in the doorway to my room. He said the word *date* like I might say *jury duty*.

"Yes." I kept my response terse, because I was determined to avoid another lecture from Jackson. Lord knows how he found out about my plans with Duane for tonight. Regardless, he'd seen fit to *throw a fit* Thursday evening when I got home. I was still driving the Mustang, so that might've contributed to his temper tantrum.

I was not in the mood then, and I certainly wasn't in the mood now. I was on my own merry-go-round of confusion because I missed Duane. And I was missing more than his face, eyes, hands, and circumcised penis.

In the end, I'd accepted the car as a loaner, but did not accept it as a gift. Secretly, I planned on working something out with Beau and Cletus, taking less for the truck as a way to compensate Duane for the use of his car.

I'd have to be careful, though. If he found out about my scheming to repay him, then he'd be pissed. Yet for some reason the idea of quarreling with Duane made me giddy. I wondered if we would disagree about the color of the sky on our date, fall into our old habit of debating and making mountains out of molehills. The possibility was exciting.

I was a little strange. Just a little… Only a little.

Since seeing him on Thursday, I'd thought about calling him approximately one million times just to hear the sound of his voice, maybe talk him into going for a drive so we could argue minutiae and kiss.

I'd always been a big fan of kissing when done right. I loved the accompanying hot pooling and heaviness in my belly, the anticipation of more, the whole experience of eyes closed, mouth open, and hot hands.

Basically, up until one week ago, my experience with the opposite sex had told me that kissing was as good as it got. All of my previous encounters went sharply downhill after the kissing.

Along with kissing, planning elaborate trips I would one day take and looking for ways to freak out my brother had been my top three pastimes when younger. Since maturing while away from home, planning trips were still at the top of the list, but kissing boys had drifted down to the low fifties. This was because ninety-nine percent of boys weren't what I would consider good kissers.

In high school everything was new and exciting. But in college the newness had worn off and kissing had grown tiresome. This was because I was doing the kissing instead of being kissed, and I wondered if that was the fundamental problem with kissing boys instead of men.

Boys usually do something not at all enjoyable that makes kissing a chore. They're either just a pair of passive lips, saliva slobberers, or tongue thrusters.

Whereas men actually *kiss*.

"You're going to wear that?" Jackson lifted his chin, indicating my outfit.

I glanced down at myself. Seeing nothing wrong with my blue jeans, hiking boots, and long-sleeved purple Henley with the top four buttons undone. I returned Jackson's scowl with a frown.

"And what's wrong with what I'm wearing?"

"Your shirt is half undone, your boobs are busting out, and those jeans are awfully tight."

I crossed my arms under my chest and glared at my brother. "Are you calling me fat?"

"No. I'm saying that outfit doesn't leave much to the imagination. I don't want that Winston boy getting ideas."

Meanwhile, I wanted Duane to get *lots* of ideas.

Because I really liked him. And Duane Winston kissed like a man, and not just any man. He kissed like he enjoyed kissing me just as much as I enjoyed kissing him. And his skills made me think kissing was just the beginning of far better things to come. It was truly the whole experience of eyes closed, mouth open, and hot hands—hands I had every confidence in.

And, just like that, *Kissing Duane Winston* jumped to the top of my favorite pastimes, my *favorites list*. Actually, debating, talking to, holding hands with, and hugging Duane Winston were also now on my list.

I tossed my long loose braid over my shoulder. "His name, Jackson, is Duane."

"I know his name." Jackson scratched his scruffy beard, sounding ornery.

"Then use it."

I was feeling ornery too. Ornery and frustrated.

I'd just lived through Thursday night and Friday without any contact between us. Even now, almost time for our date, and especially in retrospect, something about the way Duane had said, *I want to do this right,* made me think he'd be withholding kisses tonight. Or he was planning on giving me only proper kisses, and only at the end of the night, and done with respect, and mindful of who my parents were.

Lord help me, but if he denied me kisses in some misguided effort to be respectful, I was going to have to tie him to a tree and take them by force.

Jackson mimicked my stance, moving his hands to his hips, and gave me his *brother-knows-best* glare. "Now you look here, those Winston boys are a bunch of criminals and deadbeats, just like their daddy. Duane is known around these parts for driving like a bat out of hell and taking dangerous chances on those mountain roads. I'm not happy about you driving his car and I'm not happy about you spending time in the same zip code as Duane Winston, let alone going on a date with the sleazeball."

"You made your feelings perfectly clear on Thursday. And like I told you, who I see is none of your ever-loving beeswax."

"You'll see." Jackson lifted his voice, looking both exasperated and angry. "And then after he impregnates and abandons you, all those silly dreams of traveling the world will be over. Your *life* will be over."

I'm sure I was looking at Jackson like he was made of compost worms and boogers. The boy was crazy. "I don't even know where to start with you and your lunacy. I know how birth control works, big brother, and—spoiler alert—putting a wrapper on the banana is ninety-nine percent effective."

"There will be no bananas!"

"There will be entire tropical rainforests of bananas! And coconuts!" I gestured to my breasts. "And, hopefully, bananas rubbing against coconuts."

He sucked in a shocked breath. If he'd had on a string of pearls, I felt certain he would have clutched them.

Finally he managed to choke out, "Jessica James, you are being crude and unladylike." My brother's shock and outrage made him ridiculous. I knew he kept company with several girls in town, and I was sure his banana had been wrapped on more than one occasion.

Therefore I growled, "What century are you living in?"

"Going to college put wrong ideas in your head, Jess. I live in the real world and see guys like Duane take advantage of nice girls like you every day. And you think you'll be able to just travel around the world like some homeless nomad? You wouldn't last one week in the real world."

I hated it when my family brought up my plans as though they meant I was a flake. I wasn't a flake. *Having an intense desire to explore the world and travel doesn't make me a flake, damn it!*

"Oh, please." I started ticking off his ridiculous hypocrisy using my fingers. "You still live at home—"

"So do you."

I ignored that comment because I'd lived away from home and supported myself for four years in college. As well, it was an inconvenient truth.

"Momma still does your laundry. I've never seen you even make toast successfully. You're a glorified meter maid. The most excitement you get during any given day is giving people tickets for parking in front of a fire hydrant."

Jackson's brown eyes widened again and I saw his cheeks grow pink above his blond beard. I was being purposefully bratty and I didn't feel bad about it. My brother opened his mouth like he was going to launch into another argument, but was mercifully interrupted by the sound of the doorbell.

Not waiting two seconds for him to regain his ability to speak, I snatched my purse from my bed and pushed past him, making a beeline for the foyer.

I ignored Jackson's hollering from behind me as I yanked open the front door and pushed the screen door forward, almost catching Duane in the face with the wooden frame. Thankfully, he deftly stepped to the side, thereby avoiding injury.

"Oh goodness, I'm sorry," I said in a rush, reaching for one of his hands as I placed a kiss against his cheek. I was frazzled, but I still took the opportunity to smell him. He smelled good, like shaving soap and a tart hint of automotive grease. Since he had a beard, the shaving soap part didn't make much sense, but he smelled divine nevertheless. I also enjoyed the way his red beard tickled my chin when I leaned close.

"Hey, Jess. You look—"

"Let's go."

I tried to use my grip on his hand to tug him toward the edge of the porch and away from the house, but he dug his heels in and didn't move more than two steps.

"Wait a minute, is your momma here?"

"No, come on." I turned back to Duane, issuing a look

that I hoped conveyed urgency, but was stopped short when I saw him.

I'm afraid my mouth fell open, a sure sign of my surprise, as my eyes moved over his form.

He was dressed in dark jeans, boots, and a blue button-down shirt the exact same color as his eyes; he'd rolled his shirtsleeves up, which showcased his strong forearms. His beard had been trimmed short—super short—so that the line of his strong jaw was easily discernible.

My goodness, but he was delectable.

My attention snagged on a frothy cloud of white, and I saw he was holding a bunch of flowers. My eyes moved between him and the flowers, and I'm sure I looked entirely confounded.

"As I was saying…" Duane took a step toward me and I was struck by the sincerity in both his expression and tone, making me sway just a little at his ominous and heartfelt charm. He whispered, "You look beautiful, Jessica."

I think I smiled like a smitten simpleton, my eyelashes fluttering of their own accord. "So do you, Duane."

He smiled. It was small and magnetic. I took a mental snapshot; spending time with him confirmed my suspicion that Duane's smiles were few and should be treasured.

I swayed toward him again. "Did you get me flowers?"

He shook his head, his voice still low. "No. These are for your momma."

"My mom—"

"Don't you leave yet!" Jackson's voice thundered just as he appeared in the doorway, breaking our lovely moment. I couldn't help myself; I huffed and rolled my eyes. I loved my big brother, but sometimes I wanted to cover him in honey and send him into a bear cave.

Duane stiffened a little, but he didn't retreat. He turned from me, his eyes narrowing, and said, "Jack."

I lifted an eyebrow at this. No one called my brother *Jack*. Everyone called him Jackson, or Officer James.

"Duane." Jackson crossed his arms over his chest; his expression and voice were mean. "I don't much like you thinking you can take my sister out."

"Oh my God," I said to no one and tugged on Duane's hand again. "Just ignore him. Let's go."

But Duane didn't move. Instead he used our connected fingers to draw me closer while he and Jackson gave each other the evil eye.

"This might come as a shock to you, *Jack*, but I'm not losing sleep over your good opinion. Now, are the Sheriff and Mrs. James at home?"

Jackson's eyes narrowed further. "Why?"

"Because I'd like to pay my respects to the man and woman of the house before we step out."

Jackson flinched, his eyes widening as they moved up and down Duane.

I took advantage of Jackson's momentary speechlessness to answer Duane's question. "No. Momma is still in Texas taking care of my aunt Louisa, and Daddy is on duty."

Duane glanced at me while I explained, and I thought I saw something like disappointment pass over his handsome features. His disappointment made me feel guilty as well as warm all over with pleasure.

He'd wanted to talk to my parents before we *stepped out*. Goodness.

"Oh. Well then..." He frowned as he studied me, then turned back to my brother and pushed the bouquet of flowers into Jackson's hands. "Go put these in water before they die."

Wordlessly, Jackson accepted the flowers, though he was still looking at Duane like he was something strange. I didn't have a moment to dwell on any of this, because Duane pulled my hand into the crook of his elbow and escorted me down the front porch steps. We reached his car without another word between us and he opened the passenger side door. When he was satisfied I was settled, he shut the door and walked around the hood of his car.

My eyes trailed him. I watched him walk. I loved how he walked.

My heart didn't know whether to sink or swim. All I could think about was that Claire had been right last Wednesday: Duane Winston was looking to court me—good and proper. And now that the evidence was unmistakable, I felt dichotomously dismayed and dazedly giddy by the prospect.

Duane fired up the engine, and it was in this dismayed and dazedly giddy haze that I passed the first few moments of our drive. I was quite literally shaken out of my self-reflections when Duane navigated a series of switchbacks with imprudent speed. Even though I was wearing my seat belt, I slid in my seat to one side, then the other.

"Sorry," he said, pressing gently on the brake to slow our velocity, then cleared his throat and offered by the way of an explanation, "I'm used to taking these roads fast. I didn't mean to toss you around."

I braced my arm against the passenger side door. "It's fine. I just…" I shook my head. "I just wanted to apologize for Jackson, the way he acted. He was being unfair and unkind and we had words earlier. I'm sorry about that."

Duane shrugged. "Well, he wouldn't be much of a brother if he wasn't overprotective. I feel the same way about my sister..." I got the impression he hadn't quite ended his sentence and was proven right when he finally finished, "and my brothers."

Duane's gaze flickered to mine and he gave me a hint of a smile. I melted a bit at his rare smile, and I felt myself relax against the seat.

And that's when I realized how comfortable the seat was.

And that's when I finally took the three seconds required to actually look at this car I was riding in.

It was old, a classic of some sort. The upholstery was teal leather and the seat was a bench style, the kind that allowed a passenger to snuggle up close to the driver.

"Duane Winston, what kind of car is this?"

He was in profile but I saw his smile grow. "It's a '68 Plymouth Road Runner."

I studied the rest of the car, or what I could see of it. The two-door antique had a back seat, similar bench style to the front, and everything was in pristine condition.

"It's kind of small for the time, isn't it? I mean, weren't most Plymouths built at that time big old land cruisers?"

Duane's hands tightened a bit on the steering wheel, his thumb caressing the inside of the circle. "It's a muscle car, so it's built for speed."

I tried to remember what the outside of the car looked like and could recall only basic lines and shiny black paint. "It doesn't really look like a muscle car, not like the Mustang."

"It's got a four-barrel carburetor engine, pushing out 335 horsepower—but, you're right, the Road Runner doesn't have any of that flashy chrome finish or plush doodads you see with other higher-priced GTXs of the same era. It doesn't need to be showy. Its beauty is in its simplicity. Simple, straightforward design…with hidden depths." He paired this with an impressive engine growl and accelerated lightning fast along a straight stretch of road. The car certainly was responsive.

I smiled at that, glancing around the interior once more and noting the lack of fussy trimmings. He was right, it was a stunning car. Its minimalism only contributed to its effortless beauty. But I could feel the untapped potential, its restless restrained power. It was sexy as hell.

"You're right, it's gorgeous." Because I was obviously a horndog, talking about the hidden depths and restrained power of his muscle car was getting me hot and bothered. I decided to redirect the conversation toward hopefully benign territory. "Did you restore it yourself?"

"Yep."

"Even the upholstery?"

"Yes. I restored her myself, even the upholstery."

"*Her?*" I passed my hand over the bench, touching the leather with newfound respect and reverence now that I knew Duane was responsible for the flawless restoration. Based on this information, I presumed he'd also restored the Mustang I was borrowing.

I was happy to see his smile return as he halted and idled at a stop sign. Duane slid his pretty eyes to mine; I saw echoes of his *hot look* from the community center, though it appeared to be mostly restrained. "Yes, *her*. All cars are girls."

My smile was huge as I was feeling delightfully unsteady under his perusal. "And why is that? Because they're so pretty, useful, and hardworking?"

Duane's eyes drifted down my body in an unhurried

examination; the spark of heat and appreciation in his gaze made me suspicious of his true thoughts, which were only punctuated by his next words.

"Because when a guy sees a car he likes, all he can think about is getting under the hood or taking her for a ride."

This time I threw my head back and laughed with gusto and shocked delight. This was the second time he'd done this, surprised me with his audacity. On Thursday, when he'd shown up at my work with the Mustang, I figured he was just trying to get a rise out of me, but now I saw this new banter for what it was. Duane Winston was funny. And a flirt.

In all the years I'd known him, and all the arguments and shouting matches we'd had, I never would have guessed that Duane was this funny. Or a flirt.

Sly? Yes.

Smart? Certainly.

Serious and stern? Undoubtedly.

Funny and flirty? No.

He was full of surprises.

As my laughter lessened and morphed into a large grin, I turned in my seat and studied him openly. I had to shake myself a little. Before last Friday, never in my wildest—or strangest— dreams could I have imagined that Duane Winston would *ever* be interested in me, not because there was something wrong with me, but because he always left me with the impression that I irritated the bejeebus out of him.

Just like I never thought in a million years I'd be so completely drawn to him.

But here I was…

"What? What's wrong?" He frowned at my examination, sparing me a quick glance as he turned right onto the Parkway.

"Oh, nothing." I kept staring at him…but not him. I was looking for the Duane I remembered, the one who barely tolerated me, picked verbal sparring matches, and put lizards down my Sunday school dress. "I guess, it's weird. Right? I mean, you and I grew up together. We used to run around these forests with the other Green Valley kids like a pack of wild animals."

His subtle smile was back, but this time it looked nostalgic. "So?"

"So, here we are. We're adults. And we're out *together*."

"We went for a drive on Thursday and you didn't seem fazed by it."

"Yeah, but this is a date. See, I know you—I could tell anyone who asked that you're a terrible swimmer, or how you drive too fast, or how you got that scar on your right arm, or that you're better at baseball than any of your brothers—but I don't *know* you. It's like being on a date with two different people, the boy I knew and the…the…" I stuttered, then paused, stopping myself just in time. A slight rush of embarrassment made my tongue lame because I was about to say, *And the sweet, gorgeous man you've become.*

And that would have been a bizarre thing to say at the beginning of a first date. Honest, but bizarre.

"And the what?" he prompted, sliding his eyes to mine as he came to another straight stretch on the mountain road.

I cleared my throat, my chest a sudden and odd combination of achy and fluttery. "The kid I knew and the man you've become. I don't know this new you very well. It's a bit disconcerting to feel confident that I know all about you, but have no idea who you really are." I glanced down and frowned at my purple nail polish, certain I was making a mess of my thoughts. "I'm not explaining this very well."

Duane reached over and grabbed one of my hands, sending a warm jolt up my arm and to my ribs.

"You're explaining things just fine." He squeezed my fingers and gave me a quick, reassuring smile. "When we were at the lake last week and I told you we're different now, both of us have changed, that's what I meant."

"But don't you think it'll be weird?"

"So what? So it's weird. Weird can be good."

"We grew up together. I mean, when we were kids I saw you naked like"—I counted in my head—"three times. Maybe more."

"Is this your way of telling me that you don't want to see me naked for a fourth time?"

I answered emphatically and without thinking, "Oh, hell no, you should be naked all the time."

Duane's grin was immediate, but his laughter was stifled, like he was trying to contain it. I rolled my eyes at myself once I realized what I'd just said and let myself feel appropriately embarrassed. My head fell back on the seat and I closed my eyes.

"See now, here's the problem. I would *never* say anything like that on a first date, or even a tenth date."

"I still don't see a problem."

"I'm too comfortable speaking my mind around you. Speaking my mind to Duane Winston is not just my default; it's a moral imperative." I announced this to the windshield as I opened my eyes and stared at the fall foliage lining the narrow road. Brilliant streaks of red, dark purple, orange, and yellow—a beauty I'd taken for granted as a kid—blurred together as we sped by.

"That's just because you're used to arguing with me."

"Yes. Exactly. First dates are like a job interview. It's about putting your best foot forward, not arguing and speaking your mind."

"Well, I've never interviewed for a job, but I can't think of anything better than Jessica James speaking her mind."

I shook my head at him, narrowing my eyes suspiciously. "That's not fair."

"What's not fair?"

"You're saying all the right things. Whereas I'm being completely honest."

He challenged lightly, "What makes you think these right things I'm saying isn't me being completely honest?"

I blinked, then stared at him, at his profile. My heart sped at his last words and my breath caught. Pinpricks of awareness covered my skin accompanied by a nervous uncertainty. I averted my eyes back to the windshield and stared unseeingly forward.

Did I want to kiss the hell out of him? Yes, I did.

Did I want to wrap his banana and let him have his way with my coconuts? Yes. I wanted that to happen.

Did I want him to say all the right things, with sincerity, revealing his hidden depths (as well as a few of mine)?

…

…

…

I honestly had no idea.

On one hand, yes. Yes. YES! This Duane was sweet and sincere, generous and wonderful, funny and sexy. I'd known him forever; we had history. I'd thought the history would hinder a relationship between us, but I couldn't have been more wrong. Our history only added to this growing connection, provided gravity of feeling and understanding. What more could I want? What more could I ask for?

On the other hand, no. No. NO! Duane had roots. Subterranean, cavernous roots. He was a local business owner; he had a big family. I couldn't imagine him ever leaving Tennessee. This was his home, and home was a physical place for him.

But Green Valley wasn't where I belonged. I'd known I would never stay my whole life.

Regardless, I was moving deeper without meaning to, wading out of my shallow pool. And this was only our first date, a date that hadn't even technically started yet.

At some point I was going to have to tell him I had plans, and those plans meant I would be leaving. Eventually. Definitely.

I needed to be honest…but not yet.

♥

Cooper Road Trail was definitely an off-the-beaten-path kind of park. Duane's was the only car in the lot when we pulled in. I knew of this locale mostly because my momma loved to hike the trail in June, when the orange and yellow daylilies bloomed along the path. The summer air smelled sweet and warm, and was alive with buzzing bees and rushing water from nearby waterfalls.

It was a first-come, first-served kind of place, no camping reservations accepted. It was also exceedingly difficult to find if you weren't a longtime citizen of the valley. The campground was small, verging on cramped, and had roughly ten or so campsites; five of those spots were on a shallow and relatively wide clear-water stream, typical for the area.

When we arrived and Duane pulled a mountaineering backpack from his trunk, along with a big basket hamper, I abruptly remembered I'd left the beer in the refrigerator at home.

"Oh, shoot!" I grimaced, rubbing my forehead.

"What's wrong?"

"I was in such a rush to escape my brother I forgot our drinks at the house."

Duane shrugged. "No problem. I have water in the bag."

I stepped forward and moved to take the basket from his hands. "Do you have anything other than water?"

"No. Just water."

"Oh. Okay." My heart sank a little. It was the one thing I was supposed to bring and I'd forgotten. Even though he appeared to shrug it off, I felt like I'd let him down.

As we walked together past the campsites and to the hiking trail, making small talk about the park, I tried to similarly shrug off my forgetfulness. I didn't like taking advantage and I didn't like letting him down. And though it was irrational, I hated looking like a flake.

I didn't mind if people thought I was silly/weirdo, cross-dressing sexy Gandalf, but I couldn't abide anyone thinking I was unreliable. Because I wasn't. I was trustworthy and took my responsibilities very seriously.

While I was still chastising myself, Duane led me off the path when we were about a quarter mile down the trail. I was thankful I'd worn my hiking boots because we had to splash through some wet areas and over slippery rocks. Duane was careful to take my hand and plot out the driest course each time. His chivalry, care, and attention contributed to my mounting appreciation and left me feeling tongue-tied and flushed.

I finally let go of kicking myself for being forgetful when I noticed Duane's chivalry was increasingly tempered with reluctant and distracted moments of ogling.

Three times I caught him checking out my ass. Afterward he'd clench his jaw and frown severely at the ground, or the sky, or the trees lining the path. I found these little cracks in his control delightful.

"We're almost there." He glanced down at me, having just helped me hop over a few wet stones and not releasing my hand even after clearing the rough patch. "Is the basket too heavy? I don't mind carrying it."

"No. It's fine. You've got the backpack."

His eyes took a detour to the unbuttoned V of my top, and the cleavage I'd purposefully (and artfully) highlighted with a push-up bra. "Are you cold?"

I shook my head, hiding my pleased smile. "No. I'm great."

He frowned at the exposed swell of my breasts, seemed to redirect his eyes away with effort. He pulled his attention back to the narrow path. I indulged my urge to smirk. Tight jeans, strategically unbuttoned top, push-up bra…this was fun.

I'd be lying if I said his intense interest in my body wasn't a huge turn-on—for both my brain and my…other brain. It was. I liked that he looked at me and had difficulty hiding his appreciation and desire. If anything, I felt less flustered each time I spied him clenching his jaw or balling his hands into fists. I liked him so much. It was nice to see tangible evidence that he meant it when he'd said kissing me *was* something he'd wanted for a long time.

Still feeling cheered, I was surprised when we reached our destination so quickly. He hadn't been fibbing; no more than ten feet later, I was faced with a picturesque clearing at the edge of a wide still stream and I sucked in a small breath. I didn't know this place existed. If I'd known this place existed, then I would have become one of those nature people who forage the woods for sustenance and bathe in moonlit pools.

The trees overhead and their autumn brilliance reflected in the water—vivid strokes of color. We were surrounded on all sides by nature's majesty, its swan song celebration before winter. The setting was almost painfully romantic.

"Will this do?" His voice was low, just a rumble, but it held equal parts sweetness and amusement.

I moved my wide eyes to his and nodded once. His mouth tugged to the side, like he was pleased by my inability to speak, but didn't want to commit to a smile. Duane took the basket from my grip and placed it on the ground, dropping his big backpack next to it.

"There's a felled tree just there." He pointed to the embankment. I spotted a large old eastern hemlock log about as high as my knee, half on land, half in the water. "It's a good place to sit while I get all this ready."

"You don't need any help?"

"No—you go sit, relax." He appeared to be determined and was already digging into the pack, revealing a large quilted tarp and spreading it on the ground.

I studied him as he moved, pulling items out of his bag of tricks. Since I felt useless just standing there as he worked, I decided to take his suggestion…sort of. Instead of sitting on the log, I climbed it. Then I used it as a balance beam and walked the length of the old tree where it jutted out into the stream.

The early November air was crisp, just chilly enough to bite. Soon all the leaves would fall, leaving this spot bare and brown. I felt like I was looking at the pinnacle of a particularly dazzling firework as it filled the night sky, just before it lost its shape and faded into darkness. It was a fleeting moment. And I stood in the center of it.

"I hope you're not expecting me to rescue you."

I glanced over my shoulder, found Duane at the edge of the stream, his hands on his hips, his square jaw angled in a stubborn tilt.

"Rescue me? From a log?"

"No. From the water. Should you fall in."

I grinned. "More likely I'd rescue you. Are you afraid I'll steal your pants?"

I nearly lost my balance when he answered my grin with one of his own, but he quickly hid it by redirecting his attention to the ground at his feet. When he lifted his face again, a residual smile remained, but he mostly looked serious...and focused...on me.

He cleared his throat and his voice sounded different, deep and commanding—maybe a little impatient—as he said, "Come back here."

I turned carefully and picked my way back, scanning the spread he'd placed on an old large picnicking quilt. I figured the tarp was hidden underneath, meant to protect our backsides from the damp earth. I also spotted a few cushy pillows, a throw blanket presumably just in case we got cold, and an array of covered dishes to one side.

Duane Winston had come prepared.

He intercepted me where the felled tree met the land and placed his big hands on my waist. With one smooth movement, he lifted me from the log and set me on the ground.

He hesitated.

We stood still for a moment—him staring down, me staring up—our bodies separated by less than a foot.

With each passing second my heart thumped more meaningfully against my ribs. The cool November air suddenly felt warm, thick. I tilted my chin, parted my lips to say something, but words caught in my throat. Meanwhile, he stood as though frozen, his expression almost grim, but his eyes were hot.

Duane Winston was giving me a hot look.

"Duane?" I whispered, surprised when his name sounded like a plea.

He gritted his teeth, his eyelids lowering to half-mast. "We should eat." Even as he said the words, his gaze dipped to the undone buttons of my shirt, then to my mouth, and his fingers tightened on my torso.

In that moment he reminded me of his Road Runner: all hidden depths and barely restrained power. Oh yes, I liked his responsiveness. I liked it very, very much.

"Or…" I slid my hands up his arms and around his neck, annihilating the distance separating us with just a half step, and pressed my body to his. He didn't shrink back; rather he surged forward, his strong arms winding around my waist, holding me to him. My legs hit the log behind me and I felt the heat of his hard chest and stomach beneath the starched button-down of his shirt and the snuggly cotton of mine. Still holding his eyes—which had grown to firestorm levels of conflicted—I lifted to my tiptoes and licked his lips.

It was just a soft, subtle taste using only the tip of my tongue. But it seemed to shatter some wall he'd built, because Duane immediately covered my mouth, a tortured-sounding groan rumbling in the back of his throat as his lips moved against mine.

My belly twisted, feeling delightfully heavy. A shock of desire radiated from my chest to my fingertips. I'd like to say all my focus was on the slick, massaging sweep of his tongue as it expertly invaded my mouth, making me feel needy and lightheaded, but it wasn't. My mind was scattered in a hundred different directions, all of them propelled by a sudden urgency.

I needed to get his shirt off because I'd die if I didn't feel the smooth, taut skin of his shoulders, chest, and stomach.

I needed to remove my boots so I could free myself of these accursed pants.

I needed his hands on my nipples. Or his mouth. Or both. *Yes! Definitely both.*

Without my brain explicitly telling my fingers to do so, I'd untucked his shirt, managed to unlock the first few buttons, and was working on his belt buckle. I had the leather strap free in a surprisingly short period of time, with minimal fumbling, then reached for my jeans only to find Duane's hands already there.

Therefore, I leaned away for a fraction of a second and whipped off my shirt, tossing it somewhere…anywhere… didn't care where.

Our mouths met and mated again as I clawed at the remaining buttons of his shirt while he unzipped my pants. The sounds of our rough movements, heavy breathing, and frantic kisses filled my ears. It was a symphony of euphoric anticipation.

We were moving; he was moving us. At some point we'd turned and he was steering me backward toward the blanket, Duane's large hands in my pants, beneath my underwear, cupping and massaging and squeezing. I tripped a little and then I was being half pushed, half guided into a horizontal position on the soft quilted blanket. Duane covered me, nothing clumsy about his lissome movements, his shirt now open revealing a blasted white undershirt.

I growled my displeasure and tugged at the cotton, hiking it upward at his sides so I could touch his skin as he settled his muscular thigh against my center.

"Take these off," I demanded, gripping and pulling both shirts with frustrated movements.

Duane sat up on his knees and tore off his button-down, roughly pulled off his undershirt, his gaze moving over my body.

But then, horror of horrors, he stalled his forward progress and blinked, a spark of sobriety igniting behind his eyes as he caught sight of my black lacy bra, mussed hair, and unzipped jeans.

He frowned like he was confused, shook his head, and said on an unsteady exhale, "Shit."

I lifted my hands to reach for him and he shook his head again, his face twisted with what looked like frustration and anguish. He stood suddenly and walked away, leaving me on the blanket staring after him as he paced to the felled log, followed it to the stream, then stopped.

I inclined my torso and rested my weight on my elbows, watching his back, my chest rising and falling as I tried to catch my breath. My body was still…ready. Actually, *ripe* was a better word for it. And he'd looked quite ripe as well. But, despite the ripeness of my coconuts and his banana, he'd put an abrupt halt to satiating our hunger.

As I stared at his back, a song floated through my consciousness: "(Can't Get No) Satisfaction," by the Rolling Stones. Why was it difficult for him to take what he so obviously wanted? What we *both* wanted?

When I realized staring at Duane Winston's muscled back and fine ass wasn't helping matters, I stood, zipped my jeans, heaved a confused sigh, and crossed to where I suspected my shirt lay discarded.

He wanted me just as much as I wanted him, that much was clear. It was also clear we'd entered into a pattern of behavior. His withdrawal here, and in the supply closet of the garage, and at the edge of the lake, and backstage at the community center all pointed to the fact that Duane Winston wanted me—badly—but was trying to be noble. Or, something akin to nobility.

I tugged on my shirt and heaved another sigh, marinating in the oddness of the situation. When my previous boyfriends were intent on pushing me further than I was willing to go, I broke things off. But with Duane, I felt like maybe I was pushing him. I didn't want to push him. In fact, the thought of pushing him made me feel wretched. I wanted us to move together.

"You're a siren who doesn't need to sing."

I turned my head at the sound of his words, cutting through the soundtrack in my head. Duane was facing me now, his muscled arms crossed over his delicious bare chest. His expression told me he was exasperated—with himself, me, or the situation in general. I had no idea where his ire was directed.

I gave him a smile I hoped communicated my regret for being pushy, but also communicated my hope that the date wasn't over yet. "Is this your way of telling me I'm too sexy for this picnic?"

Some of his exasperation melted away and he huffed a short laugh, but then he sobered almost immediately. His focused gaze grew earnest. "Jess, doing this right, it's important to me."

I nodded once, faced him, and mimicked his stance. "I surmised as much when you brought flowers for my momma."

I saw his chest rise and fall before he continued, taking a few cautious steps toward me. "I think we're suited."

"So you've said." Something like panic tugged at my heart, and I was afraid of where this conversation was heading.

"But like you said in the car, we don't know each other anymore, not really."

"I get it," I said on a rush, because I did get it. I did.

And yet…

But then he admitted quietly, "I want to know you."

I want to know you.

I blinked at him, stared dumbly, really.

Those words penetrated some wall—around my head and heart—I didn't know existed. He came to a stop directly in front of me, his arms still crossed over his chest as his eyes roamed over my face, and they held reverence, hope. His expression and tone were distracted when he added, "And I want to be known."

That's what did it, his quiet admission. I realized I was being self-centered. And, more than that, I felt *torn*. Now that he was forcing the issue, crossing self-preservation boundaries I'd drawn without meaning to, I was going to have to be completely honest as well…and damn it all, I didn't want to. I didn't want our time together to end before it even started.

I had a plan: save money, gain teaching experience, leave Green Valley. Duane's clear-as-day intentions and my unpredictable, growing feelings were not part of the plan. His desire to court me was not part of that plan. Marriage and picket fences were not part of that plan.

I think I must've flinched or winced, because Duane straightened, and even though he didn't move, I felt him draw away. I knew at once he was misinterpreting my reaction, so I unthinkingly reached for his arm and stepped into his personal space, beseeching him with my gaze.

"I'm sorry," I said, shaking my head at my blind selfishness, realizing I should have been up front on Wednesday, when he'd asked me out originally. "I'm sorry. You're right. You're so right, and I'm… I don't know how to say this without being completely honest so, here goes: I moved home with a plan. I'm back with my parents and teaching at the school, but that's all temporary. I'm here, in Green Valley, for less than two years, tops. Just long enough to pay off my loans and save enough money to move on. I'm not ready to settle down. I don't think I ever will be. I want to see and experience things. I have wanderlust and it consumes me. If I had the money, I'd leave tomorrow. I thought… I guess I didn't really think. I just like you so much and I…" I couldn't finish my thought because my voice caught.

As I spoke, Duane's eyes widened, then narrowed. Their usual internal brilliance seemed to dim, fade, as it was replaced with a severe disappointment that completely pierced my heart. Then his expression hardened into understanding, and finally bitter, guarded withdrawal.

For the first time ever I wished I wasn't this girl. I wished I wanted to live in Green Valley and be content as a small-town teacher, a wife, a mother, a member of the community. But that wasn't what I wanted, that wasn't who I was.

I had no illusions my dreams were bigger. My dreams

weren't bigger; they were just different. I'd chosen my profession because it meant I could move anywhere; no matter the city, science and math teachers were needed. And I wanted freedom from possessions—owning them and being owned by them. I wanted to experience the world, not just one tiny corner of it.

Duane nodded, slowly at first. His eyes fell away before he turned and sauntered back to the blanket to retrieve his shirts. He pulled on the white undershirt, but didn't bother with the button-down; instead he stuffed it into the backpack. I didn't know what to do, couldn't read what he was thinking, so I stood by the log and waited for some sign.

Some selfish part of me wished I hadn't told him the truth. After all, I had two or three years left in the valley. No one understood my desire to travel the world; why would I expect him to be any different? I'd always been the odd one in my family, feeling like I didn't quite belong. I'd learned to hide this side of myself, and almost all of my other crazy instincts, from my parents years ago.

Duane and I could have dated, had fun together—me knowing it was temporary, him thinking it was leading to something permanent. I could have kept my dreams to myself, planned my trips in secret.

Then, when the money was saved and the time came, I could've just broken things off. Hell, we might not have even lasted that long. Maybe we weren't suited. Maybe it would have only been a few weeks or months.

No.

I heard the word in my head as though it had been spoken out loud. I knew with a rare certainty that Duane was right. We were suited. Withholding the truth of my dreams would be withholding myself, and that was exceedingly unfair to him. It was one thing to pretend with my folks, because they could handle me being zany from time to time and assume my wanderlust was a phase.

It was quite another matter to keep my true self from Duane. He didn't deserve that.

At length, he lifted his gaze to mine and I was saddened—but not surprised—to see it was completely shuttered.

"Are you hungry?" His tone was flat as he indicated to the cups and covered bowls with a tilt of his chin. "Because I'm hungry."

I tried to apologize with just my eyes and my chin wobbled; I managed to answer, "Yeah, I'm hungry."

He nodded again, then turned, dropped to his knees, and gestured me over with a wave of his hand. "Then let's eat."

Duane

10

> "One's destination is never a place, but a new way of seeing things."
>
> —HENRY MILLER, *BIG SUR AND THE ORANGES OF HIERONYMUS BOSCH*

"SO, HOW WAS YOUR DATE with Catastrophic Engine Failure?"

I wasn't expecting the question because I wasn't expecting my brothers' return until later in the afternoon, so I couldn't hide my automatic grimace.

I lifted just my eyes from the woodpile, found my brothers nearing the chopping block and watching me expectantly. Then, to my chagrin, Beau and Cletus shared a concerned glance when I remained silent.

"That bad, huh?" Beau scratched his beard.

"I don't want to talk about it." I picked up a new log, set it in place, and brought the ax down, splitting it with one stroke.

"Okay." Beau nodded, letting the matter drop.

"What happened?" Cletus asked, stepping forward and not letting the matter drop.

What happened...? That was the question I didn't much

want to think about. That question drove me out here to the woodshed, splitting logs we didn't need, biding my time until I could race at the Canyon this evening and burn off my aggression.

Last night after Jessica's *clarification* of the situation, what it was she wanted, we'd eaten in silence, walked back to the car in silence, driven home in silence, and I'd dropped her off. And that was that. Things were over before they'd begun, because I wasn't going to fuck around with Jessica James.

There are just some girls you can't fuck around with, because doing so would be handing over your man card. She'd own my pride first, then my heart, then my spirit. Then she'd leave, taking all three with her.

On my drive home I'd briefly considered calling Tina. But I didn't. Nothing had changed, not really. I was tired of fucking around. And the thought of touching Tina when I craved Jess… No. There was no substitution.

I frowned at my older brother. "Nothing. Nothing happened."

Cletus returned my frown and paused, as though mulling the issue over, before he asked, "Will there be a second date?"

"Cletus."

"Duane."

"I don't want to talk about it."

"Can I ask her out?"

I reckon something in my glare must've communicated the intensity of my sudden, irrational, and visceral response to his question, because Cletus lifted his hands between us as though he surrendered and took a step back.

"Hold your claws, Wolverine. I'm not going to ask Miss

James to step out. I was merely gathering data. I see your feelings for her haven't changed."

"No. They haven't."

"Then I guess I just don't understand why things aren't progressing in a satisfactory manner. Did Jackson James do something to interfere?"

"Nothing of note."

"Did her parents object?"

"No," I said through gritted teeth.

Cletus pressed his lips together, his eyes narrowing on me like I was under suspicion of criminal consorting. "Did you do something untoward?"

"No. Damn it, Cletus! Can't you just let this go?"

"No, sir. I cannot. I like things to be fixed, situated, orderly, where they belong. You and Miss James aren't situated, where you belong. As such, I feel compelled to fix the situation."

I threw the ax down so the blade cut through the earth. "Fine. You want to know what happened? She told me she's only interested in a temporary thing. She's not planning on staying in Green Valley. She wants to leave as soon as possible and isn't looking for permanent. She's got…" I paused, glaring unseeingly around the yard as I searched for the word she used; finding it, I threw my hands in the air and kicked the pile of split wood as I finished, "She's got fucking wanderlust bullshit issues."

Beau's eyebrows arched high on his forehead. "Fucking wanderlust bullshit issues? You mean, she likes to go hiking?"

"No," Cletus answered for me, his expression grave and thoughtful. "I believe our dear brother Duane means she's wanting to travel the world and doesn't want any strings holding her to one place."

"Yes, that. What he said." I lifted my chin and scanned the contents of the shed behind them for no reason. The sooner this conversation ended, the better.

Beau glanced between Cletus and me. He appeared to be confused and confirmed my suspicion when he said, "So?"

"So…" I shrugged. "So there's not going to be a second date."

Again, Beau glanced between Cletus and me like he was missing something. "Why not?"

This time Cletus and I shared a look of commiseration.

Cletus huffed his impatience, then turned to Beau like he was going to set matters straight on my behalf.

"Because…" Cletus started, but then stopped. He blinked at Beau. Then his eyes narrowed like he was thinking the matter over and reconsidering his earlier assumptions.

I frowned at them both.

"Now wait a minute." Cletus held his index finger up and pointed at Beau, then he pointed at me. "No, wait just a minute. Beau has a point."

I groaned, seething, and glanced at the darkening sky over their heads. Why were we still talking about this?

Meddling brothers. Goddamn chickens, the lot of them.

"She wants a temporary interlude, so what?"

I gritted my teeth, crossed my arms, and decided to wait for Cletus to talk himself tired. But then, surprisingly, his next statement caught my attention.

"*Everything* is temporary, Duane. This"—he gestured to our surroundings—"this is temporary. Even mountains fall. Nothing lasts forever. You got a chance at happiness, even for a week, a month, a year? You grab it and you hold on to it for as long as it lasts."

"Exactly." Beau nodded vehemently. Now he was frowning, looking as serious as I'd ever seen him. "You have a chance to be with her, even for a short time? You take it. Because when she leaves, you'll still have that."

I shook my head, not liking the cast of their words. "You want me to settle? That's fucking pathetic."

"No. I want you to seize." Cletus dropped his hand on my shoulder and gave me a little shake. "You seize that woman. You make her yours."

I examined Cletus as he spoke. I liked the words *seize* and *make*. Those were action words I could appreciate, words that made me rethink my earlier conclusions. I glanced between my brothers and actually allowed myself to consider the possibility of taking what I could get from Jess, for as long as I could get it.

She didn't want to stay in Green Valley; nothing could keep her here. Fine. I could accept that. It was her life. *But…*

I wasn't going to beg. No fucking way. I wasn't even willing to ask nicely at this point. I didn't rate on her list of priorities, and why should I? If she wanted no strings with me—and it was clear she was beyond interested in an arrangement that included the physical—what was keeping me from setting my own terms and pushing her outside of her comfort zone? Defining the timetable? Taking a bit of *her* pride and heart and spirit before she left?

Some unrealistic and idealistic dream from my adolescence?

She was here. I was here. We were adults. Mutual want, hot and desperate, existed between us. Why was I denying myself taking what I could?

Fuck that shit.

Cletus gave my shoulder another shake, pulling me from

my internal pep talk. His next sentiment echoed my thoughts, solidified them.

"You take happiness, Duane. You conquer it."

"That's right. Conquer it." Beau pointed at me and swiped his hand through the air with violent emphasis.

"And when or if the time comes for her to leave," Cletus shrugged, "*you* be the one to walk away first, with no regrets, because you captured that flag. You seized the day."

♥

Half of my bad mood and unnecessary wood chopping was because of Jessica.

Actually, more like seventy-five percent.

The rest was because of Dirty Dave and Repo's visit, and what I'd found on the thumb drive they'd given me. But I had to wait for Cletus to wander off before I could spill the story to Beau.

Beau and Cletus helped me place the newly chopped wood into the shed. We decided to grab dinner at Genie's bar—Cletus liked her chicken wings—as they filled me in on their trip to Nashville and Cletus rambled for an hour about how he'd helped the district law enforcement office unjam their mail sorter. And then he paid a call to all the local police stations to assist with mail sorter maintenance.

He was very proud of his work with mail sorters. He'd been doing it for years, pro bono, and had a strange affection for the machines.

"They're like the pre-internet internet, connecting the world and directing traffic."

He was a nut.

It took both Beau and me several attempts to steer the conversation back on track. Turns out the car they'd set out to claim, a 1963 Mustang, was in better shape than we'd thought. As well, the junkyard owner had another Mustang about the same age, in much worse shape that we could strip for parts.

They were able to rent a vehicle carrier and load it up with a few other prospects as well. All in all, it was a productive trip.

On the drive back from dinner, Beau pointed out that one of us was going to have to negotiate a price with Jessica for her Ford F-350. We were bringing in enough vintage bodywork that it also made sense to buy a large carrier.

"Should we talk to Drew first, do you think?" I glanced over my shoulder at Beau, who was riding in the back of Cletus's piece-of-shit Geo Prizm.

"I don't think we can wait that long." Beau shook his head. "It's the middle of November now. He's not getting back from the trek in the Appalachians until right before Christmas."

"When does Jethro get back again?" I asked.

"After Thanksgiving, I thought," answered Beau.

"Drew won't care about the purchases. We have the capital and he's been in favor of all our investments so far," Cletus chimed in. "The man is a PhD biologist and a federal game warden. I'm sure Drew has things on his mind other than our purchase of a vehicle carrier. Besides, he likes being a fully silent partner and trusts me to make important decisions."

Beau and I shared a look.

"You mean, he trusts *all of us* to make important decisions," Beau sought to clarify.

Cletus laughed—actually, he guffawed—as we pulled into our driveway. I wasn't really offended as I watched Cletus wipe tears from his eyes. "That's funny, Beau. Real funny."

Cletus parked, still shaking his head as he exited the small car, puffs of laughter following him as he walked to our porch. Beau unfolded from Cletus's clown car and made to follow him into the house, likely wanting to argue the point. I stopped him with a hand on his upper arm and a staying look.

Beau gave me a questioning frown and I shook my head, indicating he should be quiet. We waited, listening to Cletus as he mumbled to himself until the sounds of his trailing hilarity were cut off by the front door closing.

I counted to three, then I turned back to Beau. "I need to talk to you."

"What's up?"

"Not here. Let's go to the hangar," I whispered and lifted my chin to the Quonset hut some paces from the house.

I led the way, not waiting to see if he'd follow. I knew he'd follow. We could discern even the subtlest changes in each other's expressions, so I had no doubt he recognized the urgency in my voice.

A little-known fact about the Winstons is that we can see at night. My momma told us we were part Yuchi Indian on our daddy's side, and local legends said the tribe could see clear as day even during the blackest of nights. I had no idea if this was truth or fiction, made up to feed little boys' imaginations. Regardless, we could all see just fine in the dark.

Thus, neither of us had a problem finding the path to the hangar and navigating the obstacles along the way.

Once inside the hut—which we called *the hangar* because it resembled a small airplane hangar—I flipped on the overhead lights and navigated around the arbitrarily strewn tools and oil containers. At some point we were going to have to clean this place up. An orange 1965 Dodge Charger 273 sat ignored in the middle of our mess.

It was the car we'd been working on in August when we found out Momma was sick. We'd planned to give it to her for Christmas, after it was all fixed up and painted sky blue. Even Billy was helping with the engine work. But she'd died the first week of October. No one had touched it since.

I moved to a cluster of chairs at the back of the space and reached inside the small refrigerator to one side. Thankfully, it was still stocked with beer; I popped the top off a bottle and handed it to Beau, reserving the can of Guinness for me.

Drink in hand, I took a deep breath and tried to organize my thoughts.

"So, what's going on? Why are we hiding out here?" Beau asked.

"I had visitors on Wednesday: Repo and Dirty Dave."

Beau lifted a single eyebrow, his lips curving in to a sneer. "Those two morons? What did they want?"

I gathered a deep breath, not liking that I had no choice but to involve Beau in this. "You better sit down."

He sat down. I didn't. I paced while I drank my beer and related the story of their visit, their demands, as well as my trip into Knoxville for the disposable laptop.

"Damn," he said on an exhale, shaking his head as he absorbed the facts. His expression mirrored my own anxiety. "What was on the thumb drive? Or do I not want to know?" Beau looked like he was imagining the worst.

"You need to know. Besides, it's nothing…violent or disturbing. It's traps."

"Traps?" Beau's forehead wrinkled with confusion.

I stopped pacing, most of my restless energy spent, and

faced my twin. "Yeah. Traps. The thumb drive has a video of Jethro. A camera is following him around a garage I don't recognize, as he shows some unknown person the location of secret compartments he installed in several cars, how to access them, how to keep them concealed."

"Oh. You mean, like those vanity compartments? Like on that old MTV show, *Pimp My Ride*?"

"When have you ever watched MTV?"

"When you were off running around the woods and playing baseball with the valley kids, I was over at Hank Weller's house watching MTV and playing *Grand Theft Auto* on his PlayStation."

"Oh…"

"So, the traps?"

"Yes, so they're secret and hard to access. It's actually kind of genius. In order to open the compartment, you have to have the car off, in neutral, with the windows down, the driver's seat all the way to the front, and know where the release button is located. Then and only then will the trap open. Otherwise it just looks like regular carpet."

Beau shrugged, "So what's the big deal? So Jethro installed secret vanity compartments? How is this supposed to compel us to become the Iron Wraiths' chop shop?"

I grabbed a nearby chair and turned it around; I straddled it, facing my brother. "That's not the issue. Well, it's part of the issue. The real problem is that on the video someone tells Jethro that the traps will be used to transport drugs."

Beau frowned, his gaze became unfocused as his thoughts turned inward, and I could see he understood the implications.

I continued delivering the bad news. "Jethro cusses a few times, yells at the guy who is off camera, tells him he didn't sign up to install the traps for drug transportation. They argue a bit. Basically though, the voice reminds him that the only way Jethro can extract himself from future involvement with the Wraiths is to install the traps—which he did—and keep his mouth shut about how they're being used. The date of the video is about three years ago. They time-stamped it."

Beau closed his eyes and leaned back in his chair as he reiterated the facts. "So, they have a video of Jethro finding out the traps are being used to transport drugs, which basically makes him complicit or an accomplice to their drug running."

"Yeah. He installed the traps. Then he taught them how they're used, how to hide stuff. Then, they point-blank told Jethro that the compartments were going to be used to transport drugs and hide those drugs from the police."

Beau opened one eye, peeked at me. "And no one else is on the video? Just Jethro?"

"If you don't count the voice off camera, it's just Jethro. And the cars."

"Fuck."

I nodded, sighing at the frustrating futility of our situation.

"Did you call Jethro? Ask him about the video?"

"No. I didn't think calling him on Drew's government satellite phone, while they're off in the middle of the Appalachian Trail backwoods wilderness was a smart idea."

"Have you told anyone else?"

I shook my head. "No. I don't want anyone else to know, just in case we have to go through with this."

"I agree. No need to tell Billy in particular. He's perpetually pissed off anyway. With Roscoe finishing his last year of college, he's got enough on his plate. And I don't like the idea of messing with his life for no reason."

"And I wasn't planning on telling Cletus either." I watched Beau carefully for his reaction. If any of us were capable of seeing a way out of this mess, it was Cletus. He was too clever for his own good. Still, I didn't like dragging him into something just to have him shoulder the blame when or if we were busted.

Beau, I think, was having similar thoughts. He appeared to be considering our options. Eventually though, he came to my same conclusion. "No. Best if it's just you, me, and—when he gets back—Jethro who know about this…disaster. But I'm not ready to hand over the shop, not yet. There's got to be something we can do, even if we can put them off long enough until Jethro gets back in two weeks."

I nodded. "I've been thinking about that. The way I see it, it's the video that's the problem. If we could get our hands on all the copies, then the problem goes away."

Beau cast me a sidelong glance. "So…we what? Go to the Dragon Biker Bar and try to hack into their system? They've got to have backups on the cloud, or the mist, or whatever it's called."

"I don't think they're that advanced. I honestly don't. I bet they've got a PC someplace with the original video. Plus, if we go after their files, get a copy of everything, then destroy the machine, we might find something to use in retaliation, maybe another video we can blackmail them with, get them to back off."

"How are we supposed to access this PC?"

"I've been thinking about that, too…" My mouth turned sour because I didn't like our best option.

Beau studied me for a long moment and, unsurprisingly, he plucked my plan out of my brain. "Tina."

I closed my eyes briefly and sighed. "Yes. Tina."

Beau continued like I hadn't said anything. "Tina can get us in there. Or she can get in there on her own, no problem. She's been seeing one of the younger guys, right?"

"No. She's not an old lady. Since we broke up for good, she's now one of their girls, one of the…" I tried to think what the biker gang called women they indiscriminately used for sex.

"Sweetbutts," Beau supplied, giving me a scowl that demonstrated his dislike of the word and the concept.

The Wraiths weren't exactly known for being gentle with their women. Maybe it was because our momma regularly sported black eyes and bruised ribs at the hands of our father, but none of us Winston boys ultimately found anything remotely alluring about the biker lifestyle. The idea of fucking and then beating random women didn't strike me as badass. It struck me as dumbass and evil—like our father.

"Anyway, the point is, I think I can talk Tina into helping us."

Beau studied me before asking, "Aren't you worried about what they'd do to her? If they find out?"

"Yes," I answered honestly. "But it would be her choice. I thought we could pay her. She's always short on cash. And she's shrewd, crafty. She'd be careful. I know she could do it and not get caught."

"What if she uses this as a way to get back at you? You're right, she is shrewd. What if she takes the files for herself and then we got two people blackmailing us?"

I gathered a deep breath, let my gaze wander as I thought about this possibility—because it was a possibility. "I don't know, Beau. I guess you're right. She might double-cross us. But can you think of any other options?"

I settled my eyes on my brother, waited, hoped he'd have an alternate solution.

He looked resigned as he asked, "How much time do we have?"

"Dirty Dave said we have two weeks, and that was on Wednesday."

"Shit."

"But I think we can stall for a bit. I got the sense they'd like to do this real friendly. They'd like us to be willing. In fact, they offered to give us a cut."

"Well, we can work with that. Maybe put them off for a week or two, tell them we need to think it over, not say yes but not say no."

"Yeah, then delay another few weeks, tell them we need to get the shop ready—or even say we'll do it off-site. Maybe buy us enough time to get the files, or at least until Jethro gets back and we can beat the shit out of him."

Beau smirked at this, but it lacked any real humor. "You want to hold him down? Or should I?"

I returned his humorless smile with one of my own. "Let's take turns. No reason to be greedy."

Jessica

11

> "We all know that light travels faster than sound. That's why certain people appear bright until you hear them speak."
>
> —ANONYMOUS

I WAS IN A FUNK.

It wasn't a fun, funky-town funk. It was a full-on, pseudo-depression funk. Not even researching Aztec temples and reading travel blogs about New Zealand's geothermic sites did anything for the funk.

And it was all my fault.

Before Halloween, the majority of my fantasies centered on World Heritage sites. Now I caught myself daydreaming with alarming frequency about the time *we'd* shared. Also the reluctant curve of his smile, the shape of his torso, the cadence of his voice, the texture of his beard, and the radiance and intensity of his sapphire eyes.

Not to mention that incorrigible circumcised penis.

Accursed penis!

Making matters worse, I was second-guessing myself. Yes, I still had the insatiable wanderlust, I still desperately needed to see and know the world, but maybe there was more than one way to kill a rooster. Maybe I could save my money and go on really long vacations.

Teachers typically had the option of taking summers off; I could live the year in Green Valley and use the summer to backpack around the world. But this idea felt like settling, like giving up, and it gave me heartburn.

My point, I argued with myself, *is that it doesn't have to be all or nothing. If you really like Duane, and you do—don't try to deny it!—then you should try to find a way to make something between the two of you work…*

But with these thoughts also came fear, fear that I would be tied down, unable to travel, unable to leave. Fear that, if my intense like for him eventually turned to love, I would lose my freedom. It would be akin to having those *National Geographic* magazines read to me instead of losing myself in their pages. My dreams would be diluted and I would be stuck.

It was the fear that held me hostage, trapped in indecision purgatory.

I didn't call him after our disastrous date, and it had been a disaster. We'd consumed our food in silence; it had stuck in my throat, settled like a lump in my stomach. Duane had packed up, and this time he'd accepted my help. Our walk back had also been silent. Though he was just as solicitous and polite as he had been on the trek out, he hadn't looked at me. When we arrived at the car, he'd opened my door.

Then he'd taken me home and again opened my door when we'd arrived. He'd walked me to the steps of my parents' house, not touching me, and that's where I was left.

He gave me a short, impersonal nod, stuffed his hands in his pockets, and said politely, "I'll see you around, Jess."

Between the hot ache in my chest, the ballooning lump in my throat, and the stinging tears in my eyes, I didn't respond. I couldn't. I just stood there and watched him leave, drive away, feeling sick and sad and stupid.

And now, as I pulled my bike into the parking lot of Daisy's Nut House to meet my cousin Tina for dinner, I was still deep in my funk.

Tina had called me the Monday after my disastrous Saturday picnic with Duane. In fact, she'd called just as Claire and I were dropping off Duane's Mustang at the Winston house. We did it right after work, when I was fairly sure he'd still be at the auto shop, locking the car and slipping the keys into the mail slot of the house.

He hadn't asked me to return it, and I knew he never would. But there was no way I could keep the car. First of all, every time I looked at the thing I felt like crying. Secondly, like Duane, it wasn't mine to keep. It never had been.

As we pulled away from the house, Tina called my cell and said she wanted to get together. I was…surprised. I'd chalked up her overtures the week before to odd politeness. But now she was calling me, inviting me out.

At first she'd suggested beer and pool at the Dragon Biker Bar. I'd told her she was crazy.

In fact I'd said, "You're crazy."

She'd laughed. "What? Haven't you ever been curious about going? Meeting some of the guys? They're hot and they'd show us a real good time."

I'd shaken my head, which she couldn't see, and had repeated, "You're crazy."

I was curious about the Dragon Biker Bar and the Iron Wraiths guys like I was curious about going to jail for life.

So…not.

As the sheriff's daughter, I heard all sorts of cautionary tales about the local biker club. And, granted, if these cautionary tales hadn't included allegations of drug trafficking, prostitution, arson, and bouts of random violence, then I might have been a tad more curious.

Regardless, knowing what I did, the Iron Wraiths bikers didn't do a thing for me, except make me want to lock my doors, use the buddy system, take self-defense classes, and buy a German shepherd.

When I wouldn't budge and refused to indulge her initial idea, she relented and agreed to my alternate suggestion of dinner at Daisy's Nut House. This suited me since I didn't have a car and the diner was within walking distance of my parents' house.

Instead of walking, I opted to pedal my mom's old Schwinn Sting-Ray bicycle and arrived a full ten minutes earlier than the agreed-upon 6:30 p.m. I locked my bike up outside and meandered into the diner, happy and surprised to see Daisy behind the counter.

She waved me over as I entered and her dark-brown eyes darted between me and the sugar containers she was filling.

"Hey. I'm not used to seeing you on school nights. How's your momma's sister? I haven't heard anything all week."

She wasn't in the Nut House uniform, but rather looked like she'd just left a business meeting. Her brown skin was tinted with pink blush and her lips were bright red. As well, she'd restyled her hair since I'd last seen her. It resembled Michelle Obama's trendy straight bob.

These days Daisy ran the business side of things rather than the diner itself. Sales of Daisy's doughnuts had expanded over the last few years and were now carried by most grocery stores in the Southeast.

I claimed a stool at the counter and helped her fill the glass containers. This was an old habit from when I worked at the Nut House and Daisy used to be my boss.

I loved Daisy. First of all, she was my momma's best friend. She, her husband, Trevor, and their three kids felt more like family than some of my blood relations. Also, she was smart and funny and sassy, had been a great boss, had taught me everything I knew about fashion, and lastly, she'd taught me her secret recipe for making her homemade doughnuts.

"Last I heard, Aunt Louisa needs dialysis. The chemo is working, but it's messing with her kidneys."

Daisy made a face. "That doesn't sound good. You spent the summers with your aunt during college, right?"

"Yes. I was her personal assistant during the school year as well, but I worked remotely during the fall and spring and lived at her house during the summers."

"Her personal assistant? I didn't know that."

"Yeah. She's a big socialite in Houston now she's retired."

"What did she do before she retired?"

"She was a petroleum engineer, invented something important that lowers the environmental impact of drilling. I never knew the details. But she never married and has no kids, so she takes on a lot of charity work and special projects. Plus her house requires *a lot* of maintenance. It's a huge sprawling mansion with stables and horses."

"Yes. Your momma said something about her sister having more money than the sea has shells. Have you thought about going out there?"

"I thought about taking a visit…but, honestly? I don't think my aunt likes me much."

Daisy *tsk*ed, shook her head. "That can't be true."

"When I worked for her, when I stayed with her during the summers, she had me in the employee wing and she never ate meals with me. She didn't talk to me unless it was work related, and when she introduced me to people—and only when she had to—I was her personal assistant, Miss James. She didn't want her friends to know we were related. I'm not sore about it, but I think I must've embarrassed her."

"I can't see how that's possible. You should go visit. If not for your aunt, then for your momma. I hate to think of her lonely over Thanksgiving. Why doesn't Louisa hire a nurse?"

"She has. She has two full-time nurses and a physician."

"She hired herself a full-time physician?"

"Yes. Momma is really just out there for moral support. But I'm sure she'd appreciate a call if you get a chance."

"I'll call tonight." Daisy nodded and moved to fill another container.

"Is Daniella coming home for Thanksgiving?" I asked about Daisy's oldest daughter, now a banker or something like that in New York City.

Daisy gave me a wide smile. "She is. Simone will be home too. But Daniella will be home for both Thanksgiving and Christmas this year. I think she's bringing a boy home with her, too."

I grinned, wagged my eyebrows. "Really? A boy?"

"Yes. He works at her investment firm and, the way she tells it, they were flirting over hedge funds and gold futures for six months before he worked up the courage to ask her out."

This made me chuckle, because I could understand his

hesitation. Daniella is ten or so years older than me and always struck me as fiercely focused. She was valedictorian of her graduating class and received a full academic scholarship to Princeton.

Plus she was crazy beautiful. I'd always admired her long black dreadlocks, warm tawny skin, and Nefertiti-like bone structure.

The sound of a rumbling motorcycle pulled my attention to the front window and I watched as Tina dismounted from behind a biker and handed him her helmet.

"Are you meeting Tina here?" Daisy asked, a hint of concern in her voice.

"Yes." I nodded and hopped down from my stool. "She called me earlier this week, wanted to get together."

Daisy seemed to hesitate for a moment, her eyes moving between the scene playing outside the window and me. Tina and the biker were kissing, and if they hadn't been in a parking lot, it looked like the kind of kissing that led to horizontal fun times.

"Don't get hooked into your cousin's drama," Daisy said at last, leveling me with a penetrating glare. "She's trouble, and she's a user. If your momma were here, she'd tell you the same thing."

I grinned at Daisy and shook my head. Her advice was good, but she wasn't telling me anything I didn't already know. "Okay. I won't get hooked into her drama."

"Good." She nodded once, wiping her hands on a towel and splitting her attention between me and Tina as the latter waved goodbye to her ride. "I'll send Beverly out to take your orders."

"Thanks, Daisy."

"Mm-hmm," she said noncommittally, like she didn't want to be rude but refused to sanction my dinner with Tina.

I walked to the door just as Tina entered. As I waved and was about to suggest we grab a booth, she surprised me by yanking me forward and into a big hug. I was usually two inches taller than my cousin, but not tonight. I noticed she was wearing a pair of shiny-red spiked platform shoes. If I wore those shoes, I'd fall on my ass before I could take a step. But she walked in them as though they were slippers.

As we hugged she squealed, like she was super happy to see me, and this made me smile. We'd been good friends growing up—at least I'd thought so at the time. I wondered if, over time, our high school years would prove to be merely a friendship sabbatical.

She leaned away and gave me a giant grin. "Oh my goodness, girl! You look so great." Tina squeezed my hand one more time before releasing me. We both slid into the nearest booth, smiling at each other.

"You do, too. You're looking great."

She did look great. She looked hot. Like, superhot. Hot in a way I wouldn't even know how to go about achieving.

Tina wore false eyelashes and an impressive amount of artfully applied eye makeup. She and I looked nothing alike. When we were growing up, no one ever guessed we were related. She looked more like my daddy's side of the family, and I favored my mother's side.

But we both had brown eyes, though not at all the same color. I thought of my irises as plain brown. Whereas her eyes—with all the careful framing and highlighting—appeared to be the color of whiskey. The effect was dramatic. Beautiful. I wanted her to teach me how to do it.

The rest of her makeup was impeccable. She'd dyed her naturally light-brown hair black and wore it loose in long shiny waves around her shoulders—which was basically a miracle since she'd just been on a motorcycle. Her hair paired with her sun-bronzed skin—another miracle since the sun had been hiding for two weeks—gave her a rather exotic look.

Of course, her clothes took everything to a completely new level of conspicuous hotness. She was in black leather pants, really sexy leather pants, and a white low-cut V-neck angora sweater. Both fit her like a second skin, which was fantastic for her since she was clearly in excellent shape.

Beverly, our server, came by almost immediately with a glass of sweet tea and another of water for each of us, assuming correctly what we wanted to drink, and we both already knew what we were going to order.

Tina waited until Beverly was out of earshot before leaning forward and saying in a low, conspiratorial voice, "I was a little surprised you wanted to meet here."

"What? Why?"

She blinked at me as though the answer were obvious. When I continued to stare at her with obliviousness, she laughed lightly and shook her head.

"You know what I do for a living, right?"

I nodded and sipped my sweet tea. "Yes. I know."

"I guess I'm just surprised you didn't mind being seen with me so publicly."

I gave her a sideways glance. "Wait…I think I know what you do. You're still dancing at the Pink Pony, right?"

She nodded. "Yeah."

"You haven't joined ISIS or anything, right?"

"What's ISIS?"

"I mean, you're not actively plotting to overthrow the government?"

She giggled and tossed her hair over her shoulder. "I'm not even sure what that means." Then Tina's expression turned abruptly sober and she leaned forward, her eyes boring into mine. "But, listen, I have to talk to you about something important. It's kind of why I wanted to get together."

"Oh, okay. What's up?"

Her gaze turned speculative as it released mine and moved over my black fitted long-sleeved cotton shirt, then darted to my hair. "I always envied your blond hair. It's so pretty, just like your momma's."

"You want to talk about my hair?"

"No, silly." She shook her head, rolling her eyes. "So…you and Duane Winston, what's going on there?"

I felt my lips part and my eyebrows lift in surprise. An involuntary ache squeezed my chest, making it hard to breathe for a moment. She stared at me while I struggled to find words.

Finally I managed to say, "Nothing. I mean, we went on one date. But nothing now."

Her eyes narrowed. "You went on a date?"

"Yes."

"When? Recently?"

"Uh, last Saturday."

"So a week ago?"

"Almost, yes."

"But no second date?"

"No. No second date."

She nodded slowly, still glaring at me through narrowed eyes. "Why no second date?"

I glanced at the vinyl of the booth behind her, trying to figure out how to best explain the situation and be sensitive to the fact we were talking about her ex-boyfriend, an ex-boyfriend for whom she might still have feelings.

"We decided that our priorities weren't compatible."

She huffed and it sounded impatient. "In English, please. This ain't a parent-teacher conference."

"Um, I guess he wanted one thing out of a relationship, and I wanted something else."

Tina pursed her lips, her eyes losing focus as she considered my words. While I waited for her to finish thinking her thoughts, I sipped my tea and glanced at the specials board. Daisy's pie of the day was apple.

"I'm not jealous."

I shifted my attention from the list of pies to Tina. "Excuse me?"

"I'm not jealous of you and Duane. I don't care who he sees. You're welcome to him, if I'm the reason you decided to call things off."

I lifted my chin in acknowledgment, but said nothing. Because I wasn't sure what to say. Tina hadn't been a consideration in my decision to date or not date Duane. I wondered if that made me unfeeling. But then I reminded myself that Tina and I hadn't really spoken in over eight years, the first four of which she'd snubbed me for more popular kids at our school.

Yeah…I wasn't going to factor Tina into my dating decisions. That would be silliness.

"I just wanted to let you know that," she said, as though she were being generous. "Duane and I were together for a long time, and what we felt for each other… Well, I just think first love is really special. He'll always mean something to me. But it's over now and I've moved on. I hate to think of him pining for me."

Again, I lifted my chin in acknowledgment—higher this time—and found myself without words. Thankfully, Beverly interrupted by bringing our salads.

I changed the topic to one I hoped would be much more benign and asked Tina what she'd been up to recently. This turned into her giving me the oral history of Green Valley gossip for the last four years—who was sleeping with whom, who had divorced, had illegitimate babies, had a drug problem, was in debt. She made Green Valley sound like a sordid train wreck.

Strangely, while she spoke I found myself distracted by how incredibly hot she was. I mean, she was sex personified. Her movements were sensual, including how she chewed her food. Her smile was coy, alluring, captivating. She'd say something like, *That little fucker got what he deserved*, and I hardly heard the venom in her voice because she somehow made it sound erotic.

I was thankful when dinner was over and her biker fella arrived to fetch her, because I was…exhausted. Maybe it was a by-product of my long workweek paired with the Duane funk, or maybe it was just the tidal wave of sexual energy that was my cousin Tina.

Either way, as I pedaled home, I felt bereft and depressed and wished I'd thought to grab a slice of Daisy's pecan pie before leaving.

♥

"What's wrong, baby sister?"

I sighed, hugged the pillow I was holding a bit closer. I hadn't been able to go to sleep. The depression followed me home, and though I was tired and tried lying in bed in the dark with my eyes shut for over an hour, sleep would not come.

So I took a shower, hoping it would help me relax, and it worked. I felt a bit better when I shut off the water. But then Sir Edmund Hillary—my psychotic cat—tried to murder me with his litter box. He'd pushed it directly in front of the shower door, and I'd stepped on it, stumbled, and fallen to the floor with a squawk and a thud.

It occurred to me that, had I been living alone and Sir Edmund knew how to wield a knife, I'd be dead and no one would find me for days, maybe months.

This thought reignited my depression. So I cleaned up, dried off, and went to the kitchen. I made hot cocoa with a liberal amount of Baileys and channel surfed in the family room, hoping I'd pass out eventually on the couch, absent thoughts of my inevitable and lonely death by psycho cat.

Instead, I was still up at 2:21 a.m., which signified the end of Jackson's shift. I was never up this late, so I guessed it made sense he'd assume something was amiss.

"Sir Edmund tried to murder me," I said.

"Again?"

I nodded. "His attempts grow bolder. I think it might be time to confront him or, at the very least, move his litter box to the basement."

"Jess, the cat tries to take your life at least once a week. It's not the cat. Tell me what's wrong."

I sighed again, not sure I wanted to discuss my depression with Jackson. "I had dinner with Tina tonight."

"Our cousin Tina?"

"Yeah."

Jackson crossed the room and sat next to me on the couch.

He was still in his uniform, though his belt was gone. "She's still dancing at the Pink Pony," he said.

"Yes. I know."

"And I think she's mixed up with the Wraiths." Jackson paired these words with a sad-sounding sigh.

"Yes. I know that, too…"

"Is that what's got you down? Are you worried about her?"

I considered the question. I *was* a bit worried about her involvement with the bikers…but not really. She didn't strike me as the kind of person *anyone* could take advantage of. Rather, if anyone was going to do the taking advantage, it would be Tina.

"Kind of. I mean, I'm a little worried for her. Based on what you and Daddy have told me about the Iron Wraiths, they're certainly not trustworthy."

"They're dangerous. And she's going to get herself hurt if she keeps it up."

"But I guess I'm also thinking…" I huffed. I didn't know what I was thinking or why I was feeling so dissonant. Therefore, I didn't know how to have this conversation with Jackson. He was my brother, so any discussion about Duane and Tina would be weird. Because at some point over the last five hours I'd realized my depression was related to my Duane funk.

Tired of my hesitation, he pushed, "What are you thinking?"

I needed to talk to Claire at work in the morning, or call one of my old college roommates.

"Jess?" He prodded again, poking me in the shoulder.

"You don't want to have this conversation."

"Try me."

I glanced at my big brother, found him watching me with determination—like he was determined to be helpful—and I felt myself waver.

He was a guy after all. Maybe he could give me some perspective.

Finally, I relented. I tucked one of my legs under me as I faced him. "So, first you have to forget I'm your sister, that Tina is your cousin, and that you hate Duane Winston."

Jackson lifted a single eyebrow and his mouth flattened. "That's unlikely."

"Okay, never mind then."

I moved to stand up, but Jackson caught my arm and kept me from leaving. "Now, wait a minute. I said it was unlikely, not impossible. Fine…fine, I'll do my best. You're not my sister, Tina's not my cousin, and Duane Winston isn't a horse's ass."

I scowled at my brother. He smiled. I supposed it was the best I could hope for.

"Fine. So, here's my question…" I gathered a large breath and held it in my lungs as I tried to figure out what question I wanted to ask. When I could hold my breath no longer, my half-formed thoughts emerged. "So, here's the thing. Tina is sexy. Like, really sexy. She's got a perfect body and she's insanely beautiful. Add to that she's a stripper and erotic without trying to be and…I don't know. I guess I don't understand why Duane would break up with her when she is basically every man's fantasy. Why would he break up with her?"

Jackson studied me for a long moment, then surprised me by countering with, "Why would he break up with her? Or are you really asking me why Duane Winston would choose you over making Tina Patterson his girl?"

I straightened, started to deny what he was implying, but then stopped myself.

He was right. That was the real question even though I hadn't consciously thought it. It was the question stuck in my subconscious like a popcorn kernel buried between teeth.

I sighed. "Please don't try to reassure me that I'm pretty. I'm… It's not really a question of prettiness, is it? But, you're right. I don't understand why Duane would break up with Tina and then go out with someone like me."

Jackson examined me for several long seconds, his eyes narrowed, his mouth twisted to one side. At length he exhaled and shook his head.

"So, I might be biased because you're my sister and I think you're equal parts annoying and awesome, but it actually makes a lot of sense to me."

I scrunched my face and braced for a deluge of reassurance about my "gifts" or "talents." Instead, my brother surprised me a second time.

"Let me put it this way: Have you ever seen someone and thought to yourself, *Whoa, he's hot! I'd like to screw his brains out*? And then you talk to the guy and realize someone already has?"

I barked an astonished laugh, covered my gaping mouth with my hand, and shook my head at my brother. "I can't believe you said that. Just last week you told me I was being unladylike."

He laughed lightly at my reaction. "I'm sorry. I'm tired so I guess my gentleman filter is off. But you have, right? A guy who's super good-looking, but with not much going on upstairs? Now, Tina is… Tina hasn't ever… What I mean is Tina isn't interested in learning anything. She's interested in looking good, being the center of attention, making dramas, that kind of stuff. I'm not saying I don't love her—I do. She's family after all. But she's always been…well, she's always been shallow."

Jackson paused, allowing me a moment to let his perspective sink in before he continued. "Not all the girls at the Pink Pony are that way. Hannah Townsen dances up there, has for the last year."

"Hannah? Really?" This was surprising news. Hannah was two years behind me in school and I remembered her as being extremely shy.

"Yeah. Dancing makes good money, she uses the money to help her momma keep the homestead, and the Pony isn't like the G-Spot—you know that strip club down near the Dragon Biker Bar? Where all the girls are strung out? The Pink Pony isn't like that. Hank—you know Hank Weller? He owns the Pink Pony. Well, anyway, Hank does a good job of keeping things clean and tidy at his place, he treats his girls well, and hires good guys, bouncers to keep out the bad element. But Tina is always stirring shit up. One of these days I'm pretty sure he'll get tired of her dramas."

I assumed Jackson knew all of this startling information because of his job. Notwithstanding the local strip club politics, I tried to wrap my mind around his words regarding my cousin and Duane.

But Jackson pulled me out of my thoughts before I was able to gather them. "Now, I know you don't want me to tell you that you're pretty, but you are."

"Jackson…" I rolled my eyes.

I assumed, similar to most people, I studied myself in the mirror and saw imperfections, little things I wished I could change or wanted to target for change. But, at the risk of coming across as a complete nut, I totally thought I was pretty. I thought I had a pretty face. I thought I had a decent body. I woke up early four days a week so I could go swimming at the YMCA—because I loved swimming and I liked feeling strong. I ate fairly well (not counting my obsession with pie). I took reasonably good care of myself.

Relatively clean living paired with biological gifts meant I was on the right side of pleased with my reflection. Therefore, I didn't need to hear my older brother tell me I was pretty. But I was no personification of every man's sex fantasy.

Jackson cut me off and insisted, "You hush up and hear me out for a minute. You are a pretty girl. And pretty girls who don't know how pretty they are sometimes feel overwhelmed by attention from the opposite sex."

I rolled my eyes again, smirked at my brother's impression of me, but didn't interrupt. I was perversely curious to see where this was going.

Jackson's voice deepened and adopted a lecturing tone. "Duane Winston is…well, he's a horse's ass. I don't like him. He drives too fast and doesn't respect authority. But he's not stupid. None of those Winston boys are. And after a few years of Tina, he's got to be tired of conversations involving nothing but nail polish and gossip. It wouldn't matter if Tina looked like Angelina Jolie and—pardon my candor and potential lack of sensitivity—loved giving blow jobs every ten minutes. No man with brains would be able to put up with her brand of boring and crazy indefinitely. Not even Duane Winston."

Jessica

12

> "No matter how far you travel, you can never get away from yourself."
>
> —HARUKI MURAKAMI, "UFO IN KUSHIRO," *AFTER THE QUAKE*

CLAIRE AND I DIDN'T DISCUSS my dinner with Tina the next morning at work, mostly because I was dead tired. Plus, she'd been a witness to my Duane funk all week after we'd dropped off his Mustang. Thankfully, she hadn't commented on it so I hadn't either. I didn't want her to think I was both whiny and funky. However, I could tell she was having a hard time holding her tongue about my lingering laconic attitude.

And when we pulled into the Green Valley Community Center for jam night—she was driving—Claire turned to me after cutting her ignition and said, "You're in a funk. You have been all week. And I'm pretty sure it's why you gave Duane Winston back his pretty car."

I sighed pathetically and glanced out my window at the gathering crowd. "I know."

I could feel her eyeballs on me. "You know, he might be in there, in the community center."

"Yes. I know." My heart did a strange little stretch, then constriction thing in my chest.

"What will you do?"

"I guess I'll say hi, be polite, showcase my excellent manners."

"Why don't you drag him off someplace private and dark instead, and bend him to your will?"

I huffed a humorless laugh, turned to my friend, and answered honestly, "Because he wants more than I can give him."

I said the words without much conviction because I was still wondering if I could have my pie and not get fat; that is, figure out how to have a real relationship with Duane, not give up on my dreams, and *not* break anyone's heart.

Claire set her jaw, her eyes narrowing on me. "You know, I've been really quiet so far, about you and your situation with Duane. I understand you have dreams of seeing the world, and dreams are important. But you know what I don't understand? How is it that your dreams don't leave room for companionship? For love?"

"Claire—"

"No, hear me out. I think about my time with the man I loved—as short as it was, and all I gave up—and you know what? I wouldn't trade a lifetime of things or experiences or accolades for a second of what we had when we were together."

"Honey—"

"And you won't even consider the *possibility* that your dreams might be made better, that life and the living of it can be enriched if you have someone to share it with. Why is that?"

"I—"

"I'm not saying Duane Winston is your B—soulmate. I'm not saying that. But watching you shut down and withhold yourself from the possibility of love and being loved makes me sad. That makes me sad for you. I know you want adventure, I know you want to see the world. But love is the greatest adventure, where you risk the most for the greatest reward. What good will all this exceptional living do if you're doing it only for yourself?"

"I don't know! Okay?" I bellowed, chaotically throwing my hands around. "You're right, I don't know what I'm missing. I don't know what might have been between us if I'd gotten out of my own way and just let things be. But I do know that I will suffocate here. I know I cannot stay. And I know that being dishonest with Duane, or being dishonest with anyone—even if it's a lie of omission—isn't right. It isn't fair, not to him. He wanted to *court* me. He brought my mother flowers. His sights were set on the long term, and I…" I sighed pitifully and shook my head, glancing at my fingers.

"And you what? Is the problem that you can't see yourself with Duane Winston in the long term?"

"No. The problem is that I *can* see myself with Duane Winston in the long term. I can see a house with a garage where he fixes up old cars. I can see a home office where I grade papers and tutor kids. I see a kitchen where I bake Sunday meat loaf or roast chicken, and a deck where he grills ribs and steaks. I can see a garden in the backyard and white picket fences."

"And that terrifies you."

"And that terrifies me. Because as pretty as the picture is, I would hate it. I would hate owning stuff that owns me.

I would hate knowing the whole world was out there and I'd locked myself in a cage—even if the cage was gold and pretty, with an herb garden and a flower bed…"

She didn't respond, not for a long time. We both stared out the windshield in strained silence and watched as groups of locals passed by the front of her car on their way to jam night. Judging by the number of people, the place was going to be packed. This was a good and a bad thing.

Likely, by the time I made it to the food line, all the coleslaw would be gone. The coleslaw was my favorite of the salads.

However, on the plus side, if the place was packed and Duane was in attendance, it would make avoiding him a lot easier.

Eventually she broke our stalemate. "What if the house had a hot tub?"

I slid my eyes to the side, saw her giving me a conciliatory smile, one of surrender and apology.

I returned her smile and hoped mine conveyed similar sentiments of reconciliation. "Well, now that changes everything. I'd give up the world for a hot tub, but only if it was also a time machine."

She laughed, shook her head at me as she unbuckled her seat belt. "Why is that movie so funny? It's so stupid, and yet it makes me laugh every time I watch it. I don't understand myself sometimes."

"Beats me." I shrugged, opening my door and straightening out of the car, preparing my resolve to face whatever labyrinth of funky feelings lay ahead.

I'd braced myself for seeing Duane. I'd expected to see him around every corner or the sound of his conversation to greet me through every door.

But he didn't. He wasn't there. At least I didn't see him.

My heart seized a bit when I spotted Cletus strumming his banjo in one of the rooms, providing accompaniment for his brother Billy on vocals. I decided to torture myself by staying in the room and listening to Billy Winston sing. The man could sing. Yet this was an exercise in torture because there was something about the way he moved that reminded me of Duane.

Nevertheless, no music played that only I could hear when Billy walked by my chair during a break, stopped, and gave me a faint smile of acknowledgment. I felt nothing beyond friendly curiosity when he crossed to me, his hands in his pockets, and leveled me with his startling stare.

As I stood, I decided if Beau's eyes were the summer sky and Duane's volleyed between glittering sapphires and a swirling tempest, Billy Winston's eyes were the color of glaciers. Even his warm smile couldn't quite warm his gaze.

"How are you this evening, Jessica?" It had been a while since I'd spoken to Billy, so I'd forgotten he'd lost quite a bit of his eastern Tennessee drawl. He almost sounded like a generic person from the United States, what most would consider lacking in discernible accent. Well, generic except his voice held a soothing, melodic quality when he spoke.

"Just fine. And how are you, Billy?"

"I'm well." His gaze drifted to the empty seat next to mine. "Is Claire here with you tonight?"

"Yes. We came together. But I think she's up at the front with her father-in-law, helping with the donations."

He nodded, his gaze growing sharper in a way I couldn't help but notice. I thought it was remarkably odd, almost like he was frustrated.

But then whatever it was promptly vanished and was replaced with an unaffected air of controlled politeness. "How are things at the high school?"

"Fine...real good, actually. We now have a system worked out for all the kids bused in for calculus."

"All thanks to this little lady."

I turned my head just as Kip Sylvester, the principal of the high school and therefore my boss, shouldered his way through the shuffling crowd. Next to him was his daughter Jennifer, who I would forever think of as Queen of the Banana Cakes.

This was not an uncharitable thought on my part. She'd literally won Best Banana Cake at the county fair for the last six years and worked for her momma's bakery making the renowned cakes. Add to this her pale complexion, pale-yellow hair, and bright-yellow dress with brown polka dots, and she might as well have been a banana herself.

"Thanks to Miss James, we're seeing lots of progress in our STEM numbers already." Kip Sylvester gave me an approving nudge.

It was somewhat strange, thinking of Kip Sylvester as my boss. I'd known him since I was two. He'd been the principal when I was in high school, too. I gave Jennifer a small smile of greeting, which she returned with sunny brilliance. But then I watched as she turned her gaze to Billy; it grew noticeably bemused and dreamy.

"That's good news," Billy offered benignly, pairing his statement with a head nod in my direction.

"Are you singing tonight, Mr. Winston?" Jennifer asked prettily in a soft, sweet voice. Sweet as banana cake.

"I am. Or, I guess I was." Billy turned and glanced over his shoulder. "It depends on whether Cletus is staying for the next set. We drove together."

"Oh, I hope we're not too late to hear you sing. I think I'd die if I missed it."

Billy's expression grew a bit perplexed, maybe even a little rigid.

My boss tried to cover his grimace with an indulgent smile—which only served to highlight his grimace. "What a silly thing to say, Jennifer," he admonished his daughter, chuckling lightly and looking at Billy as though to apologize.

I felt a pang of empathy as Jennifer's face fell and her cheeks tinged pink. "I'm sorry, I'm always saying silly things I guess. I must've overdone it today in the bakery."

"See now, that's a great excuse. I usually blame all the silly things I say on syphilis." I started to laugh at my own joke before even finishing it. However, after seven seconds of dismayed stares and silence, I realized that maybe STD humor was lost on this crowd.

I reminded myself that what I thought was hilarious, like my ironic sexy Gandalf costume, was often the cause of censure and elicited abject horror from others. I was always going to be a circle peg in a world of squares.

But then I heard someone laugh, or more precisely try not to laugh. I twisted at the waist and nearly lost my breath because directly behind me was Duane Winston. He was most definitely trying his best to contain errant laughter. His sapphire eyes were glittering down at me.

And then I really did lose my breath because if I wasn't mistaken, Duane was giving me a hot look.

His gaze moved from mine to his brother's, then to Jennifer and Principal Sylvester's as he handed out customary greetings to the small circle.

I hadn't at all recovered by the time his attention swung back to me. "Jessica, do you have a spare moment?" he asked in a low voice.

I nodded.

"Please excuse us," he muttered.

Without sparing a goodbye glance for our companions, Duane wrapped his long fingers around my upper arm and tugged me toward the open door.

We were surrounded on all sides by crowds of people, music floating down the painted cinder-block- and linoleum-paved hallway. It was loud. But I was only aware of Duane. Halfway to the donations table, he slipped his hand into mine. We held hands for the remainder of our short walk to the cafeteria, causing my heart to take up residence in my throat. I was half expecting and hoping he'd drag me backstage again, but he didn't.

He steered us to one of the long lunchroom tables in the corner of the cafeteria where no one else was sitting. We were still in a room full of people, but the conversations elsewhere meant whatever words we exchanged would be indecipherable from the surrounding chatter.

Duane pulled a chair out for me and claimed the seat adjacent as I sat. Or I tried to sit. I didn't know quite how to sit. Sitting suddenly felt weird. I was superconscious of my limbs.

Thankfully, Duane spoke before I could become too obsessed with the mechanics of sitting.

"I've been thinking." He leaned his forearm along the table to his left (my right) and trapped me with his focused gaze.

"What have you been thinking?" I missed the feel of his hand and wondered if it would be weird for me to reach out and take hold of his fingers.

"You're leaving, just as soon as you can. And you estimate that at being, what? Two years?"

I felt a bit dismayed by his subject choice. I was hoping he'd want to talk about that Saturday, give me an opening to apologize and explain in greater detail. I tried to figure out how to steer the conversation in that direction. I tried and failed.

Instead, I answered the question he'd asked with honesty. "More like either one and a half or two and a half at this point, depending on how much money I can save."

His eyes narrowed and he nodded, his hand coming to his chin as he stroked his beard thoughtfully. We sat that way—him studying me while stroking his beard, me watching him study me while he stroked his beard—for several seconds.

Abruptly he asked, "What would you say if I suggested we date for the next twelve months, but only for twelve months?"

Who? What? Date?

It took me a bit to work through his words. I liked the *date* part, but the *only twelve months* part sounded fishy.

"I…um… Why twelve months?"

My question seemed to relax him and his eyes appeared to lighten a bit. "Because that way we'll be split up well before the time you need to go. It's a good stretch of time, long enough to have a bit of fun, get to know each other, but not so long that you have to be concerned about a lasting attachment."

My heart was doing strange things in my chest, but not

anything I might have predicted. It sank, like a stone. If I caught his meaning, and I was fairly certain I did, he wanted me to be his fuck buddy for the next year. I'd gone from the girl he wanted to court to the girl he wanted to see on the side, one he likely no longer respected.

I shifted in my seat, not because my body was uncomfortable but because my brain was uncomfortable.

And my discomfort didn't make sense because this is what I'd wanted…*right?*

No. This isn't what you wanted, a voice answered in my head, clear as a bell.

Sometimes I truly didn't understand myself.

"So…we'd…" I licked my lips to stall answering. When I found my voice, it was croaky and I felt the beginning of frustrated tears sting my eyes. "We'd what? Hook up a few times a month?"

He shook his head, leaned a bit closer, and I was struck by how severe his expression seemed, almost like he was angry, but not quite.

"No. That's not what I want. You would have to go all in. We would go out to dinner, see movies, call each other, text. I'd work on your car—you know, the Mustang you left at my house earlier this week—install gadgets you don't need 'cause you're my girl. You might come to the Winston place and hang out with us boys. This would be both of us, all in for all twelve months—or less if we find we don't suit."

My heart reversed positions halfway through his clarification of my misassumption and hurdled itself skyward. In fact, my entire body felt lighter, almost like I was floating.

"So, you still want to court me?"

"Yes." He nodded.

"For twelve months?"

"Yep."

I didn't try to hide my smile. "And we'd be a couple, a *real* couple?"

A touch of softness entered his expression and his eyes drifted over my face, as though cataloging it. "Yeah, with presents on birthdays, and celebrating Valentine's Day, and watching chick flicks, and all that other crap."

I gathered a deep breath, my lungs filling with both air and excitement. But then a thought occurred to me. "Wait, what if after the twelve months, one or both of us wanted to continue? Does this thing, this agreement, have an option for an extension?"

At once the softness vanished, and again the lines of his face turned severe. He leaned away, just a few inches, but the distance felt much greater. I perceived a cold kind of resolve behind his eyes.

"No. Absolutely not. The term is for a year. After that year is up, and as long as you're in Green Valley, our relationship would be over."

"But, what if I'm in town for two and a half years? What if—"

"No. Twelve months. That's it. Take it or leave it." His tone was unyielding. As though to drive home the fact that he wasn't willing to bend on this point, he set his jaw and glowered at me. His glower reminded me of the Duane Winston I used to know, the kid who used to pick apart my arguments and challenge me to think about perspectives other than my own. That Duane had been irritating. That Duane had also been right nine times out of ten.

I felt a spasm of some sort in my chest, like a spike or surge of panic, making breathing a bit more difficult. Absentmindedly, I pressed a palm to the center of my rib cage as I studied him and his stony features.

I opened my mouth, determined to try one more time, because his granite resolve on the issue didn't make much sense, but he cut me off before I could speak.

"And, if we do this, you're not to bring up the possibility of an extension again. You don't even ask about it. It's just understood. One year from today we'd be over and done and that's it."

I studied him for a long stretch, saw he was completely serious, and seeing this made me feel out of sorts.

Therefore I asked the first question my panicked heart wanted to know. "Would I still see you?"

He shrugged. "You'd see me around, I guess. This isn't a big town."

"Would we still be friends?"

"I don't know."

"Would you talk to me? If you saw me after? Or would you ignore me?"

"I'd be polite."

"But not more than polite?"

"I don't rightly know, Jess," he whispered, and his whisper sounded a bit sad.

Meanwhile, my voice lifted as I challenged, "Well, you need to know, Duane. Because I don't think I could just date you for a year and then turn my feelings off."

"But you could leave me for Timbuktu and that would be no problem?"

I huffed, my defensive hackles rising. "I don't like being made to feel guilty for having dreams and goals. I already get enough sass about this from my family."

I saw his chest rise and fall with an impressively large and silent breath. His eyes searched mine for a few seconds before he glanced to his right, shaking his head.

"This. Right here. This is the reason for the twelve-month limit." When he brought his gaze back to mine, it was clear and sober, determined. "If we limit things to the twelve months, then we both know what's up. We avoid having this conversation ever again—because you leaving won't make any difference. We'll already be done. You can go and not feel like you've left anything behind."

I considered him, his words, for nearly a full minute, seeing the sincerity painted all over his features.

"You've given this some thought." This came out sounding like an accusation and I didn't know why.

"Yeah, I have."

I felt…irritable. But then I realized his proposed plan meant he'd been thinking about me over the last week. He'd been thinking about us and what to do. And that realization made me feel gooey and sentimental.

Therefore, inspired and touched by his consideration of the matter, I blurted before thinking about what I was going to say, "What if we—" then stopped when I realized I was about to say, *What if we just do this for real, no time constraints, and I put my travel plans on hold indefinitely?*

And that was the moment I realized how much I liked—*really liked*—Duane Winston. I mean, I knew I liked him before. But my reflexive panic at the thought of a time limit with him, one set in stone, made me feel trapped by my dreams of world travel.

Oh, my dear friend, Irony. How I have not missed you…

I licked my lips, then chewed on the bottom one, again

as a way to stall speaking my thoughts. My daddy liked to say, *You can't have fried pie and not get fat.* It was a distorted and much cruder version of the popular *You can't have your cake and eat it too,* but the sentiment was the same.

"What if we...?" he prompted when I took a bit too long to continue.

Looking at him, knowing he was serious about this time limit business, I decided to take a different approach: negotiation.

"What if we did a trial period first? Before the twelve months started?"

His eyes narrowed with suspicion. "Why would we do that?"

I had no choice but to wing it, make stuff up. "Because... because it would...be weird and...depressing to pick a year from today, November fourteenth, as the day things end. Right before Thanksgiving and Christmas? No. We should do a six-week trial period and start the twelve-month countdown on January first."

His eyes narrowed more, but his mouth twisted to the side like he was fighting a smile. "You're just trying to get thirteen and a half months instead of twelve."

I shrugged. "You caught me. So what if I am? What's six more weeks in the scheme of things?"

The humor waned from his expression and was replaced with a contemplative frown. He was considering it, I could tell. He just needed a little push.

I scootched my chair closer so my legs were between his, placed my hands on his knees, and leaned forward. "Two Thanksgivings. Two Christmases. Two New Year's Eves. Think of it, this year I won't even know what to get you for Christmas. But next year…" I hoped I was giving him a winning grin.

He sighed, his almost-smile returned, and I nearly jumped out of my seat to do the moonwalk when he conceded, "Fine. A year from January first."

I didn't do the moonwalk. Instead I squealed, jumped into his lap, threw my arms around his neck, and kissed him. I made it fast, just a quick couple presses of my lips to his, then leaned away so I could see his eyes.

He was smiling at me now—a full-on, white-teeth, happy-face smile—and his arms had come around my waist, his hands on my hips. My stomach and heart were trying to out-flutter each other as I grinned down at him.

This was good. This was a good compromise. Sure, I might've been in denial. Sure, I might've been setting myself up for heartache in the long term. But…whatever. I could deal with all that later. Much later. Like, over a year from now later.

Right now I was sitting on Duane's lap and had just been given a free pass to kiss him as much as I liked for the next thirteen and a half months.

Jessica

13

> "The real voyage of discovery consists not in seeking new landscapes, but in having new eyes."
>
> —MARCEL PROUST, *THE PRISONER*

YESTERDAY WE'D SEALED OUR DEAL with a kiss at the community center, and this morning he'd texted me.

Duane: I'm taking you out tonight.
Me: Where?
Duane: Someplace where we can go fast.
Me: What time?
Duane: 5
Me: Sounds good.

I was ready to go at 4:30 p.m. even though I'd changed outfits ten times. I might have been a tad excited. Just a tad.

I decided on a white sweater dress with a built-in slip, long sleeves, and a short flared skirt. Because of how fitted the slip was over my ribs and chest, the dress was a pain to put on or take off. Not helping matters were about thirty little buttons running down the back, but I loved how it looked on me. I paired it with my tan boots and wore my hair down and wavy.

Duane was ten minutes early, and this time my daddy was home. Thankfully, Jackson was not. Daddy invited Duane in, offered him a beer (which Duane refused in favor of sweet tea, because he saw the offer for the trap it was), and they discussed sports, local politics, and cars for about twenty minutes. Then Daddy waved us off, giving me a small smile and Duane a firm handshake and squinty eyes.

Once again, Duane was driving his Road Runner. This time I was able to ogle the car as we approached, appreciate its simple, elegant lines before he opened the passenger door for me.

Even though this was our second date, everything felt different. Better. The weight of my dishonesty had been lifted. I was all in. Everything was out in the open and we had a deal. Therefore it felt more like a true date. Like I could relax and just enjoy his company because I knew we had thirteen and a half months together.

Once we were settled inside, we grinned at each other.

Feeling downright giddy, I asked, "Where are we going?"

"You'll see," he answered mysteriously, his eyes sliding over my body with blatant appreciation.

That got me warm. Yes, it did.

I really, really liked how Duane Winston looked at me. He employed every ounce of his attention and focus, like he was making plans.

Then his gaze snagged on my bare knee. "Are you going to be warm enough in that dress?"

I shrugged. "I hope so. But since you won't tell me where we're going, I guess we'll see."

Duane gave me another once-over as he brought the engine to life and we were off.

At first—for the first two minutes or so—neither of us said a word. I'd wondered about this, worried that our agreement might make things strained. Not willing to sit in silence any longer, I resolved to speak.

"So—" I said.

"So—" he said at the same time.

We both laughed, and I offered, "You go first."

Duane cleared his throat, his expression suddenly somber, and began again, "So, about that syphilis diagnosis…"

I threw my head back and laughed, was pleased when I heard his answering rumbly laughter join mine and felt him place his hand on my knee and squeeze. I was happy when he left it there.

When I was finished with my giggles, I hit him on the shoulder and *tsk*ed. "I can't believe no one thought that joke was funny last night. That joke was way funnier than they gave it credit for. STD humor is just lost on some people."

"It was funny, but I think maybe—given the fact that Kip

Sylvester is your boss and his daughter was present—it wasn't surprising he didn't laugh. And don't mind Billy. He can't laugh at anything in public. I bet he was dying laughing on the inside."

I turned my attention back to Duane. "What? Why? Why can't Billy laugh at anything in public?"

"'Cause everyone knows him, who he is. Heck, half of the guys at the jam session work for him. And I think he's considering a run for county commissioner in two years."

"Oh, goodness. That sounds awful. I can't imagine being a public servant, all those people and their opinions."

"I know, right? People are the worst."

His comment made me laugh again and I studied him for a beat, wondering what other hidden layers he might reveal.

To this end, I said, "So, Duane Winston, tell me about yourself."

"What do you want to know?"

"Tell me...tell me something I don't know. What's your favorite movie?"

"Anything with a good car chase."

I smiled at the predictability of his response, but it didn't feel quite right. "Why do I doubt your answer?"

Duane's gaze slid to mine and he gave me a half smile. "You don't like a good car chase?"

"I didn't say that. I just meant, why do I feel like there's more to you than your stereotypical guy answer?"

His hand gripped, then relaxed on the steering wheel. "There's a reason we eat popcorn during a movie. If I want to zone out, be brainless and entertained, then I watch TV, go to a movie. If I want a good story, then I read a book."

"Aha!" I poked his shoulder gently. "There it is. You're

a book person. That's probably because your mother was a librarian."

"Yeah, she likely had an influence…" Duane squirmed a little in his seat, his eyebrows tugging low over his eyes like he was deep in thought. "I reckon most people look at us Winston boys and see a bunch of hillbillies, sons of Darrell Winston, con man and criminal. In some ways, I guess we are. We like our cars, barbecue, and banjo music. But our momma wanted more for us. She demanded it. Momma basically put each of us through a kind of finishing school."

"How'd she manage that?"

"Books. Lots of books. At least one a week to expand our vocabulary and our minds. The classics were required reading. Plus table manners—all manners—were taken very seriously. Words like *ain't*, which isn't a word, weren't allowed in the house, though we've all grown lazy with proper grammar as we've grown older. She also taught us how to dance."

"Dance? She taught you to dance?"

"Yep."

"Like, what? Like the waltz?"

He nodded faintly, clearly lost in a memory of his mother. I didn't interrupt. Instead I admired his profile, feeling the depths to which I'd missed him. I'd missed him so much. For the first time in a week I felt like I could draw a complete breath. I knew I was falling hard and fast, but I didn't care. We had just over a year and I planned to abandon myself to it, to him. I was completely and totally *all in*.

At length Duane shook his head like he was coming out of a trance and added, "But really, I think I'd prefer to be out there myself. Living, doing, seeing for myself."

I was nodding before he finished his thought. "Yes, exactly.

That's exactly how I feel. I actually get frustrated sometimes when I read travel blogs or magazines. It's like, *I* want to be the one out there doing it, not reading about someone else's experience."

Duane nodded at my words like he truly understood my perspective, but then he surprised me by asking, "So then, what have you done?"

"What do you mean?"

"I mean, how have you lived? What have you done? And that crazy stuff you did while we were kids doesn't count."

Now I squirmed a bit in my seat. Duane shifted like he was about to remove his hand, so I covered it with mine, pressed it to my knee.

Eventually I admitted the sad truth. "I've done a lot of planning, getting ready. But honestly, nothing exciting so far." I added with a sad sigh, "No big trips or adventures."

His eyes were on the road, but how he'd slightly inclined his head toward me and stroked his thumb over my kneecap told me he was thinking about my response. His thoughtful expression transitioned into a frown.

"You don't need a big trip to have an adventure. There's plenty of adventures to be had right here."

I *tsk*ed. "You know what I mean."

"I guess I do…and I guess I don't. I'm just saying, if you can't have an adventure where you are, what makes you think you'll have an adventure anywhere else?"

I felt the answer was obvious; nevertheless I said, "Because it'll be someplace new. I've already done and seen everything there is to do and see here."

"Well, enlighten me then. What adventures are there to be had in Green Valley, Tennessee?"

I assumed his question was meant to be ironic, so I laughed and responded, "None."

"Wrong."

I scoffed. "No. Not wrong. We have three restaurants, three bars, Cooper's Field, and the jam session on Friday nights. Therein lies the sum total of what Green Valley has to offer."

"Wrong," he repeated, but this time the corner of his mouth tugged upward like he was fighting a smile.

"Oh really? What am I missing then?"

"Hiking, fishing, canoeing, camping."

"Come on, Duane. We hiked and explored all through these mountains when we were kids. You said kid stuff doesn't count."

He hesitated for a minute, then said, "Bungee jumping."

I nearly choked. "Bungee jumping? You've been bungee jumping?"

"Yes. And skydiving."

"Holy crap! When? Where?"

"I'll take you."

My chest constricted with a healthy dose of fear, and my immediate response was to shake my head. "No. No, thank you. I think I'll pass."

"You said you wanted adventure."

"Adventure isn't the same thing as trying to kill yourself."

Now he laughed. "It's not that dangerous."

"Says the daredevil, Duane Winston."

"So, you're telling me that when you leave and go on your wanderlust walkabouts, you're planning on having only nice, quiet, safe adventures?" He made a face, like he was disappointed in me. "That's not living. That's just more time spent planning."

Again I squirmed in my seat and grumbled, "No."

"Yes," he countered.

Mild irritation made my chest and cheeks hot, and I glared at him. "Just because I don't wish to throw myself out of a plane and plummet to the earth doesn't mean my adventures will be boring."

"You don't have to throw yourself out of a plane, because I'll be there to push you." With this he glanced at me, grinning like a devil, and winked.

My mouth fell open and a small strangled sound of disbelief emerged from my throat. But then I laughed through my outrage, because his expression was both adorably and thrillingly mischievous. Soon he was laughing too, likely at my stunned and annoyed expression.

While laughing, I reached over and squeezed his leg. "Well, I wouldn't want to be a burden."

He caught my hand. "It would be no burden at all. I'm happy to offer my services anytime you need to be tossed out of a plane."

"Or off a bridge?"

"Or a dock."

"Or a boat."

"Yes. Even a boat. I'll be happy to push you any time pushing is required." As he said these words we came to a stoplight and he turned just his head, giving me a happy smile and squeezing my hand. His smile was dazzling, and I felt my own lips curve into a wide grin.

Goodness, I loved it when he smiled, like he was doing now. I felt like finally, *finally* I was seeing the real Duane Winston, the one he only shared with a rare and worthy few. And I fell a bit more. I enjoyed this feeling of falling, the thrill and certainty of it, of his worthiness.

"I feel I must reciprocate," I said quietly, losing myself in his closeness, the genuine warmth and affection clear in his handsome face. "Please let me know if I can ever be of service pushing you in a similar fashion."

I watched him take a deep breath, his gaze moving over my features—still warm with affection—and he said in a near whisper, "My momma once told me, you don't need to be pushed in order to fall. I don't think you'll need to do much pushing, Jessica."

♥

It took us about another hour to reach our destination, during which we fell into easy conversation. He told me tales about crazy customers, and I had to guess whether they were true or false. The most outrageous stories turned out to be true, thereby shaking my faith in humanity and reminding me that fifty percent of the population fell beneath one hundred on the IQ curve.

Before I knew it, time was up and we'd arrived. I squinted out the windshield and realized where we were.

"The Canyon? You brought me to watch the dirt races?" I was not complaining, not at all. I was merely surprised, and maybe a little nervous.

Duane nodded as he pulled into a space toward the front. It was conspicuously empty, like it was his spot, though I couldn't see a marker that marked it as such.

He popped his door open as he cut the engine. "Yes. We can watch the races, but there's good food, too. And we can talk in between. Just stay close; things can get crazy."

He came around the car and reached for my door just as I

opened it, offering his hand. I took his and he kept mine. Our fingers remained entwined as we walked toward the closest of three bonfires. I wasn't usually much of a hand holder, but I liked his hands—the large roughness of them—and I liked how the contact kept us close.

"Are you hungry? There's some tailgaters up ahead. They have ribs cooking, chili, corn bread, and coleslaw, though the coleslaw isn't as good as the stuff served at the community center on Fridays."

I made a note of how wistful he sounded about the community center coleslaw. I knew Julianne MacIntyre made it every week and decided to interrogate the recipe out of her at some point.

"Chili and corn bread sound good," I responded while rubbernecking without shame, endeavoring to scope out our surroundings.

Duane was right. It wasn't even 7:30 p.m. and things already looked a little crazy. I'd never been to the Canyon before, never seen one of the dirt races, never had an occasion to do so.

This wasn't some country fair with wholesome dirt racing. This place felt dangerous, risky. The air smelled like various types of smoke—wood fire, charcoal, and engine oil—and would have been overwhelming in the hot, stagnant summer. But borne on the cool wind of late fall, it was heady, but not overpowering.

I noticed a group of punk-rock-looking folks and their girls making out next to one of the bonfires—like, *for real* making out—black-labeled bottles of bourbon lining their blanket. Two of the guys were arguing over one of the girls, and tempers appeared close to snapping.

As well, I felt a little overdressed. And by overdressed I should say *over-clothed*. The night was mild, but it was still cold; yet every woman we passed was wearing either a miniskirt or leather pants, sometimes a leather miniskirt. And their tops showed more skin than my bathing suit.

"Not everyone is friendly," Duane said, obviously noticing my gaping.

I pressed myself closer to Duane. He took the hint and wrapped his arm around my shoulders.

"The groups here segregate themselves, don't mix much, except on the track."

"Which group is yours?" I glanced up at him, watched as his eyes narrowed and he twisted his mouth to the side.

"I don't really have a group."

"Really?"

"Yeah. I mean, I know just about all the racers—the ones who take it seriously—and we have a mutual respect thing going on. But I don't usually associate with any one group."

"A lone wolf?"

He smirked, his gaze sliding to mine. "Something like that."

We passed several clusters of people, either gathered around one of the bonfires or lingering within a circle created by their cars. Several were calm, sedate, like they were tailgating at a football game. Others were rowdy—fighting, drinking, and screwing for everyone to see. I supposed everyone had a different idea of what constituted a good time.

As well, every age was represented and, seemingly, several socioeconomic strata. I saw Corvettes next to souped-up Honda Civics, a rusted-out Nissan truck parked beside a brand-new Acura. Some of the groups looked like they were my age or younger—college and high school kids—and several seemed to be at least twenty or thirty years my senior. And some groups were mixed.

After assessing the crowd, the first thing I noticed was that the Canyon wasn't really a canyon. The Canyon was an abandoned mine.

Street racing was obviously illegal, as it was almost everywhere. Racing at the Canyon, though not technically sanctioned by local law enforcement, wasn't an arrestable offense. Betting on the races, however, was illegal. But I'd heard rumors that betting was rampant and thousands of dollars exchanged hands every weekend; the race winners supposedly went home with a big cut.

We eventually approached two giant Dodge trucks with grills and tables set up just in front of the truck beds. We stood in a line of about twenty or thirty people, all waiting to grab food. The man in front of us glanced over his shoulder, and his eyes moved down, then up my body. I scowled at his blatant leering.

"Keep your eyes to yourself, Devon," Duane growled, his arm turning me so I was pressed against his side.

The man's attention shifted to Duane. Then his eyes grew large and he turned completely around, a big smile on his face.

"I haven't seen you in weeks." He reached for and grabbed Duane's hand, shaking it with enthusiasm. "Wait 'til I tell the boys you're here."

I studied this Devon person as he smiled at Duane with something like worship. He was about my age, maybe a bit older, looked like that actor David Oyelowo, and wore a black leather jacket, blue jeans, and boots. He was obviously part of some biker club, but I didn't recognize the emblem on his chest.

"Let me buy you and your lady dinner."

"No, thanks, I got it."

Devon's brown eyes glanced at me, then back to Duane, and he lifted his dark eyebrows. I heard Duane sigh.

"Jess, this is Devon St. Cloud—or just Saint if you prefer to use his club name. Devon, this is Jess." Duane made the introductions reluctantly, like his good manners required it.

Devon's strong hand enveloped mine as he gushed, "Your old man is the best. The best. Ain't nobody race like Red. We used to race Humvees around dirt tracks in Afghanistan when I was stationed there, and I thought those guys were crazy. But nobody compares to Red."

I couldn't help my smile, liking Devon a bit more now he was praising *my old man*. Plus I liked that his biker name was Saint.

"What? Red is here?"

This comment came from someone else farther up in the line, and I craned my neck to the side to see who. Turns out this was unnecessary because we were soon surrounded by several people—male and female—all anxious to see Duane, shake his hand, and meet me as well.

It became a bit overwhelming, to be honest, and everyone wanted to know the same thing: Was Duane racing? And, if so, which races? And how was he feeling?

In the end we weren't allowed to buy our dinner because a guy named Sheldon bought us a tray of food without asking permission. This caused a bit of an upset as Devon and his biker brethren had offered first. Duane used this distraction as an opportunity to move us away from the food line.

As he pulled me away, I said, "Lone wolf, huh?"

He bent and whispered in my ear, "They only like me so

much because I make them money and they enjoy watching me race."

I shook my head. "Do you know everyone?"

"More or less." He shrugged. "Or they know me."

We were stopped a few more times on our way to wherever Duane had in mind. In between greeting people and introductions, Duane explained the locale was likely named the Canyon because of the red clay and dirt making up the race track and the exposed rock faces on three sides of the track. As well, the property was private, owned by some conglomerate who'd left it abandoned years ago and clearly hadn't protested its use as a regional racing ring.

The oval track covered two acres but setup was required for each weekend night. Big industrial lights had been set into the exposed rock face earlier in the day, illuminating the track. The three large bonfires were off to one side—the side not enclosed by rock—and this was where all the cars lined up and parked. I estimated at least two hundred people were gathered around the bonfires, drinking, socializing, and trash-talking while sizing up the competition.

He was right. Everyone seemed to know or know of Duane, though we didn't loiter to talk for very long. Everyone we encountered appeared greatly surprised to see someone with him. I got the sense that he typically came alone and said very little.

We took our chili, corn bread, and sweet tea to a big boulder close enough to the track to see everything, but not so close we'd get covered in dirt. A race was about to start.

"You look tense," Duane remarked between spoonfuls of chili.

I realized I'd been frowning at the line of cars revving

their engines. I glanced at Duane and lifted my chin toward the starting lineup.

"I've heard stories about cars smashing into the rock walls, and head-on collisions causing broken bones and leaving people unconscious."

"Those rumors are true."

I felt my frown deepen. "Why would anyone do it, then? If it's so dangerous?"

He shrugged. "Because it isn't easy; it takes patience and skill. Because it is dangerous and it's fun to be a little scared sometimes."

"A *little* scared?"

He gave me a crooked grin, his eyes on my mouth. "That's right. Just a little."

I snorted my disbelief. If dirt racing made Duane *a little scared* and skydiving wasn't all that dangerous, I wondered what could possibly frighten Duane.

At the same moment, a shot went off. The cars lurched forward and sped out of the starting line like demons from hell, the engines drowning all other sound. My eyes were glued to the action in front of me, how the cars—some old, some new, all souped-up—slipped and skidded all over the dirt track. Two of the seven spun out at the first turn, one of them bouncing off the rock wall.

I sucked in a startled breath and felt Duane's hand close over mine. "He'll be fine. He wasn't going that fast."

I leaned against his solid frame and watched the remainder of the race with rapt attention. Only three of the cars made it to the finish line and it was sickeningly close. The whole affair was irresponsible and dangerous, and I thought I'd disdain it.

I was wrong. I loved it. My heart was beating fast and yet I was sitting still.

I loved the sound of revving engines, the smell of engine oil mingled with smoke and earth. I loved the general air of excitement, camaraderie, adventure. I loved how these people loved their cars and raced them hard, used them, risked them. When the cars sped by, I felt the rush of wind, the vibration in my chest.

Of course it helped seeing the people who crashed walk away from their cars with no assistance, looking more upset about losing the race and what had befallen their automobiles than about their cuts and bruises.

It was thrilling and everything seemed larger, brighter, clearer—likely a by-product of the adrenaline pumping through my veins.

I deduced the turns were by far the most dangerous part of the race. Maintaining control of over a thousand pounds of steel around a sharp corner, while traveling in excess of ninety miles per hour on a dirt track basically sounded impossible to me. But some of the cars managed it beautifully, artfully.

By the end of the fourth race I'd basically crawled into Duane's lap, and I squealed unthinkingly each time the cars rounded a curve. My squeals made Duane laugh and he held me tighter.

As soon as the—five this time—remaining competitors crossed the finish line, Duane peeled my fingers from where I'd dug them into his legs.

"Having a good time?" He nuzzled my neck, kissing it, then set me away and stood.

I turned to him and I'm sure my eyes were huge, as was my smile. "Yes, I'm having the best time and I never thought

I'd enjoy all this craziness, but it's amazing and I'm so glad you brought me."

He gave me and my run-on sentence a distracted half smile as he pulled out a pair of leather gloves from his jacket. "Good. That's good."

I glanced between him and the gloves he was pulling on, felt my own smile wane. He took off his jacket and handed it to me.

"Where are you…?" My mouth couldn't quite form the question because I already knew the answer. Abruptly, my heart thudded in my chest quite painfully, jumping around like it was trying to break free.

"Oh my God, Duane. Don't you dare."

At just that moment, movement caught my attention beyond Duane. Devon—the biker from earlier—and a woman I didn't recognize were walking toward us.

"I'll be right back." Duane brought my attention back to him, nudging my legs apart with his knee and stepping between them. He wrapped a gloved hand around the back of my head and bent to give my open mouth a kiss, and it was a great kiss. It made me feel like I was being tasted, savored, remembered. Or maybe he was trying to impart the memory to me. Either way, I wasn't going to forget it.

Too soon he straightened, holding my somewhat dazed but also panicked gaze for just a short moment—again, with plans in his eyes—then turned. Duane strolled away before I could think to protest again. As I watched him go, I stood, then sat. Then stood again. I didn't know what to do.

As Duane passed Devon, he shook the biker's hand, nodded toward me, patted him on the shoulder, and then continued on his way.

I watched the exchange with incredulity, studied Duane's long strides before he was completely swallowed by the crowd.

"Hey, Jess, this is Keisha. Mind if we keep you company?"

My eyes moved to Devon, then to his pretty lady friend, then back to Devon.

My voice cracked as I asked, "He's going to race, isn't he?"

The biker flashed me a big smile, like he thought my nerves were funny. "Yep. And I got two hundred dollars saying he comes in ten seconds ahead of the next-fastest car."

"Don't worry, baby." Keisha squeezed my arm and gave me a sweet smile. "Red ain't ever lost."

I sat back down on the boulder and placed Duane's jacket over my legs. It was still warm from his body.

He was going to race. And he'd sent a biker named Saint to watch over me.

A chill passed through me despite the added layer of his jacket. The food I'd eaten settled in my stomach like a cold lump. I was no longer having a good time.

I hardly noticed as the pair sat next to me, but I was irritated to hear how excited they were to watch *my old man's* race. It was one thing to watch people I didn't know, didn't intimately care about, risk their necks. It was quite another to sit on the sidelines and not lose my mind as Duane revved the engine of his Road Runner at the starting position.

I thought about running forward and throwing myself in front of his car. I thought about it…but I didn't. Instead I prayed and clasped my hands together. They were shaking. I was *not* okay with this turn of events.

If he hurt himself, I swore to God, I was going to kill him. And if he didn't hurt himself, I was going to demand he take me home at once. With each passing second my anxiety increased as did my feelings of helplessness.

I didn't want to watch him race. I was not amused.

By the time the starting shot echoed through the air, I'd worked myself up into a real tizzy, a temper tantrum befitting my bratty past. I wanted to close my eyes, bury my face in my hands, and wait 'til it was over, but I couldn't.

Duane immediately pulled ahead and my stomach dropped. Devon and Keisha whooped excitedly, both standing. He was the first to reach the turn and every muscle in my body tensed, my nails digging in to the flesh of my palms, and I braced myself for the worst.

But the worst didn't come.

In fact, he didn't take the turn, he attacked it. He was, by far, the fastest I'd seen around the corner, and slingshotted around to the other side completely unscathed. His engine revved, sending thrills and worry to each of my nerve endings.

But after two more turns I realized Duane really knew what the hell he was doing. He was amazing.

Now my eyes were glued to Duane's Road Runner. Devon and Keisha's excited shouts faded, as it slid around the last return cone. He was in the lead by several car lengths. Rationally, I knew it was just an old car, but something about the way he drove it turned all that metal into a sexy machine. He drove with swagger, panache, control. How he could be so unbridled on the racetrack and yet dominate with precision at the same time rang my bell—like a blaring five-alarm fire bell ringing.

But I was still mad at him.

In fact, I was furious.

Or at least I thought I was.

I felt the roar of his engine as he charged over the finish line, chased by a cloud of dust. The crowd cheered and I was up on my feet moving toward his car. I was still wound up in a tight knot of worry and tension. It was cold outside, yet I was hot all over.

My jaw clenched and worked, and I rehearsed the words I wanted to say:

How dare you make me watch you almost kill yourself! You gave me no warning, you just left me and I'm so angry that I want to… want to…

I couldn't finish the thought because what I really wanted to do was rip his clothes off, which made no sense. It seemed my main problem centered on the fact that I didn't know if I was pissed off, turned on, or both.

Peripherally, I heard Devon call my name. I ignored him.

Then I heard snippets of conversations from the horde as my furious walk turned into an urgent jog. These conversations ranged from smart-assed remarks about how he never lost, to frustrated comments regarding how he shouldn't be allowed to race anymore because he always won, to serious discussions asking why he wasn't racing professionally.

By the time I reached him, he was out of the car and surrounded by a crowd. I didn't hesitate to push my way to the front. But once I arrived, and he was there in front of me, safe and sound, I stopped short. Some emotion clogged my throat, one I couldn't identify.

As soon as he saw me his face split into a giant grin and his eyes—burning brighter than I'd ever seen them—devoured mine. Duane grabbed my hand and pulled me forward, wrapped his arm around my waist and pressed my body to his.

Then he kissed me. Hard.

Caught by surprise, I braced my hands on his chest to steady myself, and I felt his heart thundering against my palm.

And I had only a single thought: I *needed* him. Right now. I needed to know he was okay, in one piece. My need felt positively feral. I needed to feel the strength and vitality of his body beneath my hands, and I needed his hands on me.

Our kiss elicited several more smart-ass comments paired with whistles, but I didn't care. I didn't know these people, and even if I did, it wouldn't have made much of a difference.

Duane leaned backward and away, though his arms still held me. Undeterred, I kissed his neck, reached under the hem of his navy-blue shirt to touch his skin.

He grabbed my hands and he was breathing hard. "Jess, wait a minute."

"Nope." I whispered the single word in his ear right before I used my tongue to suck it into my mouth. He stiffened and I heard him release a quiet groan.

"Red, looks like you got to go, son. We can send your cash later." This sentiment came from someplace over my shoulder. The man who'd said it was laughing, his raspy voice only serving to punctuate the meaning of his words.

Duane turned us around, used his strength and size to leverage me onto the bench seat, no longer protesting my liberal pawing. We were horizontal, and he returned my fevered kisses, taking control of my hungry explorations and harnessing them, giving the hot slide of our mouths finesse and purpose.

Although, peripherally I realized he'd shut the driver's side door, cocooning us inside his sexy machine. I also heard increased/louder comments, whistling, and now banging on the roof of the car.

Kneeling over me, he dipped his head to one side, his beard rough against my cheek and jaw, and growled in my ear, "Jessica, do you think you can give me a few minutes to drive us out of this crowd? Find a private spot?"

"I don't know if I can wait that long," I answered honestly, my breathing ragged with excitement even though the progress of my reaching hand had been frustrated by his belt.

Duane made a short noise of disbelief that soon turned into loud, rumbly laughter. The sound succeeded in tugging me somewhat out of my feral cloud. I saw he was smiling at me, his face just inches from mine.

I reluctantly returned his smile. "I'm actually kind of serious. I think if you breathed on me, I'd orgasm."

My confession made his eyes widen as he laughed again; then he squinted at me. "I'm kinda breathing on you now."

"No, you mistake my meaning. If you were to breathe on me *down there*"—I glanced down at myself meaningfully, then back to him—"I would totally come apart."

He sat up, his smile now a smirk. "That sounds like a dare."

"No. It's not a dare. It's a truth," I whispered, lost in his eyes. I realized one of his hands was up my skirt, digging into my bare thigh.

He searched my face in the dark car, as though hoping to read the veracity of my statement. The crowd surrounding us grew a bit more obnoxious and were now peeping through the windows. Duane shook himself. He withdrew his hands and set me away at the same time, lifting me to a more vertical position.

He engaged the ignition, revving it, as he glanced in his rearview mirror. "Put on your seat belt. We need to move."

I used the center seat belt, and then snuggled close to him, weaving my fingers into the hair at the back of his neck and using my other hand to stroke his inner thigh. He was tense. His muscles felt tight.

"Duane," I whispered in his ear, more breath than sound, "I'm not letting you leave this car until we make it to second base. At least."

He rolled the Road Runner forward slightly, nudging the crowd out of the way, giving me his profile. "Jess, you know how good I am at baseball, right?"

I got the feeling he was waiting for me to answer. "Yes, Duane. I know you're good at baseball."

His eyes slid to the side, collided with mine. Again, I saw intense focus, like he had plans and they all involved me.

"Do you think I'd settle for second base if I was sure I could steal home?"

Duane

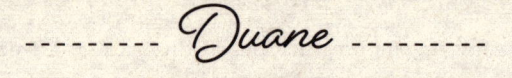

14

> "As you walk and eat and travel, be where you are. Otherwise you will miss most of your life."
>
> —JACK KORNFIELD, *BUDDHA'S LITTLE INSTRUCTION BOOK*

JESSICA JAMES TONGUING MY EAR, stroking my thigh, her knuckles brushing against my hard-on, all while I navigated back mountain roads.

It was a gauntlet.

While I drove, in between kisses she'd managed to pull off my shirt, unbuckle my belt, undo the button and the zipper of my jeans. She was single-mindedly focused on removing my clothes, but had yet to remove a single article of her own—an oversight requiring immediate rectification.

The only sound in the car was our breathing, the roar of the engine, and her soft moans of *please* and *hurry*.

But despite my earlier allusions to rounding the bases and her sexy little sounds and touches, the drive gave me the time I needed to gain perspective. I'd made up my mind a long time ago. Our first time wasn't going to be in a car.

I'd always figured, in the unlikely event Jessica agreed to my courtship, we would wait. I'd decided, likely after we'd confessed our undying love and devotion to each other and were engaged, we'd go on vacation together for an anniversary. It would be someplace I could romance her. Or maybe we would wait until we were married. That had always been my assumption.

My expectations hadn't factored in her life goals and ambitions.

We weren't going to have any anniversaries, romantic vacations, or a wedding night. We only had now. Regardless, despite her eagerness to consummate our abridged relationship, I couldn't completely shake off my years of frustrated hopes. It wouldn't be what I'd wanted, but I was damn determined to make it meaningful and memorable. Even if she didn't care about the where and how, I did.

No.

Nothing would be rushed or hurried. I would take my time, several times. We would have all night, not a quickie in my Road Runner.

Now if she would just stop dipping her fingers into my boxers, I'd be able to form a coherent thought.

I pulled into Hawk's Field. It was closer to the Canyon than it was to Green Valley. I didn't have the luxury of a forty-five-minute drive back into town. And I wasn't surprised to see we weren't the only car on the lot. But the field was massive, with several offshoots and dirt roads, plenty of space and cover for privacy.

As soon as I had the car in park and the lights off, I grabbed her hands and pulled them away from my body. I needed to think, and feeling her stiff nipples through her soft dress wasn't helping my state of mind.

"What—what are you doing?" she asked, sounding breathless.

I didn't answer. I made the mistake of releasing one of her hands so I could slide mine under her dress and she brought it down to my groin, stroking me through my boxers.

"Take off your pants," she ordered, her nails clawing at my jeans and redirecting the blood flow from my brain.

Again, I had to grab her wrist. "Jess—"

"I want you," she pleaded, biting my neck.

"Take off your dress."

"I'll take off my underwear. I thought I could just hike up my dress and climb on your lap," she said in a panting whisper.

The image her words conjured elicited an involuntary groan from the back of my throat, but I managed to say, "No fucking way, and we're not debating this. Take off your dress." I fingered one of the buttons at her back.

She freed one of her hands again and seemed to be trying to touch every inch of my bare skin on her way south. Her dress was already hiked up to her upper thighs because she was climbing onto my lap, rubbing herself on my leg. Basically, I was losing my mind.

"Duane, please. I need you. Please just let me—"

"I need your skin." I released her wrist and slid my hands from her knees to her hips, hiking the material up higher, revealing a scrap of white lace. But I didn't stop. I kept pushing the dress up, needing the weight of her bare breasts in my hands; not exactly sure what we were doing, where this was leading, and hoping I had enough sense once she was naked to rein myself in.

"Wait, Duane, wait."

The dress bunched up and became bulky. For the first time

since we entered the car, her hands moved away from my body voluntarily as she tried to withdraw them from her sleeves. I attempted to take advantage of the moment by unclasping her bra, but underneath the sweater material of her dress was a slip of some sort, and it was tight around her ribs and chest, restricting both our movements.

Not helping matters, she'd tried taking an arm out of her sleeve and her elbow was now caught between her body and the dress, immobilizing the hand. Her other arm was up and at an awkward angle, hitting the roof of the car.

I tried pushing the dress higher, but that just complicated matters, bunching it beneath her ribs.

I looked at her, and her face was red. I could tell by the set of her jaw she was frustrated. Jess was basically trapped in the material, straddling my hips, and flailing her torso from side to side as she tried to get free.

Then she started to cuss. She looked like an enraged kitten.

I couldn't help it. I laughed.

I gripped her hips, brought my forehead to her stomach just under the bunched fabric, and laughed against her bare skin.

"Duane Winston, are you laughing at me?" she growled, huffing a bit as she struggled with the dress.

"Yes. I am laughing at you." I couldn't stop laughing. I felt tears gather in my eyes. She looked so ridiculous and adorable, trapped in her dress. And I was relieved. Because the moment of levity had a sobering effect.

I heard her laugh a bit too, but it sounded irritated. "Well, if you could trouble yourself to stop laughing long enough, maybe you could help me out of this straitjacket. I'd really appreciate it."

I leaned back against the bench and studied her. "What can I do?"

"First of all, wipe that grin off your face."

I tried, I did. But instead I laughed again.

"Oh good Lord!" She paired her exclamation with an eye roll.

"Fine." I held my hands up, showing my surrender. "Fine. There are buttons?"

"Yes, but I don't think we'll be able to unfasten them with me in this position. Can you pull the dress back down?"

I nodded, concentrating on helping her untangle herself even as I mourned the loss of her skin. I pulled the slip down first, then the bulkier sweater fabric next. Her elbow was still caught, so I reached around her and tried to unbutton a few inches at the center of her back. She held my shoulder with her free hand for balance as I worked.

Pretty soon I realized I was going to need to *see* the buttons. They were round and small and slippery, and I couldn't get a good grip.

"Jess, you're going to need to get off my lap and turn around. I can't work these through the loops like this."

She huffed, released a long frustrated growl, and shouted, "This is unbelievable!"

I pressed my lips together. I wasn't going to laugh again, though I sorely wanted to. She was so angry and the cramped space of the car meant every time she twisted, the elbow caught inside her dress nearly knocked me in the nose, forehead, or chin.

I had to help her off my lap and felt her eyes on me as I set her bottom on the seat to my side.

"I can't believe you're laughing. You're still laughing."

"I'm not," I lied.

"You are!"

"It's just…" I turned her around so I could see the row of buttons running down her back; I swear there were a hundred of them. "Why would you wear this? Who helped you button up?"

"No one. I used a mirror."

"You must be crazy flexible."

"I am."

I stopped laughing. "Hush, let me concentrate."

I reached for the buttons again, but now she was laughing. And when she laughed, she shook. But her laugh was also pure magic. I let my forehead fall to her shoulder, my hands dropping to her waist, and just listened to the sound while I breathed her in.

My earlier conviction surfaced again: our first time wasn't going to be in a car. No. I wanted to be with her, make her laugh, make her crazy, take my time, take her time. Even if she didn't care about the where and how, I did.

As her laughter receded, I withdrew and gathered a fortifying breath, zipping my zipper and searching for my shirt.

She glanced over her shoulder and I noticed she'd freed her elbow from where it had been trapped in her dress, pushing it back through the sleeve. A smile lingered on her lips, but her eyebrows drew together with a question.

"What are you doing?"

"Take off your boots," I ordered gruffly, recovering my shirt and pulling it over my head.

She only hesitated for a second before I heard the zipper of her boots release and I glanced at her legs. Beneath the boots she'd been wearing long pink-and-black-striped socks that reached almost to her knees. I dug my fingers into my thighs to keep from touching her legs or rolling the socks down her sculpted calves.

"Duane?"

I lifted my eyes to hers; she was waiting for me to give direction.

"Take your panties off, Jessica."

She hesitated, then asked, "What about the dress?"

I shook my head. "Just the panties."

Her wide brown eyes studied my face for a beat and then she was lifting up her hips. I closed my eyes so I didn't have to see her shimmy out of her underwear, but I imagined her sweet center exposed and I nearly reached for her. When she finished, I felt her hesitate next to me.

I opened my eyes, found her staring at me. Her cheeks were flushed. As I suspected, she was again waiting for me to give direction. The fact she was so willing and trusting strengthened my resolve.

"Climb on my lap." My voice was softer this time.

She immediately did so, and reached for my fly at the same time.

I stilled her hands. "No. Leave it be."

"But—"

"Shhhh…" I slipped my fingers beneath her skirt, savoring the skin of her legs. Her hands came to my shoulders for balance, and her eyes grew hazy as I brushed the back of my knuckles up her inner thighs.

"Duane," she pleaded, both choking on and swallowing my name.

Lights from a passing car in the distance dimly illuminated the interior and I saw the Road Runner's windows were completely fogged.

I stroked her with the tip of my middle finger and her thighs clenched, her eyes closed, and she stutter-sighed. Moving one hand around to her ass, because she had an amazing ass, I held her in place and touched her again, parting her, entering her once, then teasing her with control and precision.

Watching Jessica was a revelation. Yeah, I was sporting angry wood at this point and my dick envied my hand, but how she responded to me, how she moved and sighed and pleaded, wound itself around my chest, filled my lungs. I experienced something akin to wonder.

She'd been right. It didn't take long. When she gripped my wrist as she panted and rocked on my lap, her mindlessness at my hands made me want to give voice to my possessive and claiming thoughts.

Your body is mine.
This is mine.
You are mine.

I didn't, though. Even as I felt her glorious body clench around my fingers and watched her come apart in beautiful waves, I swallowed the words.

Because she was mine.

But with an expiration date.

Jessica

15

> "The traveler sees what he sees; the tourist sees only what he has come to see."
>
> —G.K. CHESTERTON, *AUTOBIOGRAPHY*

I SAW DUANE AT CHURCH.

Reverend Seymour held two services every Sunday: the "fast service" at eight, and the "leisurely service" at ten.

Bethany Winston, when she was alive, and all the Winston boys went to the fast service. It lasted for an hour, tops. My momma called it fast-food religion. She complained loud and often about the regular attendees, calling them Catholics parading as Baptists.

My family had always attended the 10:00 a.m. service. It lasted anywhere between one and a half to three hours, and community worship was the name of the game. Sometimes it felt like everyone in attendance spoke at least once—asking for prayers, or saying a special prayer, or giving witness. Even after church was over, it was still going on. Groups of people met in the hall. They socialized, ate doughnuts, held prayer circles, and drank weak coffee.

For this reason I'd hardly ever seen Duane at church, and I likely wouldn't have, except my daddy unexpectedly woke me up early Sunday morning for a heaping helping of fast-food religion.

I suspected he was anxious to get Sunday service out of the way because the Cowboys were playing the Patriots at noon. This suspicion was confirmed when I spotted the fixings for nachos and a six-pack of Corona in the fridge—my father's version of wild and reckless behavior.

We arrived a few minutes early and sat in the back. Duane and three of his brothers—Billy, Cletus, and Beau—arrived a short time later and strolled to one of the middle pews. At first I was struck speechless by the sight of them: four tall fine-looking men, with broad shoulders and narrow hips, dressed in their Sunday uniform of black pants and white button-down shirts, moving with an intrinsic kind of swagger, grace, and confidence in their step.

Really, it was too much handsome. It felt like an assault.

The last time I'd seen so many male Winstons together all at once was when I was thirteen and all six of them were at a church picnic. Roscoe, Beau, and Duane had been in braces at the time. They were cute-handsome then. But now they were all grown up. I imagined it would be difficult for any red-blooded female to keep focus on the worship with an entire pew of Winston men in attendance.

As soon as my wits recovered from the Winston-handsome assault, I thought about calling out or making some sign to Duane, but I felt my daddy's narrowed eyes on me and therefore opted to remain quiet.

Furthermore, I felt conflicted about how our date had ended the night before. I'd assumed things were going splendidly. Well, it had gone splendidly until the very end when I'd tried to reciprocate his wonderful ministrations, and—instead of enthusiastically taking me up on the offer—he'd gently pushed away my advances. He drove me to my parents' house, mumbling something about having me home by a respectable time. Once there, I received a kiss on the cheek, and he left without making any new plans.

Service started and I couldn't concentrate. For me, the difficulty was having Duane within such close proximity. It's problematic for your soul when your body is recalling fleshy pursuits from the night before, and the week before that, and the week before that. I felt a twinge of embarrassment at how I'd behaved, how I'd been behaving since weeks ago at the community center, how I'd basically thrown myself at him multiple times, and how he'd gently rejected me each time.

Maybe he didn't want my enthusiasm.

Maybe he wanted to take things slow.

Or maybe my fervor—for his touch and kisses and embrace—was a turnoff.

This last theory didn't sit right. He seemed to like it, liked making me feel good, watching me lose my control. Maybe he just didn't want to lose *his* control…

As well, this behavior was not typical for me, and my thoughts turned inward as I tried to determine why I'd been acting so out of character.

Yes, I liked to kiss and be kissed, flirt and have fun. However, anything beyond kissing hadn't ever felt quite natural with anyone else. Putting on the brakes in the past had been effortless, and I'd mindfully explored at my own pace, even the guy (a.k.a. the Shetland pony) I'd lost my virginity with. In college, if I felt pressured by a boy to round the bases, I'd move on. Walking away had been easy.

Yet, with Duane…well, I realized I didn't feel in control. I felt needy. I felt urgency. I felt desperate. I wanted to be with him or close to him all the time. When we weren't together, I was thinking about him, specifically conversations we'd had as kids and adolescents, and viewing them through a new lens. He was becoming dear to me with alarming speed because I was allowing our history to tangle with our present.

And, truthfully, part of the problem was I just liked him so much.

I wasn't going to play games—games were dishonest—but I made a solemn promise to be more circumspect and careful about flinging my heart *and panties* at him in the future. He'd caught me unaware with his backstage trickery, then his vulnerable honesty at the lake. I decided I was going to slow down, adopt a more mindful attitude. If he wanted to take things slow, then I could take things slow, too.

When the service was over just thirty-five minutes after it had begun, I was surprised my father didn't rush out of church. He even placed a staying hand on my arm when I moved to leave the pew.

"Just a sec, Jess."

I glanced at him, allowing my confusion to show on my face.

My daddy gave me a small smile and lifted his chin toward the aisle where people were filtering out. "Your young man is here. Wouldn't be right, leaving without a word to Duane."

I squinted at my father, immediately suspicious of his intentions. At best my father was indifferent to all my previous boyfriends—the ones he'd met anyway—and at worst he'd been dismissive and rude.

"Daddy, is this your way of telling me you like Duane Winston?" I whispered.

"No. *This* is my way of telling you I like Duane Winston." He cleared his throat and returned my squinty expression. "Jess, I like Duane Winston."

I couldn't help the surprised laugh that bubbled forth or the smile of wonder that claimed my features as I studied my daddy. "But you don't like anybody."

"That's because ain't nobody good enough for you."

"And Duane is?"

"No. But his momma, rest her soul, was the best sort. Now, if I had my pick, I'd have rathered Cletus or Billy, but you know how Jackson and I are worthless with cars. It would be nice to have a mechanic in the family."

I'm sure my eyes bulged. "Daddy. We just started dating!"

"Yeah, but it's clear that man has his mind set on the long term, and if Duane Winston turns out to be a reason for you to stay in Green Valley instead of following through with your absurd plans, then I'll happily put up with him courting my daughter."

I gave my daddy a sad smile and my heart fell just a tad. He didn't bring up my plans to leave often, but when he did, he always used words like *absurd*, *reckless*, *preposterous*, *misguided*, and *foolish*—stopping just short of calling me stupid. I didn't like disappointing my parents, so I never brought them up.

"Hello, sir."

I twisted back toward the aisle, finding Duane standing just inside our pew with his hand outstretched to my father.

The other three Winstons were loitering in the pew to my right. I realized they were all waiting to pay their respects.

After greeting my father, Duane turned his attention to me. He didn't offer his hand. Instead he stuffed both into his pockets, nodding once in my direction and saying, "Jessica," in that way he did, with a slight whisper, and giving me the entirety of his intense focus.

"Hi, Duane." I tried to be circumspect and mindful—after all we were still in church—but it didn't work. My simple greeting sounded beyond delighted even to my ears, verging on enthusiastic. Music only I could hear switched on; this time it was "Just the Way You Are," by Bruno Mars—except the *she*s were replaced with *he*s.

Goodness, I was pathetic.

Because of the distracting music in my head and the intensity of Duane's attention, I missed most of the other conversation and the friendly chitchat between my daddy and the rest of the Winston boys. I was only able to recover when Duane shifted his attention back to my father.

"I imagine you and Jess have plans for the day?" I heard my daddy ask.

We didn't. We hadn't made any plans.

Therefore, I was surprised when Duane nodded. "Yes, sir. We do."

"What are you kids up to?" he asked, using his sheriff's voice.

"We're heading to the shop and I'm planning to teach Jessica how to change a tire."

I'm sure my face betrayed my astonishment. Out of the corner of my eye, I saw Beau try to hide his smirk, and I was glad my back was mostly to my father so he couldn't see my expression.

"Good idea, son. While you're at it, teach her how to check the fluids, change the oil, and such. Then she can teach me and Jackson."

"Be happy to, sir." Duane gave my daddy a short respectful nod, then returned his eyes to mine; once again I was struck by how he was looking at me.

He was looking at me like he had *plans*.

♥

"Brown sugar? Why would he put brown sugar in the radiator?"

"Because someone told him it would stop the leak."

"Did it?"

"No. Brown sugar doesn't work. But eggs do."

I'd left church with Duane. All the Winstons had driven their own cars. Now I was facing him, one leg tucked under me, my elbow resting on the bench seat of his Road Runner and my face propped in my palm. I stared at his profile, trying not to notice how he'd rolled his shirtsleeves to his forearms. The man had beautiful forearms.

"Eggs? People put eggs in their radiator?"

"Yep. I've done it before to stop a leak, in a pinch. Some places in these mountains it's easier to find a henhouse than it is to find electrical tape."

"Why do eggs work and not brown sugar?"

"I reckon because they're heavier when cooked, sink in hot water. Brown sugar gums up but it floats."

I stared at Duane for a long moment, thinking about his reasoning. "Huh...that's crazy."

He shrugged as we pulled into the Winston Brothers Auto Shop. "I've seen crazier. People with no money, desperate to have a working car are worse than patients with no health insurance or access to a doctor. They'll try anything."

"Tell me something else."

"Like what?" He didn't park out front, instead opting to wind the car around to the back of the building—which I thought was odd for exactly three seconds. Then I remembered it was Sunday. I surmised he didn't want anyone knowing we were here and therefore checking to see if the shop was open for business.

"Something about cars and wackadoodle customers. Tell me something else weird or funny."

Duane cut the engine and glanced at me. "Let's see… Sometimes people will complain about the cost of service, but we can't do anything about how much parts cost. So Cletus came up with the idea of adding fake line items to spread the cost around."

"Like what?"

"Like muffler bearings."

"Muffler bearings?" I asked just as Duane exited. I was already out with the door shut by the time he made it to my side, despite his hustling.

"Yeah. It's strange." Duane took my hand, frowning at the car door behind me like he was irritated with it for letting me out. "People won't question an itemized bill as long as each individual charge is small. I came up with a few fictitious charges after arguing with this one guy about the cost of a new transmission."

"What are some of yours?"

"Well, let's see…" Duane's eyes went up and to the right as we walked toward the back of the shop. "Blinker fluid."

I giggled. "Blinker fluid? You told people they needed blinker fluid?"

He nodded, a reluctant smile tugging his mouth to the side. "Or spark plugs for a diesel engine, power antenna fluid, that kind of stuff."

I shook my head, laughing harder. "I can't believe no one has caught on."

"I don't think they want to catch on. They feel like they're getting a good price on the main work, and no one really wants to know how their car works. People just want it to work; they want it fixed." He released my hand in order to open the locked door and flipped on the overhead lights as we entered. The space was just as cold as the outside and smelled like a medley of oil and actual car fluids.

"I can see that. I mean, if you told me my car needed muffler bearings, I wouldn't know enough to contradict you."

"We don't do it to everyone, just people who are perpetual complainers, or we get a sense ahead of time who might be trouble. Watch your step." His voice echoed in the cavernous shop and he squeezed my hand, lifting it as he indicated a muffler on the cement floor directly in our path.

I followed his lead, careful to watch where I stepped, and spoke as I thought. "It's interesting to me, how some people need to be pacified and don't even know it—about themselves, I mean."

"Lots of people are like that. Almost everybody, to one degree or another."

"Yeah, maybe. I can see that. I'd like to think I will always want the truth from everybody, no matter what, no matter how uncomfortable or hurtful. But I'm sure there are some situations where remaining ignorant is likely best."

"I agree, to an extent." We skirted the garage to a side door, then navigated two landings of stairs to a big room. It appeared to be a combination office, break room, and apartment. A big desk and computer sat along one wall facing the window; a small cot, counter, fridge, and sink were along the other. File cabinets lined the third, and a single round Formica table with three chairs sat in the center.

"To an extent?" I asked.

"Yeah, to an extent."

He left me at the door and crossed to one of the file cabinets. I wandered in after him, glancing around as he fished in a drawer for a few seconds. "Be more specific. What do you mean *to an extent*?"

He then withdrew something wrapped in a plastic bag and poked a hole to rip it open. "Well, take you for example."

"Me?"

"Yeah, you. You're almost too honest."

I considered him and his statement for a beat, not sure if it was a compliment, or an insult, or a complisult. When I couldn't make up my mind, I asked, "Is that a good thing or a bad thing?"

"A good thing, real good," he answered with no hesitation, drawing a set of new coveralls out of the plastic bag. "I like it. I've always liked it. But I worry for you sometimes."

Now, that made my insides feel soft and warm. I was walking toward him without realizing I was moving; obviously he had me caught in some kind of charming tractor beam. "You worry for me?"

"Yes. Most of the time what you're thinking is on your face, like an open book for anyone to read. I guess…" He paused like he didn't know whether or not to continue, but then eventually shrugged. "It reminds me of my momma and my sister. You're guileless, trusting, and that's great for me. But it can also make you a target."

"I'm not *that* trusting."

Duane's eyes narrowed and he issued me a sly smile. "Yes, you are."

"I'm not," I protested, feeling my hackles rise.

"Okay, whatever you say." He shrugged, handing me the coveralls, obviously making a half-assed effort to pacify me.

I clenched my jaw, liking and disliking the way his sly smile lingered. "You think I'm naive. I am not naive. I'm worldlier than you know." *Naive* had always sounded like an insult to me, akin to childish.

"I'm just saying, when you trust someone, you *really* trust that person. You've always been that way, ever since we were kids."

I studied him, wondering why we were talking about this. I eventually asked, "Why are we talking about this? Are you trying to tell me not to trust you?"

"I would never tell you that."

"That's not a satisfactory answer."

His features cracked with an involuntary smile. Then he took six steps forward, walking me backward until I was against the wall. Though he was invading my space, he didn't touch me. I had to lift my chin to keep administering the dirty look I'd adopted.

"Jessica," he whispered, his gaze sweeping over my face like he was attempting to memorize this dirty look I was giving him. "My priority is making sure all your dreams come true. You can trust me on that."

"But can I trust you not to push me into a lake while I'm in my Sunday best? Or switch out my travel magazines with urology journals?"

He nodded and placed a gentle kiss on my nose, but as he retreated he said, "No."

"No?"

"No. If I get a chance to push you into a lake, I'm probably going to take it, especially if you're wearing that dress." His eyes flickered down just briefly, then back to mine.

I huffed, felt my dirty look transform into a disappointed frown. "See now, I've been working under the assumption you liked me."

Duane's sly smile returned and his eyes heated. I recognized this look; it was his *I've got plans* look. "I do like you, Jessica. See now, that dress is white. And if it got wet, it wouldn't matter if you left it on or took it off."

I kept my eyes narrowed, though I felt my own involuntary smile tug at the corner of my lips. A lovely spreading warmth moved from my chest to my stomach to my thighs. I remembered the solemn promises I'd made to myself during church: not to fling my heart or my panties in his direction, to be circumspect and mindful.

He was making it very hard to keep my solemn promises, let alone be mindful.

Nevertheless, and even though I was starting to feel that uncontrollable, desperate, building sense of urgency, I managed to squeak out, "I'd like some privacy while I change, please."

The light behind Duane's eyes wavered, like I'd said something to confuse him. "You want some privacy?"

I nodded.

"Really?" He took a step back.

I nodded again.

His smile was gone and in its place was a thoughtful—verging on concerned—frown; he examined me for a bit longer, then said, "You can trust me, Jess. You know that, right?"

"I know. And I do—"

"Good."

"*To an extent*."

He smile-scowled at my use of his earlier words, then shook his head like I was a nut. "Fine, I'll meet you downstairs, Princess. We'll be changing a tire first."

I gave him two thumbs up. "Sounds good, Red."

His scowl deepened, but so did his smile as he turned toward the door and yanked it open. I heard him mutter as he left, "Maybe after we can go find a lake."

♥

We changed four tires. The shop had one of those high-powered thingamadoodles, yet he insisted we do it the old-fashioned way—with a car jack and a tire iron.

Next, he showed me how to check the oil and various car fluids, remarking on the differences between several makes and models, like the fact old VW Bugs' engines were air-cooled and didn't have radiators. I was having fun, mostly because watching Duane in his element was fun.

I realized Duane Winston loved cars. He loved how they worked, how each car was different, nuanced, a puzzle to be solved. And he told me more stories about nutty customers that made me laugh even though I couldn't quite follow them. One was about a man whose air filter was sucked into the throttle body, and another described a customer who added eight quarts of oil to his four-cylinder engine because the dipstick looked dry, except at the tip.

Some of the terms he used—like *throttle body*—made me press my lips together, avert my eyes from his big hands, and fight a blush. I'd never realized before, but automotive speak was ripe with inadvertent sexual innuendos, like *manifold*, *couplings*, *dipstick*, and *lube*.

Or maybe I just had a dirty mind.

Or maybe it was just Duane. Perhaps his mere presence did things to *my* throttle body.

Or maybe some combination of the three.

Whatever the issue, I was feeling hot under the collar of my oversized coveralls and had to unzip them to my chest, surreptitiously fanning myself after he'd used the phrases *drive shaft* and *push rod* in the same sentence. While I fanned myself, I walked over to a stereo sitting on a well-lit table. Small greasy machine parts covered the surface of the table, making me think the car part was either being disassembled or reassembled.

I switched on the stereo to CD mode and pressed Play, curious to see what had been playing last. To my astonishment, the cool harmonic melodies of the Beach Boys filled the air.

I glanced over my shoulder and found Duane watching me with not quite a smile, though his eyes were glittery.

"The Beach Boys?"

"That's right." He nodded once and strolled to where I stood, wiping his hands on a rag and stuffing it in his back pocket. He'd changed into a set of coveralls, too. However, his fit, were old with faded grease stains, and had his name embroidered over the left side. "Everyone likes the Beach Boys. At least that's what my momma used to say. Everyone likes the Beach Boys and pie."

I grinned, because Bethany Winston was right. Well, she was right about me at least. I liked the Beach Boys and pie.

I turned to face him and he stopped in front of me, smirking as he studied my appearance. I was pretty sure I had grease on my face, probably my nose, and several smudges on the new coveralls. I likely looked a mess. Yet Duane seemed to like what he saw because his eyes grew warm with what looked like affection.

"Come here," he said, holding out his hand.

I placed my hand in his as chords from "Fun, Fun, Fun" played over the stereo's speakers. To my delighted surprise, Duane pulled me into a dancing hold and proceeded to swing dance us around the garage.

I was so shocked at first that I'm sure I stepped on his toes and did more stumbling than dancing. But the steps I'd learned in college during my two-week swing-dancing phase quickly came back to me—probably because Duane was an exceptional leader—and soon we were moving together in a way that felt effortless.

The next song on the CD was "Brown Eyed Girl" by Van Morrison. I laughed out loud when he sang the words to me—because I could either laugh or swoon—and I was delighted from the tips of my ears to my toes, feeling dizzy with the force of exhilaration and happiness.

"Build Me Up, Buttercup" by the Foundations, "I Want You Back" by the Jackson 5, and "Uptown Girl" by Billy Joel rounded out the next three songs. I was out of breath, sweaty, and making no attempt to hide my euphoria when a slow song finally came on; again the Beach Boys, this time it was "Don't Worry, Baby."

Duane grinned down at me and pulled me close, pressing my body against his, his bearded jaw at my temple, and moved us in a small swaying circle. I closed my eyes, using the first full minute of the song to catch my breath. Then I used the next thirty seconds to force my heart to slow. But it wouldn't.

First of all, I could smell him and he smelled good. So, so good. Plus his arms around me felt remarkable. And the way his body moved with mine, the feel of his chest and stomach and thighs... *Oh sigh*.

I both loved and hated his embrace—loved for obvious reasons, hated because I knew I needed to keep myself at a distance when all I wanted to do was snuggle, and kiss, and grope him with abandon. But if I did that, then I'd likely have to face another of his gentle rejections.

I needed to be mindful and circumspect.

I felt the familiar building of desperation and urgency, but I pushed it away.

He wanted to go slow. I could go slow. I could do that. I could control myself. I could.

I felt Duane lean away, felt his gaze on me, so I opened my eyes and met his. He was frowning, searching my face.

"What's wrong?"

I shook my head. "Nothing."

His frown escalated in severity, his forehead creasing.

"What's wrong, Jess? And don't say *nothing*. You're all stiff and distant."

Emotion I didn't recognize felt like a swelling balloon in my throat and I pressed my lips together, not knowing how to respond.

And then he said, "Just be honest."

So I sighed and was honest. "I'm trying to go slow. But it's not easy. I, well, I really like you. Like, *really* like you. I'm thinking about you all the time and last week was difficult, when we were apart. It may sound crazy, but I missed you terribly, and not because you get me all hot and bothered. Yeah, that's part of it. But you make me laugh, and being with you feels so good, comfortable. But based on how you keep putting me off, I think you want to go slow. I'm trying to…" I shrugged, searched the space around his head for the right words, and finally settled on, "I'm trying to be less wild and reckless with you. I want to be respectful of you, of your wishes. And that's the whole truth."

Duane's mouth parted slightly and his eyebrows lifted high on his forehead. All hints of his earlier frown had vanished. Unless I was misreading his expression, he appeared to be a little lost, like maybe I'd stolen his breath and his wallet and his passport and his memories. Really, he looked stunned.

I swallowed, not sure what to say or do as the slow song came to an end and silence took its place. My heart thundered painfully in my chest. The moment felt taut and untenable, so I moved to distance myself. Duane's grip tightened, preventing me from stepping away.

Then something behind his gaze acutely sharpened, and the sharpness felt dangerous. My eyes widened in alarm just before Duane's mouth sought and claimed mine. He kissed me—wet, devouring, open-mouthed kisses—and gripped my arms a little too tight. He walked me backward until my legs connected with the hood of the Mustang. Pushing me backward, he released my arms, his hands moving to the zipper of my coveralls.

Breathing hard, I gripped his wrists and ducked my head to the side to evade his mouth. Duane's savageness caught me off guard and sucked me into a vortex of ferocious longing. "Wait…wait a minute. What's—"

"I want you, Jess. So much. You don't know…" He unzipped the jumper, pulling it off my shoulders with a yank and trapping my arms against my sides, lowering my back to the car. His mouth and tongue worked, kissing and licking and sucking from my jaw to my neck to my white lace–covered breast. I moaned and whimpered as he did something truly fantastic to my nipple with his teeth and the tip of his tongue. I didn't know if I'd ever recover, as sharp slices of hot need ran down my spine and to my lower abdomen.

"Duane, please." My arms were still trapped and I was lying on the hood of the car, writhing and arching my back, trying to get closer. He was over me, devouring my skin, pressing his thigh where I needed him.

"Don't change a thing. God, Jess. Don't change a single thing. Be wild for me, be reckless. I love your kind of wild. I love…"

His words were lost as he moved lower, his hand replacing his leg. My breath came in short, excited bursts and I briefly fought the sleeves holding my arms to my sides. But then my captivity was forgotten and I melted against the metal of his Mustang, a bundle of nerve endings and feelings and insensible desire.

He had me trapped. I was helpless to him. As he touched and tasted my body, he watched me, his gaze a mirror of the urgency and desperation I felt at his hands and mouth.

Maybe I was being absurd and reckless, misguided and foolish. I knew he would push me; I had no doubt. But I trusted him. I trusted that, even though Duane would definitely push, he'd also be there to catch me when I fell.

Duane

16

"I never travel without my diary. One should always have something sensational to read in the train."

—OSCAR WILDE, *THE IMPORTANCE OF BEING EARNEST*

SHE WANTED TO GIVE ME a blow job.

I suggested fried pie instead.

It took some convincing, but Jess finally agreed. Yet her agreement came only after I pointed out that Daisy's Nut House would be closing in an hour. If we were going to secure pie, the time was now.

While she righted herself, I grabbed my clothes, took a walk upstairs, and shoved my head and neck under the cold water faucet, thinking of England and the Queen. This was a trick Cletus taught me some years ago. When faced with a stubborn boner, thinking of all those wrinkled, disapproving monarchs in their fancy clothes usually worked.

It didn't exactly work this time, but it worked enough. I couldn't keep wearing my tented coveralls, so I switched back into my pants.

I'm not sure why I turned her down. Feeling her lose her mind against my mouth and fingers, this time lying on the hood of the Mustang I was determined to give her, was going in my long-term memory storage for frequent replay.

I should have taken her up on the offer to reciprocate, but I couldn't. *Fuck* I wanted to…but I couldn't. Not until everything was just right. Not until we had more than a few hours.

So instead I tried to recall the names of Henry the Eighth's six wives, and how each had met her demise.

Both easing and increasing the torture, on the ride over, Jess snuggled close to me, opting to use the center seat belt and laying her head on my shoulder as I drove. She sighed a lot. And she smiled a lot.

At one point she picked up my hand from where it rested on her thigh and studied my fingers, holding them close to her face and tracing my knuckles.

"I like your hands."

"My hands like you."

She smiled again. Then sighed against my neck.

"This feels good."

"What's that?" I slowed to make the turn into Daisy's, scanning the cars in the lot. It was fairly packed.

"I don't know what to call it…postorgasmic bliss, I guess."

I released a short laugh and shook my head. "Don't tell me I've given you your first?"

She shrugged. Even though we'd parked and I'd turned off the engine, she made no move to relinquish her spot curled against my side.

"No. I'm quite talented at the art of self-pleasuring."

At this statement, two thoughts warred for my attention. First, I was vehemently determined to get her to myself again as soon as possible, because I'd very much enjoy watching her talent in the art of self-pleasuring.

And second, unless I'd misunderstood, her admission meant I was the first guy who'd brought her to orgasm.

My possessive impulses were back with a sudden fierceness. I leaned slightly away so I could see her eyes.

"Jess, have you ever…? I mean, are you…?"

A small V formed between her eyebrows as I struggled to ask my question, but then her forehead cleared when she understood.

"Oh, no. No. I'm no virgin. First of all, my hymen broke when I was a teenager while horseback riding at my aunt's farm in Texas. Thank God, because I hear breaking through that thing the old-fashioned way is like getting stabbed in the hoo-hah. And secondly, I had sex with a guy in college. He was really nice, but it was…underwhelming in the extreme."

I frowned at this news, irritated someone else had touched her. But also strangely both pissed and relieved the experience had been underwhelming.

"Just one guy?"

She nodded, looking unperturbed, then asked, "What about you? How many girls have you been with?"

I studied her, bracing myself for her reaction to the truth. "Just one."

Jessica blinked several times, like I'd startled her, and she choked out, "Just…just one?"

I nodded, searching for any clues as to what she was thinking.

"Just one…" she repeated, mostly to herself and pulled away from me. After several seconds her gaze darted to mine, then away again. She laughed without humor, staring at her lap, and said, "I guess you were really in love."

"What do you mean?" I rested my arm on the bench behind Jess's shoulders, surprised by her words, wondering if it were possible she already knew how I thought of her.

"With Tina. I guess you really loved her."

I reeled back, and said much louder than I intended, "Tina? In love with Tina? Oh, *hell* no."

Jessica examined me with a questioning frown. "Then why did you…? Why were you only with Tina? For five years?"

I half rolled my eyes and tilted my head toward the door to Daisy's. "Let's go inside."

"Are you avoiding the question?"

"No. For the record, I was never in love with Tina and she was definitely never in love with me. I'd just like some pie if we're going to talk about this," I drawled, figuring it was time to return her unfailing honesty with my own.

I was happy to see Jess's answering smile and nod of agreement.

On our way in, I scanned the diner. The place was packed, especially for a late Sunday afternoon, I didn't see a free table. I was about to suggest we order our pie to go when Jess pointed to two newly vacated spots at the counter near the door.

"We can sit there."

Before I could answer, she pulled me to the empty stools. The seats were pretty good, all things considered. I could see the rest of the diner from our position, but the door was to our back. Nevertheless, it was a good place to scope out any booths that might become available.

"Do you need a menu?" she asked, reaching forward to where the laminated trifold menus were kept.

"Nah. I know what I want."

"Good. Me too." She smiled, looking at my mouth like she was planning on having it for supper.

I cleared my throat so I wouldn't groan. Closing my eyes, I pinched the bridge of my nose, trying to remember what we were discussing in the car. This was a mistake. Images of Jess on the hood of her Mustang filled my vision, the faith in her eyes, the raw want and trust.

I meant it when I'd said I loved her type of wild and reckless. It was sweet, honest, and generous. She was a good woman, and I didn't want her holding back or feeling like she needed to. Thus, I needed to settle on a place and soon. A place where we could be alone together, maybe for days, so we could do things right.

Admittedly, my motivations weren't entirely honorable; I needed to satisfy the relentless hard-on between my legs, especially when her honest words were playing on repeat between my ears:

I'm trying to go slow. But it's not easy with you.
I really like you.
I'm thinking about you all the time.
I missed you terribly.
Being with you feels so good.
I want to be respectful of you, of your wishes.

"So, you were saying about Tina?" Jess prompted, interrupting the self-inflicted torture.

I nodded, sucked in a deep breath, and opened my eyes. I found her watching me with so much trust and admiration that I almost pinched myself. This was my reality, and one day she was going to walk away.

"Tina..." I nodded, cleared my throat again.

She waited for a beat, then prompted once more, "I asked you why you stayed with her for five years if there was no love between you. Why didn't you move on? Date someone else?"

What would have been the point? No one else was you.

I shrugged, stalling, settling on one version of the truth. "Laziness and convenience, I guess. She knew what was up from the start, that I didn't want anything serious with her or anyone else. Like I've said, she wasn't my girl."

Jess's lips slanted downward on one side and her eyes narrowed. "So you've never been interested in anyone?"

"I'm interested in you." The words slipped out, her fearless honesty encouraging my own.

"Hmm…"

"Hmm?"

"Yes. Hmm."

"Why *hmm?*"

"*Hmm* because I feel like you've cheated yourself out of five years and the possibility of something great. You could have met someone, fallen in love, been loved in return. But it's like you gave up before you even started."

"I didn't give up. I was biding my time."

"For what? For who? Someone you felt suited?"

"No, not *someone*. For you."

Jess's expressive eyes widened, then she blinked. "You've been biding your time? For me?"

Maybe I had to work up to her level of brutal honesty, but eventually I got there. And now that I'd said the words, I sure as hell wasn't taking them back.

"That's right. There was no point in dating other people. No one else is you."

Her face both fell and brightened at once, like my words made her sad and happy.

"Oh, Duane…" She sounded heartbroken and elated. "What am I going to do with you?"

Stay.

I wasn't going to say that. Asking her to stay would be taking her dreams away.

Instead I shrugged. "You could buy me pie."

Jess stood from her stool and stepped between my legs, winding her arms around my neck. She pressed herself to me, giving me a tight hug and whispering into my ear, "You're a siren who doesn't sing."

I chuckled, returning her embrace, and placed a quick kiss on her neck. I couldn't quite swallow. My head was mixed up. What I wanted, knew, *and* needed didn't align.

I wanted her to stay.

I knew she had to go.

I needed to remember every day was one day closer to the end; otherwise her leaving would be my destruction. Maybe I wasn't being fair, encouraging her to lose control while I refused to cede control. But self-preservation required it.

She gave me one more squeeze, then leaned away. Meanwhile, I battled between forced numbness and a painful desire to give in, let go of my survival instinct.

Jess gave me another adoring smile. "I'll go get our pie. Be right back."

I let her go and she rushed away, though I followed her with my eyes as she walked the length of the counter and disappeared into the kitchen. My attention affixed to the swinging galley door for a long time. I finally managed to swallow around the thick discomfort in my throat, the painful desire to give in replaced with a cold certainty that I couldn't. It wouldn't be fair, not to me and not to her, because then I would ask her to stay.

"Well, looky who we have here."

I stiffened in my seat and turned on my stool slowly—not cursing, though I wanted to. I was in no hurry to see Repo.

"Repo," I said, likely sounding as irritated and bored as I was, while my eyes moved over the rest of his companions.

There were a few younger guys I didn't recognize, a few I did. One was Kip Sylvester's son, Isaac, and his presence was a surprise. He was a year or so older than me and last I knew he was still in the army. I gathered seeing him here, in the company of the Wraiths, meant he'd been discharged.

I had a few tetchy thoughts then—like wondering what his father, the principal, and his mother, the socialite, would think of his involvement with the Wraiths—before my gaze settled on Tina, my ex, near the back of the entourage.

I had to fight another eye roll because she was giving me one of her looks, all while rubbing up against one of the bikers.

"Hi, Duane," she said, flapping her eyelashes.

"Tina," I acknowledged, hoping my visible indifference toward her would hide my frustration at seeing her now. I'd been calling her nonstop for the last week. Beau had also been calling, trying to find a time to meet up so the three of us could discuss a plan for copying, then erasing the Iron Wraiths' computer files.

But she'd responded with only text messages, telling us both to come see her at the Pink Pony if we wanted to talk. I wanted to go to that strip club again like I wanted kidney stones.

"Oh, you don't mind? Do you, son?" Repo walked toward me, lowering his voice as he approached. "Your girl Tina has been keeping lots of our guys real happy."

I shrugged. "Why would I mind? She was never my girl."

Repo chortled, his hand coming down on my shoulder, and he shook his head. "You're not so bad, Duane."

"I'm not so good, either." I looked meaningfully at his hand still gripping my shoulder.

Repo's smile widened and he released me.

He glanced at his entourage and then lifted his chin toward two booths at the back of the diner. "Pay their tab and ask them to leave, nicely."

Knowing Repo, he was intending to occupy the two tables even though they were currently filled. If Daisy had been here, Repo wouldn't have been able to pull a move like this. But she wasn't.

The crowd of bikers strolled to the booths and I watched with mild curiosity as one of the Wraiths' members smiled at the occupants, withdrew several bills, and said something I couldn't hear. Almost immediately the customers shuffled out of their booths.

"I'm glad you're here," Repo said as I continued to watch the scene at the back of the restaurant. The customers were now nodding politely to the bikers as they went. "It saves me a trip to your house."

My eyes sliced to Repo's still smiling face and narrowed. "You need to borrow a cup of sugar, old man?"

Repo's eyes also narrowed. "I ain't baking no cakes. We both know why I'm so interested in your ornery company."

I examined the older biker for a minute, peripherally aware of the displaced customers as they filed out of the restaurant. They didn't look upset, but they didn't look too happy, either.

"You got three more days, son." Repo's typically friendly tone adopted a hard edge. "I'll be expecting your answer."

I thought about giving him my answer right this minute via my middle finger, but movement caught my eye, distracting me. Distraction quickly turned to dread when I spotted

Jessica making her way back. She was carrying a tray with four slices of pie and two cups of coffee.

Repo must've noticed my redirected attention because he turned and followed my line of sight. When his eyes connected with Jessica, he stood a bit straighter, his grin wavering, then falling, like the vision of her was shockingly unexpected.

Jess was smiling her big smile at me, but I saw the precise moment when her attention snagged on Repo. She blinked, her steps faltered, and the big smile fell from her face, became polite and confused. She made her final approach with hesitant steps, her eyes clearly wary.

Maybe her reaction had something to do with the fact I was currently grinding my teeth. If my outward expression came anywhere close to the lethal impulses I'd barely restrained, I wasn't surprised she'd decided to tread with caution.

Obviously, I didn't want her anywhere near the Wraiths, nor did I want the Wraiths anywhere near *her*. Thus, we needed to leave.

"Am I interrupting something?" Jess glanced between Repo and me, not putting the tray down, like she hadn't made up her mind whether or not the pie would be safe.

"Nothing at all, Miss James," Repo responded, giving her a tight smile and reaching for the tray. His voice was hoarser, softer than usual as he asked, "Can I help you with that?"

He was acting like a hypnotized loony bird and I didn't like it. So I stood and walked around the biker, stepping between them and interrupting his reaching hands by taking the tray myself.

"I'm sorry..." Her gaze flickered to me, then back to the biker, giving him a quizzical smile. "Don't I know you? You look awfully familiar."

"Maybe, around town. But I know your momma real well." Again, his voice was soft, respectful.

I tossed a furious look over my shoulder at Repo, not liking the way he was staring at Jess—all soft and revering, like she was some kind of fairy princess—then turned back to her while I set the tray on the counter, blocking her view of the biker. "Hey, can you go back and grab us some takeaway containers? We'll get this to go."

Her gentle eyes studied me and I saw a question hovering near the surface. In the end, though, she nodded and walked back to the kitchen, tucking her long blond hair behind her ears as she went.

I waited until she was back in the kitchen before turning back to Repo and lowering my voice to a harsh whisper. "Really? You know her momma *real well*? What the fuck is wrong with you? Why would you say that?"

Even though we were in a busy diner, and I imagined we were making quite a scene, no one was paying us any heed. I hoped the locals assumed our heated exchange was about my piece-of-shit father. It wasn't unusual for Winston boys and the Iron Wraiths to clash on the subject from time to time.

Repo kept his attention fixed to the spot where Jessica had disappeared and ignored my question. "The sheriff's daughter, huh?"

"That isn't really any of your concern, old man."

He turned his black eyes to me and not a trace of good humor remained. He took a step toward me and lowered his voice so only I could hear.

"*That* is my concern."

"How is Jessica James any of your concern?"

He appeared to struggle for a moment, then finally said, "Because you're going to be my mechanic soon—"

"That's not decided."

He continued like I hadn't spoken, his glare narrowing. "Do you think you'll be able to run our shop and still see that girl? Or are you thinking about double-crossing me? You think if you get tight with that family they'll let Jethro off easy? That ain't so, son. Because what we got on Jethro is a *federal* matter, not local."

"I don't run your shop," I ground out.

The muscle at his jaw ticked and his black eyes turned as mean as I'd ever seen them. "Three days, son. Three days."

"I know how to read a calendar," I replied through gritted teeth. I needed to grab Jess and get the hell out of here. Because if we didn't leave soon I was going to sucker punch one of the Wraiths' most senior members and get my ass kicked by his younger brethren. I was good in a fight, but six against one were suicide odds.

"And you're a fool if you think you can run our shop and be getting close with that girl, too. She's too good for you. Quit being a selfish fuck and leave her alone."

"Mind your own goddamn business."

"I seen it before. Some of our boys thinking they can be with her kind. It don't work out. Look at your daddy. Look what he did to your momma. He ruined her. You want that for Jessica James?"

"I'm not one of the Wraiths."

Repo's stony expression abruptly cracked with a little smile that looked more bitter than amused, and he said, "Not yet."

Jessica

17

> "The universe is a sort of book, whose first page one has read when one has seen only one's own country."
>
> —FOURGERET DE MONBRON,
> *LE COSMOPOLITE (1753)*

TWO DAYS. MONDAY AND TUESDAY.

Two days of impersonal text messages.

And all I kept thinking was that these were two days I'd never get back. We had limited time together, Duane and I, so two days without his company made me feel like I was being cheated, like he was reneging on his side of the deal.

Since Sunday, the most intimate of our exchanges had been via text message, as follows:

Me: Hey, Red, want to get together tonight?
Him: Can't.
Me: I miss you.
Him: You too.

That had been Tuesday around 4:00 p.m. Now it was Wednesday just after noon and…nothing.

Therefore, I decided to force the issue. It was early release day, so I skipped out right after the bell and I made pie.

I also bought the ingredients for meat loaf, mashed potatoes, and collards. Enough to feed eight.

I asked Claire to drive me over to the family's house that evening, intent on making those boys dinner, but also getting Duane alone so we could set a few things straight. If I was being clingy and overreacting, I needed to know. Because I wanted to see him every day of the remaining time we had left.

I wanted to see him every day, talk to him, listen to him laugh and make me laugh. I wanted to kiss him and snuggle against his delectable body. And I wanted to return the favors he'd given me. I wanted to make him feel good and treasured. All the time.

As we pulled up to the big house, I counted the cars.

Duane's sexy machine (the Road Runner) was present, as was Cletus's Geo Prizm. I was pretty sure the Ford truck was Billy's, which meant the candy-red Pontiac vintage muscle car was Beau's. Four of the boys were at home.

Claire—who'd been very supportive of my *show up and surprise your boyfriend's family with dinner* plan—helped me unload the groceries from her car and set them on the porch. I told her to drive away before I knocked on the door. They wouldn't be able to turn me away if I were stranded.

Plus, I was holding a pie. This was a strategic decision. My momma once told me no one turns away a lady bearing pie. If you want to get your foot in the door, bring pie and hold it in front of you. She called this the pie effect.

Therefore, with a pile of groceries on the big porch behind me and a still-warm apple pie in my hands, I knocked on the door to the family's house.

The main structure sat on over fifteen acres backing up to the Great Smoky Mountains National Park. The house itself had a wide curving staircase, at least seven bedrooms, and beautiful large windows lining the back. It was a big house and had once been very grand. Over the last twenty or so years, the house, and the land surrounding it, had fallen into a state of messy disrepair.

Winston was their daddy's name, but their momma came from an old established Tennessee family with the last name of Oliver, very high-cotton. The house had been called Oliver House until around ten years ago. Her father, Mr. Oliver, had been a politician, a man of business and of considerable money. Bethany Oliver had married beneath her station—or so all my momma's friends had whispered after Sunday service—by getting hitched to Darrell Winston at the very young age of sixteen.

They'd had seven kids, he was terrible, and the rest was history.

The old house had no doorbell, so I waited, only the butterflies in my stomach keeping me company. When no one answered after a stretch, I knocked again.

After knocking for the third time with no answer, I worried. I glanced over my shoulder at the line of cars and decided to swat my worry away. Surely one of the brothers was at home. Left with very few options—either walk in uninvited or do a quick survey of the property—I decided to take my pie and go around the back. I figured walking in uninvited would be my last resort.

It took me a bit to circumnavigate the house. Machine parts littered the path. I noticed a busted old CAT earthmover, dull yellow with patches of rust, that sat behind a giant detached garage. I made a mental note to check inside the garage before I walked into the house.

Thankfully, I spotted a red head with a broad muscular back about a hundred paces from the back of the house, standing on some sort of covered deck. I squared my shoulders and marched to the structure, seeing that either Beau or Duane was tending to a large smoking grill.

When I was about twenty feet away, the redhead—his back still turned—said, "Do you have the sausage?"

He was Duane. My heart knew.

The butterflies in my stomach flew to my chest, made breathing a labor. I was nervous. But I was also here, and I'd committed to this ambush. I wasn't going to shrink away now, even if dinner as bribery was the price.

But I did have to clear my throat of my nerves before responding, "No. But I have apple pie."

Clearly startled, Duane turned fully around, his eyes moving up and down my form. He was surprised and his features were a cloudy mess of stunned relief. I felt a good bit of tension leave my bones when he finally smiled like he couldn't help it and rushed forward.

Duane intercepted me on the second step leading to the deck and, paying no heed to the dish in my hand, wrapped his arms around my body and gave me a big getting-down-to-business kiss. His mouth and hands felt wonderful and possessive, one slipping under my sweater and shirt to grip the bare of my back. I liked the kiss so much, I almost dropped the pie.

Too soon, but really after a full minute or more, the kiss was over and he was nuzzling my ear. We were both breathing a bit hard.

"Goodness, I missed you," I said on a sigh, loving the

texture and feel of his beard against my jaw, and his hot breath on my neck.

"I missed you, too, Jessica." He nibbled on my ear, whispering my name like it was a dirty word—but not a curse word—a dirty word. Something erotic and scandalous. I had an odd thought then, that I liked my name on his lips more when it was whispered.

We were interrupted by a voice from behind me. "Is that pie?"

Duane stiffened a little, but didn't relinquish his hold on me. Instead, after releasing a frustrated-sounding exhale, he lifted his head from my neck. Likewise, I glanced over my shoulder and found Duane's mirror image strolling toward us, an easy, friendly smile claiming Beau's features.

But they weren't really a mirror image of each other. I decided one of the main differences between Duane and Beau was that Beau's smiles were easy, freely given; Duane's smiles were difficult, hard-won, and I'd learned to treasure each one.

"I'll take that," Beau said as he breezed past, grabbing the pie from my hand. As he crossed to a picnic table on the deck and placed the dish on top of it, he added, "I do love apple pie."

"Don't eat any of that," Duane said as we both watched Beau lean close and sniff it.

"I can't eat it. I don't have a fork...yet." Beau looked around the deck like he was searching for something.

Besides the picnic table and the large smoking grill, the twenty-by-twenty-foot deck had several Adirondack chairs, a big wooden chest that I suspected was actually a cooler (likely full of beer), and an old wooden hutch painted lime green. The exposed wood ceiling was strung with white Christmas lights, which would come in handy once the sun set.

Beau walked over to the lime-green hutch and dug through a few drawers. Watching his brother, Duane shook his head like he was disgusted.

"He's looking for a fork," he explained, his hands slipping from my body, but then—in the same movement—tucking me under his arm. "Don't eat any of that pie. It'll ruin your dinner."

"I'm just going to taste it."

Duane looked like he was going to protest again, but I cut him off with my question, "When did y'all get this deck? I don't remember it being here."

"Drew, Billy, and Jethro built it for Momma two years ago. She likes having dinner out here when the weather is nice."

Duane was still speaking about his mother in the present tense. It made my heart hurt a bit. I didn't correct him, but I did give him a squeeze.

"I hate to ask, because I don't want you to think I'm not happy to see you"—Duane pulled away, just far enough that he could look into my eyes—"but what are you doing here other than to bring me pie?"

Cletus walked past us at just that moment, and Billy wasn't far behind. This was good timing because now I could announce my plans to all of them.

"I'm actually here to make dinner for you and your brothers," I responded happily, gesturing to the pie Beau had placed on the picnic table. "The pie is for dessert. I hope you like meat loaf."

"Oh, Jess…" Duane appeared to be completely torn and his voice held true regret. "I wish you'd talked to me about your plans ahead of time. Tonight is sausage night."

"Sausage night?"

"Yes. Cletus Winston's famous sausage is *famous*." Cletus uncovered a heaping platter of raw sausage that he'd set next to the smoking grill. "These boys have been looking forward to my sausage *all…week…long*."

"Cletus." Billy's tone held a warning as he claimed the Adirondack chair nearest the grill, nodding to me as he sat. "Evening, Jessica."

I noted that Billy's Tennessee accent was back, thicker.

Cletus cocked an eyebrow at his older brother, clearly not impressed with Billy's tone. "You're going to tell me you haven't been salivating for my sausage?"

I had to cover my mouth with my hand and press it there, hard. Otherwise I was going to launch into a fit of hysterical giggles.

Duane scowled at his older brother, then squeezed my waist, drawing my attention back to him. His mouth curved to the side when he saw me struggle to contain my laughter, but he made no remark on it. Instead he moved us to the picnic table, set me on his lap, and opted to clarify the situation.

"See now, since there's five of us left here—with Ashley back in Chicago, and Roscoe at school—we each have a night of the week where it's our responsibility to cook, then we fend for ourselves on the weekends."

Beau, unable to find a fork, gave up his search and pulled three beers out of the wooden chest, setting two down in front of Duane and me before claiming a seat across from us.

"Thank you, Beau."

"You're welcome, Jess."

"Cletus takes a trip to Texas twice a year to spear hunt wild boars, and so once a month, he feeds us wild boar sausage," Duane continued.

"Spear hunt?" I knew my eyes were bulging out of my head. "Wild boar? Aren't those things huge?"

"Let's just say they make a lot of bacon. And sausage." Cletus indicated to the plate of sausage again, then poked at the smoking coals in the grill with a long grilling fork.

"I can't believe you spear hunt. Isn't that terribly dangerous?"

He shrugged. "Well, now. I don't think it's respectful to shoot a boar from the comfort of a hiding place and while wielding a firearm. That's not a fair fight. Nowadays I feel like people are too far from the food they eat. How many people do you know would eat a steak if they had to slit its throat, electrocute it, and watch all the blood drain out."

"Ugh, Cletus! Really?" Beau made a face. "I *was* hungry, before you started bringing up slaughterhouses."

"My point is, if I'm going to kill a wild animal, I don't see why I should make things easy on myself."

"He does it with a bunch of Native American fellas, good guys. They all get together and run around the forest in loincloths," Duane supplied before tipping his beer back and taking a long pull.

I watched with fascination how his lips wrapped around the bottle, how his throat worked as he swallowed. By the time he took it from his mouth and caught an errant drop with the tip of his tongue, I felt a little dazed. As well, I'd completely forgotten what we were discussing.

When he finished, he glanced back at me, but then his brow furrowed in question—likely at my dreamy expression. "Hey, Jess. You okay?"

I nodded, sighed, and wished he'd been licking an errant drop of something off me. "Yeah. I'm fine."

"You look a little hot." This came from Beau and I found him watching us, mischief behind his eyes. So I frowned at him and his teasing. He mimicked my frown, though not quite successfully because his mouth curved into an impish smile immediately after. "Maybe Duane should show you around the house; it might help you cool off."

"Sitting so close to my sausage likely has you overheated and excited," Cletus mumbled as he indicated to the grill with his chin.

"As I was saying..." Duane's tone held a note of exasperation as he swept Beau and Cletus a hard look before turning his attention back to me. "Billy cooks Mondays, Beau is Tuesdays, then Cletus on Wednesday, me on Thursday, and Jethro on Friday."

"We have a schedule," Cletus volunteered. "We like our schedules. They keep things orderly."

"So, who's filling in for Jethro on Friday?"

"He left casseroles—lots of them—in the deep freezer," Billy answered in a flat tone.

"Hey, you could make us dinner on Friday. If you want," Beau suggested.

Duane shook his head before I could answer. "No. Jess and I will make dinner together tomorrow, on my night."

"That's cheating," Billy protested.

"There's no rules. And are you really going to turn down Jess's meat loaf?"

Billy didn't respond to Duane's question verbally, but instead allowed his icicle eyes and disapproving silence to answer for him.

"Can you come back tomorrow?" Duane turned me in his arms slightly, his voice low and gentle.

"Yeah. I can come tomorrow. No problem. Do you mind if I leave everything here tonight?"

Duane shrugged. "We have plenty of space in the fridge, now Cletus has removed his sausage."

"Okay," I nodded, leaned forward, picked up my pie again, and made to stand. "Well then, I guess I'll go—"

A chorus of "No!" and "What? Where are you going?" and "Put that pie down," and other protests kept me from going back to the front porch to collect my things.

"You should stay." Billy gave me a half smile that was completely unexpected, as were his words. "Stay and have dinner with us. Your company would be a welcome change."

"Yes. Stay. Even if you're a big eater, there's plenty of my sausage for you."

"Cletus!" His name was exclaimed in a unified shout by the other three brothers, each shooting him their own unique version of a dirty look.

"Well…" I glanced at the pie in my hands, biting my lip so I wouldn't laugh, and turned my attention to Duane. "I guess everything will keep until tomorrow."

"Oh, no. We'll eat that pie tonight. You make a new one for tomorrow to go along with your meat loaf." Cletus nodded like this was already decided.

"If you're taking requests, I'd really like another apple pie." Beau gave me a wink from across the table.

"She is not taking any pie requests from you," Duane barked at Beau.

"Fine, fine! No need to get your britches twisted; it's not as though I was offering her my sausage, like some people. I'm just saying, since she has to make a new pie irregardless, she might as well make another apple pie."

Billy lifted his beer toward Beau, his tone completely condescending as he remarked, "I feel I must tell you, Beau, that there is no such word as *irregardless*. It's just *regardless*."

"Stop correcting Beau's terrible grammar and go get the bigger bag of charcoal." Cletus kicked Billy's chair. "These flames aren't adequate to cook my sausage."

I was fighting another grin when Duane leaned close, removed the pie from my hands, and set it back on the table. He slid his hand back around my waist, sending lovely tendrils of warmth through my body. "Ignore them," he whispered, his hot breath on my neck making me shiver. "They're just trying to get you to make more pie."

"I don't mind," I whispered back. "The crust recipe made enough for two, so it's just a matter of making the filling."

"Go show Jessica around." Beau flicked his wrist toward us, waving us off while giving me a conspiratorial look. "She hasn't been here in years. Go show her the upstairs."

"The upstairs?" Duane made a face. "There's nothing upstairs except the bedrooms."

"He means, go spend some time being physically intimate with your pretty girlfriend until dinner is ready," Cletus supplied, not sparing us a glance. He was frowning at his coals. "We'll make a ruckus and call you down when it's time to eat."

Duane scowled at Beau. Beau shrugged. The arch of his eyebrows and his pleased smirk were positively devilish.

"We'll go inside and *unpack the groceries* for tomorrow," Duane said pointedly, and continued to glare at Beau.

"You do that. You go unpack those groceries." His twin nodded, still looking unrepentant. "You unpack those groceries so hard."

Before Duane could lean over the table and assault his

twin, I added with my biggest, cheekiest smile, "Then we'll go upstairs and be physically intimate until dinner is ready."

I heard Billy choke on his laugh. Beau guffawed.

Duane glanced at me, his eyebrows half suspended between wonder and disapproval. I winked at him.

"That all sounds just dandy," Cletus agreed, his tone level, as though I'd just said Duane and I were going inside to wash the floors. Then he added, "But work up an appetite, woman. Because you've never tasted fine meat until you've eaten my sausage."

"CLETUS!"

♥

We did unpack the groceries.

But other than a few quick kisses in the kitchen, we weren't physically intimate and Duane didn't take me upstairs.

I didn't mind. I wanted to talk to him, make sure we were okay. Thankfully, things between us were easy and fun, leaving me feeling silly that I'd planned my elaborate dinner ambush. Looking back over the last few days of minimal contact, I realized I'd overreacted. I could have stopped in at the auto shop or called him after work.

I decided he hadn't been avoiding me. I'd inflated the meaning of his lack of contact in my head.

After unpacking the groceries, he walked me to the woods surrounding their house and we used familiar trails to navigate the forest.

"This path leads to the creek," he said, holding my hand in his and helping me over a felled log with unnecessary—but not unwelcome—solicitousness.

"The one that feeds the lake?"

"Yep."

I grinned. "I haven't been out there in…goodness, in years."

"Want to go?"

I vehemently shook my head. "No. You'll just push me in."

He grinned briefly in response, the short smile quickly waning into a frown. "Ashley spent a good amount of time on these trails while she was here. Every now and then, when she wasn't holed up inside the house, taking care of Momma, one of us would walk with her down to the creek."

I glanced at Duane, saw his mood had turned introspective. "Do you miss your sister?"

He nodded, frowning at the path. "Of course. I missed her when she left the first time, and I miss her now she's gone again."

I stepped closer to him and squeezed his hand, giving his side a quick hug. "I bet she misses you, too."

He nodded once, then turned his face away as though searching the trees to make sure we were on the right trail.

Then out of the blue, he asked, "Do you really need more than three restaurants?"

I faltered a half step, but then quickly recovered. "What do you mean?"

"I mean, Daisy's place serves great breakfast and pie. The Front Porch makes a first-class prime rib. I don't see why you need more restaurants."

I realized he was making a reference to our conversation on Saturday, when I'd stated that Green Valley only had three restaurants.

"It's not about the number of restaurants."

"I know." He frowned, shook his head. "I guess I don't see what's *out there* that's so much better than what's here. Is Green Valley so boring that all you can think about is escape?"

As I studied him I realized his question didn't necessarily denote a change in subject. His sister, Ashley, had left home when she was eighteen and hadn't returned until just recently. And then she'd stayed only long enough to take care of their dying mother during the last six weeks of her life. Ashley had left again on the day of the funeral, left Green Valley and her six brothers for her life in Chicago.

"There's nothing bad about Green Valley—"

"But nothing great either? Nothing worth sticking around for?" Duane pulled us to a stop. His eyes pierced me and his gaze felt almost physical, like a beseeching touch. I knew he wasn't trying to make me feel bad about my dreams. He was trying to understand both my motivations and perhaps the reason why his sister had left so many years ago, and kept leaving.

But I didn't see Ashley's desire to leave Green Valley as anything resembling my desire to see the world.

I sighed, my eyes skittering away so I could gather my thoughts. I didn't know how to explain my longing to wander and how it had nothing to do with my hometown. If I'd been born in New York City or London or Paris, I would still want to leave. I wanted to *explore* and experience and know.

"Have you ever heard of the German words wanderlust or fernweh?"

"You used wanderlust on our first date. And I read a book some years ago about hiking, and the title had the word wanderlust in it. It was about people who love to hike and cataloged some of the great hiking trails around the world."

"Wanderlust in German basically means to love hiking, but it's been repurposed by English speakers to mean a love of wandering. I remember the first time I heard the word fernweh; in German it means *farsickness*.' It's like some people have homesickness and that's considered normal, acceptable. Missing one's family and friends, what's familiar... I think everyone can understand longing for home. But I realized that the strange anxiousness I've always felt to be elsewhere was called fernweh. I have fernweh. How most people long for the familiar, I've always longed for the unknown. Heck, if I could manage it, I'd love to see Mars. I love to explore. And don't think it's an easy concept to explain or, for people who don't have the same desire, to grasp."

Duane frowned and nodded, his eyes moving away from mine. He was lost in thoughtful contemplation, but I could see he didn't really understand. Usually I accepted my friends' and family's lack of comprehension, wrote it off as me just being too nutty, too much of a circle surrounded by squares. But for some reason I felt a swelling, desperate need for Duane to understand. Therefore I grabbed his other hand and tugged on it until he was looking at me again.

"This desire, to explore, has nothing to do with where I am. It has everything to do with where I'm not."

"So, it's about newness? Being in a new place?"

I shook my head, carefully entwining our fingers. I found I needed to touch more of him, I needed the connection. "No. Not really. It's like, here we are"—I glanced around the brilliance surrounding us, fading colors of autumn on the Smoky Mountain path, dusky-blue sky overhead giving way to nightfall—"someplace awesome and spectacular. But, can you imagine if you had the chance to see a thousand places that were equally spectacular? I want to see the Colosseum in Rome, and St. Peter's. But I don't want to go on a tour during a vacation. I want to live there, know the city, learn the people, eat the food. I want to sketch Michelangelo's paintings—even though I'm no artist. Then after a time, maybe a year or more, I want to see the Yangtze River, see the Great Wall of China. And after that, the redwood forest. And after that, go diving in Fiji, or maybe visit castles in Ireland."

I glanced at him and saw he was watching me openly. Duane's frown had been replaced with not quite a smile, and his eyes held appreciation; however, it was the perceivable glimmer of understanding there that sent my pulse racing.

"I think I'm starting to get it. You're more than curious about the world, and I see it calls to you." His quiet voice was laced with empathy, and I saw he truly did *get it*.

I didn't temper my heavy sigh of relief, or my immediate grin, or attempt to hide my pleasure. This pleasure was quickly followed by a sudden and deep sense of gratitude. I'd tried to explain this desire to my family and friends on more than one occasion. Invariably my parents would always ask, *But what about a house and a nice car and nice clothes and a TV and a familiar bed?*

They couldn't fathom that I wanted to fill my life with experiences, not with things. I had their core values, but in so many ways we were completely different. They'd never understood my dramatic, wild side. Consequently, I'd spent my childhood trying to suppress or ignore it. But it was no use. I craved freedom, they craved structure. I didn't know why my dreams and goals were so different from my family's. They just were.

Until this moment, I hadn't realized how lonely I'd been,

having no one to share my dreams with, and no one to understand. It was Duane's understanding that pushed me over the edge. I stared into his brilliant eyes and knew with absolute certainty I was in love with Duane Winston.

And it didn't feel like a burden or a weight, something holding me down. Loving him made me feel paradoxically phenomenal and reckless and safe and strong and capable—because Duane was all of those things.

My big smile was beginning to hurt, but I didn't mind. I wanted to hold on to this moment for as long as possible, because it was the first time—and maybe the only time in my life—I felt truly seen, known, and understood. And I wanted to give him everything in return. I wanted him to know I saw him. I *knew* him, too.

Duane's almost-smile turned wry and his eyes narrowed. "You looking at me like that makes me feel ten feet tall."

"Aren't you?"

He laughed. I laughed. We laughed together.

Duane tugged me forward and captured my lips for a quick kiss, sending a thrill of warmth to my toes, then whispered against my mouth, "I guess I am, when I'm with you."

"You say sweet things."

"Do I?"

"Yes. Like when you said I was a siren who doesn't need to sing." I imagined my expression mimicked the dazed and floaty feeling of my heart. "That was a sweet thing to say, even though it implied I sought your destruction by tempting you with my body."

He shook his head, leaning away, one of his reluctant smiles teasing over his lips. Duane released me and pushed his fingers into my hair, his strong hands moving against my scalp and down to my neck. "That's not what I meant when I said it."

"Then what did you mean?"

"Have you read *The Odyssey*?"

"No. Have you?"

"Yes. It was required reading in my house. Remember, we didn't have a TV growing up. All we had were books and our imagination."

"Lord help us all, the Winston boys left to their collective imaginations," I teased lightly, enjoying my view because Duane was my view.

"How much do you know about the story?" His eyes studied me and he cocked his head to the side. "Do you know the basics?"

"Of *The Odyssey*? It was about Odysseus's travels. His journey home."

"What about the sirens in *The Odyssey*?"

"I know a bit. I know the sirens are beautiful. Their beauty and their song inspire lust in Odysseus's men and tempt the sailors to crash their ship against the rocks, more or less."

"Nope. That's not what happens. It's not lust they inspire that drives sailors toward their own destruction."

I squinted at him. "Then what do the sailors feel?"

"The sirens are beautiful, yes. But their song and their beauty call to the soul, not to the body. The sirens don't inspire lust. They inspire longing. A deep, wrenching longing. Bone-deep, so the sailors would rather die than live without the siren."

I stared at him as he stared at me. I could tell he was waiting for me to catch on to his meaning. It didn't take me very long because he voluntarily filled in the blanks.

"Your wanderlust, or *farfigneugan* or whatever—that's your siren's song." He tilted his head to one side, then the other, as though studying me from different angles before adding, "I get that."

Again my heart bloomed, and I wanted to give him a similar gift. So I asked, "And yours is going fast? Is speed your siren's call?"

He shook his head and his smile fell away, even as he continued to study my face with his trademark intensity and focus.

"No, Jessica," he whispered, gaining a step forward and pulling me into his arms.

"Then what is?" I lifted my chin.

He didn't answer. Instead, he kissed me.

♥

Dinner was great. Cletus's sausages were delicious, and the boys ate all of my apple pie.

But I was extremely cognizant of my 5:30 a.m. Thursday morning alarm, so I had to leave much earlier than I would have liked. Duane asked Billy if we could use the truck, and when it was time for me to go, Billy, Cletus, and Beau stood on the front lawn and waved goodbye. It was actually really sweet, and a thought occurred to me as we pulled on to the main road, the Winston boys still visible in the truck's rearview mirror: these boys needed a woman at the house.

They missed their momma. And they likely missed their sister. I decided I would make a habit of cooking with Duane every Thursday night.

Also, it wasn't right that all five of Duane's brothers were single. Goodness, they were a handsome and sweet bunch. Their collective singleton lifestyle was a crime against women everywhere. I further decided I would take it upon myself to find each of them suitable girlfriends over the next year.

"What are you plotting over there?"

I glanced at Duane in the driver's seat. We were paused at a stop sign; he was studying me with knowing eyes.

I shrugged and tried to suppress my guilty smile. "Nothing much."

"That's a lie. You're planning something." Duane pulled through the intersection and I lamented the fact that our houses were so close.

"I just thought it would be nice for me to help you cook on Thursdays." I turned in my seat and rested my elbow along the back of the truck's bench seat so I could stare at his profile.

"Mm-hmm," he said, like he didn't believe me.

"And what do you mean by that *mm-hmm*, Duane Winston?"

"I can see the gears turning. You forget, I know your face by heart. You're scheming."

I laughed, loving everything he'd just said. "You know my face by heart?"

"Don't change the subject." Duane made an unexpected right on to a dirt and gravel road, just a half mile from his house. It appeared to be one of the unmaintained roads used by park rangers and hunters.

"Where are we going?"

"I want to show you something. It's why I borrowed the truck. Don't worry, this won't take long. I know you have to get up for work early in the morning."

"Can you give me a hint?" We were swallowed up by trees and pitch-black night on all sides.

"Sure. In fact I'll just tell you. It's a hunting cabin. Billy and I built it four summers ago. No one else knows about it."

"Not even Beau?"

Duane shook his head. "No. Not even Beau. Billy…well, Billy suggested I keep it a secret."

"Why?"

"Probably because both Billy and I aren't as social as Beau or Jethro, or even Roscoe. We both used to have a habit of losing our tempers when kept in close quarters. At home. Cletus goes on long trips—boar hunting and whatnot—but Billy and I aren't in that habit. He suggested we use it as a place to lay low, cool off."

"Why don't you stay there all the time?"

"It doesn't have electricity, and it's small. It's got an outhouse and an outside well, but not plumbing."

I studied as much of Duane's profile as I could, given the lack of light. "But you're showing me now…?"

He nodded once. "That's right."

"Is this national park land? Or are we still on your family's property?"

"My family's property."

"Basically, you and Billy share it?"

"More or less. He doesn't use it much, since he works all the time. Our house, the big house, is really just a place for him to store his stuff and sleep."

"So this cabin, it's like your fortress of solitude."

He shrugged, his eyes flickering to mine. "I like to think of it that way."

A slow-burning thrill gradually warmed my belly as my

overactive imagination ran away, stripped naked doing wild cartwheels, and made salacious plans. This place meant privacy. Time we could spend together, just the two of us, sharing hopes and dreams. Maybe this place would be where I admitted how much I felt for him, how I loved him. Maybe we'd use it to make plans for our future beyond the next thirteen months.

He pulled the truck off the gravel road and took a path I would never have noticed. After another few minutes, the truck's headlights illuminated a rough-hewn stone staircase leading to a dark wooden cabin.

I didn't wait for Duane to open my door. Instead, I jumped out of the truck as soon as he stopped, but before he'd engaged the emergency brake. He left the headlights on, and they were the only source of light.

Duane called after me, "Slow down, Jess. Those steps aren't as solid as they look."

I forced myself to pick my way more carefully, which allowed Duane to catch up and place a protective hand at my back. When we reached the door, I tried it and found it locked.

"I have keys," he said gruffly, unlocking the door, and stopping me from bolting forward by gripping my upper arm. He waited until I was looking up at him before pressing the keys into my palm. "Here, these are for you."

"For me?" I grinned. I couldn't help it.

He laughed lightly and shook his head, walking past me into the cabin and disappearing into inky darkness. I hesitated at the door, listened to the sound of his boots scuffing on the floor, then the strike of a match. Pale illumination filled the small space as he lit a candle. I stepped in and closed the door behind me as Duane walked around the rectangular space, lighting wax candles as he went.

It was small. Really small. Maybe two hundred square feet. The walls were finished—which was surprising—but were painted plain white and held no photos or paintings. A stone wood-burning fireplace took up most of one wall, a small table with two chairs took up another, and a queen-sized bed ran along the third.

"Are you cold?"

"No," I said on a sigh, imagining us spending countless days and nights here, enjoying each other's company, sharing more of ourselves.

Finally, I lifted my eyes and met Duane's schooled expression.

He was studying me, my reaction to this place. Despite the careful coolness of his features, I could read his thoughts as clearly as though he'd spoken. He wanted to know if this place would do. If I would consent to him taking liberties with my body in this cozy cabin.

He was so silly.

So I said, "Duane, you are so silly."

"I'm silly?" He lifted an eyebrow and crossed his arms over his broad chest.

"Yes. See now, this place is great. But I'd just like to point out that if you've been waiting for a room and a bed for us to start doing mattress cartwheels, then I think you're being silly. Do you think I need candles and romance?" I waved a hand around the cabin. The place was small, but it was undeniably romantic. Add a fire in the fireplace, a bottle of wine, and naked cartwheels on the bed—it was basically a rustic den of seduction.

Regardless, I continued my tirade. "Baby, I do not need those things. You need to realize I don't want to be put on a pedestal. I don't want you to keep a respectful distance. I just need you. I like you wild and I love you reckless. Outside on a picnic blanket, inside the cab of your Road Runner, on the bed in this here cabin…where we come together makes no difference to me. It's you I want."

Each word was true. I didn't want or need romantic gestures or pretty things. I just wanted him. I was in love with him and nothing else mattered to me, not the where and not the when.

As I spoke, I saw the corner of his mouth lift of its own accord, and his gaze grew warmer. When I finished, he studied me for a long moment, his scorching stare skating up and down my body in a protracted perusal.

Good Lord, I was getting hot. Fleetingly I hoped he would take my words to heart and just take me now, fast and hard against the wall. The thought made my knees weak.

But then he crossed to where I stood with slow measured steps. And he didn't stop coming until he'd backed me up against the door. He placed one hand on the frame behind me and the other possessively on my hip.

His eyes glittered and smoldered. He gazed specifically at my mouth, as he said in a rumbly whisper, "Jessica, I've been thinking about making love to you for a real long time. And I won't settle for our first encounter being rushed—on a blanket outside, in a car, before dinner in my bedroom at home. I plan on taking my time with you…"

He leaned forward and to the side, the friction of his beard against my jaw and hot breath dancing beneath my ear making me shiver again. His fingers on my hip slipped under my shirt, his thumb rubbing a slow circle on the skin just above the waistline of my jeans.

"Duane," I whimpered, my hands grabbing fistfuls of his sweater. "We don't need to wait."

"But we do, Jess. Because I plan on taking your time as well." He licked my earlobe, nibbled it, and I trembled. "A whole night, and a whole day…"

"Please." My grip tightened and I yanked him toward me, needing his weight and warmth.

But instead he leaned away. This time his eyes connected with mine and they were fiercely sober and stern as he said, "You're already on that pedestal, Princess. And I respect the hell out of you, whether you like it or not."

♥

Like Saturday and Sunday, when Duane dropped me off, he walked me to my door and gave me a very respectful kiss. But this time he left me with a big grin. I wanted to call after him and say, *I'm in love with you, Duane Winston!* Instead I let him go. Though I felt warm and tingly, certain of having good dreams. The anticipation of admitting my feelings was going to kill me dead…in the best possible way.

I floated into my parents' house, not quite finished with my happy sigh, when I heard my daddy call to me from the family room.

"Jessica, is that you?"

"Yes, it's me."

"Can you come in here?"

I hung up my purse, kicked off my boots, and strolled—still ensconced in my happiness daze—into the family room. My daddy was standing in the center of the room when I entered, his hands in his pockets and his expression grim.

I felt my smile fall. "What's wrong?"

He sighed, looking resigned, and said, "There's no easy way to break the news, so I'll just tell you outright. Your momma called this evening. Aunt Louisa died this afternoon around five. She took a turn yesterday and didn't wake up."

My good mood deflated like a violently popped balloon. I covered my mouth with my hand. "Oh no…oh goodness. But she was just… I thought she was getting better?"

He shook his head.

My eyes lost focus as I thought about Aunt Louisa, my mother's younger sister, still so young at forty-two. Even though she'd always kept me at an arm's length, even though we'd never formed a real bond during our summers together, I still loved her. She was family.

"I can't believe she's gone," I whispered, without knowing I was speaking my thoughts.

My father crossed the room, pulled me into a hug, then led me to the couch. Once there he tucked me under his arm and let me cry a bit through my confusion. When I was mostly finished, he handed me a box of tissues and patted my hand.

"I've already purchased our plane tickets and called Kip Sylvester at the school to explain things. We'll leave tomorrow morning. Your momma will need your help."

I nodded numbly. "Yeah. Thank you. That makes sense."

My daddy stirred a bit in his seat, then leaned away. I sensed his eyes on me so I lifted my gaze.

After a long moment, he said, "This might be unseemly to discuss before your aunt is laid to rest, but I think I need to warn you about something before we get to Texas."

"Warn me? About what?"

I watched as my daddy gathered a deep breath, then

released it slowly. His words were halting as he said, "The thing is, Jessica, your aunt Louisa... She was your... Well, she was very wealthy. And you spent a lot of time with her, more than anyone else. I think you need to prepare yourself for a significant inheritance."

"Uh...what?"

If possible, my father looked even more mournful as he explained. "Your momma has seen the will. Baby girl, I don't know how else to break this to you, but Louisa left you everything. She left you the house, her engineering patents, the farm, and all her money. We're talking several million dollars."

Duane

18

> "I love to sail forbidden seas, and land on barbarous coasts."
>
> —HERMAN MELVILLE, *MOBY DICK*

WE WERE CUTTING IT CLOSE.

After dropping Jess off, I drove back to the house and jumped into Beau's car. He'd been waiting for me, sitting in the dark inside his red 1967 Pontiac GTO, drumming his fingers on the steering wheel. He didn't say anything; he didn't need to. I knew we were running late. If we were lucky, we'd arrive at the meeting spot just on time.

Jessica James was distracting. She'd been occupying my thoughts with more and more frequency. And now I was making new plans. These plans only served to increase my level of distraction. Showing Jess the cabin hadn't been premeditated. But when I realized I would need to borrow Billy's truck in order to take her home, I'd exploited the opportunity.

"Smart move, taking Billy's truck." My twin checked his rearview mirror as we pulled onto Moth Run, the paved road adjacent to our property. "The Wraiths know not to come within ten feet of Billy; no way in hell they'd follow his truck."

I nodded, because it had been a smart move. I didn't share that avoiding the Wraiths hadn't been my only reason for taking the truck. But avoiding the Wraiths *was* the reason I hadn't given the Mustang back to Jessica yet.

Both Beau and I were quickly proven right about taking Billy's truck when four motorcycles separated from the darkness and easily caught up with Beau's Pontiac.

"These guys are so stupid." Beau's face was twisted with irritation and impatience, an unusual expression for him. "What do they think we're going to do? Try to leave town undetected in my red GTO? Everyone knows this is my car. What a bunch of morons."

Before I could add a layer of colorful trash talk, my cell rang.

"Who is it?" Beau's eyes flickered between me and the road.

"I don't know. I don't recognize the number."

Beau glanced at the screen, then back out the windshield. "It might be Repo. He uses burners."

Burners, of course, being disposable cell phones thrown away before they can be traced.

Figuring Beau was probably right, I swiped my thumb across the screen and answered, "What?"

"You're finally leaving the house." Repo's raspy voice emerged from the other end.

"Yeah, so?"

"So, you're late."

"Not yet."

Repo chuckled. "I guess you still have a few minutes.

While I have you, why don't you tell me what Claire McClure was doing at your house earlier?"

I frowned and answered automatically and truthfully. "I don't know what you're talking about. I didn't see Claire at the house."

"Our boys saw her pull into your drive around five this evening and then leave a few minutes later. You know her daddy is my president, right? I don't think he'd like one of you Winston boys messing with his daughter."

"Like I said, I didn't know she was there. What and who my brothers do is none of my business, and it ain't yours either. And why are your recruits watching our house?"

I knew I was being followed, but I didn't know the Wraiths were watching the house. And I wasn't going to volunteer that Claire must've been the one to drop off Jessica. Given the fact the Wraiths had our driveway under surveillance, I was relieved Jess hadn't driven over on her own. If she'd borrowed her daddy's car, I was certain I would now be getting shit from Repo about my relationship with the sheriff's daughter. Again.

I'd been avoiding her for the last few days for this very reason, hoping they'd stop shadowing me after tonight's meeting.

Instead of answering my question, Repo lowered his voice and said, "None of your brothers better be *doing* anything with Claire. That girl is the property of the Wraiths."

My instinct was to argue, point out that Claire McClure hated them almost as much as we did and would raise hell if she heard anyone say she was property.

Instead, I fought my urge to throw the phone out the window or smash it against the dashboard. "I have to talk to your ugly face in ten minutes, so I'm hanging up now."

And I did.

Beau smirked at me. "I fucking hate that guy."

"Nothing to like," I agreed, my tone flat, still tempted to beat the shit out of my phone. Something needed to be smashed.

"Tina returned any of your calls yet?"

I shook my head, deciding to place the phone in the glove box, out of my reach. "No. Just text messages telling me to bring you to the Pink Pony. You?"

"Nope. I figure she wants us to go to the club and have a chat in person."

I glanced out the side mirror at the four motorcycle headlights and flexed my jaw. "I think so, too. We'll have to pay a visit."

"Tomorrow night, you think? Or Friday?"

I shrugged. Either would work. Since Tina wouldn't return my messages with anything other than invitations to watch her dance, I'd called Hank Weller, the owner of the Pink Pony, and asked for Tina's schedule. She was no longer stripping Sunday through Thursday, only on Thursday, Friday, and Saturday nights. Hank also volunteered that she'd been spending more and more time at the Dragon Biker Bar, entertaining the Wraiths.

At this point I wasn't convinced she'd help us at all. Her loyalty might rest firmly with the bikers—what little loyalty she had. Still, it was worth a shot to feel her out, see if she'd be willing.

"You ready to do this?" To anyone else, Beau would probably sound like his normal, good-humored self. To me, his levity sounded fake, forced, a cover for anger and determination.

"I'm ready."

I wasn't nervous or afraid. These morons didn't scare me. They pissed me off. And I was ready for this annoying game to be over.

♥

As soon as we pulled up to the meeting spot—an abandoned barn about three miles from the Dragon Biker Bar—bikers swarmed our car and "escorted" us inside. Repo was sitting calmly by the door. Dirty Dave was pacing the dirt floor. In total, there were ten of them and two of us.

I sized each one up with detachment and decided if all six of us Winston boys had been present, we'd likely be evenly matched.

"You ain't stupid, but you're reckless. Which can be difficult to tell apart, especially when the end result is the same." Repo greeted me with these words, not standing as we entered. His expression was outwardly friendly, but I could see simmering anger behind his black eyes. He didn't like that I'd hung up on him, and I couldn't bring myself to care.

"Let's get this over with," I mumbled, rolling my eyes.

"Now hold on, Duane." Beau gave both me and Repo a valiantly convincing smile. "I haven't seen Uncle Repo in a while."

My response to these staged words was authentic. I tried not to gag. How Beau could say such shit with a straight face—and believably—was a miracle.

Most of the fury behind Repo's expression eased and he stood to shake Beau's hand. I crossed my arms over my chest. No fucking way I was shaking hands with these douche canoes. Luckily, my honest reaction was also the part I'd been assigned.

I was bad cop. Beau was good cop.

Thus, I stood passively as Beau and Repo exchanged pleasantries, noticing that the other nine bikers appeared to take their cues from Repo. They all visibly relaxed when they saw how friendly Beau and Repo were. Even Dirty Dave smiled at Beau, shaking his hand, calling him *son* instead of *boy*.

My twin had this effect on people because he was so gifted at being insincere. I was convinced he could bullshit his way out of a federal prison if the need ever arose. He'd inherited our father's gift of artless charm. Jethro, my oldest brother, had similar abilities. Roscoe, the youngest, was a close third.

Cletus, Ashley, and I possessed my mother's temperament, too candid for our own good. And Billy turned his charm on and off like a switch. He used it when it served his purposes, but I could tell he hated every minute of it.

But unlike our father, and despite their charisma, my siblings were good people, worthy of my respect and trust. Well, actually...Jethro *was* questionable at times. Regardless, I'd do just about anything for all of them.

Eventually I grew tired of watching Beau make everyone laugh. "Are we going to get down to business anytime soon?"

The laughter tapered and Repo's eyes slithered back to me, though he now appeared to be in a much better mood. "Sure thing, Duane. You boys ready to discuss terms of the partnership? I think you'll find our offer of a thirty-seventy split more than fair."

"Depends on who gets the thirty percent and who gets the seventy percent," Beau quipped, making Dirty Dave chuckle like a bashful schoolgirl.

"Now hold on." I shook my head and stepped forward. "We haven't agreed to anything."

"Then what are we doing here, boy?" Dirty Dave lifted his fat finger like he was going to wave it in my face. But something in my expression must've given him pause, because he settled for sticking out his chin and barrel chest.

"Like I said, we haven't agreed to anything."

"You're trying my patience, Duane," Repo said, sounding more tired than angry.

Beau cut in, "What Duane means is, we can't agree to something we're not sure we can deliver."

Repo narrowed his eyes—with confusion, not suspicion—and glanced between the two of us. "What does that mean?"

"It means we can't use our shop for this operation. Its location is too public, and I don't think anyone here wants us to get caught before we get started." Beau's words were entirely reasonable.

Repo nodded. "Okay. Fair point. I'm listening."

I spoke next, because the plan was for me to break the bad news in a completely irritating way while Beau reexplained it, making it sound more palatable.

"So we're not going to do it," I stated, maybe with more belligerence than was called for.

"What Duane means"—Beau glanced at me like he was exasperated with my attitude—"is that we can't do it, not until a suitable location is found."

Dirty Dave shrugged and said just as we thought he would, "That's easy. Use Brick and Mortar's shop."

"Can't." I shook my head stubbornly. "First of all, it's associated with the Wraiths. Secondly, I overheard Jackson James mention their office is working on a warrant for that place."

Repo's eyes narrowed further. "You overheard?"

"Yep. Why do you think I've been so friendly with his sister?" I hoped Repo would believe this explanation for many reasons, not the least of which was that—if he did—then I'd be able to go about my business with Jess and not have to suffer through Repo's reprimands and disapproval. But more than that, I hoped this version of my motivations would keep Jessica safe. I needed her safe and far away from this mess.

Thus, I was surprised by Repo's answering thunderous expression and raised voice. "You're using that girl, boy? You hurt her, I will break you in two!"

Beau stepped between us. "Now come on, Repo. You've known us since we were babies. You know Duane. Do you think *Duane* would be able to run a con on someone as clever as Jessica James?"

I should have been insulted by Beau's insinuation that Jessica was my superior in intelligence, but I wasn't. This was because he was likely right. Jess was smart. But I wasn't intimidated by her intellect, likely because—when paired with her sweetness—it turned me on so much.

Beau continued. "All he's saying is that he's taking advantage of a rare opportunity—access to the James's household. That's not using Miss James. That's being resourceful to all of our benefit."

Repo didn't look entirely convinced, and I was busy trying to figure out why he felt so invested in Jessica's well-being. I thought about his comment last Saturday at Daisy's and wondered just how well Repo knew Jessica's momma.

Beau pushed the conversation back on track. "So, that's where we are. We've been busy over the last two weeks. If your fine brothers here have been keeping tabs on us, then they've probably told you about how Duane and I have been scouting locations."

Repo glanced at Dirty Dave. Dave gave him a short nod. Repo frowned and exhaled loudly, searching the floor as he considered the matter.

Finally he said, "You should have contacted us. We have properties everywhere. One of them is bound to suit."

I shook my head. "No way. Like I said, we're not doing this using one of your properties."

"Why the hell not?" Dirty Dave lifted his chin again.

"Because nothing could be more obvious, old man. Suddenly you have two Winston brothers, auto mechanics, making frequent visits to one of your warehouses right after Brick and Mortar are put away? That's just stupid."

Luckily Beau didn't have to interpret because Repo nodded thoughtfully at my tirade. "He's right. Better these boys find the space themselves, outfit it. The less evidence of a partnership between us the better. Bringing Brick and Mortar into the Wraiths was a mistake. It made things difficult over the years, trying to get things done without police always doing random searches."

No one else noticed, but I saw Beau's shoulders relax at Repo's words, and his smile came a bit easier. I was still outwardly scowling, but took Repo's agreement as a victory.

Jethro was due to return in two weeks. If we could hold the Wraiths off for another two weeks, then maybe Jethro could help us sort this mess out without getting our hands dirty. Or maybe Tina could be convinced to wipe their files and bring us a copy.

Either way, this was the stay of execution we needed.

"All right, looks like we have a plan." Beau rubbed his hands together, nodding at Dirty Dave, then at me.

"Yeah…" Repo scrutinized Beau. "But this search can't go on forever. You two need to find a place this week."

Beau chuckled, like this demand was made as a good-natured joke. "This week? Repo, we're coming up against Thanksgiving. Ain't no one going to meet with us about property this week. We need at least until January first."

"If no one will meet with you before Thanksgiving, then ain't no one going to talk to you around Christmas neither. You have until the second week of December and that's it."

I shook my head, but grumbled, "Fine. Second week of December."

Luckily, I was much better at pretending to be irritated than I was at pretending to be nice.

Duane

19

> "Nothing travels faster than the speed of light, with the possible exception of bad news, which obeys its own special laws."
>
> —DOUGLAS ADAMS, *MOSTLY HARMLESS*

Jessica: You're probably still asleep and I didn't want to wake you. On my way to Texas for a funeral, my aunt died yesterday.
Jessica: Tell your brothers I'm sorry about dinner.
Jessica: I'll call you later today, I need to talk to you.
Jessica: I miss you.

I DIDN'T SEE JESSICA'S TEXT messages or her three missed calls until Thursday afternoon, not until Beau and I were on our way home from the shop, because I'd left my cell in Beau's glove compartment all day.

When I did see them, I spent the next several minutes using every curse word in my arsenal as I listened to her voicemails.

"What the hell happened?" Beau eyeballed me from the driver's seat.

"Hush, I'm trying to listen." I waved him off, restarting Jessica's first message.

"*Hey, Duane. It's Jess. We just landed in Houston. I wanted to talk to you before we left the airport because the reception out at the farm can be spotty. It'll take us about an hour and a half to drive out there. Call me when you get this.*" She hesitated, her voice cracking a little when she added before clicking off, "*I really miss you.*"

The second message was short: "*Hey, it's me. We're on the road now. Call when you can.*"

And my heart was in my throat as I listened to the third message: "*Hi. We're at the farm now; this number is the direct line to the house. If you call, one of the staff will answer and I left instructions that they should come get me if you do. So…call me? Did I mention I miss you? …Bye.*"

I immediately hit Redial, praying she'd be available to talk. As she'd warned, one of the staff picked up and placed me on hold, apparently searching the house for her.

I could feel Beau's split attention—between me and the mountain road—and he finally asked, "Is that Jessica? What happened? Is she okay?"

"Shhh…" I didn't want him distracting me. With each passing second, I grew more agitated—with the wait and with myself for leaving the phone in Beau's car.

But relief flooded my chest when I finally heard her voice. "Hello?"

"Jessica, it's me. It's Duane. I am so sorry I didn't get your messages. My phone was in Beau's glove compartment and… You know what? It doesn't matter. How are you? Are you okay? Do you need me to fly out? I can leave today."

This was a thoughtless promise and I knew Beau was

looking at me like I was crazy, but I didn't care. If she needed me, I would fly out. The Wraiths and their threats could go to hell. Then they could go fuck themselves and go to hell again.

She sighed softly, but when she answered, her tone was low and stiff, like she was trying to keep from being overheard. "Thanks for calling. I–I'm glad you called."

I paused for a second, then asked, "I'm guessing you're with people?"

"That's right…"

I guessed she was hoping I'd lead the conversation, do most of the talking, since she was being listened to on her end.

"Can you call me tonight? Nine my time?"

"Yes!" Her loud and enthusiastic response made me smile despite the situation. "I mean, yes. I can do that."

"Good. You call me at nine. I'll keep my phone on me."

"Okay…" I heard her struggle, like she wanted to say more, something in particular. Instead she sounded resigned as she said, "Talk to you later."

I guessed what she wanted, so I said it. "I miss you, Jessica James."

"Me too," she said immediately, like she was anxious I wouldn't say the words, but relieved I had.

"I mean it. I miss you. You're too far away. If you need me to fly out, I can get on a plane tonight."

"Don't do that. Things are… Well, anyway." I heard her take a deep breath, then say, "Okay, sounds good. Talk to you later."

I hesitated, wondering if I should just go. In the end I decided I'd be talking to her that night and could reassess the situation then, fly out Friday if needed.

Eventually I said, "Okay, okay. We'll talk tonight."

"Yes. We will. Bye."

"Bye."

I set the phone on my lap, staring at the screen for a long minute before adding the Houston number to my contacts.

Beau exhaled loudly next to me. "You mind telling me what's going on?"

"Jess's aunt died. She's in Houston, can't make dinner tonight."

"That's terrible."

I nodded absentmindedly.

"So…no pie?"

I glared at my brother. "No. No pie for you, Beauford Fitzgerald."

"No need for that tone, Duane Faulkner. I was just double-checking." When I continued to glare, he added, "The woman makes good pie. You can't blame me for wanting more of it."

"You'll get her pie only if and when I say it's appropriate."

He grumbled something under his breath I didn't catch. I ignored him in favor of glancing out the window and I saw the flashing police lights behind us through the side mirror just before the siren gave a yelp, making Beau jump in his seat.

"God in heaven!" Beau, obviously startled, frowned and squinted at his rearview mirror. "What the hell? Is that Jack?"

I nodded, grinding my teeth. Jessica's brother, Jackson, was pulling us over and the hairs on the back of my neck abruptly itched. Something about the situation didn't feel right, almost like it was an ambush, like he'd been waiting for us.

"Just pull off." I sighed, closed my eyes, and rubbed my forehead. "Let's get this over with."

"I wasn't even speeding, and this car doesn't have a broken taillight. He is *such* a jackass!" My brother hit his steering wheel with obvious frustration, but slowed the car, navigating two more switchbacks before pulling carefully onto a mountain overlook.

Beau was now repeating all my earlier curse words under his breath as we waited for Jackson to approach the car. I was not surprised that Jackson, being the complete jackass that he was, shined his high-powered flashlight in Beau's face even though the sun was still out.

"Which one of you is Duane?" he asked, then pointed the flashlight at me. I'd averted my eyes so I wouldn't be blinded and was reminded how much I seriously hated this guy.

"You can't pull cars over just because you're looking for somebody, Jack," Beau said, nice and friendly and with a shit-eating grin. "Not unless that person is missing or under arrest."

"You're Beau," Jackson said, lifting his chin toward my brother. He redirected his attention back to me as he holstered his flashlight, still leaning against the car and into the window. "Duane, did you know my sister is out of town?"

I sat a bit straighter, surprised Jackson had pulled us over just to share his sister's whereabouts with me, and glanced at Beau before answering. "Yes. I just spoke with her."

"My aunt died, my momma's sister. Jess is out in Houston with my parents, sorting everything out."

Beau and I shared another look, and I read Beau's thoughts perfectly because they mirrored mine: *Why the hell is he telling us this?*

"I know all this, Jackson. Like I said, I just spoke to Jessica."

Jackson nodded, and I realized he was schooling his expression, keeping his tone flat. Something dark and cold settled in the pit of my stomach. This was a setup. I was sure of it. Jackson was setting me up, but for the life of me, I couldn't figure out how.

Abruptly I knew we needed to leave before Jackson could say anything else.

"Well, thanks for the info. We'll just be on our way." I motioned to Beau to restart the car.

"If you know about the funeral, then I guess you know about the money, too. Right?"

I almost flinched. Almost. Instead I swallowed and nodded, bluffing. "That's right. Know all about it. Start the car, Beau."

Beau did as I instructed, but Jackson didn't move away from the window. He just kept on talking.

"Oh. Did Jess tell you how she inherited all my aunt's money? That she's now independently wealthy and will be leaving Green Valley after Christmas?"

Beau's eyebrows lifted, just a fraction of an inch, but otherwise he did an admirable job of hiding his surprise. Outwardly dispassionate, I stared at Jessica's brother. Meanwhile my heart was beating out of my chest and I'd broken into a cold sweat.

Fear.

I was feeling fear.

The last time I felt fear, really and truly, was when my daddy locked me in the woodshed for two days with no food or water as punishment for sitting in his chair.

I couldn't breathe.

Beau answered for me. "Like he said, Duane just talked to Jessica. He already knows all this. Now if you'll step away from the car, we'll be on our way home, *Officer*."

Jackson frowned, looking disappointed and confused by my lack of outward reaction, then nodded once and backed up so we could pull away.

Beau rolled up his window, being careful to check for

traffic and using his blinker before pulling onto the mountain road. We drove in silence for a full minute and I was thankful for the quiet.

At first I considered the possibility that Jackson was lying. I dismissed this, as one quick call to Jess would be enough to disprove any false claims.

No, he was telling the truth.

Staff had answered the phone at her aunt's house, now her house. It was a farm, she'd said. Jessica had mentioned horses on the property. Horses weren't cheap to maintain. And she'd told me that her aunt had just died. She didn't want to talk to me when others were present on her end. I pulled up the text messages she'd left earlier.

> I'll call you later today, I need to talk to you.
> I miss you.

"Fuck..." My forehead hit the window at my side. I closed my eyes as something sharp and intangible stabbed my heart. The pain was unbearable, spreading up my neck and down my spine. I held my breath, waited for it to pass.

"Did you know she was leaving? After Christmas?"

I shook my head and my voice was rough when I answered, "No. I don't think she had plans to leave, not yet."

"Not yet?"

"She'd planned to leave, just not yet. Not 'til she had enough money saved..."

I heard Beau mutter a curse, then clear his throat. "It's sad about her aunt."

"Yes...it is." I wondered if Jessica was close to her aunt. I wondered if she was hurting. As much fear and, frankly, despair

I felt at the idea of Jessica leaving, the thought of her hurting, and me being powerless to help, was worse.

"Do you think it's true? You know, Jackson is a little bitch. He could be trying to mess with you, now he knows you have it bad for his sister."

I ignored Beau's last statement and addressed the former. "He's not lying. If she had the money, she'd leave tomorrow. She told me so on our first date."

Beau shut his mouth after that. Again I was grateful for the silence. I didn't want to talk about Jessica leaving, debate the truth of it.

She had the means. She was leaving. There was nothing more to say.

♥

I'd planned to ignore Jessica's call at nine by switching off my phone, letting it go to voicemail.

I wasn't afraid of what she would say. I knew what she was going to say. I just didn't want to hear it over the phone, when she was hundreds of miles away, and be expected to respond calmly...when all I wanted to do was rage.

I didn't want to rage at her, didn't want to part ways with that between us, so I'd planned to ignore her call.

I figured she'd either leave me a voicemail—tell me she was never coming back and spare me the conversation—or she'd write me a letter—tell me she was never coming back and spare me the conversation. Either was preferable to having the conversation because I could delete a voicemail and burn a letter, but I couldn't take back words said in anger.

Regardless, my good intentions were ignored, because when she called, I answered.

"Duane?"

"Jessica."

I heard her sigh when I responded, like she was relieved I'd answered. Meanwhile, I couldn't swallow even though my throat was on fire.

"Oh my goodness, it is so good to hear your voice. I know I texted it to you and left you a voicemail, but I can't tell you how much I've missed you. I…" I heard her sigh again, then sniffle. When she spoke next, her voice was full of tears. "Duane, I need to tell you something."

"Go ahead." I imagined this was what it was like just after the hangman's noose was fitted over one's neck, but just before the floor gave way beneath the condemned. I knew the end was coming. I wondered if the finality of it would be a relief or a burden.

But then she said, "Duane Winston, I love you."

I opened my mouth to respond to the words I'd expected to hear—we were over, she had her means, and she was leaving sooner rather than later—but the reality of what she'd *actually* said rendered me speechless. I stared ahead, frowning at the wall of my room, feeling like she'd just thrown my swim shorts up a tree.

"I love you and I'm in love with you and I realize you're probably upset with me for saying it over the phone, but something happened. I found out something…and I felt like I needed to tell you. Like you needed to know. I love you. Life is so short, too short for secrets and things left unsaid. I know we haven't been together very long, but I've known you most of my life and I think I've always loved you, even though you were ornery and mean and argumentative. Even though you were never the safe choice…"

Now she was crying, big heavy sobs, making my chest ache in response. My fingers tightened on the phone. I wanted to hold her, soothe away her pain, but she was a thousand miles away and I wasn't prepared for this conversation. I hadn't planned on her love, hadn't counted on it.

More accurately, I hadn't thought it was in the realm of possibility.

Maybe Jackson had been lying. Maybe she had no plans to leave after Christmas. Maybe she did. But if she had the means to go, then I was the only reason she would consider delaying…

I didn't feel elation at this news. I felt only misery.

"So…I love you," Jessica repeated for a fifth time. I closed my eyes, shaking my head, rejecting the chant that called to my soul—bone-deep—and tempted me with my own destruction, and hers as well.

Still unable to swallow, I cleared my throat instead and closed my eyes, gathering my resolve. Self-preservation finally kicked in and I knew what I needed to do.

"Jess, we'll talk when you get back. Okay?" My voice was steady and calm.

A muffled sob sounded from the other end and I nearly relented, I nearly gave in and told her how I loved her, how I adored her. But then I forced myself to imagine how she might look at me five or ten years from now. I would be the source of her misery because I would be the focus of her resentment.

My mother had looked at my father that way. He'd been the thief of her dreams, of her life. She'd loved us kids, but we all knew she'd longed for more. That road wasn't one I was willing to travel.

"Okay," she said finally, her voice small and dejected.

"Okay. Bye, Jess."

It took her another moment and I knew she was covering the phone with her hand, possibly so I couldn't hear her cry, but then she said in a rush, "Goodbye, Duane," and hung up the phone.

I removed the cell from my ear and stared at the screen, at the number I'd saved earlier in the day, one I'd labeled as *Jessica—Texas funeral*.

I'd been an idiot.

Jessica wasn't going to break my heart.

I was going to break hers.

Duane

20

> "Travel brings wisdom only to the wise. It renders the ignorant more ignorant than ever."
>
> —JOE ABERCROMBIE,
> *LAST ARGUMENT OF KINGS*

WITH A DARK CLOUD OVER my head, Beau and I arrived at the Pink Pony at 10:30 p.m. The lot was full, but that wasn't unusual. This place was by far the best strip club in eastern Tennessee. I was no connoisseur, but Beau was, and I trusted his opinion.

The interior of the Pink Pony was mostly pink. The walls were pink, as were the carpet, tables, and chairs. The dancing platforms were a shiny black lacquer, and four white fiberglass carousel ponies decorated the stage. Girls would use the attached carousel poles in their act, and sometimes they would "ride" the ponies.

I knew the bouncer on duty from my days of picking up Tina after work. He waved us in and I immediately crossed to the bar. I didn't notice any of it as we entered—the glitz, the tits, the girls, the patrons. Hank typically manned the bar on weeknights. We'd need his permission to go backstage and I wanted to get this over with.

As soon as he saw me, he gave me a smile that was equal parts pleased and disappointed. He finished pouring two shots from a bottle with a black label, then crossed to meet us.

"Aww, man. I was hoping to never see you here again." He reached his hand out and shook mine over the bar, politely ignoring my foul mood, then turned to my brother. "Beau, are we still fishing on Sunday?"

"Yep. Butt crack of dawn," Beau shouted over the noise, sliding onto one of the stools and grinning at his old friend.

Hank was four years our senior. Growing up, he was only around for the summers; his parents shipped him off to boarding school during the year. Now he was living it up, a Harvard Business School graduate turned local strip club owner, and a source of extreme embarrassment to his parents.

"Based on your phone call last week, I'm guessing you're here to see Tina?" He sounded like he hoped his assumption was wrong.

"I'll take some whiskey first." I pulled a twenty out of my wallet and lifted my chin to the Jack Daniels behind him.

I didn't miss the way Hank glanced at Beau as though asking for permission before turning for the bottle on the wall and pouring three shots.

"One for each of us?" Beau leaned forward and passed me one of the small glasses.

"Nope." Hank shook his head. "Duane here gets three shots and that's it. I'm pouring them now so he won't ask for more later. And they're on the house."

I wasn't going to argue. If and when I wanted to get

drunk, it wouldn't be at the Pink Pony right before talking to Tina Patterson about serious business.

"Thanks." I passed one of the shots to Beau. "Here. I only want two."

I picked up my shot and lifted it, but before I could down the amber liquid, Beau clinked his glass against mine and said, "To making new plans, better plans."

I stared at my brother for a long moment and he held my glare. I appreciated the sentiment even though I was disposed to reject it in my present mood. I'd spent so long wishing for something that ultimately brought me misery.

No…I wouldn't be making any more plans. Not for a while.

I finished my two shots in quick succession while Beau and Hank fell into an easy conversation about boats. I didn't pay any attention. Instead, I used the time to scan the Pink Pony's patrons. I didn't see any Iron Wraiths members, but that wasn't unusual. Rumor had it the Iron Wraiths owned a stake in the G-Spot, a dirty little strip club down by the Dragon Biker Bar. Plus they had to behave at Hank's club; he didn't take their shit.

After scanning the crowd, I waited another five minutes for Beau and Hank to finish their conversation, but they were engrossed and I was too impatient to wait for a polite opening. Thus, when the pleasant numbness of whiskey took its hold, I interrupted.

"We need to talk to Tina. Any chance we could go in the back?"

Again, Hank looked to Beau as though asking permission, prompting my brother to add, "We both need to talk to her. It shouldn't take longer than a few minutes, twenty at the most."

Hank nodded. "That's fine. Y'all can use my office."

He motioned to one of the bouncers and handed Beau the keys to his office; we shook hands again; then we followed Hank's employee out of the main lounge and into the back area.

I half listened, but not really, as Beau greeted all the girls we passed, only half heard them coo and flirt with my brother. I had no pleasantries for anybody and was relieved when we finished the gauntlet of barely covered breasts, glitter, and tall hair.

Beau unlocked the office and the bouncer left us, stating he'd bring Tina. Once we were inside, Beau shut the door and walked to the desk. I stood by the door, leaned against the wall, and waited.

Inevitably, my thoughts turned to Jess. Without meaning to, I conjured her face, was entranced by the slant of her mouth, mesmerized by the small freckles on her collarbone. She was a sickness, my sickness.

I decided, once this was over, I was definitely getting drunk. Maybe for a couple days. At least through Monday.

"You're going to have to fake it."

I glanced at my brother, knowing he'd spoken but unsure what he'd said. "What?"

"With Tina. You're going to have to find some charm and fake it. She's not interested in me, wouldn't help me out of a shallow ditch. But she'd do anything for you, if you asked nicely."

I frowned. "She wouldn't."

Beau smirked. "She would. Yeah, like Cletus says, she's a crazy bitch. But she's got real feelings for you—as real as she can manage—and you're going to have to use them if you want her to help us."

I gathered then released a large breath, wiping my hand over my face. "This was a bad idea."

"Why?"

"Because I'm no good at bullshitting."

"Then don't bullshit. Tell her the truth—or some version of it. You need her help. Tell her that. That'll make her feel good, important."

I opened my mouth to respond, but at that moment the door opened and Tina walked in. As soon as she saw me, she stopped, her mouth parting in surprise. I straightened away from the wall and crossed to her, reaching around and closing the door.

She swayed toward me, her big eyes made bigger with paint and fake lashes. "Duane…?"

"Tina." I tried to force some warmth into the word, but I couldn't. Too many years of drama and stupid shit were between us. I looked at her now and saw nothing but a black hole of aggravation and tedium. Why I put up with her for so long was a mystery.

At my greeting, she stiffened. I heard Beau sigh and saw him drop his head into his hands. Gritting my teeth, I shook my head, searching for some inner strength or hidden powers of bullshit.

"What do you want?" she spat.

I studied her for a long moment. She was dressed in tight jeans and a blue halter top, real clothes, like she was on her way out.

"I need your help," I said simply.

She blinked at me, my words obviously not what she expected.

"You need my help?" Her tone was softer than it had been.

"Yes. I need your help."

"Oh…I…" Tina appeared to be flustered by my admission, but she rallied after a few seconds, giving me what I recognized as a look meant to entice. "Well, you must need my help, seeing as you've been calling me for two weeks and you're here now. You must need me real bad."

She strutted toward me and lifted her hand as though to place it on me; I caught her wrist before she could.

"No," I said.

"No?" I'd surprised her again.

"No." I shook my head. "Never that. Never again."

"Then, w-what…" she stuttered, then huffed her impatience. "What could you want me for?"

Beau finally spoke. "Tina, honey, there's more to you than your snatch. You have a brain upstairs, might be worth dusting it off every once in a while."

This earned Beau a venomous look, and I realized he and I had switched positions. I was now good cop…well, my version of good cop.

"Shut up, Beau, and let me talk to Tina alone."

"You want me to leave?" Beau straightened from the desk, sounded appropriately surprised.

"Yeah. Give us a minute."

Tina glanced back to me, her expression curious and uncertain.

Beau made a show of his disgust on his way to the door. "I hope you know what you're doing, because I told you this was a mistake. We never should have come here. She can't be trusted, Duane."

"Just leave," I said, holding Tina's gaze.

He snorted, all part of the show, then stormed out of the office.

When he'd gone, I let go of her wrist and walked to one of the chairs in front of Hank's desk, motioning her to follow. "Please. Sit down."

She didn't move, but said in a rush, "You *can* trust me, Duane. You know you can. Beau never liked me and he never understood us."

I nodded, but made no verbal response. I was starting to think *I* never understood us.

Again I motioned to the chair. "Please sit down. We need to talk."

She gave me a hopeful smile then crossed to the seat, sitting as I'd instructed. I sat in the other chair, positioned it so we were facing. I couldn't bullshit. That wasn't my strength. But I could be focused, and I could be precise, and I was good at honesty.

Thus, I focused on pushing distracting thoughts of Jessica's sobs from my mind.

I explained the situation to Tina in precise—but not explicit—detail.

And I was honest.

I didn't have a choice. My family needed her help. And there was nothing I wouldn't do for my family.

Jessica

21

> "See the world. It's more fantastic than any dream made or paid for in factories."
>
> —RAY BRADBURY, *FAHRENHEIT 451*

I WASN'T MAD.

I was hurt and sad and confused by…well, everything. But I wasn't mad.

My aunt's funeral took place on Friday.

Except she wasn't my aunt. She was my birth mother. This devastating tidbit had been revealed as soon as I arrived at her house from the airport. My daddy traveled with me and both my parents—the only parents I'd known—and Aunt Louisa's lawyer pulled me into the office on the ground floor and told me the truth.

A big part of this truth was that she'd purposefully waited to tell me until she'd gone, and no one knew the identity of my biological father. Aunt Louisa hadn't seen fit to share my paternal parentage with anyone.

In light of the fact that Louisa had waited until *dying* to tell me she was my birth mother, I was feeling understandably emotional. And reflective. And reckless. And angry I'd been cheated out of knowing the truth while I had time to do *something* other than accept a huge inheritance from a woman who hadn't liked me much.

So I told Duane the truth, and he'd responded by saying nothing. *Nothing.*

I'd told him I was in love with him and he hadn't reciprocated. I'd been foolish. I'd allowed myself to fall too hard and too fast, and he probably thought I was crazy. Maybe I was. Maybe Aunt Louisa was crazy, or maybe my biological father was a whack job who fell in love too hard and too fast, who valued freedom and wanderlust over lasting relationships and responsibilities.

Maybe I was the person I was because my biological parents were circles surrounded by good, generous, reliable square pegs. It certainly would explain a lot.

When the will was read on Saturday, I was again named as her daughter, and therefore the official sole beneficiary. I'd had two days to adjust to the truth of my biological beginnings, but it was still a shock when the executor said, "To my daughter, Jessica James, I leave my entire estate. All patents, holdings, accounts…"

After the word *accounts* I'd zoned out, feeling sick to my stomach.

My daddy left on Sunday, needing to return to work. Before leaving, he told me that I was his daughter. He told me he held me the day I was born and made me his, and nothing would ever change that fact. I cried. He cried. We hugged. He cleared his throat and told me to take care of my momma, and let her take care of me.

Momma stayed and tried to help me get things sorted. I'd decided it didn't matter whose uterus I'd inhabited; my parents were my parents. They'd raised me. They'd bandaged my cuts and kissed my hurts and attended my school plays. Aunt Louisa might have left me her empty, cold estate, but she'd never tucked me in at night. She wasn't my mother because she hadn't *been* my mother.

I tried calling Duane again on Sunday. He didn't pick up and he didn't return the call. My heart splintered a little more.

By Tuesday evening, Momma was anxious to get back for Thanksgiving, so we took one of my new-to-me cars—a new model Jaguar F-Type—and split up the fourteen-hour drive. I'd never driven a luxury sports car before. It was fun. Or rather, it would have been fun, if I hadn't been so sad.

I told Aunt Louisa's lawyer I would return after Christmas to make arrangements. I'd decided to wait the month because I honestly didn't know what I was going to do.

Momma and I left early Wednesday morning and pulled into our driveway just before 10:30 p.m. We talked very little on the drive. I asked her all the obvious questions—*Do you know who my biological father is? Why didn't you tell me? Why didn't Louisa tell me before she died? Why did you adopt me?*—and she had very few answers.

She did reassure me that she chose to adopt me. That she loved me as her own and always had. But every question made her cry like the world was ending, so I stopped asking questions.

Exhausted when we arrived home, I excused myself after receiving a round of hugs from my daddy and brother, numbly took a shower, and readied myself for bed. I pulled on my favorite sleep shirt—a black silk nightshirt that fell just above my knees—and woolen socks, and climbed under my covers.

Except, now I was settled and should have been feeling comfortable, but I couldn't stop thinking. The money, what to do with it, what to do about the house and all the land, wasn't what kept me awake. I wasn't ready to wonder about my aunt Louisa, or why in tarnation she'd kept me at arm's length while she was alive and took the secret of my father's identity to her grave. Maybe I was simmering in these questions, but I wasn't ready to confront them. Regardless, she wasn't at the forefront of my thoughts either.

The truth was, I couldn't stop thinking about Duane.

During the drive home I'd decided, on I-20 someplace between Tuscaloosa and Birmingham, I was going to search him out. He missed me; he'd said so. He'd offered to fly out to Houston. We'd made plans before I left, plans that included a whole night and a whole day and a rustic den of seduction in the woods. We'd made thirteen months of plans.

Now at home, I tossed and turned, wondering if I'd misunderstood or misinterpreted things between us. I replayed every conversation—every touch and every look—over and over in my head, all the words he'd said that felt like promises.

I think we're suited.

I've always wanted you.

When we make love…

The house fell quiet and still I fretted. Unable to stand the sound of silence any longer, I grabbed my coat, my car keys, and the keys to Duane's cabin.

On the way out, I also nabbed a small flashlight from the kitchen drawer and pulled on my tennis shoes, not bothering to tie the laces.

Finding the turnoff from Moth Run proved to be relatively easy. But I began to doubt myself and the sanity of taking a sixty-thousand-dollar sports car on a unpaved Tennessee mountain road until I spotted the rough path that led to his place. Less than three minutes later, I spotted the cabin, and my breath caught in my throat.

I was momentarily paralyzed by the sight because light flickered through the windows, and what I guessed was smoke from the chimney rose into the air, made visible by how it blotted out the stars in the sky above.

Inexplicably, I was suddenly quite furious.

Riding the wave of intense anger, I put the stick shift in first gear, forcefully engaged the emergency brake, and turned off the headlights, opting to traverse the remaining distance by foot. No car was in sight—not Billy's truck and not Duane's Road Runner. I didn't dwell on this trivia because with each step, I grew more agitated. By the time I'd silently picked my way up the rough stone steps, I was good and pissed off.

I didn't knock before I tried the handle, found it locked, then laughed to myself maniacally as I searched for the cabin's keys.

"No keeping this crazy lady out..." I muttered nonsensically to myself. "Hide all you want. I have a key, a key you gave me, you stupid hillbilly. You shouldn't give a girl keys to your man cave if you don't want her to open the door..."

No sooner had I found the keys and exclaimed, "Aha!" with wild satisfaction than the door swing open. My head whipped up, a ready frown on my face, and I was assaulted with the image of a sleepy, peeved Duane Winston in nothing but unzipped blue jeans and black boxer shorts.

Of course, my frown gave way to wonder as my eyes moved

over his body. Warmth permeated my bones. Goodness…I loved his body. It called to me. It wanted me to touch it. It promised to hold me and provide the comfort and reassurance I desperately needed.

"Jessica?" The truly perplexed way he said my name cut through my wishful thinking and I lifted my gaze to his, found him looking at me, stunned. Like I might be a figment of his imagination.

"I'm not drunk!" I yelled at him.

I don't know why I volunteered this bit of information. Maybe because showing up in the middle of the night to his cabin in the woods, dressed in my pajamas and coat and untied tennis shoes, seemed like something only a drunk person would do.

His eyebrows drew together.

"Duane Winston, I–I…" I swallowed, my throat working without success. My chin wobbled, my eyes stung, and not knowing what else to do, I punched him as hard as I could in the shoulder.

"Ow!"

"Ow?"

"What'd you do that for?" He was rubbing his shoulder, now looking at me like I was crazy.

I wasn't crazy. I was simply a woman scorned, in the Shakespearean sense.

"I'm mad at you!"

"You're mad at me?"

"Yes! I needed you and you don't love…" I let my voice trail off, unable to complete the sentence, and moved to punch him again even as tears blurred my vision.

Obviously anticipating my intent, he easily intercepted my

wrist and used my momentum to pull me forward into the cabin. He kicked the door shut and caught me around the waist before I could face-plant on the floor in front of the fire.

"Stop—"

"I'm so mad at you." I thrashed against his hold, the tears now streaming freely down my face. "I thought we were in this together; I thought you wanted me; I thought you'd be there for me when I needed you! But I tell you how I feel and you want to talk about it *later*? Was this all a setup? A big lie? Did you ever want me at all?"

He snaked his arm around me and managed to keep my arms from flailing. My back was pressed to his front and he had me in a tight hold.

"Jess—"

"You are such a bastard!" I had just one goal: hurt Duane Winston. Hurt him just as badly as he'd hurt me with his cool dismissal of my confession.

"Just calm down for a second," he growled in my ear.

"Calm down? *Calm down?*"

"Yes, calm down." He dragged me farther into the small space.

I tried to wrench myself free, digging my nails into his bicep and scratching viciously as I bellowed, "I AM NEVER GOING TO CALM DOWN!"

With one smooth movement, he twisted me around and pushed me backward. I thought I was going to land ass first on the hard floor, but instead my back connected with the soft mattress. A split second later he was on top of me, holding my wrists above my head and pressing me against the bed with the weight of his body.

I bucked beneath him to no avail. His breathing was ragged

and so was mine. I took the opportunity to glare daggers at his skull. But it wasn't long before I realized he appeared to be just as angry as me.

As soon as I comprehended his fury, Duane's eyes lowered to my mouth, like my lips distracted him. Then his expression changed, teetered between furious, hungry, and lost.

"Jessica…" he whispered.

I wasn't mad anymore. Well, I was mad, I just didn't feel mad. I felt tired, and all the hurt beneath the anger bubbled to the surface.

"I am so mad at you," I repeated, like the watery words might protect my heart, and I felt hot tears slide past my temples into my hair.

His gaze lifted to mine and he winced; his hold on my wrists loosened and he let them go. Duane cupped my face with his big hands and I felt his thumbs lightly wipe away the wetness at my temples.

"Don't be mad, Jessica. And don't cry. Please don't cry."

He brushed his lips against my forehead, pressed a lingering kiss between my eyebrows. Then he moved over me, trailing kisses from my eyebrow to my cheek, to the corner of my mouth, my jaw, my neck. Once there, he licked and bit the exposed skin, making me shiver and tense.

His hands slipped from my cheeks, lower to my neck, my shoulders, tugging at my coat. Instinctively I lifted myself and he shifted his weight to accommodate the movement, his mouth capturing mine, making my head swim. I loved his mouth, loved how he kissed. I wanted to lose myself in him and he was making it easy for me to do so.

Unwilling to break contact, together we worked to free me of my jacket. I heard him toss it to the floor and I climbed on his lap, straddling his legs and kicking off my untied tennis shoes. Duane's fingers sought my skin, caressing my thighs, slipping into my panties to squeeze my bottom.

I decided, just as soon as we finished kissing, I was going to demand an explanation. But first we would kiss, because my brain told me I needed it. My heart seemed to think so, too, because it warmed and expanded, making my chest feel airy and achy in the best way.

My hips, however, seemed to think I needed more than just kissing and his caressing hands, because they rocked against his middle.

Okay, that's not quite right.

I grinded against him. Multiple times.

I did that.

I'm not ashamed.

The friction felt necessary.

My grinding made him groan, which made me moan. His fingers dug into my hips, encouraging me, and mine fisted in his hair like we were anchoring ourselves together. Like maybe, if we could just hold on, we could hold on to this moment, being wrapped in each other.

The moment lasted. And it was glorious. But I needed more. A lot more. In fact, I needed everything. No more in between. I needed to know I wasn't alone in risking everything.

Given our historical pattern—my need followed by his retreat—I also needed to stop giving him all the say, all the power. If he couldn't give me everything, then I wanted nothing. I couldn't keep bashing myself against a door he kept firmly closed. It hurt too much. Therefore, despite how glorious this kissing and grinding and touching business was,

I pulled myself away, pushed against his chest, and stumbled from his lap.

"Now just…just wait a minute." I held up my finger and backed away two steps. My legs were wobbly and I was still gathering my thoughts. Therefore, I didn't get very far before he caught me, brought me back to the bed, and climbed on top. He lifted my nightshirt until my chest was exposed, and then went to town biting and sucking and licking.

"Hush," he breathed against my skin. "Just for tonight, Jess. Just give me tonight."

Just for tonight? I couldn't focus, didn't understand what he meant.

Instead of deciphering Duane code, I moaned mindlessly, grabbing his hair and keeping him in place. Goodness, I needed him. I needed this. I needed the comfort and reassurance that *he* wanted me as badly as *I* wanted him. I'd grown accustomed to feeling as though a part of my heart was perpetually vacant—yet he had filled that empty hole, or I thought he had.

Duane understood me. He wanted me. I wasn't strange. We fit together. We fit perfectly. We were suited. And I loved him. I loved him so much.

He was tugging at my panties so I lifted my hips, felt them slide down my legs. I shivered, not from cold, but needing his heat. My fingers left his hair and fumbled for the waistband of his jeans.

Each time we were together and things turned passionate, each time I felt the promise of his skin, I also felt a maddening kind of urgency. It didn't make sense. But there I was, grasping his pants and boxers, shoving them down with my hands and eventually my feet.

Likewise, Duane pushed my nightshirt over my head, forcing me to lift my arms when all I wanted to do was grab him and hold on. I hadn't had access to his body before, not really. I'd never seen his bottom as an adult. Nor his thighs or calves. I wanted to see them, touch them, spend quality time getting to know them and all their hopes and dreams.

But I was trapped, my wrists held down and tangled in my silk shirt. Granted, I was sexy-trapped—unable to move as I would have liked because Duane's hot, hard, naked body covered mine—but I was still trapped.

"You are so beautiful, Jessica," he whispered, his muscular thigh between my legs pressing against my center. Spirals of erotic heat twisted low in my belly, making me arch and whimper. Duane kissed his way down my body, biting and licking, like I was being savored. He was exploring me in much the same way I'd longed to explore him.

But now I was teetering on mindless selfishness, needing him to keep working his magic, stiffening with delighted suspense as he kissed my hip, the front of my thigh, the inside of my thigh, and then…

Hell and tarnation, I couldn't stand it. He was breathing on me, his mouth and tongue so close, but no lollipop action. I wanted to scream. I felt him hovering and I lifted my head, determined to give him whatever encouragement he needed to make this happen, and found his sapphire blues looking back at me.

As soon as I gave him my eyes, I saw the pink of his flat tongue lick his lips. Really, this man should have been employed by the CIA, because the sight was torture. I was so primed, my legs were shaking. Therefore I was about to either holler at him or beg—I wasn't sure which—but before I could, he lowered his mouth to my center and we both moaned.

My head fell back and I sighed the big sigh, the sigh of *Thank you, Jesus!*

I didn't think much about the fact I was thanking Jesus for my building orgasm, because—again—selfish mindlessness. It had me tilting and lifting my hips, rocking them against his mouth, chasing and cherishing all the prickles of sensation.

When I came, it felt like being tossed skyward, the feelings of belonging, the spikes of heat and rightness and desire and fulfilled longing coursing through my body.

Then he was gone.

Then I heard the very distinct sound of a condom wrapper ripping open.

Then there was a pause.

Then he was back.

I opened my arms to him, wanting to cuddle and lose myself in his strong arms, and confused by his placement of the banana wrapper. My confusion was short-lived because he didn't come to my arms, not exactly. He hovered above me, his sheathed erection rubbing against my sensitized flesh.

I sucked in a shuddering breath, my eyes flying open, and I stared at my beautiful man. He was so…everything. So sweet and handsome and passionate. So wonderful and kind and…I was so desperately in love with everything about him.

"I need you." He kissed me, his hot mouth claiming mine, the hardness of his length separating me and nudging at my entrance. "Can I have you? Just for tonight."

"Yes! You can have me forever." I nodded, my fingers digging into his torso. In this position, I might be able to fondle his bottom like I'd wanted. I wouldn't be lost to selfish madness, because I'd already had my orgasm. I could use this lovely invasion as a chance to explore, show Duane how I cherished every inch of him.

Yeah…I thought that for exactly two seconds.

Because as soon as he pushed inside, the selfish madness returned, and my mouth opened with soundless wonder. He was moving in a particular way, his body high over mine, so that with every stroke I was feeling him like I'd felt his tongue. My body was hot and damp and so was his.

"Oh…what are you doing to me?" I panted, bracing, feeling completely out of control.

"I'm making love to you." Duane's eyes moved between mine, his soul completely bare, and I knew. I knew he loved me. He hadn't said the words yet, but it didn't matter. His eyes told me everything and the certainty was bone-deep.

"I love you. I love you. I love you," I chanted, holding on to him, hoping my saying the words would encourage him to open his heart and admit the truth.

He didn't. Instead he kissed me. The friction between us became a smooth glide and I moaned into his mouth, not recognizing the sound I made *at all*. I closed my eyes.

It was at this point I realized I was teetering on the edge of my release, and I wanted desperately to share it with him. I wanted us to move together. I didn't want to push. I wanted him to come with me in tandem, of his own free will.

I opened my eyes, found him watching me, and was nearly made breathless by the intensity of his focus, the force of his gaze.

"Jessica, I…" he whispered, starting then stopping. It was enough.

I moaned in response, higher pitched this time, and again not a sound I recognized as one I'd ever made before. Nonsense words and promises I didn't know I was going to say tumbled from my lips.

He didn't respond, just continued his delectable conquest, spreading my legs wider and bringing my knees to my shoulders.

"Duane. I need you; I love you so much, so much…"

He cursed, tensed, growled in a way that sounded like a surrender, burying his face against my neck and biting my shoulder. I was tossed skyward again. This time he was with me.

And we held on to each other, like the world was ending and beginning, long after our shared ecstasy was over.

Jessica

22

> "Never did the world make a queen of a girl who hides in houses and dreams without traveling."
>
> —ROMAN PAYNE, *THE WANDERESS*

"CAN I ASK YOU A question?" I asked, breaking our hour-long silence of touching and petting and kissing.

"Sure…" he said, his voice sounding drowsy and not at all sure.

We were cuddled together in the bed, my back to his front. I faced the interior of the cabin, the fireplace directly in front of me. I was completely relaxed. Really, *malleable* was the right word for my present state, caught in that dreamy world of satisfied to the point of exhaustion, but too excited for sleep. Not yet. Again, I wanted to hold on to the moment.

"Do you always have condoms in your wallet? Or only when you come to your fortress of solitude? Are there random wood-women who come to the cabin and service hillbillies?"

I felt his tension ease, and he chuckled while nuzzling the back of my neck. "That's three questions."

"Okay. Forget the last two."

"Yes. I always have condoms in my wallet."

"Hmm…"

"What? What does *hmm* mean?"

"It's just that I never took you for an optimist."

His renewed laughter made me smile.

He clarified while stroking my hip possessively beneath the covers. "I'm not. Billy does random wallet checks. And every year for Christmas he stuffs our stockings with condoms. I think he'd sterilize us all if he could."

Now I was laughing, and that meant we were laughing together.

My laughter tapered and I spoke as I thought. "I really like your brothers."

Duane was quiet for a beat; his beard tickled my shoulder when he finally spoke. "Yeah. They're okay."

I smiled at his affectionate and dismissive remark, letting the subject drop. I wasn't ready to invite anyone else—not even via discussion—into our lovely slice-of-heaven pie. Not yet.

The fire was burning low, just coals at this point, embers of red glowing in chalky black cinders. I loved how wood fires smelled, tart and smoky. They reminded me of dessert, s'mores and hot lemon curd baked in a pie iron. My daddy was my Brownie pack leader growing up; he'd taught me all the campfire dessert shortcuts.

"How did you get here, Jess?"

"Pardon?" I'd been lost to my thoughts, desserts and campfires. Now I'd associate wood fires with Duane. This thought made me happy.

I felt him shift behind me, lean up on his elbow. "Did someone drive you?"

"No. I drove. I have...well, I have a car now. It's a long story." I frowned, remembering I hadn't spotted his parked car when I arrived. "By the way, where's your car? Where's the Road Runner?"

Duane dithered, his body tensing behind me. At last he cleared his throat and said with a sigh, "I wrecked it."

I choked on nothing, my eyes bulging, certain I'd heard wrong. "You...*you what?*"

"I wrecked it, last weekend at the Canyon."

I twisted in his arms so I could see his face, a rush of alarm making my muscles tense.

I rested my palm on his cheek, needing to touch him, as my eyes moved between his. "Are you okay? Are you hurt?"

"No. I'm fine."

I wanted to search his body, see for myself. But then I reminded myself of the sex cartwheels we'd just finished. If he'd been injured, then he could hardly have accomplished such a physically demanding activity.

He didn't look sad or mournful about the car, and his lack of reaction did not compute. "You loved that car."

His expression didn't change, not really, but he shrugged. "It's a good car."

"Why aren't you more upset?"

"It's not a person, Jess. It's a thing. Things can be fixed. Eventually, maybe, I'll fix her up."

"But...that car is awesome. And you never lose."

"I wasn't quite myself last weekend," he mumbled distractedly, his attention dipping to my chest as his hand lifted to cup my breast. He touched me like he appreciated my texture, using his thumb to draw circles on my skin.

"Then why would you risk it?" I ignored the pleasure

radiating from where he enjoyed my body because I wanted to understand how Duane could be so dismissive of his badass car.

"I only risk what I'm willing to live without," he said, still with an air of distraction. He moved, guiding me so my back was against the mattress and he was above me again. Just before he bent his head to my chest, he licked his lips. The wet, slick heat of his mouth closed over my nipple and he sucked, swirling his tongue in a circle.

Despite my best efforts to remain focused, my breathing became erratic.

"Duane." I struggled to remain sensible. "Duane, that's not real risk at all. It's only real if you risk what you need."

"I need to be inside you again, Jessica," he half whispered, half growled and I felt his need press into my inner thigh.

"Okay…" I sighed, adding absentmindedly. "But you should know I'm still mad at you for not taking my call on Sunday."

"I shouldn't have done that. I should've taken your call." He nipped the underside of my breast.

I squirmed, my eyes closing. "You have to promise me, I need you to promise you'll never do that again."

I sensed him falter, his movements stilled, and several long seconds passed where the only audible sounds were our combined breathing and the crackle of the dying fire.

His continued stillness prompted me to open my eyes and lift my head. He was still over me, his mouth parted like he was going to speak, but needed to think first on the words. Duane's sumptuous eyes examined my face, searching. His expression was enough to give me pause, and I was about to withdraw, push him further for the needed promise.

But then he said, "As long as we're together, I'll never ignore your call, I promise."

Something about the assurance felt off, too careful. I was groggy, therefore I replayed his words in my head three times before I caught the disclaimer.

"No." I shook my head, narrowing my eyes in an attempt to stay focused. "No, no disclaimers. Just a promise. You need to promise me you will never ignore me again. For the rest of our lives, you will call me back, 'til we're dead and buried."

He continued to stare at me, and as he stared I watched Duane war with himself. After a protracted minute, he rose to his knees, his eyes conducting a quick but heated sweep of my face, hair, body, and then he climbed off the bed.

He paced the short distance to the fireplace, then the table. He halted there, his hands on his hips, giving me his glorious backside. I watched his broad shoulders rise and fall and propped myself up on my elbows, waiting. The longer I waited, the heavier the sinking sensation twisted in my belly, giving me vertigo.

"Duane?"

Abruptly he turned and stalked back to the bed, careful not to touch me. He sat on the edge, grabbing his boxers from the floor, and pulled them on. I watched him dress, at a complete loss as to what he was thinking.

"What are you doing?"

He gave me his decidedly stormy gaze. "You're asking too much. I can't promise that."

Again, I replayed his words in my head three times before I understood. When I did, I'm sure my expression mirrored the explosion of anger catching my brain on fire. I scrambled from the bed, taking the sheet with me, and stood over him as he yanked on his jeans.

"Why the hell not?"

"You know why not."

"I don't. I really don't." My hand fell against my thigh with an exasperated smack. "Sometimes you talk to me, and sometimes you don't. You tell me you've been waiting for me, for five years, biding your time. You're hell-bent on courting me, but heaven forbid I give you a blow job! We make this deal for thirteen and a half months, meanwhile you're straddling the line. I'm all in and you're half in, half out."

He stood from the bed, buttoning and zipping the fly of his jeans, and I lifted my chin to maintain eye contact. I decided he was too tall. And imposing. And unreachable.

"You're leaving, Jess. You're not all in. You're dipping your toes in the water until it's time to go."

I felt that remark in my spine, between my shoulder blades like a knife.

It took me a moment, but I finally managed—albeit more loudly than I'd intended—to respond, "That is complete bullshit, Duane, and you know it. When have I ever given you any reason to think I'm not completely invested?"

"What I know is when you leave, you can't expect me to have friendly feelings about it. When you leave, you shouldn't call me. Ever. Because I am *not* returning your calls. I won't want to see or talk to you."

This time the pain was in the front and the back, my spine and my chest, and I'm pretty sure I flinched. His words felt like a blow, a slap across the face, especially after what we'd just shared. I knew tears were gathering in my eyes but I didn't care.

Duane studied my features only briefly before turning around and walking back to the table, like he couldn't stand looking at me. I swallowed my emotion, but it continued to rise, making my scalp feel hot and my skin overly tight.

And then I heard his frustrated grumble. "This was a mistake."

I couldn't think. All the air had been sucked out of the room. I backed up to the mattress and sank to it. He was a pendulum and I couldn't keep up with his perpetual-motion mood swings. One minute we're cuddled up in bed and the next…

"I don't understand." I stopped, then decided just to say what I felt. "I don't understand why you offered me a year when you obviously had no intention of following through. Can you explain that?"

He glanced at me, examining me from over his shoulder. He appeared to be confused by my question, or maybe the vulnerability behind it. Finally, he turned completely around, scratching his beard as he did so.

"Jess…" he started, released a short breath, his face screwed up like I was a lunatic, then began again. "Jessica, I know about your plans."

"My plans?"

"Your brother told me about your aunt. About the money. About your plans."

"What?"

"To leave. After Christmas." These words were stated as cold fact.

"To… Christmas? What?" I shook my head. "What are you talking about?"

Duane stopped scratching his beard, but his eyes narrowed,

like he was studying my reaction closely. "Your brother, Jackson. He pulled Beau and me over on our way home, Thursday afternoon, right after you and I finished talking. He told me you inherited all the money you'll ever need for your world travels. He told me you were planning to start after Christmas."

I blinked twice, shaking my head in an automatic rejection of at least half his words. "Well, that's a lie."

Duane straightened, his abruptly wide eyes evidence of his surprise.

I rushed to clarify. "Not all of it. I mean, my…*aunt* did leave me with money. From the looks of it, and with good investments, enough for me to travel the world and not work if I so decided. But I have no plans to leave Green Valley imminently, and certainly not just after Christmas."

His eyes dimmed and his mouth flattened. "Why not?"

Now I studied him, how he appeared to be restraining himself, holding himself away from me, and everything clicked. He'd been so cold, so aloof when I'd told him I loved him. He thought I was leaving. He thought I was just going to leave and never come back.

"Wait a minute." I jumped to my feet, my mouth opening and closing as I tried to decide which part of this tangled mess to address first. "You thought…and then you…and we just…" I gestured to the bed, and decided to settle on my last thought. "So Jackson tells you about the money and you assume things are over between us? Do I mean so little to you? Did you ever want me? Or was that a lie?"

Duane frowned, balled his hands into fists, and said nothing. Yet behind his frown, I perceived a restlessness to contradict.

But I wasn't finished. "Or is this about you not trusting me? You don't trust me. And that's why we made love tonight. You don't trust me to stay. *'Just for tonight, Jess.'* That's what you said."

He didn't deny it. He just continued to watch me piece everything together.

"Admit it! The only reason you gave in tonight is because you thought I was going to leave right away. Now that I can leave, you don't trust me to stay. You don't trust me at all."

"I trust you," he countered quickly.

I ignored his statement, desperation making me say, "We are far, far from over, Duane Winston!"

"Jess," he shook his head, looking visibly torn. "We have an expiration date. In fact, we are over. I don't see where we go from here. You're going to be making plans to leave. We had this trial period before the twelve months started and I'm calling it off."

"You don't get to call it off!" I charged forward, waving my index finger around like it was a sword.

"I am calling it off. I'm walking away because I'm not going to keep you from doing what you need to do."

"What do I need to do?"

"Leave."

I flinched again; my next words were accusatory, half outraged question and half statement. "You want me to leave?"

"I'm not answering that."

"Didn't you hear me? I'm in love with you. Why don't you ask me to stay?" I demanded with a frustrated shout and a firm push against his chest.

"You don't ask someone you love to give up on her dreams!"

I reeled back, my mouth falling open—wide, wide open—and I'm sure I looked a bit like an astonished owl. Two fat tears trailed down my cheeks, hot and unwieldy.

Duane gritted his teeth and looked away, his eyes focusing on a spot behind me. Shifting on his feet, refusing to make eye contact, he appeared to be regretful. He was obviously wishing back his hastily shouted admission, and that made me immeasurably sad.

Meanwhile, none of my internal organs knew what to think. They wanted to have a *He loves you! He finally said it!* party, but the manner of his confession and immediate withdrawal afterward made my heart hesitate to place the catering deposit.

My voice wasn't entirely steady as I asked, "Were you ever going to admit the truth if I hadn't pissed you off?"

"We're not discussing this."

"Why not?" I cringed at how needy I sounded, how lost.

I finally had his eyes again, but now they were blazing with fury. "Because you're leaving, and we're over, and it's pointless. That's why!"

"And everything has to be perfect, right? Everything has to be just right. Heaven and all the angels forbid Duane Winston *ever* does anything without precision and guaranteed success."

I must've struck a nerve, because his gaze morphed from heated to incensed, and he advanced on me. "Fine. Fuck yeah, I love you. What do you think this is all about?"

"Well, now we're finally getting somewhere. In case you didn't hear me the first hundred times, I love you, too!"

He ignored me, or maybe he didn't hear me. "I look at you and I see my future, and it is something great. But I can't do anything about the fact that our dreams don't align. And since I *do* love you, I want you to live yours."

He'd backed me into the bed, but I held my ground, catching his arm before he could turn away. "So what about you?"

"I'll be fine."

"Fine? *Fine?* Screw fine!"

"Yes. Fine. I'll be just fine knowing you're somewhere in this world following your siren call."

He was withdrawing again, so I held on to him tighter, not allowing him to turn away. "Why are you like this? Why do you insist on being so noble? Why does everything have to be defined?"

His chest rose and fell with a large breath, his eyes darting away, and I knew I was pushing him beyond his level of comfort. But I couldn't help it.

I tried softening my voice, coaxing, "Duane, I have been nothing but honest with you. The least you can do is tell me—"

He interrupted, bringing his flashing eyes back to mine. "My father always took whatever he wanted, whenever he wanted it. He took my momma, us kids. He'd take and take and take. I promised myself I was never going to be like that. Because when you have a father who is a selfish bastard, who takes what he wants whenever the fuck he wants it, the last thing you want to be is without honor."

My heart hurt for him, but I didn't know what to say, how to make it better. Regardless, he didn't give me a chance.

Duane peeled my fingers from his arm and cradled my hand between his. "You want to go out there and live your dreams, so I'm going to remove myself from the equation.

I'm not going to stand in your way. Because I would rather see the sadness in your eyes now than resentment in your eyes months or years from now. We are over. And I have to be the one to end it. I have to be the one to walk away. It has to be my decision. You need to give me that at least."

He dropped my hand and stepped away, his eyes moving around the cabin like he was searching for something. Finding his shirt, he pulled it on. I watched numbly, part of me still cuddled up with him in bed, as he sat in one of the chairs by the table and put on his socks and boots.

I was feeling so many things, but none of them were eloquent. Broken. Sad. Broken and sad. That's what I was. Silent tears slipped through my eyelids while he slipped through my fingers.

I didn't have the brainpower or the heart for an impassioned speech. I was tired and my heart was bruised. But I couldn't let him go. Not without exploring every option. Not without a Hail Mary pass.

I couldn't keep bashing myself against a door he kept firmly closed, but I could leave a note.

Therefore, on a desperate whim, I asked with an unsteady voice, "Truth or dare, Duane?"

He shook his head, his eyes closing briefly to cover his discomfort, like the sound of my voice caused physical injury. "Truth or dare? You want to play truth or dare now?"

"Yes. Pick one, truth or dare?"

"Fine." He clenched his jaw, then gave me his eyes; they were cool and distant. "Dare."

I nodded once, making a decision to be vulnerable just once more. "I dare you to extend the term of our relationship to indefinite."

His expression didn't change. He just stared at me. The line of his mouth flat and straight.

So I pushed, begging, "Stay with me tonight; don't leave. Stay with me, and not just for twelve months. Stay with me always."

He winced and I could see his hackles rise. Before he could speak, I lifted my hand to stop him.

"I see you don't understand my meaning."

"I understand you perfectly," he ground out, his tone rough, unyielding.

"No. You don't." I waited a beat, wanting to be sure he saw I was serious before I handed him my heart on a platter. "Come with me."

That made a dent. He blinked his surprise before he could catch himself and blurted, "What?"

"Come with me. I dare you to come with me. Next month, next year, whenever. I dare you to come with me when I go. And stay with me, stay with me always."

Duane

23

"To travel is to live."

—**HANS CHRISTIAN ANDERSEN,** *THE FAIRY TALE OF MY LIFE: AN AUTOBIOGRAPHY*

I WALKED HOME.

I left Jessica wrapped in a sheet.

I left Jessica.

I left.

And I left part of myself in the cabin. I sensed the emptiness in my middle, in my gut, as soon as I crossed the threshold and entered the cold night. Her suggestion—that I leave with her, travel the world and share her life, her adventures—sounded like a fairy tale. A perfect fairy tale. And I'd been so surprised by the proposition that my mind actually considered the possibility.

But then I remembered the shop, my brothers, my obligations, the shit with the Wraiths, and how everyone had been affected when Ashley ditched us years ago. I remembered my father and how he took what he wanted, without a care for his family. He came and went as he pleased.

Leaving *with* Jessica was a fairy tale. Perfect in theory, but completely impractical in reality. Beau and Cletus relied on me, needed me. They couldn't handle the workload on their own. My savings were invested in the auto shop, and I wasn't going to travel the world using Jess's aunt's money.

Was I too proud? Fuck. Yes.

I was too proud to take money from Jess or anyone else without working for it.

So I left before I reconsidered, before I heeded *my* siren call.

But even then I'd been undecided. I kept seeing her face, the tears shining in her beautiful eyes as I walked out. The image of her called to me, to the depths of my soul. Each step was a burden. I turned back to the cabin at least three times and the tightness in my chest made breathing near impossible.

That was until I spotted her car. Jessica's new-to-her car was a brand-new F-Type Jaguar. 5-liter V8. Manual transmission. All-wheel drive. 495 horsepower. I knew my automobiles like most people know their ice cream, so I knew the MSRP (manufacturer's suggested retail price) was just under a hundred thousand dollars.

I stared at it for at least a full minute.

Then I walked the remainder of the way home without looking back, taking satisfaction in the sound of every twig that snapped violently under my boots. By the time I arrived at the house, I was in desperate need of breaking something; no way was I going to be able to sleep.

Getting drunk was an option, but I'd been drunk for most of the last five days. And it was our first Thanksgiving since Momma died. Besides, getting shit-faced an hour before dawn wasn't my style anyway. Concluding the only option available to me at present was splitting more wood we didn't need, I decided to veer toward the woodshed once the house was in view.

But as I cleared the trees, I stopped short. Jethro, my oldest brother, was walking up the porch steps to the front door, carrying a large duffel bag slung over his shoulder. I was too surprised by the sight of him, and too caught in the momentum of my misery, to call out before he entered the house. But the sound of our front door shutting pulled me out of my stupor.

My mind was a mess as I quickly jogged to the porch and rushed through the screen door. I needed to speak with him, bring him up to speed. But I was also five different shades of pissed off with my oldest brother. Somehow, likely because violence was already on my mind, the five shades of pissed off won out over being sensible.

Thus, when I entered the house and he turned around—a big carefree grin eating up his face—and he said, "Hey, Duane. Did you miss me?" I punched him in the face.

I pulled my punch at the last minute. I didn't want to knock him out; I just wanted to beat him up a little. Maybe get knocked around myself.

He staggered back—more from surprise than from the force of my fist—and threw a completely perplexed frown at me while clutching his jaw. "What the hell was that for?"

I didn't answer. I let him read the intent in my eyes, gave him a few seconds to prepare; then I charged at him. Jethro was a good fighter. We all were, but he was better than most of us. Being the oldest and spending a good part of his youth fucking around with the Wraiths, he learned to fight fierce and dirty. But he'd taught me all his tricks long ago, and his fight now wasn't fueled by weeks of frustration, of dealing with biker threats and Jessica James's confession I could do nothing about.

Perhaps he was trying to defend himself against my assault, but that didn't deter me any.

We crashed around the living room, banging into walls, sending picture frames falling to the floor. He had me in a headlock and I used the position to elbow him in the ribs, then administer a kidney punch as he struggled to contain me.

My nose was bleeding and I took satisfaction in the sight of his split lip when we were interrupted by a harsh whisper. "What are y'all thinking?"

We glanced up in unison. Cletus's furious expression had an instantly sobering effect. He stood on the stairs, looking as upset as I'd ever seen him, and loud-whispered down at us. "Making a big ruckus at five in the morning? Making a mess of things? On Thanksgiving? Today is turkey day! Plus you know how Billy needs his beauty sleep. Otherwise he'll be whining at us 'til dinner. I don't want to listen to that swill on my day off. And besides, you interrupted my quiet time."

Jethro grimaced, shooting me a dirty stare—which I returned—and loud-whispered his response. "Sorry, Cletus."

Cletus's hands were on his hips and he gave us both a hard look, his eyes sticking to me a bit longer than Jethro. "Take your fight outside."

I nodded, staggering to the front door and whispering contritely, "We will."

"And now you owe me pancakes, Duane Faulkner Winston," Cletus added with a reprimanding whisper. "Blueberry pancakes." Then he pivoted and disappeared down the upstairs hall.

I didn't know what Cletus did during his quiet time, but Beau seemed to think it was yoga.

I opened the front door, then turned and gestured for Jethro to exit the house.

"You first." He lifted his chin, covered with three weeks' worth of unkempt beard. His hands were still balled into fists. He'd never been the trusting sort; then again, I had just attacked him in our living room.

I shrugged and exited to the porch, walking to the far corner. I waited until he followed and shut the door before saying, "You've always been a selfish asshole."

Jethro nodded once, working his jaw back and forth. His steps were measured as he crossed to me. "Everybody knows that. And you always could start an argument in an empty house. Now why don't you tell me specifically what I did to inspire such an unforgettable welcome home?"

"Traps," I growled, closing the remaining distance between us and keeping my voice low. "You installed traps in four cars for the Iron Wraiths, so they could run drugs without getting caught."

Jethro's eyes widened even as his brow pulled low. "How do you—"

"Because, dummy, they videotaped the whole thing. And now Repo is exploiting your shitty decisions as blackmail. He wants to use the Winston Brothers Auto Shop as their new chop shop, or else he's sending you to federal prison."

"Oh shit…" Jethro said on a shocked and defeated exhale, then sank to the rocking chair to his left. I watched dispassionately as his elbows came to his knees and he buried his face in his hands.

I was quiet, something I knew how to do well, and waited for my brother to process reality.

"Did you do it? Did you agree?" He didn't lift his head, so his words were spoken to the wooden porch floor.

"No. We've been stalling."

Jethro's shoulders rose and fell, and he nodded. "Good. Good." He was silent for a beat, then asked, "And Cletus doesn't have a plan?"

"No. Cletus doesn't know."

Jethro lifted his head from his hands, his eyebrows knit together. "What do you mean, Cletus doesn't know? You didn't tell Cletus?"

"No, Jethro. I didn't tell Cletus. Why would I want to bring him into this god-awful mess of yours if he can keep his hands clean? Isn't it bad enough that Beau and I have to deal with it?"

My oldest brother jumped to his feet. "Duane, Cletus installed the traps."

Now he'd surprised me. I straightened from the wooden beam where I'd been leaning and stared at him. He was half smiling.

"Come again?"

"Cletus was the one to install the traps in those cars, not me. Do you think I'd be able to install those contraptions? Did you see how they work? You have to…" He appeared to be searching his memory for the description. "You have to wire them just so—where they won't open unless the car is off, but the key is in the ignition, and the seat belt is fastened, and there's a hurricane in Florida, and no beer left in the fridge, and everyone's favorite dessert is banana cream pie—or some such complicated nonsense."

I was still stuck on the fact that Cletus—not Jethro—had been the one to install the traps, too stuck to admire the genius of how they worked.

"So…Cletus knows? He knows all about this? How you got out of the Wraiths?"

Jethro nodded. "Yeah. When I decided enough was enough, and those biker boys told me what I needed to do, the cost of my freedom, the first person I thought of was Cletus."

I frowned at my brother. "Was he there? When you showed them how the traps work?"

"No. He installed the traps, showed me how to use them. I went to the Wraiths on my own, took credit for the installations. I was trying to minimize his involvement."

"So he doesn't know they're being used to smuggle drugs?"

Jethro made a sound in the back of his throat and shifted on his feet. "I mean, he probably guessed it. I knew, of course, even before the Wraiths told me so. Why else would they want secret traps?"

"But on the video you start cussing them out when they tell you."

"Because I had plausible deniability up until that point. Once they told me, and I knew for sure, I became an accomplice. That's why I was so pissed off. If they didn't tell me, then I could always claim ignorance."

Jethro was good at that, claiming ignorance, shifting blame. Or he used to be, before he got himself straight.

"We need to tell Cletus," Jethro said with a kind of certainty that gave me my first glimmer of hope. "He'll definitely know what to do."

♥

We took turns in the downstairs bathroom wiping blood from our faces.

I walked into the kitchen once I was finished assessing the damage and rehanging fallen pictures. I found Jethro making coffee and icing his lip. Thus, after grabbing myself a bag of peas for my eye, I set to work making enough blueberry pancakes to feed a small army.

Without prompting, Jethro good-naturedly related his adventures trekking the Appalachian Trail. I was amazed how he was able to keep from fretting about the Iron Wraiths' blackmail attempt.

I'd been twisted up, either thinking about how to outsmart the Iron Wraiths or debating what to do about Jess. Or counting the hours until I could see her again. Or trying to figure out how to get her alone. Or wondering how the hell I was going to survive without her. Thus, Jethro's tall tales were a welcome distraction.

We had to wait until Cletus emerged before approaching him. Having interrupted his quiet time earlier, I had no desire to provoke his wrath further. Cletus's retaliation was always unanticipated and devious. He was a fan of polite revenge, knowing how to get his point across with very little fuss.

We both stilled when we heard footsteps on the stairs, and Jethro poked his head out of the doorway.

"What the hell? What happened to you?"

Recognizing Billy's voice, my shoulders sagged and I turned back to the griddle. Jethro didn't answer. Instead he walked back into the kitchen and reclaimed his spot at the kitchen table.

Billy entered the kitchen seconds later, his eyes moving from the bruise high on Jethro's cheek to the cut on his lip. "Did that happen on the trail?"

"Yeah. I was assaulted by a gang of ninja raccoons." Jethro took a sip of his coffee.

Billy gave him another long look, then turned to the coffee. But he stopped again when he saw my face and the less-than-subtle swelling around my eye.

He lifted an eyebrow, glanced between the two of us, then left the kitchen without his coffee, saying as he went, "Never mind, whatever it is, I don't want to know. But do let me know when the hotcakes are ready. And there better be a turkey today, because I already made the stuffing, and something or someone is getting stuffed."

"Getting the turkey was Cletus's job this year," I called after him.

No sooner did Billy leave than Beau shuffled in, scratching his balls and yawning. "Do I smell pancakes?"

"Yes." I nodded, then tilted my head toward Jethro. "You also smell skunk."

Beau lazily glanced where I indicated, then did a double take when he saw our oldest brother. Beau was suddenly awake, his brow pulling low and the set of his mouth grim as he studied Jethro, perhaps trying to determine whether he was going to be sensible or violent. Prior to Jethro's miraculous reformation, seeing him with a black and blue face was a normal occurrence. But since he'd changed his ways a few years ago, he hadn't come home with more than a scratch.

"What happened to your face?" Beau finally asked, and not kindly.

"Your twin happened to my face."

Beau nodded, his features relaxing, then crossed the kitchen to the coffee machine. "Good. Saves me the trouble of doing it myself. So what's the plan, Duane?"

"We're waiting for Cletus to get up."

Beau halted his coffee pouring and glanced between me and Jethro. "I thought we weren't going to involve him."

"He already knows. He did the initial installations."

"Well, I'll be..." Beau shook his head, his eyes losing focus someplace over my shoulder. Then he abruptly snapped his fingers. "That makes sense. Ain't no way Jethro could have installed those traps. I don't know why we didn't figure it out earlier."

Just then, Cletus walked into the kitchen, obviously still in a temper. "Don't speak to me until I've had my hotcakes. I'm still angry at both y'all."

Jethro jumped up from his chair, Beau set his coffee cup down on the counter with a loud *thunk*, and I straightened to attention. All of us were standing like statues staring at Cletus, wanting to speak but knowing better than to disobey his request. It took him a bit to notice our rigid readiness, but when he did, his eyes narrowed and bounced between the three of us.

"All right...I take that back. Y'all are making me nervous. Maybe somebody should tell me what's going on."

Duane

24

> "Life is an experimental journey undertaken involuntarily."
>
> —FERNANDO PESSOA, *THE BOOK OF DISQUIET*

THE FOUR OF US TOOK our breakfast to the Quonset hut, escaping the house before Billy knew we were leaving. By some silent agreement, Jethro and Beau appointed me as the storyteller—likely because they both had a habit of extreme and unnecessary embellishment.

I explained the situation, provided the timeline, and described what steps we'd taken so far. All the while Cletus ate his pancakes and drank his coffee, nodding at intervals, and frowning at other intervals. For example, when I mentioned I'd enlisted Tina's help, he scowled.

"Are you finished?" he asked at length, his eyes on my untouched plate.

"With the story or with my food?" My pancakes had gone cold, but I wasn't hungry.

"Both."

"Yes. You can have them." I passed him my plate and rubbed my hand over my face. I was tired and the thought of eating made me nauseous. But it was more than the exhaustion. Everything hurt, and not because of my fistfight with Jethro.

Cletus took three bites, making us all wait in suspense, and then asked, "What I want to know is, why didn't you come to me in the first place? And also, how do you get these to be so darn fluffy? It's like eating a blueberry-flavored cloud of awesome."

"We didn't tell you because we didn't want to make you an accomplice, just in case we had to follow through," Beau answered for me.

"I see. Thank you. I appreciate your thoughtfulness and concern for my well-being," he said, using his most formal tone. Then added, "But that was really stupid of y'all."

"So what are we going to do, Cletus?" Jethro got right to the point, giving our brother a charming smile despite his split lip.

"Nothing to do." Cletus shrugged, sipped his coffee, and then set it down.

Beau and I exchanged looks of despair. If Cletus didn't have a plan, then we were going to have to rely on Tina.

Cletus must've seen our expressions and understood what they meant, because he added, "Let me clarify that last statement. There's nothing to do because it's already been done. In these cases, federal law requires the installer to inform local law enforcement when traps are suspected of being used for illegal purposes. The police have already been informed about those secret compartments because I informed them years ago when I first installed the traps."

Now Beau and I exchanged looks of astonishment. I don't think either of us were capable of speech at that moment.

However, Jethro narrowed his eyes on Cletus and sounded half insulted. "What do you mean, the police already know? Did you rat me out?"

Cletus *tsk*ed at Jethro and scrunched his nose like my oldest brother smelled badly. "No. Well…" His eyes moved up and to the right, as though reconsidering his answer. "Not in the way you mean. I informed the police when I installed the traps because I suspected they'd be used for illegal purposes. Whether or not the police actually *know* about the traps is a different matter entirely."

I was too tired for Cletus's riddles. "Cletus, would you just speak plainly? What did you do? And what does it mean for us? Should we be worried about the Iron Wraiths?"

"I'll answer your questions in reverse. First, you do not need to worry about the Iron Wraiths. They have no power over you, Jethro, or me, or Beau for that matter. In fact we are in a position to blackmail them, should we so choose."

"Well, thank heavens." Beau sat back in his chair and heaved a loud sigh of obvious relief.

"Second, what this means for 'us'"—Cletus used air quotes around the word *us*—"is that we should, the four of us, go to the Dragon Biker Bar and meet with Repo, or even Razor himself. One of us will need to explain the situation, that the Winston boys are immune to their threats, so they'll quit their harassing and stay on their side of the schoolyard."

"You want to talk to Razor?" Jethro asked like Cletus was certifiable.

Razor was the Iron Wraiths' president and one truly dangerous motherfucker.

"No. I did not say that. I said one of 'us.'" Again, he used air quotes around *us*, but this time his eyes slid to me and he looked at me with meaning.

"What?" I asked, shaking my head. "You can't mean me?"

Now all three of them were looking at me, and they were nodding.

"It makes sense," Beau said encouragingly. I was not encouraged.

"It does," Jethro agreed. "Razor hates my guts already, because of…well, the past. He doesn't know Beau, but he can spot a bullshitter a mile away."

"Are you calling me a bullshitter?" Beau frowned at Jethro.

"Yes. Yes, I am," Jethro admitted smoothly.

"Okay. Just making sure. Carry on." Beau's smile was back and he looked quite satisfied, likely because it took one to know one.

"And Cletus…well, no offense, Cletus, but Razor won't respond well to your style, either."

"Agreed." Cletus nodded once and took another bite of my cold pancakes. When he spoke next, he spoke around a full mouth. "It has to be Duane. He's abrupt, irritable, and those charlatans don't scare him any. He's perfect."

It was my turn to exhale loudly, shaking my head, but not willing to argue the point just yet. We'd have plenty of time to debate this later. Right now I wanted answers. "So, what did you do, Cletus? How did you inform the police without them knowing?"

"You know how I help with those mail sorter machines at the police stations and the central office? I maintain them for three counties. Just one of the many ways I spend my time helping the citizens of Tennessee."

"Yes. We know," Jethro answered for all of us.

"Well, funny thing about those machines. Letters get stuck and unstuck all the time. When a machine breaks and needs fixing, I sometimes find letters that are years old."

Beau and I quickly shared a glance. "Are you telling me that you planted a letter in one of those machines? Down at the station?" he asked.

Cletus shook his head. "No. Of course not. I didn't plant anything in any of the machines. But I did slip a certified letter in with a stack of old mail, mail found in one of those machines during a service call and then subsequently placed into storage unopened. I even know the box and shelf number where it's kept. I believe I even have the receipt for the certified letter upstairs someplace."

Again, Beau and I were rendered speechless. And this time Jethro was as well. The three of us sat in stunned silence for several seconds, watching Cletus eat my pancakes like he didn't have a care in the world.

Jethro stirred from our trance first. "Well then, I guess Duane will just explain to Razor that the police have a certified letter in their possession detailing the existence of the traps…?"

"That's right," Cletus agreed. "I included pictures of the cars, their VINs, and the traps. As well, I described the sequence for opening the compartments. I have a copy of the documentation in my room…someplace."

Beau shook his head and barked a laugh. "I can't believe you, Cletus."

"Believe me, Beau. But there is one more thing," Cletus said grimly, moving his eyes to me. "You never answered my original question."

"Yes, I did. We didn't tell you because—"

"Not that one." He waved his hand in the air as though swatting my words away. "The pancakes. How do you get them to be so light? It's amazing."

I shook my head at my eccentric older brother and answered honestly because I was so tired. "Egg whites."

"What?"

I stood and stacked the plates. "It's egg whites. I keep them separate. Then I whip them 'til they're stiff and fold them in at the end. It makes the pancakes super light."

"Oh…" Also standing, he nodded, as though deep in thought. But then unexpectedly asked, "Why do you look like that, Duane?"

"Like what, Cletus?"

"Like your heart is diseased. I told you, we're in the clear. No need to worry any longer. And your egg-white secret is safe with me."

"I know." I nodded, but didn't respond further because I had nothing to say. I wasn't going to whine about Jessica. I was going to suck it up and move on…eventually. In about thirty years.

Unfortunately, Beau liked to gossip. "He's upset because Jessica James just inherited a mountain of money from her aunt and now she's leaving."

I glared at my twin, promising retribution at a later date. He gave me a sympathetic look in exchange, which only fueled my ire. I didn't want pity.

"Miss James is leaving? In the middle of the school year?" Cletus appeared to be genuinely distressed. "But we were just getting to integrals."

I shrugged. "I don't rightly know."

"What do you mean, you don't know? Jackass James pulled us over, told us both a week ago." Beau pressed the point while Jethro raised an eyebrow and glanced between the two of us.

"Jessica James..." Jethro said her name thoughtfully, as though trying to recall her image. "Didn't she wait tables at Daisy's Nut House? You've had a thing for her since I can remember."

"Thanks for the reminder, Jethro." I gave him a hard look and set the plates back on the table in front of him. The Iron Wraiths blackmail problem might be close to solved, but I was still feeling very little charity where my oldest brother was concerned.

"Well, is she leaving, or not? Because we have a test next week and I feel pretty good about the material," Cletus pressed.

I stuffed my hands in my pockets and shook my head. "I don't know. She said she doesn't have any plans to leave immediately, but she doesn't have any reason to stay."

Cletus and Beau's frowns were severe.

"No reason to stay? What kind of swill is that? What are you—pig liver? What a heartless doxy."

I huffed, not liking Cletus's uncharitable assessment, because if memory served, I was pretty sure *doxy* meant the same thing as *floozy*. I was also growing impatient and needed this conversation to end.

"Look, she wants me to go with her, okay? She's not heartless. She's following her dreams, and I can't fault her for that. And I can't hold her back, so I broke things off."

Beau and Cletus shared a look, then Beau said, "So... what's the problem? Why don't you go with her?"

Dumbfounded, I stared at my twin, then my older brother. They were watching me as though expecting me to explain myself when the reasons were perfectly obvious. I looked to Jethro for help, but he was staring at me like he didn't understand the problem either.

I growled at their thickheadedness and turned away, shaking my head and making for the exit. Cletus stepped in front of me, blocking my path.

"Now, hold on. Beau's question is valid. We all know how you've been pining after Miss James. What's the problem? Maybe I can fix it."

I answered through gritted teeth, "The problem, Cletus, is that I'm part owner in the shop, in case you've forgotten."

He shrugged. "So?"

"So, you and Beau think you can keep up with business without me?"

He shrugged again. "Maybe. Maybe not. If I'm honest, I'd say probably not. But then we could always hire a replacement."

I stared at him, again dumbfounded, and added, "What would I live on, huh? If I went off with her? All my savings is in that shop."

"We'd buy you out if you want." This answer came from Beau. "Or you could get a job wherever you and Jess land. Auto mechanics—good ones—aren't easy to find. Plus, there's your racing, and there's always circuits out there, especially if you stay in the South and Midwest for a bit."

"Or you could stop being such a proud douchebag, let Miss James and her inheritance keep you in style, earn your keep the old-fashioned way." Jethro grinned as he said this, cocking an eyebrow, then winked at me.

I was tempted to punch him in the face again.

"Sign me up for some of that," Beau said, also grinning.

But then his smile fell and he cleared his throat, looking away when I glared at him.

"The point, my dear brother, is that there's nothing keeping you here other than your own stubbornness." Cletus's tone was instructive and gentle and incredibly irritating.

"What about honor? Huh? Obligation?"

"To whom? Us? Beau and me?" Cletus shook his head. "You think we want to look at your grumpy face for the next twenty years, regretting your decision every day? No, thank you, sir. You're already ornery enough as it is."

Cletus wiped his mouth with the corner of his napkin, then placed the used paper towel on top of the plates stacked in front of Jethro.

"You better get started on those dishes," he said to Jethro. "It's the least you can do, given the trouble you've caused. And you"—he turned to me—"you need to call Tina and tell her we got it covered. We can't have her messing things up or making complications."

I nodded.

"What about me?" asked Beau, sitting back in his chair, looking mighty relaxed and pleased.

"Well now, Beau. You and I…" Cletus clamped his hand on my twin's shoulder. "We need to go find ourselves a turkey."

Jessica

25

"Falsehood flies, and the truth comes limping after it."

—JONATHAN SWIFT

TINA BROUGHT HER NEW BOYFRIEND to Thanksgiving dinner. He wanted us all to call him Twilight.

This was an odd and difficult adjustment for our family because his real name was Isaac Sylvester and my brother had known him since kindergarten. His father, Kip, was my boss and his mother, Diane, ran the bakery in town and read poetry at the library on Thursday nights. His sister, Jennifer, was the baker of those infamous award-winning banana cakes.

And he wanted us to call him Twilight.

I was too tired and melancholy to truly feel the level of bafflement this request deserved. However, I did notice the initial exchange between my brother and Isaac/Twilight when they arrived with Tina's momma. It went something like this:

Jackson: "Tina. I didn't know you were bringing Isaac. Good to see you, man."

Isaac/Twilight: "It's Twilight."

Jackson (looking bemused): "No it ain't; it's not even noon yet."

Isaac/Twilight: "No. My name is Twilight."

Jackson (still looking bemused): "Say what?"

Isaac/Twilight: "My name. Call me Twilight."

Jackson: "You mean like that *My Little Pony* character?"

Tina: "Jackson! I didn't know you were a *My Little Pony* fan."

Jackson (scowling then motioning to Isaac/Twilight): "Jessica was always watching it growing up, and I'm not a fan—not like Twilight Sparkle over here."

Isaac/Twilight: "The name is Twilight, not Twilight Sparkle."

Jackson (irritated): "If you want me to call you Twilight, then don't be surprised if I slip up a few times and call you Pinky Pie."

A similar conversation ensued when Twilight was brought in to greet my dad, except my dad said, "That's not a name, son. That's a time of day."

It didn't take long for us to realize that the Isaac Sylvester we used to know wasn't this Twilight fella. Last I'd heard, Isaac had joined the army and was stationed in Afghanistan; that was six years ago. But now the leather jacket he wore covered with Iron Wraiths patches quickly told us everything we needed to know.

My father's method of solving the inherent awkwardness was to put a beer in all empty hands and turn on the football game so loud no one could speak. Tina stayed with the men in the family room, basically sitting on Twilight's lap.

Meanwhile my momma, my daddy's sister, and I made

dinner. It was just as well. Mashing potatoes was a good outlet for my gloomy aggression, and neither my mother nor my aunt expected me to talk much.

I was feeling hollowed out, like Duane had removed some essential part of me and had taken it with him. I had no way of getting it back.

Therefore, Thanksgiving was spent in a distracted haze of sadness and self-doubt. My family attributed the depression to my *mother's* death. Several times during the day my momma put her hand on my back and rubbed the space between my shoulders.

Then she'd say, "I know. I know it hurts," give me a quick hug, and walk away fighting her own tears. I'd watch her go, grimacing to myself, because I wasn't preoccupied mourning the loss of Louisa. I mean, I mourned her. I was sad she'd died, but she'd spent all my life, especially while I was in college, keeping me at arm's length.

I guess now I knew why…but not really. Her actions still didn't make sense to me and I was too exhausted to contemplate Louisa's decisions. The reality of Louisa's betrayal—because it was starting to feel like one—was too fresh.

My momma seemed to think I was feeling a great deal more despair about Louisa than I was, and contradicting her assumption felt wrong. It felt heartless, especially in the face of her genuine pain. So I kept my mouth shut and accepted her sympathy, offering my shoulder as a safe place for her to cry.

Meanwhile, the focus of my conscious desolation was of the red-bearded man-troubles variety.

Matters were not helped when Tina sauntered into the kitchen after dinner. I'd offered to do all the dishes. All of them. All. On my own, with no help, because I really just needed to be by myself. I didn't hear her come in because I was scrubbing the roasting pan and trying not to cry.

"Hey, Jess. Want company?" she asked right before her arm wrapped around my shoulders and gave me a squeeze. "I am so sorry about your aunt."

I stiffened, then sighed, relaxing and giving an odd sideways lean into her embrace. I couldn't hug her without drying off my hands and that just felt like too much effort. She obviously didn't know the truth yet. I made a mental note to talk to my parents about the plan going forward, how they wanted to proceed, if they wanted people to know I'd been adopted.

"Thanks, Tina." I acknowledged her sympathy with a head nod. "But no need to keep me company in here. I imagine your boyfriend can't be feeling too comfortable with Jackson poking fun at his new name."

Tina leaned against the counter at my side and giggled. "Twilight isn't my boyfriend. We've been hooking up a lot lately, is all. I brought him to ease my momma's mind. She thinks I'm some kind of biker whore, so I figured bringing a familiar face from the Wraiths would make her feel better."

I slid my eyes to the side and scrutinized my cousin. "What do you do with the Wraiths anyhow? When you're there at the Dragon Biker Bar?"

She shrugged. "We play pool. Get drunk. Have fun, fool around. Sometimes I put on a show."

"Do you ever feel like you're in danger? I mean, they don't have the best reputation."

She shrugged again and this time when she giggled it sounded nervous. "Well...not in *danger* exactly. I mean, things can get pretty intense and scary—like some of the guys can be really rough—but I think I like it, most of the time. I really like it when they fight over me. I like that part a lot."

I nodded thoughtfully. I was trying not to judge. Trying *really* hard. Because watching two men fight over who would be having sex with me didn't sound all that appealing. And I didn't know how to ask the questions I suddenly wanted to ask but knew would be imprudent, not to mention impolite. What Tina did, and who she did it with, and why in tarnation she did it were none of my business.

I felt her eyes on me. Apparently she misinterpreted my struggle, because she said, "Duane and I aren't back together."

I stiffened with surprise and dropped the roasting pan I'd been holding, splashing water on my apron. "What? What did you say?"

"I said, Duane and I aren't back together. Despite what you may have heard, we aren't. He came to see me on Friday at the Pink Pony, and I know how some people like to gossip. I'm sure you heard about it."

I felt many things at that moment and all of them were of the ugly, jealous variety. I recognized something about myself just then: I wasn't enlightened or open-minded. Not even a little.

I didn't want Duane going to the Pink Pony, watching and admiring naked women, and I didn't want him seeking out Tina. Just the thought of it made me angry. And feeling more and more like a woman scorned—in the Shakespearean sense. And lots of crazy-woman-scorned thoughts bounced around my brain, making me dizzy. The room tilted and I gripped the edge of the sink.

Maybe Duane didn't want to leave Green Valley because he didn't want to leave Tina and all the dancers at the Pink Pony.

Maybe I wasn't enough for him. Maybe he'd been expecting me to conform to some role, where he raced cars and got lap dances on the weekends while I stayed home, knitted him socks, and folded his laundry.

But that wasn't right. That wasn't the Duane Winston I knew and fell in love with. That wasn't even the Duane I grew up with. Reason raised its hand and suggested I doubt my cousin, or doubt her version of events at least.

Reason had a calming effect, and that's when I realized she was still speaking.

"So just because he'd been texting and calling me like crazy for the last three weeks didn't mean I was open to restarting anything between us. Like I said, I've moved on and so should he. I told him—"

She stopped talking abruptly, frowning as she pulled her phone from her pocket. Helplessly, I watched as she smirked at the screen of her cell.

"He just can't stop calling me," she *tsk*ed, then showed me the incoming number.

It was Duane's number. And he was calling her.

I watched her send it to voicemail. I felt her eyes on me, though mine were affixed to the phone. Duane *was* calling her; he'd left her messages. Now maybe I was being willfully blind, but I could not swallow the notion that Duane cheated with Tina, or with anyone for that matter.

He loved me. He did. I knew it. And no one could convince me otherwise. And he wasn't a cheater. I *knew* him. Therefore, with cold conviction, I turned my tired gaze back to Tina.

"You're lying."

Her full lips parted, like she was offended, and she stuttered for a bit before managing, "What? You just saw his number flash on my phone. You just saw him call me."

I shook my head. "I'm not doubting the calls or the messages, Tina. But you're still lying. This smells like a skunk in a perfume shop. First of all, you come in here on Thanksgiving, the day after I come back from my…Louisa's funeral, and tell me how Duane has been visiting you at the Pink Pony, waving that phone in my face, wanting to stir shit up. I don't buy it. You're trying too hard."

Tina was giving me her angry bitch face, which was actually pretty scary, but I was too numb to feel fear or intimidation.

After an intense and drawn-out staring contest, Tina rolled her eyes, flipped her hair, and snorted. "Whatever. You believe what you want. But that don't change the fact—"

"That's right, nothing you can do or show me will change the fact that I *know* Duane Winston, and he is a good man. He's not his father. He's not a cheater. He wouldn't do that to me or to anyone. And I know he loves me, I *know* it. I trust him, and I love him and…" And now I was crying.

I didn't know why she was doing this, why she wanted to make me believe that Duane had been running around behind my back, but I didn't care to know her reasons.

Using still wet hands, I turned from Tina and grabbed a paper towel, using it to wipe my eyes and nose.

I could feel her stare, feel her intense dislike, as she pressed. "I thought you weren't together. Isn't that what you told me at dinner a few weeks ago? Or were you lying?"

I shook my head, sniffled, and squared my shoulders as I faced her. "Not that it's any of your business, but we weren't together when you and I had dinner. Then we worked things out a few weeks ago."

"So why are you crying now?" she spat, pursing her lips, her eyes narrowed slits.

Suddenly, I was too tired for this conversation, for her brand of crazy, so I said, "That's also none of your business."

I turned away from my cousin and the remainder of the dishes, needing the solace of my dark room and softer tissues.

"Hey! Wait, we're not done here."

I turned and walked backward, shaking my head at her nasty audacity. "You are my cousin, Tina. I will always love you, notwithstanding your spitefulness. I will. If you ever need my help, I'll be there for you. But we're not friends. I don't like being lied to, and I don't like you trying to cast aspersions on Duane's good character. So, we *are* done here. I'm finished, and now I'm leaving."

♥

Duane,

I think you've broken my heart. I've never had my heart broken before, but I'm pretty sure this sick sadness is it. I didn't sleep after you left. I cried for a long time though. I feel like I kept trying to give myself to you and you kept withholding yourself from me, and now I guess I know why.

I'm not so good at letting go. Once I get an idea in my head I hold on to it with both hands, so you'll have to pardon my inability to just walk away now without saying my piece. You said a few things on Wednesday night/ Thursday morning that weren't true, so now I want to set the record straight.

I meant it when I said I have no immediate plans to

leave Green Valley. I still have the rest of the school year to finish, and there's no one who can fill in or take my place. I may have the wanderlust, my soul may long to see and live in the world, to explore and have adventures, but that doesn't make me a flake. That doesn't mean I don't take my obligations and promises seriously.

Tina came to Thanksgiving at the house yesterday and told me you've been chasing after her for the last three weeks. She showed me text messages that you'd sent and then you called her phone, left her a message while I was standing there with her. Just so you know, I don't believe her. I know you, Duane. You're not anything like your father. You're not a cheater.

I love you and want to be with you all the time, so, yes, I asked you to come with me when the time comes. Maybe I shouldn't have done that. Maybe that's asking too much. But I want you to belong to me and I want to belong to you.

I wish you would ask me to stay, or help me try to find a compromise. Compromise isn't dishonorable. Asking me to stay isn't either. Please ask me to stay.

*Love always,
Jess*

I read then reread the seventeenth iteration of my letter.

Presently, it was the day after Thanksgiving. I'd been working on the letter all day and had discarded the other sixteen because after getting past the part where I told him how much I loved him, my mind invariably returned to the moment when he'd left the cabin.

He'd left me standing in that sheet, with a dead fire and a

cold bed. He'd just walked away from me. So I would become spitting mad. I was still mad now, but I recognized calling him insulting names in the letter—like shit-for-brains—might be counterproductive to the letter's purpose. I needed him to read it. It was a way for me to monologue and share my thoughts without the unhelpful shit-for-brains comments slipping out.

Plus name-calling wasn't likely to inspire affection and an open heart.

I set the letter back on my desk and rubbed my eyes, reflecting on how complicated life had become over the last month. Likely it was the ghost of J.R.R. Tolkien making me crazy as retribution for the blasphemy of my sexy Gandalf costume.

"Knock-knock."

I turned from my desk and found Claire poking her head in my bedroom door, her mouth flattened in sympathy.

"Hey. How are you holding up?"

I sighed, twisting to my desk and quickly flipping the letter over. "Come in and shut the door."

She did, moving to sit on the edge of my bed nearest my location. I turned fully in my seat to face her.

"I'm so sorry about your aunt. Your momma says you two were really close."

I stared at Claire for a beat, then shook my head. "That's not true. We weren't close."

"Didn't you work for her? Live with her over the summer during college?"

"Yes, but we weren't close. When I lived with her, she had me stay in one of the maid's rooms, and we never took meals together unless Momma was visiting."

Claire's face screwed up with confusion. "Well, that's a strange way to treat family."

It must've been strange for Claire to label it as such, especially considering Claire's experience with her own extremely dysfunctional family.

"I organized her house and schedule. When she had visitors, she'd tell people I was *on staff*. She never once referred to me by my name, let alone admitted I was related. I just figured she was embarrassed by me." I shrugged, trying to ignore the twinge of hurt feelings I'd long ago set aside, but that now felt remarkably fresh, given the fact *she'd* given birth to me.

At first, during the early days of my employment, my feelings had been hurt. I'd thought working for Louisa would bring us closer together. Ironically, in retrospect, I'd thought she'd be like a second mother. I'd thought we'd talk to each other about topics other than hiring a new driver, replacing the tile in the blue damask bedroom, and her various nail and hair appointments.

But working for my aunt had only served to segregate us into the roles of employer and employee. I'd never grown attached to Aunt Louisa because she didn't want me to be attached. She'd distanced me in a way that had felt purposeful.

"Huh…" Claire sat back on the bed, crossing her arms. "That is so bizarre. The way your momma spoke just now, she made it sound like your aunt loved you most in the world."

I sighed again. I was doing a lot of sighing. I wasn't ready to tell Claire that my aunt was actually my birth mother. I wasn't ready to talk about Louisa because I didn't know how to feel about her. So, once again, I pushed my feelings away.

I decided to tell Claire the truth minus the maternity reveal. "I never figured her out."

"But she left you all that money."

"Yeah. She left me everything."

Claire tilted her head to the side, her bright eyes assessing my face. "Is that why you look so forlorn? Don't tell me you're feeling guilty about your aunt's money?"

I shook my head, biting my lip so I wouldn't speak the truth about my mood. If I'd learned anything from this disaster, it was to be considerably more guarded with my heart. I'd always thought that if I were open to love, then love would find me. As it turns out, if you're open to love, then heartbreak finds you and leaves you naked in a cabin with no electricity or indoor plumbing.

But Claire knew me too well. Her eyes narrowed on my lip and she tilted her head the other way, her assessment becoming full-on scrutiny.

"Jessica, what are you hiding?"

I shook my head faster.

"What's going on? You're miserable and it isn't your aunt and it isn't inheritance guilt. Something has happened."

I shook my head even faster, but now Claire was a blur of red hair and white skin, because my eyes were filling with tears. And, crap, I just sobbed.

She reached forward and pulled me into a hug, stroked my hair and held me tight. "Goodness gracious, what is going on? You're shaking."

I grabbed fistfuls of her shirt and cried on my friend. Cried and cried. I don't know how long I cried, but it was a good while and it was embarrassing. She hushed me and spoke soothing words. Her shirt at the shoulder was soaked by the time the tears ebbed.

"Can you talk now? Can you tell me what happened?"

I opened my mouth to speak but hiccupped instead. I needed a moment, or an hour.

Therefore, I straightened away and grabbed letter number seventeen from my desk; I handed it to her and managed to squeak out, "Read this. I'm going to wash up," then hurried from the room.

I took my time in the bathroom, scrubbing my face, blowing my nose, giving myself a mirror pep talk. I felt a bit less pathetic when I stepped back into my bedroom. Crying and being sad is like an upper respiratory infection; snot makes me feel pathetic, and the absence of snot makes me feel less pathetic.

"Oh, Jess. I'm so sorry." Claire looked both sympathetic and confused when I entered the bedroom. She crossed to me and squeezed my shoulders. "I feel like I pushed you into this thing with Duane. But I just can't imagine… I would never have… He left you in a sheet?" She sighed, befuddlement winning out over sympathy.

I finally felt stable enough to explain the entire situation, so I did. We sat on my bed and I told her everything—about how I'd called him from Texas, how I'd tracked him down to the cabin, how we loved each other, how he was using honor to abandon me to my empty dreams. When I finished, Claire was staring at me, her fingers halfway covering her open mouth.

I shrugged, not sure what else to do. "It's all right. I'll be fine."

She nodded, frowning, and it was clear she didn't believe me. "Fine. You'll be fine. You pack a bag, come stay with me tonight."

I gave my friend a small smile. "That actually sounds really nice."

Claire's frown intensified, then she *tsk*ed. "Well, come on. Let's get a bag packed. We'll stop by the Piggly Wiggly on the way for some ice cream."

♥

We were just pulling out of the store parking lot when my phone rang. I glanced at my screen, but didn't recognize the number. I stared at it for one ring longer, then swiped my thumb across the display and answered, figuring it was likely a wrong number.

"Hello?"

"Jess? Jess, is that you? Jess, it's me, Tina. I…your help… real big trouble. I need you to…totally fucked…and they found…"

"Tina, wait a sec. I can't understand you, you're cutting out. Where are you?"

I heard some static on the other line, then she said, "The Dragon and you have to hurry. I stole this phone and…"

"Are you at the Dragon Biker Bar? Do you need me to come get you?" I glanced at Claire, found her watching me with alarm.

"Yes! I need—"

But that's all I got, because her side clicked twice, then the line went dead. I brought the phone to my lap and pulled up the recent calls list. Not only did I not recognize the number, but the area code wasn't local.

"What was that all about?"

"I'm not sure. It was Tina and she sounded frantic. I think she was calling from the Dragon Biker Bar. At least she said yes when I asked. She wants me to come get her."

"She wants you to go to the Dragon? To pick her up?"

"Actually, she sounded like she was in trouble."

I took a deep breath, staring at my phone for a stretch, trying to figure out what to do. Then I dialed Jackson's cell number.

"What are you doing?"

"Calling Jackson. I'm going to ask him to meet me there."

"At the Dragon? You want to go to that hellhole?" She sounded incredulous and a little panicked. The bar served as the club headquarters for the Iron Wraiths. Since her daddy was the club president and her momma was his old lady, Claire had spent much of her early adolescence at the infamous biker bar with the MC members and club girls.

If memory served, she hadn't seen or spoken to her folks since marrying Ben McClure years ago.

As I waited for Jackson to pick up, I tried to calm Claire. "Listen, don't come. Just take me back to my house and I'll drive over on my own."

"The hell you will. You're not going there by yourself." She glanced in her rearview mirror and started her car. Backing up, she maneuvered the small parking lot. "But we're stopping by my house first. I need to get something."

"Claire, take me home. I know that place doesn't have good memories for you." Jackson's phone clicked over to voicemail, so I hung up and decided to text him about what was going on first.

Her grip on the steering wheel tightened and I noticed her eyes were a bit wider, but she dismissed my suggestion. "No. I'll go. It'll be...fine."

I didn't know if she was trying to convince me or herself.

Jessica

26

> "I can't think of anything that excites a greater sense of childlike wonder than to be in a country where you are ignorant of almost everything."
>
> —BILL BRYSON, *NEITHER HERE NOR THERE: TRAVELS IN EUROPE*

AS I WAITED IN CLAIRE'S truck for her to grab whatever she needed from her house, I called Jackson again and this time I left a voicemail. Then I called my daddy and did the same. I rationalized it was sufficient they know where we were. It wasn't unusual to get their voicemail, especially when they were on duty and driving around the mountains; and most especially on a holiday weekend when all the drunk drivers were celebrating by smashing into trees.

Finished with my messages to the law enforcement members of my family, I looked up just in time to see Claire coming out of her house. She was carrying two handguns.

Wordlessly, she opened the driver's side door, leaned over me, and put them both—and an extra magazine—in the glove compartment. Then she buckled her seat belt, started the car, and backed out of her driveway. Meanwhile I was staring at her the whole time, wondering what the heck she was thinking.

About two minutes down the road, I finally asked, "What the heck are you thinking?"

Her eyes flicked to mine, then away. "I'm thinking I'm not going near that place without a gun."

"Claire!"

"I have a concealed weapons permit."

"So do I, Claire. But I'm not bringing my gun to the Dragon Biker Bar."

"I'm not taking any chances, okay?"

"I said I'd go by myself."

Claire slowed at the stop sign—one way leading us down to Green Valley, the other way leading us up the mountain to the Dragon Biker Bar—and turned to face me. Her jaw was set, her eyes were determined, but the panic fraying the edges of her typically calm demeanor made me nervous.

"Look, I know these people. I grew up in that place. I know what it's like to be inside that compound with no way out. We're not going in there and we're not getting near the place without a plan, a weapon, and a means to escape, and I'm not letting you go without some kind of protection."

"I called my brother and my dad. They know where we're going. You can't tell me these guys are dumb enough to do anything to the sheriff's daughter?"

"Honey, they're dumb enough and dangerous enough to do just about anything."

"Then what should we do? Should we wait for Jackson or my daddy?"

She sighed, her fingers flexing on the steering wheel, then

turned the truck up the mountain. "No. No, we need to go get Tina before it's too late."

"Too late? Should I call 911?"

Claire hesitated, then shook her head. "We can call 911 when we get there, but maybe it won't come to that. Maybe just the threat of your brother and father being on their way will be enough for them to hand over your stupid cousin. Plus they won't do anything to me, nothing lasting anyway."

"What? What does that mean?"

"It means I know too many of their secrets."

♥

Claire pulled her Nissan truck into the parking lot of the Dragon, choosing a space near the edge of the lot and far from any of the motorcycles. It was cold and the weatherman had threatened snow on top of the mountain. As I exited Claire's truck, a gust of frigid wind whipped my hair in all directions.

It was going to snow, sooner rather than later. That meant all the leaves would fall and autumn would officially be over. I would miss the vibrancy of color, but part of me was looking forward to the white blanket of winter, when everything is either desolate or covered. It would match my mood.

Claire put both weapons in the back of her jeans along with the extra magazine, covering them all with her bulky sweater. We walked to the main entrance together, holding hands. I'm not sure which of us reached out first, but I was glad to have her next to me. I'd never been to the bar before, though I knew where it was located, perched at the tippy top of the highest peak. Everyone knew where it was, and what it was about, and to avoid it unless you were looking for trouble.

A giant dragon was painted along the front side of the cinder-block building, and not one of those friendly Chinese dragons used in parades. This dragon looked mean and it had metal spikes coming out of its tail and the top of its head as horns; its claws were also metal spikes. I surmised all the metal spikes were iron, which explained the name of the club. The dragon was in the midst of decapitating a person, blood gushing over the mystical creature's claws in a gratuitous display of artistic violence. *Real nice.*

Row after row of motorcycles were lined up in front and loud music reverberated from behind the closed doors. A rough interpretation of the Iron Wraiths emblem hung in the window as a neon sign right next to two other neon signs advertising BUD LIGHT and JACK DANIELS.

Certainly, the music, the murderous dragon mural, the rows of motorcycles, plus the austere cinder-block exterior gave a less-than-friendly aura to the place. But the outside was tidy, no trash in the lot or littering the building, and the surrounding area was covered in trees and underbrush.

As we approached, I spotted two men coming around the side of the building, apparently deep in discussion and also apparently related to giants. These men weren't big. These men were huge. Like, basketball-player tall plus rugby-player wide. I was more than a foot smaller than the shorter of the two. Claire must've seen them as well because I felt her stiffen, then pull us abruptly to a stop.

"We're close enough," she said, even though we were a good twenty feet from the building.

I glanced at her in question, but her eyes were fixed on the two men and her stance was rigid, primed to flee.

"Listen, you go back to the car and I'll—"

"No. You're staying right here with me." She shook her head, but before I could object she called out to the men. "Catfish, Drill. Hey. Over here."

The two giants—who apparently called themselves Catfish and Drill—glanced up. Neither frowned, nor did they smile. But it was obvious they were surprised as their gazes moved over Claire.

Almost reluctantly they broke away from the side of the building and crossed to where we stood. They glanced behind us and around at the woods lining the perimeter of the lot, as though checking for a trap or potential hidden accomplices.

"It's been a long time, Scarlet. You here to see your daddy?" the shorter of the two asked. His head was bald and his eyes were a sharp blue color. Maybe they appeared so sharp because he was dressed in all black—black leather pants, black leather jacket, black leather boots, black shirt beneath.

"That's close enough." She lifted her hand when they were about ten feet away, her tone stern. "I'm not here to see anyone. This is Jessica James. Her daddy is Sheriff James and her cousin called her earlier from inside the Dragon, wants to be picked up."

The two men stopped where she'd indicated, approximately ten feet from where we stood, and their eyes moved over me again. The shorter one asked, "Your daddy is the law?"

I nodded. "Yes, sir. But all we want is my cousin. She called about twenty minutes ago."

"What's her name?" This time the taller one spoke. His skin was dark brown but his eyes were nearly hazel, and his voice was so baritone it was almost too deep for my ears, making his words sound slurred together.

"Tina. Her name is Tina Patterson," I supplied.

"She dances at the Pink Pony," Claire added and I saw recognition ignite behind both of their expressions. Claire continued, her explanation sounding like a command. "She called. She wants to leave. We're here to get her."

The two men exchanged a look that I didn't understand, then the shorter one made like he was going to reach out and offer his hand to me. "I'm Drill; this here is Catfish."

Automatically, I moved to step forward, but Claire pulled me back and somewhat behind her. She had steel in her voice as she ground out, "She don't need to shake your hand. She just needs her kin."

"Come inside, Scarlet. Have a drink. I'm sure your daddy would—"

"What's going on here?" A third male voice interrupted Catfish's overtures, its owner walking quickly from the entrance of the bar to where we stood. He was about six foot, no taller, and was older than the other two, but they both stepped to the side as though deferring to his authority. I recognized the newcomer almost immediately as the biker who'd been talking to Duane the night we stopped by Daisy's Nut House for pie.

His dark-brown eyes snagged on mine and his steps faltered, his mouth parting. He was definitely surprised and he definitely recognized me.

"Scarlet is back and she brought a friend." Drill motioned to me.

"I am not back." From my vantage point, I could see Claire was speaking through clenched teeth and her blue eyes flashed as she appealed to the newcomer. "Repo, this is Jessica James, and her daddy—"

"I know who her daddy is. What are you two ladies doing

here?" The man Claire had addressed as Repo still hadn't taken his eyes off me, and his stunned surprise seemed to have morphed into disapproval and anger.

"We're here to pick up my cousin, Tina."

Repo's eyes narrowed and he didn't respond for several seconds, opting to scrutinize me instead. Meanwhile Drill and Catfish were looking at Repo as though they were waiting for direction.

"What makes you think Tina is here?" Repo finally asked.

"She called me."

"She called you?" He sounded doubtful.

"Yes. So I called my brother and my daddy, told them I was coming up here to pick up my cousin."

At this news, Repo's glower turned into a smirk. "You called the sheriff and the deputy? They know you're up here?"

"Yes, Mr. Repo, they do. Now, for the fourth time, could one of you please bring Tina out? Then we'll be happy to leave."

His smirk widened into a smile when I called him *Mr. Repo*. Then he chuckled, like he thought I was funny. "Smart girl," he said under his breath, shaking his head. He turned, the smile waning from his face, and lifted his chin to Drill. "Go get Tina. Bring her here. And don't go volunteering that Scarlet is here. That ain't nobody's business."

Drill seemed surprised by the orders issued, but said nothing to contradict. He nodded once, then Catfish and Drill walked back to the building. They didn't use the main entrance; instead they took the same path they'd come from and disappeared around the cinder-block corner.

This left Claire, Repo, and me standing outside the bar. Claire was glaring at Repo. Repo glared at Claire. I split my attention between the two of them. I figured we were going to spend the next several minutes in silence as we waited. Neither of my companions seemed inclined to talk. Dislike as thick as sausage gravy rolled off my friend; whether her ire was pointed at this man, or this place, or both, I had no idea. She didn't discuss her childhood, just a few slips and scraps of information here and there, enough for me to extrapolate that she'd never had it easy and considered the Wraiths part of a dark past.

But then Repo cleared his throat and said to me, "I heard your…uh, your aunt died."

I nodded once. "That's right."

He studied me for a long minute, so long I thought he was finished. Unexpectedly, he said, "I knew her when we was kids."

I'm sure I looked as surprised as I felt. "My aunt?"

"Both the Franklin sisters, in Texas. Your granddaddy was my daddy's boss."

"At the ranch?"

"That's right."

"Huh." I frowned at the coincidence and said, "Small world."

"Not so small," he mumbled under his breath, but I caught the words.

My curiosity was piqued. In fact, a prickle of cold something slithered down my back, so I asked, "So, what was she like? My aunt?"

His small smile was framed by a well-groomed salt-and-pepper goatee and reflected in his dark eyes. "She was very pretty—beautiful—and smart. Smarter than me. And she was funny; she used to make me laugh."

I narrowed my eyes at him; the cold slithering something

settled in my belly. "Really? How'd she do that? What'd she do that was funny?"

"Play tricks, pranks mostly. She got me good a few times."

I huffed a humorless, disbelieving laugh. "I can't imagine Aunt Louisa being funny."

"She was…she was wild, and she sure liked to piss off her daddy," he responded absentmindedly, like he was talking to himself. His gaze lost focus, turning inward with nostalgia.

"Sounds like you," Claire whispered, nudging me with her elbow.

I blinked. It did sound like me, and I felt an odd lightness in my chest, but it wasn't a good feeling. I'd always considered myself an outsider in my own family. All my relatives in both Tennessee and Texas were the traditional type—well, everyone but Tina, but Tina and I weren't much alike either. And now I knew Tina and I shared no blood.

My relations thought I was a bit strange, my sense of humor odd, my ideas about traveling the world a phase, and that my good sense would eventually prevail.

Maybe my birth mother had been like me when she was younger. In her case, I supposed that good sense did eventually prevail. She'd settled down, never got married, but she'd grown roots. After making millions with her ingenious patent, she spent her life organizing charity functions and getting her nails done. I shuddered at the thought.

"She changed," I said and thought at the same time.

"Pardon?" Repo asked, like I'd woken him from a trance.

A harsh gust of wind sent my hair flying, so I gathered the chaotic strands at the base of my neck and twisted them, raising my voice over the music and the sudden breeze. "She changed. My aunt changed. I never saw her wild side."

His expression blanked, then shuttered; he studied me for a beat, then shrugged, his voice sounding abruptly distant as he said, "She did change."

"Do you know why? Did she…I mean…did she ever have any boyfriends? That you remember? Like a high school sweetheart? Or maybe someone in college?" I ignored Claire's confused expression as I interrogated Repo.

He didn't answer. His eyes darted away, then back to mine, more distant than before. "You ask too many questions. A woman should know her place."

I lifted an eyebrow at this odd shift in subject and the sudden impatience in his voice. Of course I'd heard the phrase *A woman should know her place* before, always from an asshole. But something in me couldn't help playing dumb and poking a stick at this particular asshole.

So I asked, deadpan, "*A woman should know her place?* You mean, like her address?"

"No, baby girl. A woman should know her *place*. You know, on her back or on all fours. Wherever her man wants to take her."

I grimaced. "You're joking."

"I ain't joking."

Claire huffed.

"You're serious? You really think that?" My voice raised a half octave, unable to contain my disgust.

"He's serious," Claire deadpanned from her place at my elbow.

I sneered at him. "And your…your old lady? She thinks this way too?"

He shrugged. "I don't have an old lady, not anymore."

"What happened to her?"

Claire tugged on my elbow and warned, "You don't want to know."

I ignored her, horrified and curious. "No. Tell me. What happened to your old lady?"

"She didn't like my fun, so I cut her loose." Repo's dark eyes seemed to be watching me closely as he said this, gauging my reaction.

"Your fun?"

"He means, his woman didn't like him…" Claire struggled for a moment, like she didn't know how to proceed. Finally she settled on, "She didn't like him fucking the club girls. So he told his old lady to get lost."

"That's revolting."

Repo grinned, his white teeth now menacing. "Baby girl, that's club life."

"That's revolting," I repeated, then added, "and you're revolting."

I didn't want to look at him anymore.

I didn't want to talk to him.

I wanted to find Tina and get the hell out of here.

And just at that moment, Catfish and Drill reappeared. This time they came out of the main entrance to the bar and four other bikers were with them. I felt Claire stiffen at my side and take a step back.

"What the hell?" I heard Repo say, glancing over his shoulder. He turned completely around as they neared, his hands on his hips, standing between us and the approaching gang. "What the hell is this?"

The men kept advancing, and something about the set of their jaws and the steel in their eyes made my stomach drop.

"We need to go." Claire backed up another step, pulling me with her. "Shit, we need to run. Run!"

But we were too late. They read our intentions before we could gain distance and these men moved like athletes. I'd only managed ten sprinted steps before I was lifted off my feet, big arms closing around my torso and turning me back to the bar.

I heard Claire screech and cuss, realized she was also being carried. Drill had thrown her over his shoulder like a sack of potatoes.

I also heard Repo rage against the giant who was carrying me. "What the fuck is this? You get your goddamn hands off her right fucking now or I'll break every finger in your fucking hand!"

"Sorry, Repo." Catfish's baritone rumbled behind me as I fought fruitlessly against his hold; I might as well have been clawing at a boulder. "Razor wants the girl."

Duane

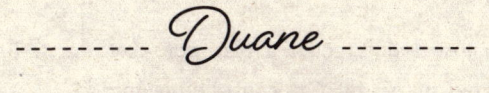

27

"Travel far enough, you meet yourself."

—DAVID MITCHELL, *CLOUD ATLAS*

"HAVE YOU CALLED JESS YET?"

I shook my head, staring out the driver's side window of Beau's GTO. It was the Friday after Thanksgiving. Instead of heading to the jam session and delicious coleslaw, we were on our way to the Dragon Biker Bar, unannounced and uninvited. We were presently stopped at the convenience store because Cletus needed duct tape. Jethro escorted Cletus into the store to ensure he didn't dawdle. And I was driving because I was by far the best driver in case we needed to make a quick getaway.

I heard Beau curse under his breath next to me, then say, "You're such a dummy."

"I didn't say I wasn't going to call her. I just haven't called her yet."

"Well, why not?"

"Because I don't have a plan yet, that's why. I need to come to her with a plan, not just being stupid."

"You are being stupid. What you need to do is call her, tell her you were wrong, beg for her forgiveness, say you're ready to go whenever she is, and then meet some place for make-up sex. That's how you do it."

"She's not going to forgive me that easily. That's why I need a plan. Besides, I want all this mess with the Iron Wraiths over and done with before I set things straight. They've taken too much of my time, been too much of a distraction."

"You need to stop waiting for everything to be just right, Duane. Haven't you wasted enough time already?"

"I'm not asking for your opinion," I ground out.

Beau shook his head and singsonged under his breath, "You're making a mista-*ake*."

The buzz of my phone offered an alternative to Beau's meddling. Tina.

My message to her yesterday was clear: she was no longer needed.

She hadn't responded. Not 'til now.

Tina: Tina can't come to the phone right now. You should probably call your uncle Razor, he's got something you want.

I frowned at the short text, reading it twice, then cursed.

"What? What is it?" Beau glanced between me and my phone.

I showed him my screen.

He cursed, then said unnecessarily, "I bet she got herself caught."

Luckily Jethro and Cletus walked out of the Piggly Wiggly at just that moment and made a beeline for the car.

"Sorry that took so long. They had a wide selection of duct tape. And Cletus bought Silly String." Jethro sounded irritated as he settled in the car behind me.

"You can't rush a duct tape purchase." In my rearview mirror, I saw Cletus clutching the shopping bag to his chest. "Duct tape is man's answer to electrons and protons. It's how we keep matter together."

Once Beau was back in the car, he grabbed my phone out of my hand and passed it to Cletus. "We may have a problem."

Cletus frowned at the message, then nodded, pushing his thick-rimmed glasses farther up his nose. "Well. Okay then. You can't make an omelet without heat."

"You mean, you can't make an omelet without breaking some eggs," Beau corrected.

"No. I meant what I said, you can't make an omelet without heat. If you have no heat, then it's just watery raw eggs. That's not an omelet."

"Why are you wearing those stupid glasses, Cletus? You don't need glasses," Beau asked impatiently.

"It's a fashion statement," Cletus responded while he typed something into his calculator watch.

"And to think, I was actually missing y'all last week, before I got home." Jethro's sarcasm was Cool Whip on whipped cream—completely unnecessary.

"Whatever," Beau said, straightening in his seat. He was anxious.

I should have been, but other than hoping Tina hadn't done anything too crazy, and a measure of guilt for involving her in the first place, all I felt was impatience to have this mess sorted.

I wasn't anxious. Not at all.

Not until the moment I spotted Jessica James and Claire McClure being carried against their will into the Dragon Biker Bar by two huge men in black leather, trailed by four more men and a shouting Repo.

The situation didn't look friendly.

"What the fuck?" Jethro's voice was tight. I knew he recognized Ben McClure's widow by her red hair. Part of me suspected Ben's death years ago had been the catalyst for Jethro's abrupt desire to clean up his act.

"Park the goddamn car, Duane!" Jethro's voice was now frantic.

"Give the man a minute," Cletus reprimanded. "Can't you see his woman is up there, too?"

But she wasn't, not anymore. They'd both been carried into the bar and swallowed up by the black doors.

I raced the GTO as close to the entrance as I dared and had already parked when Cletus spoke. I didn't move my seat up to let my brothers out. Instead I ran to the entrance and yanked the door open, scanning the inside for any sign of them and paying no heed to the dozens of bikers staring at me.

I heard Repo's angry voice but didn't see him, so I charged toward the sound. My way was immediately blocked by several gang members.

"Out of my way!" I growled my frustration, readying my fists for a fight. Somewhere in the background, "Honky Tonk Blues" rattled over an old speaker system.

"Wait, wait a minute." I heard Beau from behind me, but I ignored him.

"Get out of my fucking way!" I shouted, drawing my hand back. I didn't really register the men's faces, didn't need to.

"Whoa! Hold on!" An older woman with flaming-red hair jumped between me and the wall of bikers, her hands held up. "Just cool your shit, Winston. This ain't no way to show respect."

I'd never hit a woman before. But this woman was between me and Jess, and that meant she might as well have been a man. Before I could take action, Jethro was suddenly there, standing in front of me.

"Christine, we just saw your boys grab Claire McClure and Jessica James from the parking lot and carry them inside. You need to bring those women out here right now."

Christine shoved her face into Jethro's and spat, "You don't order me, Jethro Winston. Claire is my daughter and I'll remind you who you're talking to, boy. Coming in here, acting crazy. You wanna die today?"

I gave the woman another look and immediately registered the resemblance between Claire and Christine. I remembered that I'd met Christine before, years ago at a club picnic when I was a kid. And I'd seen her around town many times, never realizing who she was.

But none of this information was getting me any closer to Jess. I took a deep breath and gritted my teeth, forcing myself to talk even though all I wanted to do was burn this place to the ground.

"Look, we're here to see Razor," I cut in, glaring at Claire's momma, then the barrier of bikers behind her. "I got a message he has something I want. And I guarantee I've got something he wants. So enough of this standing-around chitchat bullshit. Which of you is going to take us to see the big man?"

Christine's eyes moved to me, face still twisted in a sneer. Her glare traveled down, then up, as though appraising me for a fight. The bar was eerily quiet and I noticed the music, wherever it had come from, had been turned off. I also noticed we were the center of attention. No man was sitting and no woman was talking.

"I know he's expecting *you*." Her tone was cold and measured. "But he wasn't expecting four of you boys, just the twins."

"Well, we're all here, and we're all telling the same story. So let's go."

She studied me, her shrewd eyes moving over my face like she could read my secrets.

At last she nodded once. "Fine. Follow me, Winston."

Christine turned and the impenetrable barrier of bikers split down the middle, creating a straight path through the crowd. I looked beyond Christine, saw we were headed toward a hallway at the back of the bar.

I heard Cletus from someplace behind me say, "Gentleman, ladies."

The walls were black. The doors were black. Everyone was dressed in black. Moving through the crowd was like swimming in a midnight sea surrounded by sharks. I could feel their eyes on me, their stares menacing and hostile.

Once we entered the hall, I glanced behind me. Though the wall of bikers loitered at the edge of the hallway, eight were following us. Christine stopped abruptly, turned, and lifted her chin toward me.

"Put your hands on the wall and spread your legs."

Clenching my jaw, I did as instructed, realizing we'd made it pretty far into the club without being frisked.

My three brothers also complied, but then after a half minute, I heard Cletus say, "That's Silly String."

I glanced over my shoulder, watching the interaction between Cletus and one of the bikers patting us down.

"What's it do?" the biker asked.

"It's silly," Cletus responded. "And it makes a mess."

The club member glanced at Christine and she shrugged, addressing her question to Cletus, "You planning on making silly messes?"

"No, ma'am."

"Then why do you have it?"

"Just in case you have cameras in the room where we're being taken."

She frowned at Cletus, her eyes narrowing. "You planning on covering the lenses with Silly String?"

"Yes, ma'am."

"No, you ain't." She lifted her chin and the Silly String was confiscated.

Once the pat-down was complete, Christine led us further into the winding corridor. We descended a flight of stairs, passing more black walls and more black doors. Nothing was labeled and all the hallways looked the same. I had no idea how we were going to get out of here without a guide.

With every step, my fear mounted, a sensation I wasn't accustomed to. Panic threatened to either choke me or send me into a blind rage. All I could think about was Jess, somewhere in this hellish labyrinth. But I stopped myself from imagining the worst, because if I did, then I would most certainly yield to blind rage.

Finally, we stopped in front of a door. I strained my ears, heard voices on the other side, and a shot of adrenaline traveled through my system like a lightning bolt when I recognized one of the voices as Jessica's. I had to clench my jaw and ball my hands into fists to keep from charging forward.

"After you, handsome," Christine said, opening the door wide and giving me a sinister smile.

I didn't need to be told twice.

I walked into the room and scanned it, my eyes immediately latching on to Jessica. She was sitting on a black leather couch, and next to her was Claire. They both looked pissed, but unharmed. My chest eased and some of the panic I'd been fighting dissipated. The girls weren't looking at us. They were looking at the man on the adjacent couch, a man I recognized as Razor Dennings, president of the Iron Wraiths.

"So you boys made it," he said without turning his head. Razor's eyes were on his daughter but he lifted his chin toward Jess. "I knew you'd come if I invited your girl here for a visit."

Jess's attention finally moved to where I stood, her eyes telling me most of what I needed to know. She wasn't surprised to see me. And she was scared, and feeling stupid for some reason, trying to apologize without saying the words.

"I don't see why all this was necessary," Repo drawled. I glanced to my right, found him sitting on a stool in front of a black lacquer bar. He had a whiskey or a bourbon in front of him, but it looked untouched.

I forced myself to see beyond my Jess tunnel vision and took a quick survey of the room. Besides the eight-biker escort behind us, Razor, and Repo, there were two other Wraiths members in the room, both as big as mountains. I recognized one as Catfish. I knew him because he liked to fish and sometimes went out with Hank Weller and Beau. He was difficult to overlook.

"This is all necessary, Repo, because you take too fucking long to get shit done," Christine spat as she strolled past me and crossed to her old man, giving him a sloppy kiss and whispering something in his ear.

"I have the situation under control," Repo responded through gritted teeth, glaring at the back of Christine's head.

"Enough. This shit needs to be settled." Razor pushed his old lady aside and she fell into the couch. He stood, stepped over her legs like she was a nuisance, and scanned us.

Razor was tall, but he wasn't big. He'd never been thick or burly. He was lanky and reeked of evil. Looking into his blue eyes, I'd always felt like I was looking at death. Repo had told me once, when I was just a kid and he was over for dinner, that Razor got the name from his preferred method for punishing insubordination.

His dead eyes settled on me, his face without expression, and he lifted his black beard–covered chin. "You. What's your answer? Yes or no?"

"No." I didn't hesitate. This fucker was scary as hell, but bullshitting or delaying was only going to piss him off.

"No?" He didn't sound surprised, more like he wanted to confirm my final answer.

"No."

From the corner of my eye, I saw Repo's face fall into the palm of his hand and he shook his head.

Razor nodded once, again with no expression. "Then your brother is going to federal prison. But first, my boys are going to fuck you all up."

"No," I said again. "None of that's going to happen either."

"You're going to give me a compelling reason, son?" The first note of inflection entered Razor's voice. He sounded interested, like he hoped I would surprise him.

"Yes."

"And what is that compelling reason?"

"When Jethro installed the traps, he alerted the law, sent pictures of the cars, VIN numbers, and a letter stating he suspected the traps were being used for the transport of drugs."

Razor's eyes narrowed, just a tad, and something like a small smile made his lips curve. "Is that so?"

"Yes."

"If that's so, then why hasn't the law interfered with our operations?"

I paused, thinking about Cletus's confiscated Silly String. He obviously thought we were being recorded or videotaped. I didn't want to say anything incriminating.

"No answer?" Razor's smile grew.

To my relief and surprise, Cletus stepped forward and answered for me. "The law hasn't interfered with your operations because they've been informed, but they don't know it. The certified envelope is in a safe place at an off-site facility and we have copies, including a receipt—dated three years ago—of the certified letter, signed for by the law. All we need to do is place a phone call. Or you could murder us."

"Say what?" Repo asked. He'd abandoned his stool and crossed to stand next to his boss.

"Murder us," Cletus responded slowly and loudly, like they were hard of hearing. "If you murder us, then the police will also be notified about the location of the certified package. As well as other information pertaining to your...activities."

"Other information?" Repo sounded skeptical.

Cletus nodded. "Yes. That's right. I make a hobby of covert surveillance. And I imagine no one in this room wants the police to know what happened on the night of January seventh, two years ago."

Razor's humorless smile melted away. His eyes no longer looked dead; they looked murderous.

"Are you threatening me, boy?"

"Not precisely," Cletus started, and I knew it was time for me to cut in, before Cletus explained the semantic differences between a fact, a promise, and a threat.

"We're not here to threaten you. We're here to decline your offer. If you push the issue, then we'll have no choice but to call the law." I spoke plainly because it was clear the club president didn't respond well to anything but plain speaking. "Now, we'd rather not do that, for obvious reasons. If you leave us alone, and Miss James and Mrs. McClure alone, then we'll have no reason to go sharing."

Razor's eyes flashed as he returned his attention to me, and I clenched my jaw, bracing for whatever came next. This guy was crazy enough to hold Jess, the sheriff's daughter, against her will. He was likely crazy enough to do much more than that.

"You don't think you can just walk out of here, do you, boy? I can't let y'all leave without one of you receiving a souvenir."

I swallowed a fair amount of dread, but also relief. We would be walking out of here, not limping, not carried out on stretchers. Walking.

If the rumors were to be believed, Razor's boon of choice was a cut, or several cuts, usually on the lower back and in a crosshatch pattern. Sometimes he wrote his name. I could do that if it meant all of us, especially Jess and Claire, were going to *walk* out on our own two legs.

I felt rather than saw Cletus stiffen next to me, knew he was about to object, but I lifted my hand to stay his outraged speech and addressed the club president. "Fine. I see you need to save face. That's fair."

Jessica's strangled squeak met my ears and I ignored it, fought the urge to look at her.

"That's *not* fair," Cletus objected through clenched teeth.

"I'll do it." I stepped forward.

"Duane..." Beau's protest was choked, and I heard him say, "No, I'll do it."

A hand closed over my shoulder and I turned my head to find Jethro behind me, his eyes unusually serious. "It should be me."

The president pulled a straight razor from one of his pants pockets, flipping it open at the hinge. He was smiling again. "Should I give y'all a few minutes to decide who gets the honor?"

"No," Claire shouted, standing and bringing Jessica with her. "No one will have the *honor*. There won't be any of that shit today."

"Dearest daughter, I didn't mean *you* would be leaving. Remember what I said? You ever come back here, you ain't leaving again. This is where you belong."

She shook her head slowly and lifted her hand, and that's when I saw the 9-millimeter handgun in her grip. My eyes darted to Jess, and despite looking scared, she didn't look surprised. She looked determined. In fact, at that very moment she lifted her arm as well, and in her hand was another 9-millimeter.

"You didn't frisk her?" Razor thundered at Catfish and the other mountain-sized biker. "What the fuck is wrong with you? She's *my daughter*. Of course she's got a weapon."

Truly, you could have knocked me over with a feather.

"We're leaving, those Winston boys are coming with, and no one is getting carved today." Claire's voice was unnervingly calm.

"You try my patience, baby girl." Razor took a step toward his daughter and she responded by flicking off the safety, murder in her eyes. He stopped dead in his tracks.

"You dare raise a gun to your daddy?" Christine stood as well; her eyes and voice were full of loathing.

"Like I said, we're leaving. And there will be no retribution either." Claire ignored her momma. She and Jess moved in unison to where we were standing. Jess's gun was trained on our eight biker escorts and Claire was covering Razor, Repo, Catfish, and the other mountain-sized Wraiths member.

"Boss?" Catfish questioned, his eyes darting between us and Razor.

The club president squinted at his daughter for a long moment, his expression unreadable. At last he shook his head. "Let them go."

"All the way?"

"Yeah. All the way." Razor nodded once, his eyes still on Claire as he addressed her. "I'm only doing this 'cause you're my blood, girl. I still got a soft spot for you. But don't you forget, you don't come back unless you plan to take your place."

Claire shook her head, her lip curling with disgust. "I won't be back. But don't *you* forget, Cletus ain't the only one who knows where the bodies are buried."

Duane

28

"A man with outward courage dares to die; a man with inner courage dares to live."

—LAO TZU, *TAO TE CHING*

CLAIRE SAVED US.

She guided us out of the compound via a much faster route than the maze we'd taken. It exited through a pair of aboveground cellar-like doors, opening to the outside at the edge of the parking lot. The temperature had dropped in the last half hour and we were dusted with big, fat snowflakes.

Once we were all outside, Jessica handed her gun over to Jethro, her eyes cutting to mine for the briefest of moments, and then the two of them were off running to Claire's truck, which was parked nearby.

"Wait!" I started to follow, but Cletus stopped me with a hand on my arm.

"No time for that right now. Claire knows what she's doing. We need to leave."

I pulled out of his grip. "No. No fucking way. I need to see—"

"Duane, let her go. We ain't got time for this and she ain't got time for this. Claire will keep her safe."

I wasn't so sure. Not because I didn't trust Claire or have faith in her level of badass, but I had a choking need to be the one to save Jess. *I* needed to see her to safety, witness it with my own eyes, hold her, and know with certainty she was okay. But Claire and Jess were already in the Nissan Frontier and Claire was already maneuvering it out of the lot.

Cursing, I nodded. Cletus was right and I hated it.

We sprinted to the GTO, Jethro covering us with the gun Jess had passed him. I heard rather than saw Claire's truck peel out and the engine rev as she sped away.

The outside of the bar was vacant, no soul in sight. The four of us quickly piled into Beau's car and I sped off like a demon, hoping to never lay eyes on the godforsaken Iron Wraiths headquarters again.

Twenty minutes later, no one had said a word and we'd had no sighting of Claire's truck. I was still glancing in the rearview mirror, half expecting to see motorcycles tailing us. But I didn't. I saw only tourists' rental cars, trucks, and campers. I couldn't stop thinking about Jess.

We were just about fifteen minutes from home, but I couldn't take it anymore. I needed to know she was safe.

So I broke the silence. "Jethro, I need you to call Claire, find out where they are."

"I texted Claire five minutes ago. They're good. Jackson is meeting them at the James's house. He'd read them both the riot act over the phone, she said. Claire is staying with Jess for the night in their guest room."

I blew out a breath, nodding, a new wave of relief passing through me. For the first time in my life I was thankful Jackson James existed. "Good. That's good."

Jethro turned in his seat and addressed his question to Cletus. "What I want to know is, what happened two years ago the night of January seventh, *Cletus.*"

"That's the night Tommy Bronson went missing, a.k.a. Lube."

"Lube?" Beau asked.

I saw Cletus nod in my rearview mirror. "Yeah. His biker name was Lube,..an unfortunate nickname. But he got it because he was so slippery."

"You have proof? The Wraiths killed him?"

"No. I have no proof. I was bluffing. But everyone knows Razor did it." He waved his hand in the air like this was a fact and this fact was common knowledge.

"Well, what I want to know is"—Beau met my eyes in the mirror briefly before turning to Cletus—"why did you tell Razor all that stuff when you were so sure we were being recorded? About how the police have been informed about the traps, but don't know? Can't he just use that to blackmail us again?"

Cletus took off his thick and unnecessary glasses, handed them to Beau. "You see this? This is an FPV video scrambler. It renders recording equipment useless. They might have been recording us, but all they'll get is static."

Jethro huffed a laugh and shook his head. "Then what the hell was the Silly String for?"

"Like I said, it's silly. And it makes a mess. I like to be prepared for all eventualities."

I didn't know what to say. Apparently, neither did anyone

else because everyone was silent. Naturally, my thoughts turned back to Jess.

I needed to speak to her. Instinct told me to go to her, wrap her in my arms, and take her away from all this craziness. Take her back to our cabin and keep her there until things between us were sorted. I wanted her to look at me with certainty again. Not anger. Never hurt.

But first I needed a plan.

"You want us to drop you off at Jess's?"

I glanced at my oldest brother, then shook my head.

"Why the hell not?"

I tightened my grip on the steering wheel and gave Jethro my stony profile, and said nothing.

"I agree with Jethro," Cletus chimed in, then added, "For the record."

"Me too," Beau agreed.

Jethro continued to push when I remained silent. "That woman loves you. I saw the way she looked at you when we walked in, saw the fear in her eyes when you volunteered to get cut."

I shook my head, rejecting his words. "I have no plan. I've got nothing. I need to figure things out first, figure out—"

Jethro cut me off. "See, this is your problem."

"I don't have a problem."

"Yeah, you do. You're always planning, but getting nothing done, waiting for a sure thing. You love that woman, you go get her, Duane. You don't wait 'til the time is right."

"Pot, meet kettle." Beau's retort sounded almost cheerful.

"Shut it, Beau. We're not talking about me." Jethro turned in his seat, facing me, and added in a more persistent tone, "She loves you something fierce. She does. You don't wait for that kind of love to cool off, believe me. You strike while the iron is hot."

♥

It was the middle of the night and I was about to throw rocks at the window of Sheriff James's house. Specifically at his daughter's window. Now these were small rocks, pebbles really, and I wasn't trying to break anything. I just wanted her to let me inside.

I didn't know what I was doing. This kind of recklessness was completely foreign to me. I had no plan, no idea if I was about to make things a hundred times worse. But something about Jethro's pushing, when he'd said, *You don't wait for that kind of love to cool off. You strike while the iron is hot,* rang true.

Jethro's odd words of wisdom, plus a restlessness that felt like heartburn, pushed me to make my second spur-of-the-moment decision in the last month. The first being tricking Jessica James backstage at the community center.

I jogged over to Jessica's house—with no strategy, no confidence that this would work—only knowing I needed to see her. I needed to make this right before she'd slept another night on the angry words between us and decided I'd pushed her away too many times to forgive.

I tossed three pebbles at her second-story window, waited, then threw two more. She didn't appear, so I tossed another two. I was warring with doubt and eyeballing the tree next to the house, considering the likelihood of climbing it without killing myself, when I saw her light flip on. I didn't know whether I was relieved or distraught when she opened the window.

She poked her head outside, her long blond hair dangling over one shoulder, and scanned the rooftop.

Not allowing myself to think about it, I cupped my hands to my mouth and loud-whispered, "Jess! Down here."

I saw her frown in my general direction, but no focus in her features. She couldn't see me.

"Duane…? Is that you?"

"Yes. It's me."

Her eyes were still searching for me as I again studied the hemlock tree next to the house. I decided to climb it.

"Where are you?"

"I'm coming up."

"You're…what?"

I didn't answer because I was already climbing the tree. Now, this tree was really two trees, split down the middle. I was able to leverage myself between them using my upper body strength exclusively. Luckily, there was a branch just out of reach, so I jumped for it and grabbed on.

"Oh my God!" I heard her whisper, and she sounded frantic. "Please do not tell me you are climbing that tree."

"Hush, I'm almost there." I pulled myself up until I was finally kneeling on the branch.

"Duane Winston, you are the craziest person I've ever met." I don't think she meant for me to hear those last words, but her voice carried, and they made me smile and gave me hope because along with exasperated, they sounded affectionate.

I climbed one more branch, though I wasn't sure it would hold my weight. It made a cracking sound just as I straightened and I heard Jess squeak, which made me laugh.

"Are you laughing?" she accused with a harsh whisper. "I can't believe you're laughing. After what happened tonight.

You are the only person on the face of the earth who would laugh while risking a broken neck. Everyone knows hemlock trees aren't climbing trees..."

Her tirade continued as I stepped on the steepled roof and carefully made my way across. She was still fussing at me as I climbed into her window, keeping my footfalls as soundless as possible.

"All this risky behavior, you're going to kill yourself. Or I'm going to kill you for making me a witness to it. You are completely thoughtless about your own safety..."

I closed the window behind me and surveyed her room. I crossed to the light switch and flipped it off. Then I moved back to where she stood. Her hands were on her hips, the slant of her mouth even more pronounced now that she was frowning.

She was still talking, something about medical insurance and hoping I had a good policy, so I kissed her to hush her. And also because I needed to. I needed to know she was safe, whole, unharmed. I needed to feel her body, her heartbeat against my chest.

I missed her. Oh, how I'd missed her.

After a stunned second, she kissed me back. My fingers slipped under her nightshirt—another silk button-up that fell to her thighs—and hers fisted in my sweater.

I loved her petal-soft skin, her curves, how hot she felt beneath my hands. She burned up every place I touched. I needed to touch her everywhere.

I loved her taste and how responsive she was, like she couldn't think past what we were doing.

But then she stiffened and pushed me away, maybe just realizing what was happening. She turned and darted to the other side of the room, placing the bed between us. The back of her hand came to her mouth and Jess stared at me with big eyes.

"What are you doing here?" she asked, shifting from foot to foot like she was ready to bolt.

My mind wasn't prepared for talking, so I said stupidly, "We didn't finish our conversation earlier."

"When?"

"Before now."

"When before now? You mean when you walked out on me at the cabin?" Her chin lifted, like my walking out was a sore spot for her. "Or when we were trapped at the biker compound?"

Being reminded of the cabin made my chest hurt, but being reminded of the danger I'd put her in at the compound made my blood pump cold and furious.

"Both," I managed through my self-loathing, hating she'd been in danger because of me.

"Now? In the middle of the night? At my parents' house? You know my daddy is the sheriff, right?"

"Yes. I know."

"So, what's the plan, Duane? Do you think it's a good idea getting caught sneaking into the house of a man who shoots people for a living?"

I flattened my lips into a straight line so I wouldn't smile, because she sounded so serious. "Your daddy doesn't shoot people for a living."

"Well, it's in his job description."

I ignored her irrelevant but funny statement and put the conversation back on track. "The truth is, I have no plan. I came here with no plan. And I know you can scream bloody murder at any moment and your brother and daddy will come flying in here, maybe with their guns, shooting first and asking questions later. But I need to talk to you—not later, right now—and I'm asking you to listen."

She was frowning at me like she was concentrating, or torn, or both. Abruptly she blurted, "Tina showed me her phone over Thanksgiving. She implied you were calling and texting her because you wanted her back, were still in love with her."

"I was never in love with Tina. She was…convenient and willing…and a headache. When I found out you were coming back to town I called things off with her, and I haven't looked back. And you were right. I should have done it years ago."

"I believe you. I told her on Thanksgiving to go to hell, that I trusted you," she said, but she was frowning. "But I don't understand; why'd you go to the Pink Pony last Friday? Did you really want her to spy on the Wraiths?"

I stiffened. "Where did you hear that?"

"When Claire and I were downstairs in that room with her father, Claire's daddy told Repo that you and Beau had visited Tina at the Pink Pony last week, asked her to spy on the Wraiths. She was the reason I was even there tonight. She'd called me and pretended to be in trouble."

"Tina called you tonight?"

"Yes. Well, she called late this afternoon while I was with Claire. Tina acted like she was in trouble and asked me to come to the bar to pick her up. But Claire's father said it was a setup. Tina set me up so you would go to the bar."

Jess then proceeded to fill in the blanks, explaining that she'd called Sheriff James before approaching the bar, and that Claire had insisted on bringing the guns. She also told me Repo didn't seem to have any idea that Jess was being used as bait.

"I'm sorry," I said, shaking my head and biting my tongue. What I wanted to say was, *If I ever see your cousin again, I'm going to kill that bitch*.

"For what?"

"For getting you involved. For putting you in danger."

"That wasn't you. That was my shitty cousin." She waved away my apology. "But I'd like to know what this was all about. I couldn't follow most of the conversation. Something about traps and drugs?"

I gathered a deep breath and returned her frown with one of my own. I needed to tell her the truth, but couldn't tell her the whole story.

"You don't want to tell me," she said, her tone held a sharp edge of disappointment. "You still don't trust me."

"No. I trust you. But part of this story isn't mine to share. I can tell you that the Iron Wraiths were blackmailing Beau and me for the last month or so, trying to get us to do something illegal. We've been stalling and I thought maybe Tina could help. She wouldn't return our calls or text messages, so Beau and I went to see her. I asked her for a favor and she said yes."

"What was the blackmail?" Her frown deepened and she appeared uneasy.

I pulled my hand through my hair and scratched the back of my neck, knowing she wasn't going to like my answer. "I can't tell you."

She stiffened, her eyes narrowing into slits of distrust, so I quickly added, "But I can tell you it was about Jethro. It had nothing to do with Beau or me. Just Jethro."

Her expression cleared and a knowing smile curved her

pretty mouth on one side. "Ah...that makes sense. I'm guessing it relates to some missing cars?"

"Not exactly. Long story short, turns out what they were trying to blackmail us with wasn't actually illegal. So we were going there tonight to set the record straight, tell the Wraiths to back off."

"And Tina double-crossed you."

I nodded. "I never lied to you, Jess. Not about how I... what I want."

"I know," she responded softly, looking unhappy. "I know you."

My hands ached to hold her, touch her, but she was still so far away.

Jessica glanced around her room and gathered a deep breath before lifting her eyes to mine. "Thanks for coming here to clear up tonight's events. I... Thanks."

I acknowledged her thanks with a short nod and stared at her. Uncertainty clogged my throat. I didn't know what to do next.

"Well, you can use the front door instead of the tree if you want. My daddy isn't even home. Jackson is, but he's not going to make a fuss, especially if you're leaving." Her eyes dropped, like she couldn't look at me anymore.

I didn't want to leave. What I wanted to do was eliminate the distance between us. I hadn't taken any time to prepare so I stood there, in the dark, watching her, knowing I needed to say something.

So, finally, I said something.

"I don't want to let you down. I don't want to let anyone down. I don't want to take without asking permission or deserving what I get. I need to take responsibility—for me, for my family—and I don't want any handouts or free rides."

Once again I had her eyes, but now she looked surprised. Her voice was halting as she asked, "Is this why you won't even consider the possibility of coming with me? Because it wouldn't be like that. I'm the one who wants to travel. How could I ask you to pay for—"

"Please, let me finish."

She bit her lip and nodded—though I knew she held her tongue with a great deal of reluctance.

"I want to…" I started, stopped, and shook my head because the word *want* was wrong. I started again, "I *need* to go with you."

She gasped, her hand coming to her chest and her pretty lips parting in surprise. I had no earthly idea how she could be surprised.

Even so, having confessed the truth, I said, "You've been it for me since you threw my shorts in that tree and left me naked in the lake, laughing at your prank and my misfortune—though I admit, I deserved it. You were right. I was trying to court you on our first date, nice and slow. I was trying to do everything right, guarantee my own success. I had a plan, one that wasn't ever going to work because I didn't take your dreams into consideration."

"Duane—"

"And then I came up with a new plan. I thought if I could dictate the how and for how long we were together, then I would be able to walk away, risking nothing I can't live without. You were right again. I wasn't all in. I wasn't even half in. I was ready to leave the whole time, looking for a reason. Because every second we spent together was better than the last."

Jessica took a step forward, like she wanted to rush over,

but stopped herself and gathered a quick breath. "We don't have to end. And I know I'm being selfish, asking you to leave when your roots are here."

Unable to stand the distance between us, I crossed to her, needing her skin and warmth. "But you did ask. And I'm glad you did, because I wouldn't have. I won't ask you to stay, and I would never ask to go with you. But since you asked…"

Her eyes grew round and she pressed her lips together like she was afraid to make a sound. And she let me touch her. She let me hold her in my hands and it felt so good I never wanted to let go.

"Since you asked, and since I need you, and if you're still willing—"

"I am!"

I smiled down at my girl, pulled her body against mine, and—even though nothing was really resolved, and we had no plan, and I had no clue how this was going to work—I said, "Then let's go."

"But what about the shop? What about your brothers?"

"I've talked to Cletus and Beau. We'll work something out with the shop."

"You already talked to Cletus and Beau? About leaving?"

"Yes."

"What will they do?"

"We'll figure it out. They want me to be happy."

"But do you think you'll be happy? Really? I've been thinking we could compromise. Stay here during the school year and travel over the summer."

"I'm not okay with that. I'm not asking you to compromise your dreams."

"But what about your dreams?"

"You're it."

She blinked, her mouth parting.

"You're it, Jessica James. And that's the truth. Not racing or going fast. Not fixing up old cars. I want to spend my life with you. And maybe that makes me wrong in the head and unhealthy, or old-fashioned, but when I think of my future and what I want, all I see is you."

Her smile was wide and hopeful, so the tears in her eyes didn't alarm me much. Seeing her so happy took my breath away. And looking at her now, something in me shifted. Actually, it was more than that. It was a blow to my chest, an earthquake, a fundamental rearranging of my foundation.

Not thinking about anything other than what I wanted right then, at that moment, I kissed her. I kissed her like I meant it because I did. I kissed her and moved my hands under her shirt to the hot skin of her stomach. I pressed my hips against her lower belly and tugged at her underwear, grabbing and squeezing handfuls of her body as I worked them down her thighs.

She gasped against my mouth as my hand cupped her sweet spot and stroked her with my middle finger, a long assertive touch.

Fucking hell, I wanted her beneath me, needed it. I needed her fighting sweet moans as I filled her, her hands held hostage, bare to me, taking and claiming this woman as mine. I wanted her fast and hard, and I wanted her slow and sweet.

"Duane!" She pushed lightly against my chest, breathing my name on an exhale. "Wait a minute, wait—what are you doing? My momma is right downstairs. Claire is next door."

I filled my other hand with the weight of her breast and massaged her through the silk of her shirt, all the while fondling her heat.

"I want you," I said simply; maybe I paired it with a growl to show my desperation.

Her big eyes moved between mine with a question, even while her breathing came in short chaotic bursts, her hips rocking against my hand.

"Was this part of your plan?" she panted.

"Jess, like I said earlier, I have no plan. All I know is, I need inside you, now. I want you. And I'm not thinking about who's downstairs or next door."

Her pretty mouth slanted upwards with a dreamy smile even as a shuddering breath escaped her lungs. "You're really going to climb in my bedroom window in the middle of the night and have sex with me in my parents' home?"

"Yes. That's what I'm doing." I bent to claim her mouth again but she tilted her head to the side, giving me a sly gaze.

Jessica's hand smoothed from my shoulder, down my chest. Then she grinned, cupping and rubbing me through my jeans with her palm.

I didn't want her teasing. I wanted satisfaction. I pushed her, advanced until her knees hit the bed and she was forced to fall backward on the mattress. She gazed up at me with enormous excited eyes, her mouth slightly parted.

"Take off your shirt," I said, nudging her knees apart, "and open your legs."

I dispatched my shirt, took off my boots, unbuttoned and unzipped my jeans, and pushed them to the ground.

All the while her hungry stare watched me undress, and fuck me, I loved it.

Jess's fingers unfastened her buttons, giving me a glimpse of the valley between her breasts, and she whispered, "Duane, you're being terribly disrespectful."

I climbed between her spread thighs, spreading her wider, stroking her need with mine, then whispered in her ear, "If you're willing, I'd like to disrespect you all night long."

♥

"What are you thinking about?"

I blinked at the ceiling, her question unexpected only because we'd been lying in silence for so long. We should have been asleep. I was tired enough. And though we were still in her bedroom and I'd just spent the last three hours disrespecting the hell out of her, my mind was finally content.

Yet she kept reaching for me—mostly for kisses and touches, petting and embracing—and I wasn't inclined to deny Jessica anything. So I waited. For her to settle. For her to relax. For her to sleep. And I used the time to appreciate the feel of her in my hands.

"I was just thinking your skin is awfully soft," I answered honestly.

"Really?" Jess's leg was between mine and she was on her stomach, one arm over my chest. Her face was turned toward my neck and I felt her breath against my shoulder.

"Yep."

She propped her elbow on the mattress and lifted her head, held her cheek in her hand and gazed down at me. "Do you want the name of my moisturizer? I can get some for you, maybe for Christmas? A stocking stuffer?"

I made sure my expression was as flat as my tone. "My stocking doesn't need stuffing."

She gave me a little smile, one that didn't quite reach her

eyes. I would have missed the subtle sadness if I hadn't been able to see so well in the dark.

Jessica shifted like she was going to lie down again, but I stopped her by gripping her arm. "Hey. What's wrong?"

She blinked. "Can you see my face?"

"Yes."

"How can you see my face? It's pitch-black in here."

"I just can. Why don't you tell me what you're thinking?"

"Can you see in the dark?" Now her eyes were narrowed.

"I'll answer you when you answer me."

Jess hesitated, and in her hesitation I saw more unhappiness. My chest constricted with dread.

But then she said, "My aunt Louisa...she was my mother."

Before I had an opportunity to process these words, her face crumpled and she sucked in a breath. Tears and sobs soon followed. Jessica flung herself down on me and I automatically wrapped her in my arms. I was confused. But once I sorted out what she'd said, I was mostly astonished.

"She was your mother?"

Jess nodded, burrowing herself against my neck.

"How long have you known?"

"Just found out last Thursday," came her muffled response.

I cursed, holding her tighter, my chest again constricting. I wasn't one for regrets, but if I could have rewound the last week and done everything over, I would have.

"I'm so sorry. I should have... I'm so sorry."

She shook her head and pulled away, sniffling. "No. No, it's fine. Really. It's just—"

"I should've been there for you. I should've gone to Texas for the funeral."

She continued as though I hadn't spoken or she hadn't

heard me. "It's just, I don't know why she never told me, you know? She gave me to her sister, treated me like an employee every time I visited—which, technically, I was, I know that—but I don't understand why she didn't want me to know until it was too late."

"What does Mrs. James say? Or the sheriff?"

Jessica's eyes came back to mine and she wiped a tear from her cheek, her lips pressing into a wobbly smile. "My daddy says it changes nothing. He says I'm his, have been since the day I was born and he held me."

Though it was a strange thing to remark upon while naked in bed with Jessica under the man's roof, I said, "I've always liked Sheriff James."

She nodded, then continued, "Momma says Louisa never gave her a reason. One day, Louisa called and said she was pregnant, said she wanted to give the baby up for adoption, but wanted to check with her first to see if she wanted me."

"And your momma and the sheriff wanted you."

"Yes. They did. And Momma says Louisa never wanted to talk about it, about me." She heaved a watery breath. "My birth mother didn't want me, and when she was alive she...she made me feel so inferior. Is it wrong I'm so sad about this? Is it strange that it hurts so much?"

I shook my head, cupped her cheeks between my palms, and gave her a firm kiss before responding. "No. It's not wrong. Our situations aren't the same, but I might as well have been a goat to my father."

Jessica half laughed, half sighed. "Duane—"

"It's true. All us kids were property to him. He didn't want us, except when he did. I know a thing or two about being left, discarded. But I've had my whole life to grow accustomed to it."

Even in her sadness, Jessica grew fierce and angry. "Your daddy is a pathetic excuse for a human being, not worth your time or thought. If he couldn't see how amazing you are, then he should be horsewhipped, then covered in paper cuts and lemon juice, then shot, then—"

"Hey now, Annie Oakley, settle down." I slipped my fingers through her hair and brought her cheek back to my chest. "All I'm saying is that you get to live through this however you decide. There's no right or wrong."

She nodded and heaved a full breath. "I don't know if I want her money. It feels like a payoff."

Her words settled around us, both heavy and light, making me frown and smile. She was so stubborn.

"If you want my vote, I think you should take the money."

"*Hrumph*."

My smile widened. "Just because it came from bad beginnings doesn't mean it can't be put to good use."

"How about I'll only take it if you agree to spend it with me?"

"Nice try, Jess."

She shrugged. "It was worth a shot."

We were silent for a stretch. Though we were two people, in that moment we were really one unit. We were unified. I didn't like Jess having this new sorrow, but I was glad to help. Maybe it was selfish on my part, but I liked that she needed me.

As though reading my thoughts, Jess kissed my chest and said on a sigh, "You know you're essential to me now, right? There's no escape, Duane Winston."

"Good."

I felt her small smile, still a bit sad, against my skin. "Do you promise? Do you promise you'll always take my calls? Do you promise you'll always be there for me when I need you?"

"Yes," I responded straightaway.

"No matter what?"

"No matter what or when. I promise."

With that said, Jessica settled. She relaxed. She fell asleep.

And so did I.

Jessica

29

> "It is good to have an end to journey towards;
> but it is the journey that matters, in the end."
>
> —URSULA LE GUIN,
> *THE LEFT HAND OF DARKNESS*

ONE MONTH LATER...

I WAS NERVOUS. WITH BETHANY Winston's passing, Ashley was now the matriarch of the Winston family and I *really* wanted to make a good impression.

I'd known Ashley—Duane's only sister—when I was a kid. She and Jackson had been real good friends growing up, and I'd been his annoying younger sister gawking at the local beauty queen. I hadn't seen her in years, almost a decade.

And now she was home for Christmas. Duane had spent all of Christmas Eve up at Drew Runous's house on Bandit Lake with his brothers, Drew, Ashley, and some of Ashley's friends from Chicago. He'd invited me but I felt strange about it. I figured the family needed time together to remember their momma without the introduction of new girlfriends. But I did accept Duane's invitation for Christmas Day.

Therefore I was nervous. "Basket Case" by Green Day was on repeat in my head. I'd been so anxious I made four pies and hadn't checked first before stepping out of my shower. Sir Edmund Hillary, once again, had tried to murder me with his litter box.

Duane came over for Christmas brunch, visited with my daddy, and swapped dirty looks with Jackson. When I was satisfied that the man-time had been adequate, I pulled him into the kitchen and showed him my pies, asking which one he thought Ashley would like best.

He shrugged one shoulder, kissing my cheek, then the back of my hand, entwining our fingers and drawing me close. "Ashley likes all kinds of pie, as far as I know. These look great."

I sighed, lamenting his lack of specificity and helpfulness. "Well then, maybe pie isn't the answer."

"Pie is *always* the answer." He grinned down at me, lowered his mouth to mine, and gave me a sweet, soft kiss. "You need to relax. Ash is good people. She's going to love you."

I swallowed, pressing my lips together. "It's just I'd really like for us to be friends. I mean, if she's moving back here from Chicago in March, then I'd like for us to—"

"She is moving back. She and Drew will probably get married sometime this year, start working on a dozen kids of their own." Duane's mouth hooked to the side and his gaze grew fuzzy and warm.

I squeezed his hand, the look on his face making me feel fuzzy and warm.

Over the last month, Duane and I had been making plans, lots and lots of plans. I hadn't expected him to embrace the idea of world traveling with such gusto, but he had. He texted me links during the day, articles or blog posts discussing potential destinations for our world tour or travel tips for nontourists.

When asked, he flat out told me he wanted to go to Italy first, specifically Maranello. In fact, he'd purchased the Rosetta Stone software and started learning how to speak Italian. I was confused by his choice until I realized Maranello is the home of Ferrari and the Scuderia Ferrari Formula One racing team.

Of course.

So that was our plan. We found a few villas for rent just outside of Modena, an ancient city in North Italy dubbed "the capital of engines," and Duane was researching potential employment possibilities.

"I didn't know Ashley and Drew were a thing, not 'til you told me two days ago. When did that happen?"

"When Momma was sick and Ashley was down here taking care of her at the end of the summer. But I don't reckon either of them were ready to admit it, not until a few days ago. Pair of dummies, both of them, wasting all that time. We should've just locked them in a room together back in September."

I smirked at his pronouncement. "You know, the same could be said for us. We wasted a lot of time, too."

Duane's gaze cut to mine and his mouth was curved with a half frown, half smile. "And whose fault was that?"

"Yours," I answered immediately.

His eyes narrowed, but now the curve of his mouth was a full smile. "That's right, and don't let me forget it."

♥

We held two pies each and I carefully picked my way along the path leading to the Winstons' front porch. I was in my fancy boots and didn't want to track mud into the house, so I tried to step on thicker patches of dying grass to avoid puddles.

The tops of the mountains were blanketed in snow. However, moderate morning temperatures lower down in the valley had melted most of the overnight precipitation, leaving some ice on the ground, but mostly just cold mud. I glanced toward the house and smiled, seeing that the Winston boys had left up the garlands, holly, and white twinkling lights lining the porch and the roof of the house. As well, the wreath I'd made still donned the front door.

I'd been over to the house last week to make dinner with Duane, and had been appalled by their lack of holiday decor. They didn't even have a Christmas tree.

That night Duane had made chicken and dumplings; meanwhile I tasked the brothers, set them to work adding wreaths and lights and garlands to the house facade as well as the big staircase and fireplace. Cletus, in particular, had grumbled the entire time, calling me an *interfering female*.

I wondered if they'd kept the bough of mistletoe hanging up between the kitchen and dining room. Regardless, despite the mess of the front yard, the grand old house looked great, festive and welcoming.

"It does look nice," Duane said at my shoulder; I saw he was looking at me, reading my expression and my mind.

"Yes. It does. I'm glad we took the time to do it."

"Me too. Thanks for being such a bully."

I flattened my expression. "I wasn't a bully. I was merely a persistent peddler of holiday cheer."

"You told Beau if he didn't help put up the Christmas lights on the roof, then you wouldn't make him apple pie ever again."

I shrugged, climbing the steps to the porch. "So? He needed some persuasion. And he's a complainer."

Duane laughed, a good robust, rumbly chuckle, and the sound made me smile.

"Besides," I added, "he only complains and resists because he likes being threatened."

"Is that so?"

"Yes. He needs a firm hand."

Duane stopped laughing, but I heard teasing in his retort. "You keep your firm hands where they belong."

"And where is that?"

"On my drive shaft."

Now I barked a laugh, almost dropping the pumpkin pie in my left hand, and then snorted because I was laughing so hard. Dirty automotive double entendres were now my favorite.

I remembered my nerves just as Duane leaned around me and knocked on the front door with his boot, calling, "Open up. Our hands are full of pie."

Not three seconds later, almost as though he'd been lying in wait, the door flung open, revealing a grinning Jethro in a hideous reindeer sweater. "Well, hello, beautiful."

Before I understood what was happening, Jethro bent down, wrapped his arm around my waist, and planted a big old kiss on me.

My eyes bulged and frantically cut to Duane—who looked startled at best, murderous at worst. I felt Duane's boot brush past my leather-clad calf on its way to administering a swift kick to his eldest brother.

"What the hell are you doing?"

Duane's boot must've connected with Jethro's shin,

because the kiss abruptly ended with Jethro stumbling back two steps, his grin now a happy grimace.

"Ow, damn, that hurt."

Duane stepped in front of me, balancing a pie in each hand, and bellowed, "I didn't know you wanted a broken nose for Christmas, Jethro."

"Relax, Duane." Jethro laughed, bending over to rub his shin as he pointed toward the ceiling. "We moved the mistletoe; it's right there."

"Duane, you're standing under the mistletoe, and you have pie." This comment came from Cletus, who'd appeared out of nowhere, swooped forward, and grabbed a pie out of Duane's hand. Then he called over his shoulder, disappearing with the pie, "I'd kiss you but I don't want our beards to tangle."

Duane glanced at the ceiling briefly, then back at Jethro. I could see my man was not amused. Meanwhile, I had to roll my lips between my teeth to keep from laughing.

Beau sauntered over, leaning to the side and giving me a smile though he addressed Duane. "Well, come in, dummy. Don't keep your woman standing out in the cold."

Duane shoved the remaining pie at Beau. Then he turned, took both pies out of my hands, and gave them to Jethro. Then he turned again, wrapped an arm around my waist, and kissed me. Actually, he kissed and dipped me. My arms automatically went to his neck and I kissed him back with fervor. When we finally straightened, I was dizzy and smiling like a well-kissed goof.

"There. Now she's been kissed under the mistletoe." Duane pressed me close to his side. "No need for any more liberties."

"She's been kissed under *that* mistletoe," Jethro corrected, his mischievous hazel eyes—which looked almost green this evening—shifting to mine just before he gave me a wink. "But we've got mistletoe all over the house. You can thank Jess for the original idea, and Cletus for running with it."

I felt Duane's hold on me tighten, saw his jaw work and clench just before he abruptly pulled me forward, giving his brothers the stink eye as we passed. "Come on, Jess."

"Where are we going?"

"We're going to find all the mistletoe in the house and disarm it."

We'd managed only a few steps before the sound of new arrivals made him stop and turn. Ashley Winston and Drew Runous had arrived.

The Winston boys grew suddenly both alert and boisterous, pulling their sister in for hugs and passing her around like she was a national treasure. The noise brought Billy, Cletus, and Roscoe out from wherever they'd been hiding—not that they'd actually been hiding. I suspected Roscoe had been hovering near the front door, probably ready to pounce on me as part of their practical joke.

Billy and Cletus came from the direction of the kitchen, so I guessed they'd been busy cooking.

It was nice to see that all the Winston boys appeared to be just as eager to greet Drew as they'd been to greet their sister, passing out profuse handshakes, smiles, and salutations of *Merry Christmas*.

I stood stock-still and waited for my turn, certain I looked like an indecisive statue as I debated what to do with my hands. Did I try to give her a handshake? Or was I expected to hug? Or some combination of both? Kiss on the cheek? Kiss on both cheeks?

Drew made it to us first. I'd seen him only a handful of times before and always from a distance at the community center for jam night. He played the acoustic guitar and sang when the occasion called for it, but he wasn't the outgoing sort.

If he wasn't singing or playing guitar, he wasn't making noise. As well, Drew Runous was a tall man, taller than all the Winston boys by an inch or more, his beard was bushy and blond, and his eyes were a steely gray. He reminded me of the Viking god Thor, if Thor had been a reclusive federal game warden from Texas with excellent manners.

"Duane," Drew said as they shook hands, and Duane bestowed one of his rare smiles on his friend.

"Drew, do you know Jessica James?"

Drew's attention swung to me and he offered his great paw. "Jessica James…you teach at the high school and your daddy is the sheriff."

I nodded, slipping my fingers into his, expecting a firm and efficient handshake. Instead, he held my hand in his, not moving it.

"That's right, I teach math."

"She teaches calculus," Cletus said from someplace. "And she doesn't grade on a curve."

I laughed lightly and Drew gave me a smile that made his eyes shine. Then he pulled me forward into an unexpected bear hug.

"Welcome to the family, Jessica," the big man said as he set me away, sounding and looking more sincere than a man had a right to sound or look. To my astonishment I felt my chin wobble.

I didn't get a chance to respond because Ashley was there,

bumping him out of her way with her hip and saying, "Jessica James, is your cat still trying to kill people?"

I opened my mouth to respond, but she cut me off by pulling me into a warm, soft, lovely-smelling hug. In truth, she smelled like pancakes. Delicious, buttery, fluffy vanilla pancakes.

And when she'd finished with our tight embrace, she slipped her arm through mine and pulled me away from the congregation of beards, walking us toward the living room. "You're a sight for sore eyes. I'm so glad you're here. I was hoping to see you yesterday, but understand you had a family commitment. Duane was telling me about your plans to go to Italy in the summer, and then after that he said something about Greece?"

"Yes, but Greece might be next year, depending on how long we stay in Italy."

"Well, if you're still in Italy *next* summer, then maybe I can talk Drew into a trip." She grinned down at me, her big blue eyes excited. "I've always wanted to go, and there's this yarn from Italy, one hundred percent cashmere, called S. Charles Collezione…"

I turned and glanced over my shoulder as Ashley told me about this special yarn she wanted to procure from Italy and I found Duane standing next to Drew. The two men were watching us with mirrored expressions of amusement and adoration.

I gave Duane a bright smile, which he returned, and I found myself truly at a loss.

He was giving this up—this amazing family, with their holiday pranks and steady love and support—just to be with me, just to travel the world and share adventures. I felt both astonished and blessed.

But most of all, I was humbled. He was giving up his home. And so I made him a silent promise that he'd never regret giving up so much. Not for one second.

♥

Duane went through the house and systematically removed all the mistletoe.

Well, all the mistletoe he could find.

He missed a bunch in the pantry and had to fight his way to the front of the line to rescue me from his brothers—all of whom had lined up except Billy. Billy had caught me earlier under another bunch hanging just outside the downstairs bathroom. However, like a gentleman, he'd been content with a kiss on the cheek.

Ashley pocketed every bunch Duane removed, slipping them into her bag. She planned to hang them up all over Drew's house. She wanted to catch him unaware for the next week before she had to fly back to Chicago.

She really was planning to move back to Tennessee and hoped to return for good no later than the end of March. I was glad to hear it because it would give us a few months of getting acquainted before Duane and I were off. Plus I still thought these boys needed someone. They needed a good woman to keep them safe, and Ashley already loved them with her heart and soul.

Dinner was nice. Actually, it was great. The boys were lively and animated, telling stories about Ashley and Duane, hoping to embarrass their siblings. This may have worked for Ashley, but I already knew most of the stories they told about Duane. Therefore I didn't hesitate jumping in and adding details they missed.

My eagerness earned me high fives from his siblings, but only heated glares from Duane. And it was totally worth it. Each hot look ignited a simmering thrill low in my belly because each promised delicious retribution. I had a feeling I was going to enjoy his version of revenge.

After dinner I served my four kinds of pie. When all the dust settled, not a single slice remained. Truly, there is no feeling quite like making four pies and leaving with no leftovers.

Dessert was followed by an impromptu family concert. Cletus played his banjo and Drew accompanied on his guitar while Billy and Ashley sang folk duets of Christmas classics. They looked like twins, Ashley and Billy, and their harmonies were beautiful, like they'd been singing together all their lives, like they knew each other from the inside out. I guessed, when I reflected on it, they did.

From the time the music started until it ended, Duane had me wrapped in his arms on his lap. I leaned in to him, enjoying his easy affection. He touched me with contentment, with wistful sighs and smiles, melting my heart with each cherishing pass of his fingers through my hair and stroke of my back.

Midnight came and went. Around 1:30 a.m. Duane told me it was time to go. Leaving took another twenty minutes as sleepy hugs were handed out and Ashley made me promise to have lunch with her before she flew back to Chicago. The entire brood gathered on the porch to wave as Duane pulled the Mustang out of the drive and turned on Moth Run.

I yawned, eyeballing Duane in his bucket seat.

"I miss the Road Runner," I said, my words a little slurred because I was dead tired.

"Why?"

"Because it was a bench seat. This car has bucket seats."

"Fair point." He nodded solemnly, then took the turnoff for the cabin.

I gave him a small smile and shook my head. He hadn't mentioned we'd be staying the night at the cabin, hadn't discussed his plans with me, but I couldn't say I was surprised. He'd been doing this with regularity over the last month, taking us out to his fortress of solitude.

Sometimes we'd have picnics, go on walks, talk, play cards. The cabin was where we'd discuss my aunt Louisa and my feelings on the subject. I'd lost it a few times, cried tears I didn't know I needed to cry. And he'd held me close, reassuring me that I was wonderful and her absence in my life was her loss. I talked through my messes and he listened, giving advice if and when I asked. He talked through his frustrations and I listened, giving advice if and when he asked.

But most of the time we ripped each other's clothes off.

Yep. That's what we did. And I finally got to spend some quality time with his buttocks, thighs, and calves. They were wonderful.

Duane pulled up to the stone steps and cut the ignition, then jogged around to my side of the car. I was barely on my feet before he swept me up into his arms and kicked the door closed behind him. I snuggled against his broad chest and placed a kiss on his neck; meanwhile, he had the keys ready and unlocked the cabin door, crossed to the bed, and placed me gently on top of the covers.

I sat up and fumbled to remove my clothes, the room spinning a tad, likely the effect of too much moonshine eggnog and the late hour. Duane quickly built a fire and turned back to me when he was done, giving me a pleased grin when he saw I was naked except for my socks.

"Get under the covers," he said, peeling off his own clothes.

I did as he instructed. My eyes were heavy but I managed to keep them open long enough to watch him undress.

Sleepy tipsiness meant I was saying and thinking in tandem, "I like watching you take off your clothes. It's like unwrapping a present."

My stream-of-consciousness nonsense was rewarded with a broad smile, his glittering sapphire eyes just visible in the dim cabin.

"How do you think I feel? Having you to myself, naked? It's like winning the lottery."

I giggled at this and turned my face into the soft pillow. A moment later the bed dipped and I felt him climb in next to me, one of his legs moving between mine, his strong arms bringing my chest against his, and his hands smoothing down my body.

"Go to sleep, Jessica," he whispered as he stroked my hip. "Go to sleep and have sweet dreams."

"So, dream of you and your hot looks?" I mumbled, relaxing into his skin, my eyes already closed.

His hand paused on my hip and I felt his lips curve against my temple.

"Or dream of you and your sassy back talk?"

His smile grew.

"Or dream of you and your goodness? Your...*yawn*... irksome integrity."

This earned me a chuckle and a squeeze.

"Or maybe I'll just dream of us, like this, forever." I shifted against him so I could get closer. "Yeah…that's what I'll do. I'll dream of home."

"Is this place home?" He kissed my cheek and I discerned the lingering smile in his voice.

"No, Duane." I shook my head and confessed just before tumbling into blissful sleep, "You are."

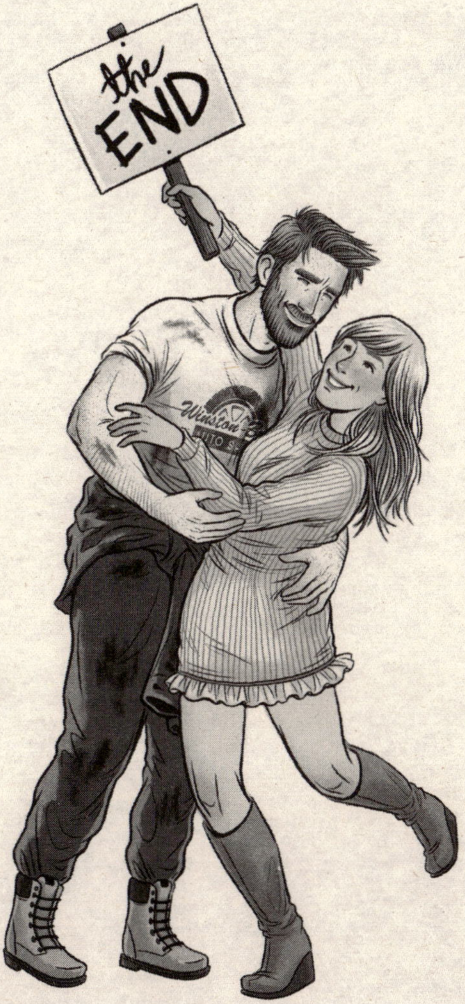
the END
Winston

Bonus Features

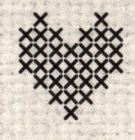

Explore the world of the Winston Brothers with these special features

WINSTON FAMILY TREE

DATING PROFILES

PLAYLIST

BONUS SCENES

```
        BETHANY —— DARRELL
                 |
          ┌──────┴──────┐
         BILLY        ASHLEY
          |             |
       JETHRO        CLETUS
```

Winston Family Tree

BEAU

ROSCOE

DUANE

Book 1

JESSICA

Dating Profile

Duane Winston

24
6'1
Gemini
"Go fast or go home."

Hobbies: Dirt racing at the Canyon, fixing up old cars,
   driving the getaway car
Likes: Coleslaw, The Beach Boys, dancing, Jessica James, my family, making blueberry pancakes
Dislikes: Basically everything else

Duane Winston is the fifth Winston brother and the (younger) twin to his brother Beau Winston. He spends his days fixing cars at the Winston Brothers Auto Shop and the weekends dirt racing (and winning) at the Canyon. Some people would call him the "grumpy twin," and they'd be 100% correct.

Duane doesn't fight against his own surly nature, but he's generally well regarded around town by everyone except Jessica James's older brother, Jackson. It's okay, because the feeling is mutual.

Dating Profile

Jessica James

22
5'6
Virgo
"Not all those who wander are lost."
J.R.R. Tolkien

Hobbies: Planning trips I'll never be able to afford, reading travel blogs
Likes: Travel, math, travel, pie, travel, picnics, travel
Dislikes: Students who don't put their name in the upper left hand corner of their homework assignments.

Jessica James is the youngest daughter of Sheriff Jeffrey James and elementary school teacher Janet James. Her protective older brother, Jackson, is a sheriff's deputy. Born and raised in Green Valley, TN, she's always longed to leave and travel (literally) anywhere. A recent college graduate and presently the calculus teacher at Green Valley High School, Jessica is biding her time, paying off her student loans, and waiting for the day she can afford to travel the world.

Truth or Beard Playlist

- "Monster Mash" (Rerecorded)— Bobby 'Boris' Pickett
- "Eternal Flame"—The Bangles
- "Dream Weaver"—Gary Wright
- "Creep"—Radiohead
- "I Am Weary (Let Me Rest)" (from the *O Brother, Where Art Thou?* Soundtrack)—The Cox Family
- "Thriller"—Michael Jackson
- "(If You're Wondering If I Want You To) I Want You To"—Weezer
- "True" (Single Edit)—Spandau Ballet
- "I Want You Back"—The Jackson 5
- "Brown Eyed Girl"—Van Morrison
- "Eyes Without a Face" (Remastered 1999)—Billy Idol
- "Touch the Sky" (from the *Brave* Soundtrack)—Julie Fowlis
- "Maybe I'm Amazed"—Jem
- "The First Time Ever I Saw Your Face"—Roberta Flack
- "You Could Be Happy"—Snow Patrol
- "Uptown Girl"—Billy Joel
- "Locked Out of Heaven"—Bruno Mars
- "Hey Ya" (Solo Version)—Obadiah Parker
- "Riptide"—Vance Joy
- "I See Fire"—Ed Sheeran
- "Higher Education"—Will Dailey

- "Home"—Phillip Phillips
- "Bury Me Beneath the Weeping Willow"—Ricky Skaggs & Tony Rice
- "The Bad Days"—David Ramirez
- "Have You Ever Seen the Rain?"—Creedence Clearwater Revival
- "Fortunate Son"—Creedence Clearwater Revival
- "Mammas, Don't Let Your Babies Grow Up to Be Cowboys"—Waylon Jennings & Willie Nelson
- "What'll I Do"—Lisa Hannigan
- "Tennessee"—Jimmy Martin
- "Wouldn't It Be Nice"—The Beach Boys

Additional Scenes

Author's Note: *This was one of the first scenes I wrote, and subsequently the first big scene I cut while writing* Truth or Beard. *I didn't like all the "dramatics" of this confrontation between Duane and Jess, what they left unsaid, and felt they'd be more mature than how they're portrayed here. And so, it had to go...*

I JOGGED OVER TO WHERE Jess and Claire were standing, the fear becoming both better and worse the closer I got.

Better because she seemed completely unharmed. Worse because she was glaring at me something fierce.

I reached for her arm and ignored her glare; the momentum of my fear causing my words to be more demanding than intended. "What are you doing here?"

"Don't touch me." She twisted away; I saw her throat was working like she was trying to swallow but couldn't.

"Fine. Fine." I removed my hand, though what I really wanted to do was toss her over my shoulder, carry her back to Beau's car, and speed away. "I'm not touching you. Now tell me why you're here."

"None of your business," she spat. Her glare was narrowed and mean.

"I think the lady wants you to leave her alone." Repo squinted at me, his tone held an unmistakable threat.

But Jessica turned her angry glare to the older biker. "I

think you can shut your mouth, Mr. Repo, and allow the lady to talk for herself. Despite what you're accustomed to, there are women in the world who are quite capable of speaking their own mind, no assistance from an ignorant caveman biker required."

His eyebrows lifted about two inches on his forehead and, to my amazement, he smiled. He smiled at her like he was proud.

She spun back to me, her beautiful face twisted with rage; but I also saw the hurt she tried to hide, and the hurt made my teeth ache and my neck stiff, like when someone scratches their nails on a chalkboard. I heard my brothers' footsteps behind me slow, then come to a stop.

"I'm guessing you're here because of Tina?" she asked, and something about the way she asked reminded me of a rattlesnake about to strike.

I shook my head, hungrily cataloging her features, unable to help myself. "No. We're not here for Tina."

"Lies." This statement was matter-of-fact, like she considered me a liar. She was now looking at me with disgust.

I'd expected her to be upset, but I didn't expect her to this upset. I didn't expect her to hate me. I stared at her, dumbfounded and not able to draw a proper breath. Her contempt was akin to being repeatedly pummeled in the chest.

Beau must've recognized I was unable to form words, because he stepped forward and said, "No, Jess. It's true. We came to speak with Razor about…well, about something."

Her eyes sliced to Beau and she gave him a hard look. "Whatever. I don't care. I'm just looking for my cousin so I can leave."

"Now wait a minute. You boys have business to discuss,

you talk to me." Repo stepped forward to insert himself between me and me.

In my peripheral vision I saw Cletus take his place at my shoulder. "I don't know if that's going to be sufficient, Repo. Things might have escalated beyond your ability to negotiate."

Movement at the corner of the building caught my attention, then it caught everyone's attention because Tina was making a giant fuss. She was screaming. Two massive bikers held each of her arms impassively as she tried to claw and kick them. She wasn't successful.

"Here's Tina now. We'd be happy for you to take her off our hands." Repo gestured to Jess's cousin as the two men pulled her along.

Claire tsked. "She better not be black and blue under those clothes."

"She's not. But let's just say she should be grateful you arrived when you did."

Tina's fussing muted abruptly as her eyes connected with mine and widened with surprise. Some of my guilt eased as I surveyed her. Other than black trails of makeup running down her face, she appeared to be unharmed.

"What did she do?" asked Cletus, sounding mildly curious. I studied my brother, confused by his manufactured ignorance.

"She pissed off the wrong person too many times." Repo's eyes flickered to Claire then away. "Let's just say some old ladies don't know their place…and are indulged."

"She pissed off Momma?" Claire asked. She didn't sound surprised.

"Scarlet, your momma ain't hard to piss off," Repo answered just as Tina and her captors were within ear shot.

"She's an old bitch!" Tina screeched. "She's just jealous."

Beau sighed and muttered, "Drama, drama, drama."

I was relieved Tina's woes with the Order had nothing to do with my request. She'd always been good at finding trouble, no help required.

"Duane, baby." Tina's eyes moved between Jess and me in a way that made my stomach turn cold. As soon as the bikers released her, she rushed to me and threw her arms around my chest. Then she lifted on her toes like she was going to kiss me. I stopped her, placing my hands on her shoulders and setting her away.

"What the hell are you doing?"

Her eyes darted to Jessica again and her neck flushed hot and red. "Just saying hello to my guy."

"Tina, I told you on Friday, we're never getting back together. That's never going to happen."

Tina flinched like I'd slapped her, but then her chin lifted in defiance. "Yeah right, Duane. That's why you kept texting and calling me for weeks."

I glanced at Jess, found her watching us with wide, watchful eyes. The cold lump in my stomach became cold certainty, and I returned my attention back to the viper in front of me.

Before I could interrogate Tina, Beau spoke. "So did I. I texted and called you twice daily, but that didn't mean I wanted in your crabby panties. Tina Patterson, have you been telling Jessica James tall tales?"

Tina's mouth fell open, like she was truly outraged, and she snorted. "Shut up, Beau Winston. You always did hate me."

"Because you'd do anything to make drama, and your kind of drama is boring," he shot back. "Now answer the question: did you twist Duane's friendly request into something untoward? Did you do that to your cousin? And here she is, coming here trying to rescue you. She's got your back, meanwhile you're stabbing hers with lies."

I saw the exact moment Tina decided betray my trust. Her act of innocence dissolved, leaving a sort of cruel determination. "You want to talk about lies? Then let's talk about lies, Beau Winston." She spun on her heel and faced Repo, pointing to me. "Duane and Beau came to me on Friday at the Pink Pony. They came to me and wanted me to spy on the Order. But I told them no. I would never do that. My loyalty has to count for something."

Repo frowned at her hollering and shook his head, slowly at first then with more conviction. "Girl, you are crazy. Let your cousin take you home, and don't come back here. You leave us alone, we'll leave you alone."

My eyes were drawn to Jessica. She was staring at Tina, looking shell-shocked and confused. I watched as comprehension dawned behind her pretty eyes. Then her stare shifted to me. Gone was the anger and spite and contempt, leaving only hurt and sadness. Jessica James's hurt and sadness was also akin to being pummeled in the chest.

I took a step toward her. "Jess—"

She held her hand up and shook her head. "No. I'm done. I'm so done. I'll leave you all to your business."

Instinct told me to go to her, wrap her in my arms, and take her away from all this craziness. Take her back to our cabin and keep her there until things between us were sorted. I wanted her to look at me with certainty again, not disgust. Not anger. Never hurt.

Instead I clenched my jaw and balled my hands into fists. She didn't want me to touch her and I didn't want to do this with an audience.

"Come on, Tina," Jessica said softly, her stare unfocused and introspective. "We'll take you home."

Cletus stepped forward and offered her his arm. "May I escort you and Mrs. McClure to your car? I've no doubt you'd be able to manage on your own, but I would like to ask you about the radius of convergence and the test is on Tuesday." She glanced at him like he was something new, something good and recognizable, then gave him a soft smile.

"That'd be fine, Cletus." Jessica slipped her hand into the corner of his elbow.

Cletus offered his other elbow to Claire and she took it. Her smile was a good deal larger, easier.

"Come now, Tina. Try to keep up." Cletus turned from where we were gathered and escorted Jessica and Claire from this clusterfuck, his voice trailing off. "Now then, what I want to know is, if half the width of the interval inside which a power series converges absolutely…"

Tina hesitated for a moment, her teeth grinding as she sent hateful glances to all who remained. "I don't care. I don't care and you can all go to hell!" she screeched.

Lifting her chin, she spun and walked away with her head held high. We all silently watched as Cletus opened Claire's door first, made a little bow, then walked Jessica around to the passenger side. I noted that Tina slipped into the cab behind the driver's seat, sitting on the back bench. But my eyes were fixed on Jess.

A hand closed over my shoulder and shook me gently. "You're just going to let Jess go?"

I looked at my twin, not registering his words at first. When I did, I shook my head at his questioning. "She doesn't want to talk to me."

"So you're going to stand there like a dickless asshole." This statement came from Repo, who was now glaring at me like I was a moron.

I returned his glare, though I'm sure a certain measure of surprise registered on my face, but I said nothing. He was a meddling old man—first angry I was associating with Jessica, now inexplicably giving me horse shit for not running after her like a fool.

Don't get me wrong, I was a fool for her. But I wasn't going to air any more of our dirty laundry in public. I would wait until she'd cooled off, approach her when she was feeling more inclined to listen. Plus, we had a plan to follow. We needed to sort this mess out with the Order.

But then Repo read my thoughts with uncanny accuracy. "You love that woman, you go get her, son. You don't wait 'til the time is right."

My temper slipped. "Are you fucking serious? A few weeks ago you were warning me away from Jess, like you have a say. And now you're telling me to go after her?"

"That's right. I am. That woman loves you. She loves you something fierce. You don't wait for that kind of love to cool off. You strike while the iron is hot."

I stared at him for a beat, then waved him off. "What do you know about it?"

"I know a hell of a lot more than you. I know waiting for the right time means it'll never come."

"What is going on?" I muttered under my breath, glancing at the cold sky.

Repo took a step closer and dropped his voice. "The past is in the past. Best thing you can do is forget about your mistakes, the secrets you've kept, and go after what you want.

I see you and I see myself, a fool for a girl I'll never deserve. But the difference between you and me is, you're a good man. You deserve her more than you think, more than you know."

"I agree with Repo." Jethro tipped his head toward the older biker. "You are such a dummy. I can't believe we're related."

"Now you're agreeing with Repo?"

"When he's right." Jethro nodded.

"Do you want to sort this shit out with the Order now? Or do you want me to go after Jess?"

My oldest brother shrugged. "Go take care of your business. We'll handle this."

"What happened to me being the only one Razor will listen to?"

Beau pushed my shoulder. "We'll figure it out. Maybe we'll just sort through the mess with Repo, not involve the big guy at all."

I stared at Beau, then Repo, then Jethro. For good measure I glanced at the two, silent biker giants who'd escorted Tina from the premises. Everyone wore similar expressions of *what the hell are you waiting for?*

"How am I supposed to get there? Hitchhike?"

"Take one of my bikes." Repo offered, digging in his pocket then withdrawing a set of keys and tossing them at my chest. I feel like I am in an alternate universe. "The Harley, third one along."

Beau nodded at the older biker, his smile of gratitude was genuine.

Repo waved off Beau's thanks. "I'll pick the bike up from the shop on Monday. Now let's go inside and talk business."

"Y'all still have Hap and Harry's on draft?" Jethro and

Beau turned away from me to follow older biker into the bar. The two lackeys followed.

The next thing I knew, I was left standing outside the Dragon Biker bar by myself in the freezing cold, holding the keys to Repo's Harley in my hands, not exactly sure what had just transpired.

Cletus's voice awoke me from my stupor; he didn't pause as he walked passed, just called over his shoulder. "What are you waiting for? An invitation?"

Duane's Letter to Jess

Author's note: *Originally written right after I finished* Truth or Beard *for a Valentine's Day post. More or less, it's meant to give you an idea of Duane and Jess's happily ever after and how they fare on their adventures together.*

Jessica,

I don't remember what happened last night after Roberto opened the third bottle of wine (these Italians sure know how to make good wine). But I woke up this morning and you were laying on top of me, naked except for a crushed crown of flowers on your head.

My body is sore in odd places. I have a terrible headache. Part of my beard is missing. I feel like roadkill.

And I've never been happier.

I don't care what we do or where we go. As long as I'm with you and you're with me, being sore in odd places don't bother me any. This headache is nothing compared to the thought of missing out on you.

I don't need my beard, but I do need you in my life.

So, the next time Roberto opens a third bottle of his wine, I might decline. I don't want to miss or forget a single second of our time (especially if it's time spent naked).

Watching you sleeping like a creeper,
Duane

ABOUT THE AUTHOR

Penny Reid is the *New York Times*, *Wall Street Journal*, and *USA Today* bestselling author of the Winston Brothers and Knitting in the City series. She used to spend her days writing federal grant proposals as a biomedical researcher, but now she writes kissing books. Penny is an obsessive knitter and manages the #OwnVoices-focused mentorship incubator/publishing imprint Smartypants Romance. She lives in Seattle with her husband, three kids, and dog named Hazel.

Website: pennyreid.ninja
Facebook: pennyreidwriter
Instagram: @reidromance
TikTok: @authorpennyreid
Mailing List: pennyreid.ninja/newsletter/
Goodreads: ReidRomance
Patreon: patreon.com/smartypantsromance
Email: pennreid@gmail.com... Hey, you! Email me 😉